LONELY HAUNTS

LONELY HAUNTS

SIX GHOST STORIES
Sir Thomas Graham Jackson

THE DEATH MASK AND OTHER GHOSTS
Mrs. H. D. Everett

COACHWHIP PUBLICATIONS

Greenville, Ohio

Lonely Haunts: Six Ghost Stories / The Death Mask and Other Ghosts
© 2014 Coachwhip Publications
No claims made on public domain material.
Six Ghost Stories published 1919.
The Death Mask and Other Ghosts published 1920.
Cover: Quiraing Mountains, Scotland © Martin Molcan

ISBN 1-61646-249-3
ISBN-13 978-1-61646-249-9

CoachwhipBooks.com

CONTENTS

SIX GHOST STORIES

Sir Thomas Graham Jackson

PREFACE

THE FOLLOWING TALES were written in idle hours for the amusement of the home circle, without, at first, any idea of publication. As they proceeded, it was thought that they might perhaps amuse a wider circle as well.

The author of *Ghost Stories by an Antiquary* lays down two conditions for a good story of the kind.

Firstly, the setting of the scene must be in ordinary life. This gives the story an air of reality, so that one may say, "This might happen now, and to me."

Secondly, the ghost should be malevolent. This is necessary if the reader's flesh is to creep and his blood to curdle.

I have ventured in two cases to violate the Provost's second rule, and to make my ghost benevolent. It seems but fair that ghostly society should be able to show a creditable side to its communications with mankind, as well as the reverse.

If any reader should wish to know more about the cult of *La vecchia religione* in Tuscany he will find a full account of it in *Etruscan Roman Remains in Popular Tradition* by C. G. Leland. I learned something about it myself when last in that country.

The scene of the last story will probably be recognised by some readers. But although the tale

is purely fictitious, it may be mentioned that Mr.
Dawes was a real person, and really wrote that letter, which is in my possession, though the name of
the person to whom it was addressed is altered.

> T. G. J.
> Eagle House,
> Wimbledon
> September 30, 1919

THE LADY OF ROSEMOUNT

"And so, Charlton, you're going to spend part of the Long at Rosemount Abbey. I envy you. It's an awfully jolly old place, and you'll have a really good time."

"Yes," said Charlton, "I am looking forward to it immensely. I have never seen it; you know it has only lately come to my uncle and they only moved into it last Christmas, I forgot that you knew it and had been there."

"Oh! I don't know it very well," said Edwards. "I spent a few days there a year or two ago with the last owner. It will suit you down to the ground, for you are mad about old abbeys and ruins, and you'll find enough there to satisfy the whole Society of Antiquaries as well as yourself. When do you go?"

"Very soon. I must be at home for a week or so after we go down, and then I think my uncle will expect me at Rosemount. What are you going to do?"

"Well! I hardly know. Nothing very exciting. Perhaps take a short run abroad a little later. But I shall have to read part of the Long, for I am in for Greats next term. By the way, it is just possible I may be somewhere in your direction, for I have friends near Rosemount who want me to spend part of the vac. down there."

"All right," said Charlton, "don't forget to come over and see me. I hope I may still be there. Meanwhile, au revoir, old man, and good luck to you."

Charlton remained some time at his window looking on the quad of his college. Term at Oxford was just over and the men were rapidly going down. Hansoms were waiting at the gate, scouts and messengers were clattering down the staircases with portmanteaux and other paraphernalia proper to youth, and piling them on the cabs, friends were shaking hands, and bidding goodbye. In a few hours the college would be empty, and solitude would descend upon it for four months, broken only by occasional visitors, native or transatlantic. The flight of the men would be followed by that of the Dons to all parts of Europe or beyond, the hive would be deserted, and the porter would reign supreme over a vast solitude, monarch of all he surveyed.

Charlton was not due to go down till the next morning. He dined in the junior common-room with three or four other men, the sole survivors of the crowd, and then retired to his rooms to finish his packing. That done, he sat on the window-seat looking into the quad. It was a brilliant night; the moonshine slept on the grass, and silvered the grey walls and mullioned windows opposite, while the chapel and hall were plunged in impenetrable shadow. Everything was as still as death; no sound from the outer world penetrated the enclosure, and for the busy hive of men within, there was now the silence of a desert. There is perhaps no place where silence and solitude can be more sensibly felt than the interior of an Oxford college in vacation time, and there was something in the scene that appealed to the temperament of the young man who regarded it.

Henry Charlton was an only child. His father had died when he was a lad, and his mother, broken down by grief, had foresworn society and lived a very retired life in the country. At Winchester and Oxford he naturally mixed with others and made acquaintances, but his home life was somewhat sombre and his society restricted. He grew up a self-contained, reserved lad, with few friendships, though those he formed were sincere and his attachments were strong. His temperament—poetical, and tinged with melancholy—naturally inclined to romance, and from his early youth he delighted in antiquarian pursuits, heraldic lore, and legend. At school and college he revelled in the ancient architecture by which he was surrounded. His tastes even carried him further, into the region of psychical research, and the dubious revelations of spiritualism;

though a certain wholesome vein of scepticism saved him from plunging deeply into those mazes, whether of truth or imposture. As he sat at his window, the familiar scene put on an air of romance. The silence sank into his soul; the windows where a friendly light was wont to shine through red curtains, inviting a visit, were now blind and dark; mystery enveloped the well-known walls; they seemed a place for the dead, no longer a habitation for living men, of whom he might be the last survivor. At last, rising from his seat, and half laughing at his own romantic fancies, Henry Charlton went to bed.

A few weeks later he descended from the train at the little country station of Brickhill, in Northamptonshire, and while the porter was collecting his traps on a hand-barrow, he looked out for the carriage that was to meet him. "Hallo! Harry, here you are," said a voice behind him, and turning round he was warmly greeted by his cousin, Charley Wilmot. A car was waiting, into which he and his belongings were packed, and in five minutes they were off, bowling along one of the wide Northamptonshire roads, with a generous expanse of green-sward on each side between the hedges, and the hedgerow timber. The country was new to Henry Charlton, and he looked about him with interest. The estate of Rosemount had lately come unexpectedly by the death of a distant relation of his uncle, Sir Thomas Wilmot, and the family had hardly had time yet to settle down in their new home. His cousin Charley was full of the novelty of the situation, and the charms of the Abbey.

"I can tell you, it's a rattling old place," said he, "full of odd holes and corners, and there are the ruins of the church with all sorts of old things to be seen; but you'll have lots of time to look about and see it all, and here we are, and there's my dad waiting to welcome you at the hall-door."

They had turned in at a lodge-gate, and passed up an avenue at the end of which Henry could see a hoary pile of stone gables, mullioned windows, massive chimneys, and a wide-arched portal, hospitably open, where Sir Thomas stood to welcome his nephew.

Some years had passed since Henry had seen his relatives, and he was glad to be with them again. A houseful of lively cousins rather younger than himself, had in former days afforded a welcome

change from his own rather melancholy home, and he looked forward with pleasure to renewing the intimacy. His young cousin
Charley was just at the end of his time at Eton, and was to go to
university in October. The girls, Kate and Cissy, had shot up since
he used to play with them in the nursery, and were now too old to
be kissed. His uncle and aunt were as kind as ever, and after he
had answered their inquiries about his mother, and given an account of his uneventful journey down, the whole party adjourned
to the garden where tea awaited them under the trees, and then
Henry for the first time saw something of the Abbey of Rosemount.

This ancient foundation, of Sanctus Egidius in Monte Rosarum,
had been a Benedictine house, dating from the twelfth century,
which at the Dissolution was granted to a royal favourite, who
partly dismantled and partly converted it into a residence for himself. His descendants in the time of James I had pulled down a
great part of the conventual buildings and substituted for the
inconvenient cells of the monks a more comfortable structure in
the style of that day. Many fragments of the Abbey, however, were
incorporated into the later house. The refectory of the monks was
kept, and formed the great hall of the mansion with its vaulted
roof and traceried windows, in which there even remained some
of the old storied glass. The Abbot's kitchen still furnished Sir
Thomas's hospitable board, and among the offices and elsewhere
were embedded parts of the domestic buildings. North of the refectory, according to the usual Benedictine plan, had been the cloister and beyond that the church, which lay at a slightly lower level,
the lie of the ground inclining that way from the summit of the
Mount of Roses on which the habitable part of the convent had
been built. Of the cloister enough remained, though much broken
and dilapidated, to show what it had been, but the greater part of
the church was destroyed for the sake of its materials when the
Jacobean house was built. A considerable part of the nave, however, was still standing, part of it even with its vaulted roof intact,
and of the rest, enough of the lower part of the walls was left to
show that the church had been of a fair size, though not on the
scale of the larger establishments.

Henry Charlton, with the greedy eye of the born antiquary, took in the general scheme of the Abbey with his tea and buttered toast under the shade of the elms that bounded the lawn on that side of the house. But he had to control his impatience to visit the ruins, for after tea his cousins insisted on a game of tennis, which lasted till it was time to dress for dinner, and after dinner it was too late and too dark for exploration.

They dined in the great hall, once the monks' refectory, but not too large for modern comfort, the Abbey having been one of the smaller houses of the Order, and the number of the brotherhood limited. Henry was enchanted and could not restrain the expression of his enthusiasm.

"Ah!" said his aunt, "I remember your mother told me you were crazy about architecture and antiquities. Well, you'll have your fill of them here. For my part, I often sigh for a little more modern convenience."

"But my dear aunt," said Henry, "there is so much to make up for little inconveniences in living in this lovely old place that they might be forgotten."

"Why, what do you know about house-keeping?" said his aunt, "I should like you to hear Mrs. Baldwin, the housekeeper, on the subject. How she toils up one staircase only to have to go down another. The house, she says, is made up of stairs that are not wanted, and crooked passages that might have been straight, and it took the maids a fortnight to learn their way to the food-store."

"It's of no use, mother," said Charley, "you'll never convince him. He would like to have those old monks back again, and to be one of them himself with a greasy cowl on his head and sandals on his naked feet, and nothing to eat but herbs washed down with water."

"No, no!" said Henry, laughing, "I don't want them back, for I like my present company too well. But I confess I like to call up in imagination the men who built and lived in these old walls. I believe I shall dream of them to-night."

"Well, Harry," said his uncle, "you may dream of them as much as you please, so long as you don't bring them back to turn us out.

And you shall have every opportunity, for you are to sleep in a bit of the old convent that the abbey builders of the modern house spared; and who knows but that the ghost of its former occupant may not take you at your word and come back to revisit his old quarters."

Harry laughed as they rose from table, and said he trusted his visitor would not treat him as an intruder.

The long summer day had enabled them to finish dinner by daylight, and there was still light enough for the old painted glass to be seen. It was very fragmentary, and not one of the pictures was perfect. In one of the lights they could make out part of a female figure richly dressed; she had been holding something that was broken away, and beside her was the lower half of an unmistakable demon, with hairy legs and cloven hoof. The legend below ran thus, the last word being imperfect:

QVALITER DIABOLVS TENTAVIT COMITISSAM ALI . . .

The next light was still more imperfect, but there was part of the same female figure in violent action, with the fragment of a legend:

HIC COMITISSA TENTATA A DI . . .

Other parts evidently of the same story remained in the next window, but they were too fragmentary to be understood. In one light was a piece of a monk's figure and part of a legend:

HIC FRATER PAVLVS DAT COMI . . .

The last of all was tolerably perfect. It represented a female robed in black, and holding in her hand a little model of a church. She was on her knees prostrate before the Pope, who was seated and extended his hand in the act of benediction. The legend below said:

HIC COMITISSA A PAPA ABSOLVTA EST.

Henry was much interested and wanted to know the story of the sinful Countess; but none of the party could tell him, and indeed, none of them had till then paid much attention to the glass. Sir Thomas had once made a slight attempt to trace the identity of the Countess, but with little success, and had soon given up the search.

"There is an antiquarian problem for you to solve, Harry," said he, "but I don't know where you should look for the solution. The annals of Rosemount are very imperfect. In those within my reach I could find nothing bearing on the subject."

"I am afraid, sir," said Harry, "if you failed I am not likely to succeed, for I am only a very humble antiquary, and should not know where to begin. It seems to me, however, that the story must have had something to do with the history of the Abbey, and that its fortunes were connected with the wicked Countess, or the monks would not have put her story in their windows."

"Well, then, there you have a clue to follow up," said his uncle, "and now let us join the ladies." The room where Henry Charlton was to sleep was on the ground floor in one corner of the house, and looked out upon the cloister and the ruined abbey-church. It was, as his uncle had said, a relic of the domestic part of the Abbey, and when he had parted with his cousin Charley, who guided him thither, he looked round the apartment with the keenest interest. It was a fair-sized room, low-pitched, with a ceiling of massive black timbers, plastered between the joists. The wall was so thick that there was room for a little seat in the window recess on each side, which was reached by a step, for the window sill was rather high above the floor. Opposite the window yawned a wide fireplace with dogs for wood-logs, and a heap of wood ashes lying on the hearth. The walls were panelled with oak up to the ceiling, and the floor, where not covered with rugs, was of the same material polished brightly. But for the toilet appliances of modern civilisation the room was unaltered from the time when the last brother of the convent left it, never to return. Henry tried to picture to himself his predecessor in the apartment; he imagined him sitting at the table, reading or writing, or on his knees in prayer;

on his simple shelf would have been his few books and manuscripts, borrowed from the convent library, to which he had to return them when they met in chapter once a year, under severe penalty in case of loss or damage. As he lay on his bed Henry tried to imagine what his own thoughts would have been had he himself been that ghostly personage five centuries ago; he fancied himself in the choir of the great church; he heard the sonorous Gregorian chanting by a score of deep manly voices, ringing in the vaulted roof, and echoing through the aisles; he saw the embroidered vestments, the lights that shone clearer and brighter as the shades of evening wrapped arcade and triforium in gloom and mystery, and turned to blackness the storied windows that lately gleamed with the hues of the sapphire, the ruby and the emerald. Pleased with these fancies he lay awake till the clock struck twelve and then insensibly the vision faded and he fell asleep.

His sleep was not untroubled. Several times he half awoke, only to drop off again and resume the thread of a tiresome dream that puzzled and worried him but led to no conclusion. When morning came, he awoke in earnest, and tried to piece together the fragments he could remember, but made little of them. He seemed to have seen the monk sitting at the table as he had pictured him in imagination the evening before. The monk was not reading but turning over some little bottles which he took from a leathern case, and he seemed to be waiting for some one or something. Then Henry in his dream fancied that someone did come and something did happen, but what it was he could not remember, and of the visitor he could recall nothing, except that he felt there was a personality present, but not so as to be seen and recognised; more an impression than a fact. He could remember, however, a hand stretched out towards the seated figure and the objects he was handling. More than this he could not distinctly recall, but the same figures recurred each time he fell asleep with slightly varied attitude, though with no greater distinctness. For the monk he could account by the thoughts that had been in his mind the night before, but for the incident in his dream, if so vague a matter could be called an incident, he could trace no suggestion in his own mind.

The bright summer morning and the merry party at breakfast soon drove the memory of the dream out of his head. After breakfast there were the horses and dogs to be seen, and the garden to be visited, and it was not till the afternoon that his cousins let him satisfy his longing to visit the ruins of the church and cloister. There they all went in a body. The cloister lawn was mown smoothly and well tended, and here and there barely rising above the green sward were the stones that marked the resting places of the brotherhood. Part of the cloister retained its traceried windows and vaulted roof, and on the walls were inscribed the names of abbots and monks whose bones lay beneath the pavement. At the end of the western walk a finely sculptured door led into the nave of the church, the oldest part of the building, built when the ruder Norman work was just melting into greater refinement. Henry was in raptures, and vowed that neither Fountains nor Rievaulx could show anything more perfect. The girls were delighted to find their favourite parts of the building appreciated, and led him from point to point, determined that he should miss nothing.

"And now," said Cissy, "you have to see the best bit of all, hasn't he, Kate? We don't show it to everybody for fear strangers might do mischief."

So saying she pushed open a door in the side wall and led them into a chantry chapel built out between two of the great buttresses of the nave aisle. It was indeed a gem of architecture of the purest fourteenth-century Gothic and Henry stood entranced before its loveliness. The delicate traceries on wall and roof were carved with the finish of ivory, and though somewhat stained by weather, for the windows had lost their glass, had kept all their sharp precision. Part of the outer wall had given way, weeds and ivy had invaded and partly covered the floor, and a thick mass of vegetation was piled up under the windows against the masonry.

"What a pity to let this lovely place get into such a mess," said Henry. "I have never seen anything more beautiful."

"Well," said Charley, "it wouldn't take long to clear all this rubbish away. Suppose we set to work and do it?"

So while the girls sat and looked on, the two men fetched some garden tools, and cut, hacked and pulled up the weeds and ivy and brambles, which they threw out by the breach in the wall, and soon made a partial clearance. Henry had begun on the mass that stood breast-high next the window, when a sudden exclamation made the others look at him. He was peering down into the mass of vegetation, of which he had removed the top layer, with an expression of amazement that drew the others to his side. Looking up at them out of the mass of ivy was a face, the face of a beautiful woman, her hair disposed in graceful masses, and bound by a slender coronet. It was evident that under the pile of vegetation was a tomb with an effigy that had long been hidden, and the very existence of which had been forgotten. When the rest of the vegetation had been cleared away there appeared an altar tomb on the top of which lay the alabaster figure of a woman. The sides bore escutcheons of heraldry and had evidently once been coloured. The figure was exquisitely modelled, the work of no mean sculptor; the hands were crossed on the breast, and the drapery magnificently composed. But with the head of the figure the artist had surpassed himself. It was a triumph of sculpture. The features were of perfect beauty, regular and classical, but there was something about it that went beyond beauty, something akin to life, something that seemed to respond to the gaze of the observer, and to attract him unconsciously whether he would or not. The group of discoverers hung over it in a sort of fascination for some minutes saying nothing. At last Kate, the elder girl, drew back with a slight shiver, and said "Oh! What is it, what is the matter with me, I feel as if there was something wrong; it is too beautiful; I don't like it; come away, Cissy," and she drew her sister out of the chapel, in a sort of tremor. Charley followed them, and Henry was left alone with his gaze still fixed on the lovely face. As he looked he seemed to read fresh meaning in the cold alabaster features. The mouth, though perfectly composed in rest, appeared to express a certain covert satire. The eyes were represented as open, and they seemed to regard him with a sort of amused curiosity. There was a kind of diablerie about the whole figure. It was a long time before he could remove his eyes from the face that seemed to understand and return his gaze, and it was not without a wrench that at last he turned away. The features of the image seemed to be burned into his brain, and to remain fixed there indelibly, whether pleasurably or not he could not decide, for mixed with a strange attraction and even fascination he was conscious of an undercurrent of terror, and even of aversion, as from something unclean. As he moved away, his eye caught an inscription in Gothic lettering round the edge of the slab on which the figure lay.

HIC JACET ALIANORA COMITISSA PECCATRIX
QVÆ OBIIT ANO DNI MCCCL CVIVS ANIMÆ
MISEREATVR DEVS.

He copied the epitaph in his notebook, remarking that it differed from the usual formula, and then closing the door of the chantry he followed his cousins back to the house.

"Well, here you are at last," said Lady Wilmot, as Charley and his sisters emerged on the lawn. "What a time you have been in the ruins, and the tea is getting cold. And what have you done with Harry?"

"Oh, mother," cried Cissy, "we have had such an adventure. You know that little chantry chapel we are so fond of; well, we thought it wanted tidying up, and so we cleared away the weeds and rubbish, and what do you think we found? Why, the most lovely statue you ever saw, and we left Harry looking at it as if he had fallen in love with it and could not tear himself away."

"By Jove!" said Charley, "just like old Pygmalion, who fell in love with a statue and got Venus to bring it to life for him."

"Don't talk so, Charley," said Kate, "I am sure I don't want this stone lady to come to life. There is something uncanny about her, I can't describe what, but was very glad to get away from her."

"Yes, mother," said Cissy, "Kate was quite frightened of the stone lady and dragged me away, just as I was longing to look at her, for you never saw anything so lovely in your life."

"But there is one thing I noticed, father," said Charley, "that I think wants looking to. I noticed a bad crack in that fine vault over the chantry which looks dangerous, and I think Parsons should be sent to have a look at it."

"Thank you, Charley," said Sir Thomas, "I should be sorry if anything happened to that part of the building, for archeologists tell me it's the most perfect thing of its kind in England. Parsons is busy on other matters for the next few days, but I will have it seen to next week. By the way, we shall have another visitor to-night. You remember Harry's college friend, Mr. Edwards; I heard he was staying at the Johnstons and so I asked him to come here for a few days while Harry is with us, and here I think he comes across the lawn."

Edwards had some previous acquaintance with the Wilmots, and was soon set down to tea with the rest, and engaged for lawn tennis afterwards, a game in which he had earned a great reputation.

Harry Charlton did not appear till the party were assembled in the drawing-room before dinner. On leaving the Abbey he was possessed by a disinclination for the lively society on the lawn. His nerves were in a strange flutter; he felt as if something unusual was impending, as if he had passed a barrier and shut the gate behind him, and had entered on a new life where strange experiences awaited him. He could not account for it. He tried to dismiss the finding of the statue as a mere antiquarian discovery, interesting both in history and in art; but it would not do. That face, with its enigmatical expression, haunted him, and would not be dismissed. He felt that this was not the end of the adventure; that in some mysterious way the dead woman of five centuries back had touched his life, and that more would come of it. To that something more he looked forward with the same indefinable mixture of attraction and repulsion which he had felt in the chapel while gazing at those pure alabaster features. He must be alone. He could not at present come back to the converse of ordinary life, and he set off on a swinging walk through field and woodland to try and steady his nerves, so as to meet his friends in the evening with composure. A good ten-mile stretch did something to restore him to his usual spirits. He was pleased to find his friend Edwards, of whose coming he had not been told, and when he took his place at the dinner table next to his aunt there was nothing unusual in his manner.

The conversation during dinner naturally turned on the discovery that had been made in the Abbey that afternoon. It was singular that so remarkable a work of art should have been forgotten, and been overlooked by the Northamptonshire Archæological Society, which had so many enthusiastic antiquaries in its ranks. There had been meetings of the society in the ruins, papers about them had been read and published, plans had been made and illustrations drawn of various parts of the building, including the chantry itself, but there was no mention or indication given of the monument either in the text or in the plates. Strange that no one should ever have thought of looking into that tangle of brambles by which it was concealed, till that very day.

"I must go first thing to-morrow," said Sir Thomas, "to see your wonderful discovery. The next thing will be to find out who this pretty lady was."

"That I think I can tell you, sir," said Henry, who now spoke for almost the first time, "and I think it helps to solve the mystery of the sinful Countess in the painted windows opposite, which puzzled us last night."

All eyes were turned to the fragments of painted glass in the hall windows, as Henry continued. "You see in the first window the devil is tempting the Countess ALI—, the rest of her name being lost. Well, on the tomb is an epitaph, which gives the missing part. She is the Countess Alianora; no further title is given. But whoever she was, the lady whose tomb we found is the same no doubt as the lady whose adventures were depicted in the windows."

"Now I know," broke in Kate, "why I was frightened in the chapel. She was a wicked woman, and something told me so, and made me want to go away from her."

"Well," said Lady Wilmot, "let us hope she mended her ways and ended her life well. You see, she went to Rome and was absolved by the Pope."

"Yes, but I bet she did not get absolution for nothing," said Charley. "Just look at her in the last picture and you will see she has a church in her hand. Depend on it, she got her wicked deeds pardoned in return for her gifts to Rosemount Abbey; and I daresay she rebuilt a great part of it and among the rest her own chantry."

"Charley," said Edwards, "you ought to be a lawyer; you make out such a good case for the prosecution."

"At all events," said Sir Thomas, "Charley gives us a good lead for our research. I will look out the old deeds and try to find what connection, if any, there was between Rosemount Abbey and a Countess Alianora of some place unknown."

The rest of the evening passed in the usual way. A few friends from neighbouring houses joined the party; there was a little impromptu dancing, and it was near midnight by the time they retired to rest. Henry had enjoyed himself like the rest, and forgot the adventure of the afternoon till he found himself once more alone in the monastic cell, looking out on the ruined Abbey. The recollection of his dream of the night before then for the first time recurred to him; he wondered whether it had any connection with his later experience in the chantry, but he could trace none whatever. The dream seemed merely one of those fanciful imaginings with which we are all familiar, devoid of any further meaning.

He was not, however, destined to repose quietly. This time his dream showed him the same monk, he recognised him by his coarse features and shaggy brows, but he was in the nave of a church, and in the massive round pillars and severe architecture of the arches and triforium, Henry knew the nave of Rosemount Abbey, not as now, in ruins, but vaulted and entire. It was nearly dark, and the choir behind the pulpitum was wrapped in gloom, in the midst of which twinkled a few lights before the high altar and the various saintly shrines. The monk held something small in his hand, and was evidently, as on the night before, waiting for somebody or something. At last Henry was aware that somebody had indeed come. A shadowy figure draped in black moved swiftly out from behind a pillar and approached the monk. What the figure was he tried in vain to discover. All he could see was that just as had happened on the night before, a hand was stretched out and took something from the monk, which it promptly hid in the drapery with which the figure was covered. The hand, however, was more clearly seen this time. It was a woman's hand, white and delicate, and a jewel sparkled on her finger. The scene caused Henry a dull terror, as of some unknown calamity, or as of some crime that he had witnessed, and he woke with a start and found himself in a cold sweat.

He got up and paced his apartment to and fro, and then looked out of the window. It was brilliant moonlight, throwing strong shadows of the broken walls across the quiet cloister garth where the monks of old lay quietly sleeping till the last dread summons should awake them. The light fell full on the ancient nave walls

> "Where buttress and buttress alternately
> Seemed framed of ebon and ivory"

and the light touched with the magic of mystery the delicate traceries of the chantry where lay the Countess Alianora. Her face flashed upon his memory, with its enigmatical expression, half attracting, half repelling, and an irresistible desire impelled him to see her again. His window was open and the ground only a few feet below. He dressed himself hastily, and clambered out. Everything was still; all nature seemed asleep, not a breath of wind moved the trees or stirred the grass as he slowly passed along the cloister; his mind was in a strange state of nervous excitement; he was almost in a trance as he advanced into the nave where the shadows of column and arch fell black on the broken pavement. He paused a moment at the gate which led into the chantry, and then entered as if in a dream, for everything seemed to him unreal, and he himself a mere phantom. At last he stood beside the tomb and looked down on the lovely countenance which had bewitched him in the afternoon. The moonlight fell upon it, investing it with an unearthly mystery and charm. Its beauty was indescribable: never had he conceived anything so lovely. The strange semi-satirical expression of which he had been conscious in the afternoon had disappeared; nothing could be read in the features but sweetness and allurement. A passionate impulse seized him, and he bent down and kissed her on the lips. Was it fancy or was it real, that soft lips of warm life seemed to meet his own? He knew not; a delirious ecstasy transported him, the scene faded before his eyes and he sank on the floor in a swoon.

How long he lay he never knew. When he came to himself the moon had set, and he was in darkness. An indefinable terror seized him. He struggled to his feet, burst out of the Abbey, fled to his rooms, scrambling in through the window, and threw himself panting on his bed.

Henry Charlton was the last to appear next morning at the breakfast-table. He was pale and out of spirits, and roused himself with difficulty to take part in the discussion as to what was to be done that day. After breakfast he pleaded a headache, and retired with a book to the library, while the others betook themselves to various amusements or employments. The girls were in the garden where they found old Donald the gardener, whose life had been spent at Rosemount, and in whose eyes the garden was as much his as his master's, and perhaps more so.

"Yes, missy," he was saying, "the weeds do grow terrible this fine weather, and as you was saying it is time we cleaned up a bit in the old Abbey. But I see the young gentlemen has been doing a bit theirselves, chucking all them briars and rubbish out on the grass just as I had mown and tidied it."

"Why Donald," said Cissy, "you ought to have thanked them, for that chapel was in an awful mess, and they have saved you some trouble."

"Well, miss, I suppose they pleased theirselves, but that's not where I should have meddled, no, no!" and so saying he moved away.

"But why not there," said Kate, "why not there of all places?"

"Oh! I say nothing about it," said Donald. "Only folk do say that there's them there as don't like to be disturbed."

"Indeed; what do they say in the village about it?"

"Oh! Ay! I say nothing. I don't meddle with things above me. And I shan't tell ye any more, miss, it's not good for young women to know."

"But do you know, Donald," said Cissy, "what we found there?"

"What did you find, miss? Not her? Oh, Lord! She was found once before, and no good come of it. There, don't ask me any more about it. It's not good for young women to know." So saying Donald wheeled his barrow away into another part of the garden.

"Father," said Kate, to Sir Thomas who now came up. "Donald knows all about the tomb and the statue, and he won't tell us anything, except that the people think it unlucky to meddle with it. Have you ever heard of any superstition about it."

"Nothing at all," said he. "I have just been down to look at your discovery. The statue is a wonderful piece of work. I have never seen anything finer either here or in Italy. But the chapel is in a bad way and part of the roof threatens to fall. I have just sent word to Parsons to come tomorrow morning and attend to it."

They were joined presently by Edwards and Charley, and the day passed pleasantly enough, with the usual amusements of a country house in holiday time. Henry did not take much part with them. He was abstracted and inattentive, and altogether out of spirits. He had but a confused idea of what had happened the previous night, but there seemed still to linger on his lips that mystic, perhaps unhallowed kiss, and there still floated before his eyes the mocking enigma of that lovely countenance. He dreaded the approach of night, not knowing what it might bring, and did his best to divert his mind to other things, but without much success.

His friend Edwards was much concerned at the change in his behaviour, and asked Charley whether Henry had been upset in any way during his visit. He was assured that till yesterday afternoon Henry had been as happy and companionable as possible, and that it was only that morning that the change had come over him.

"But I can tell you one thing," said Charley, "I believe he was out of his room last night, for the flower beds show footmarks, and the creepers are torn outside his window, showing some one had been getting in and out, and there certainly has been no burglary in the house. Do you know whether he walks in his sleep?"

"I have never heard that he does," said Edwards. "We can't very well ask him whether anything is wrong, for he does not seem to invite inquiry, and has rather avoided us all day. But if it is a case

of sleep-walking we might perhaps keep a look-out to-night to prevent his coming to mischief."

"All right," said Charley. "My room is over his and looks out
the same way. I'll try and keep awake till midnight, and will call
you if I see anything of him."

"That's well," said Edwards, "but we must be careful and not
be seen, for it is dangerous to wake a somnambulist I believe."

And so they departed to their several chambers.

The first part of the night passed peacefully enough with Henry.
He had no dreams to trouble him, but towards midnight he began
to turn uneasily in his bed, and to be oppressed by an uneasy feeling that he was not alone. He awoke to find the moon shining as
brilliantly as on the previous night, and bringing into view every
detail of the ancient buildings opposite. A dull sense of some sinister influence weighed upon him: someone was with him whom
he could not see, whispering in his ear, "You are mine; you are
mine." He could see no form, but to his mental vision was clearly
visible the countenance of the figure in the chapel, now with the
satirical, mocking expression more fully shown, and he felt himself drawn on he knew not whither. Again the mocking lips seemed
to say, "You are mine, you are mine." Half unconsciously he rose
from his bed, and advanced towards the window. A faintly visible
form seemed to move before him, he saw the features of the countess more plainly, and without knowing how he got there he found
himself outside the room in the cloister garth, and entering the
shade of the cloister. Something impalpable glided on before him,
turning on him the face that attracted him though it mocked him,
and which he could not but follow, though with an increasing feeling of terror and dislike. Still on his ear fell the words, "You are
mine, you are mine," and he was helpless to resist the spell that
drew him on and on farther into the gloom of the ruined nave. And
now the shape gathered consistency and he seemed to see the
Countess Alianora standing facing him. On her features the
same mocking smile, on her finger the jewel of his dream. "You
are mine," she seemed to say, "mine, mine, you sealed it with a
kiss," and she outstretched her arms; but as she stood before him

in her marvellous and unearthly beauty, a change came over her;
her face sank into ghastly furrows, her limbs shrivelled, and as she
advanced upon him, a mass of loathly corruption, and stretched
out her horrible arms to embrace him he uttered a dreadful scream
as of a soul in torture, and sank fainting on the ground.

"Edwards, Edwards, come quick," cried Charley, beating at his
door. "Harry is out of his room, and there is something with him, I
don't know what it is, but hurry up or some mischief may happen."

His friend was ready in a moment, and the two crept cautiously
downstairs, and as the readiest way, not to disturb the household,
got out into the cloister through the window of Harry's room. They
noticed on the way that his bed had been slept in, and was tossed
about in disorder. They took the way of the cloister by which Charley had seen Harry go, and had just reached the door that led into
the nave when his unearthly scream of terror fell on their ears.
They rushed into the church, crying, "Harry, Harry, here we are,
what is it, where are you?" and having no reply they searched as
well as they could in the moonlight. They found him at last,
stretched on the ground at the entrance to the fatal chantry chapel.
At first they thought he was dead, but his pulse beat faintly, and
they carried him out, still insensible, into the outer air. He showed
some signs of life before long, but remained unconscious. The
house was aroused and he was put to bed, and messengers were
sent for the doctor. As they watched by his bedside, a thundering
crash startled them; looking out of the window they saw a cloud of
dust where the chantry had been, and next morning it was seen
that the roof had fallen in, and destroyed it.

Harry Charlton lay many weeks with a brain fever. From his
cries and ravings something was gathered of the horrors of that
fatal night, but he would never be induced to tell the whole story
after he recovered.

The fallen ruin was removed, and Sir Thomas hoped that the
beautiful statue might have escaped. But strange to say, though
every fragment of masonry was carefully examined and accounted
for, no trace could be found of any alabaster figure nor of the tomb
of the Comitissa Alianora.

THE RING

Two Englishmen were sitting one autumn evening in the garden of the inn at Corneto. The sun had just set over the sea, and the short Italian twilight had begun. The plain down below was already in shadow, but hues of purple and violet still tinged the hills, and invested them with all the ineffable charm of a Tuscan landscape at eventide. The elder of the two men was an Oxford Don, a well-known antiquary and student of ethnology. The younger had been a Fellow of the same College, but had settled in London and taken to literary pursuits, in which he had already made his mark. They had spent the morning in the museum, examining with the help of the courteous curator the rich collection of Etruscan antiquities, and in the afternoon had visited the famous necropolis on the plateau behind the town, and penetrated into a score or more of the painted tombs. They finished the day by crossing the valley to the bare plateau on the opposite hill, where once stood the proud city of Tarquinii, which gave kings to Rome, when Rome itself was but a thing of yesterday, sprung from an upstart settlement of outlaws and robbers. As they sat and sipped their coffee in the gathering dusk, their minds were full of what they had seen; of the mystery of that strange people who came to Italy from nobody knows where, whose written language nobody had ever interpreted, whose gloomy religion coloured the whole ritual of the Romans, and of whom the best record is to be found in their graves.

"I can imagine nothing more delightful," said the younger man at last, "than to penetrate into an untouched Etruscan tomb,

30

another Regulini-Galassi discovery; where, though the body may have turned to dust—though, for the matter of that, glimpses have been seen of one before it fell to pieces—the ornaments that had fallen off show how the man lay amid the votive offerings to his gods, with his cherished possessions and trinkets all standing around him or hanging on the walls just as they had been left by his relatives three thousand years ago. But I fear there is no chance of such a piece of luck nowadays. The tombs everywhere seem either to have been rifled in bygone ages, or stripped in modern times, to enrich museums and collections."

"Well, I don't know," said Dr. Morton, the elder man; "it may be, as you say, too late for discovery, and yet— But, at all events, I agree with you that nothing could be more interesting."

"You were here some weeks before I joined you," said Archie Bryant. "I think you came mainly to study the folk-lore of Tuscan peasantry. How have you been rewarded?"

"Fairly well. It is not easy to get below the surface with the Italian peasant when you try to fathom his beliefs. But it is curious how much has survived of something older than the Catholic faith he shows to his priest."

"Indeed," said Bryant. "Do you mean he has not forgotten Tinia, Fafluns, and Teramo, and the other Etruscan deities whom we have been looking at on vases, and in the tombs?"

"So far from having forgotten them," said Morton, "many of the old peasants, though they are Catholics outwardly, have much more real faith in *la vecchia religione*, the outworn creed, as you would think it, of Etruscan mythology. There are still many women *streghe*, witches, who know and practice incantations, but of course all that is under the ban of the Church, and though luckily the Holy Office can no longer burn them, they are very timid and afraid of attracting notice. However, I have managed to get into the confidence of some of them, and have learned a good deal that would surprise you, as it certainly did me. It is even said that it is usual for a family to have one of their number brought up in the old religion, in order that they may have friends in all quarters."

Bryant laughed, and said it was like the way families in the time of the Wars of the Roses took care to have some of their relatives in each camp, so as to have a friend on either side in case of accidents.

"But to return to what you said just now," said Morton, "about visiting an untouched Etruscan tomb, do you know that I have great hopes we may really manage it. One of the women into whose confidence I have got, and who has given me a host of spells and incantations which I hope some day to publish, is a *strega*, or witch, and my belief is that she knows of such a tomb. She says, however, it is dangerous to visit it, no doubt from some superstitious views about the old gods—Tinia, the god of thunder, and the rest. But we shall know more to-morrow, and I have no doubt we shall manage to open the tomb with the aid of a golden key."

They laughed, and rose from their seats, and, after a turn or two in the alleys of the garden, went to bed.

The next morning was spent partly in the museum, and partly in the communal library.

Bryant's interest was excited by the subject of Etruscan mythology, which was new to him, and under Morton's guidance he dipped into the ample stores of literature that bore upon it. As they walked away in the evening Bryant said:

"And you really mean to tell me that Tinia and other members of the old Etruscan Olympus still have their followers among the descendants of the people whose tombs we have visited. I can hardly believe it."

"I don't wonder you should be incredulous," replied Morton. "They do not have it all to themselves, for the saints have their share of popular favour; but, besides the prayers that they offer to the saints, many of the peasants believe in the *folletti* or spirits of the past; charms and incantations are addressed to them, and legends are preserved of their potent aid. But in a few minutes I will convince you beyond all doubt. We are going to visit an acquaintance I have made—the woman of whom I told you last night; and there she is waiting for me. I doubt, by the way, whether she is actually one of the *streghe*, or witches, but she knows most of their lore."

Bryant saw a peasant woman seated at her door, spinning with distaff and spindle as her ancestors had done before her from time immemorial. She rose at their approach, pushed the end of the distaff through her belt, and greeted them with the dignified courtesy that sits naturally on the Italian of the humblest degree, his heritage from an ancient civilisation. She seemed to Bryant a woman of sixty years, or perhaps rather younger, for women age more rapidly in Italy than with us, and she retained much of the classic beauty of her youth.

"Antonietta," said Morton, "I have brought a compatriot, a lover of your country and people."

"The Signore is welcome," said Antonietta, with a smile and a slight inclination, and she invited them to enter her house. A young girl who was sitting there rose as they entered, whom Antonietta presented as her daughter Chiarina. She was a Tuscan beauty, with blue eyes and a rich complexion burned by the sun to a tint like the bloom on an apricot, set off by the bright-coloured handkerchief thrown over her head and fastened with silver pins.

"I have been telling my friend," said Morton, "what you told me the other day of a tomb which—"

"Ah!" said Antonietta, interrupting him. "Scusi, Signore. These things must not be spoken of lightly," and she looked furtively round and shut the door carefully. Returning to Morton's side, she continued in a low voice:

"And is the Signore really bent on what he proposed? Is he not afraid of disturbing those we dare not speak of?"

"We should make no disturbance, Antonietta," said he. "I only want to see a tomb of one of the old people just as it was finished and left by those who made it. I think you said you knew of one that had never been disturbed."

"There is such a tomb, Signore, and Chiarina knows it as well as I. No one else does. But it is dangerous for strangers to visit it, as I have warned you, Signore."

"But you and Chiarina go there safely," said Morton.

"Yes, but that is different. There are reasons," and she nodded her head sagely. "We are known. They would not harm us."

"Is that why you wear a guard against evil spirits?" said Bryant, pointing to the silver cross that hung on her bosom. "They cannot touch a good Catholic, I suppose."

"*Si, si, sicuro; sono buona Cattolica*," replied Antonietta. "I am a good Catholic, though I do not believe all the priests tell me." And then in a lower voice to Morton, "You know what I believe."

"*La vecchia religione*, the old religion?" said Morton.

She nodded two or three times, but said nothing.

"But now about this tomb," said Morton, returning to the object of his visit.

"Signore, be advised. Think no more about it. There are those there who would not welcome you. It would not be wholesome for you to go. I speak for your good."

"But I will be careful to give no offence," said Morton. "I am bent on going, and trust to you to help me," and as he spoke he slipped two gold pieces into her hand. Antonietta looked at them for a minute, and then said:

"Well, if the Signore is resolved, I can certainly guide him, but, no! I will not be paid for it," and she laid the money down on the table and pushed it towards him. "Neither dare I take you myself. Chiarina knows the way, and she is not bound like me. She shall take you, but it must be by night and secretly, and there must be no more than you two."

Morton faithfully promised to obey her conditions, and it was arranged that Chiarina should meet them after dark at the town gate which gave on to the necropolis.

THEY WERE PUNCTUAL at the rendezvous, and found Chiarina waiting for them. She was dressed in black, and had a black shawl or hood over her head which concealed her features. She made a sign of recognition, and preceded them without a word.

It was a lovely starlit night, without a moon. Not a breath of air stirred the trees, and the silence was unbroken save by the silver tone of the bell in the Palazzo Comunale, tolling the hour of twenty-three. A few belated wanderers returning to the city passed them on the high road, but as their footsteps died away in the distance, the dead silence settled down again. When they had proceeded about a mile Chiarina turned off by a by-path, that led across the solitary waste. Around them lay the unseen city of the dead; the ground was honeycombed with tombs, where, amid pictured scenes of dancing and revelry, a mockery as it were of mortality, lay the dust of Lucomos and warriors, people of that mysterious race whose history and language are alike forgotten.

"And yet," said Morton, "one may believe that they are the same people still; mixed, no doubt, with Goths and Lombards, but mainly derived from the old stock that worshipped Tinia here before the days of Romulus."

"I like the idea," said Bryant, "and, according to you, they still pay him a divided homage, though he has many rivals in Catholic hagiology. But I like to think that Chiarina's ancestors followed Lars Porsena of Clusium to the siege of Rome—"

Their guide caught the mention of her name, and looked round with her finger on her lip to enjoin silence. They were traversing a thick wood of undergrowth by a path obscurely marked, which might easily be overlooked by one who was not familiar with the route, but Chiarina never faltered or hesitated on her way. They now descended slightly into a thicker grove; the trees met overhead, and it was with difficulty they saw their guide before them. At last she stopped and turned to her companions. Taking Morton by the hand and signing to Bryant to follow, she drew them through a thicket and then, striking a match, lighted one of the earthen lamps that the peasants still use, exactly like those found in the tombs of their ancestors and placed there three thousand years ago. They found themselves facing a ledge of rocks, about ten feet high, that had evidently been scarped by the hand of man to a smooth face.

Here Chiarina turned to them, and in a whisper warned them to be silent.

"The Signori will be so good," she said, "as not to speak while we are here. There are those whom we must not disturb, or they will be angry. But I will do what is wanted to appease them."

They promised to do as she bid them, Bryant much interested in her seriousness and her unfeigned alarm, and amused at the idea of two prosaic Englishmen in the twentieth century assisting in a religious function of thirty centuries ago.

Pulling away a bundle of brushwood, Chiarina showed by the feeble light of her lamp a descent of steep steps leading to a doorway at the foot of the rock, and following her they entered an excavation imperfectly visible till their eyes had become more accustomed to the darkness. They then found themselves in a vaulted chamber, cut in the rock, with a square pier left in the middle to support the roof. On this pillar, as Chiarina held her lamp high above her head, they saw a huge figure of Typhon, with twisted serpents for legs, and outstretched wings, grasping a thunderbolt as if to hurl it at an intruder. The walls presented to their delighted eyes a series of paintings as perfect as when the artist had given them his last touches. On one side were rural scenes, harvest and vintage, with jocund peasants and oxen. On another were pictures of banquet and revelry, youths piping and maidens dancing. All spoke of the joy of life, of nature, and contentment. On another wall were scenes more appropriate to the place: there sat Hades black and gloomy, and beside him Persephone with snakes bound in her hair, while Charon, *con occhi di bra gia*, with his bark stood awaiting his freight of souls. All this, however, was like what the visitors had seen in other tombs during the preceding day, though nowhere so brilliantly preserved as here.

But what was their wonder to see around them the treasury of the dead, untouched by the hand of man since the last inmate of the tomb had been laid to rest. His golden collar and breastplate and other ornaments lay on a bier of bronze, though the body that wore them had melted away from within them into dust. On the wall hung his weapons, and around were arranged painted vases, such as form the priceless treasures of countless museums. Morton and Bryant had indeed their wish satisfied to the full.

As they stood in the death-like silence of the tomb, the mystery of the ages weighed upon their senses; the unknown occupant whose dust undisturbed no doubt lay still on the floor: the things he had used in life, that had hung idly beside his bier for countless centuries; the inscriptions on the walls intended to tell who and what he had been, which could be read but which no one could understand, all combined to make an indescribable impression on the imagination. Pictures of the gods of the outworn creed of ancient Etruria surrounded them—outworn, but no! What was Chiarina doing? At the far end of the cell she had lighted a little flame on a bronze tripod, and while dropping on it pinches of incense, was muttering some charm or incantation of which only a few words reached them. The ancient deities, then, still had their worshippers.

As Bryant looked on in amazement, a strange sense of unreality clouded his mind: he was for the moment as it were transported back to ancient days, the present was confused with the past, and the intervening centuries vanished as a dream. Before he recovered himself something fell on his foot. He stooped to pick it up. It was a ring, and he half-unconsciously put it on his finger. As he rose he met the gaze of the Typhon painted on the central pillar. In the flickering light of the lamp it seemed instinct with life; its expression seemed changed, and it appeared to regard him with malevolence and deadly hate. Its gaze fascinated him, and he could not remove his eyes till the touch of Morton on his elbow recalled him to himself, and he saw that Chiarina had finished her divinations and was anxiously urging them to depart. As they mounted the steps that led to the upper world, a vivid flash of lightning was followed almost instantaneously by the crash of thunder. Chiarina clung to them in terror.

"Go, go, Signori," cried she. "It is Tinia. He is angry. I must go back to appease him." and she pushed them through the thicket into the pathway and then disappeared into the darkness. Left without a guide, they scrambled as best they could through the wood and into the open country, and with some trouble found the high road. A few lights of the town twinkled in the distance to direct them, and they hurried onward with a strange sense of insecurity. The heavens were black with clouds, the lightning was incessant, a deluge of rain caught them while they were still in the open, and they arrived at the inn drenched to the skin.

"A strange adventure," muttered Morton as they parted for the night. "A trifle uncanny, eh? One might almost imagine there was after all something in their creed, were it not too absurd. But what is that on your finger?"

Bryant looked at his hand. He had forgotten the ring he picked up, and he now examined it with curiosity. It was a curious piece of Etruscan goldsmith's work with some letters inscribed round the rim which he could not decipher.

"Oh! the ring," said he. "It fell at my feet from somewhere or other. I suppose I brushed against one of the bronze tables and knocked it off, and I picked it up and slipped it on my finger, and then forgot all about it."

"H'm! well, you know best," said Morton, "but I think you would have done better to have left it there. However, good-night, I am longing to get dry again."

BRYANT WAS OF AN IMAGINATIVE TURN OF MIND, as befitted his literary vocation, and the adventure of the night made an impression on him that kept him for some time awake. The whole scene presented itself to his memory; the silent walk, the wood, the mysterious tomb with its contents, and above all the countenance of the Typhon with its scowl of concentrated hate. This last pursued him into dreamland, and caused him to pass a troubled night.

Next morning they thought it right to go and see whether their young guide had got safely back, and had not suffered from the storm. Chiarina, however, it appeared had fared better than they, for the storm ceased about the time they reached Corneto. But Antonietta was anxious and troubled. Something she said was wrong, and the storm showed displeasure on the part of the powers on whom they had intruded. As they were leaving Corneto that afternoon, Morton shook her by the hand, and said, "You see, Antonietta, no harm but a wetting has come of our visit, which you thought so dangerous."

Antonietta said nothing, but when Bryant offered his hand her eye caught sight of the ring. Dropping his hand she made an exclamation of horror.

"Signore," she cried, "do you know what you have done, you have brought a curse upon you; restore the ring at once, or mischief will befall you."

"But we are leaving Corneto to-day," said Morton, "and have no time for another visit. And what harm can come of the ring."

"Besides," said Bryant, "on further looking at it, I think it is a very curious piece of work; and I mean to give it to the Museum when I get home."

"If you keep it," said Antonietta in great excitement, "perhaps you will not get home. And you will never give it to the Museum, for it will not leave you till you restore it to the place you took it from. The hand that took must be the hand to restore."

"But that is impossible," said they both. There was no time to go back to the tomb. And besides Bryant had taken a fancy to it, and looked forward to presenting the Museum with a genuine antique, of whose authenticity there could be no question. He even declined to give it to Antonietta who said she herself would take it back, and that would suffice. At last she threw up her hands in despair, and retreating into her cottage slammed the door behind her.

Early in the afternoon they parted; Morton for Rome, and Bryant for Viterbo, by way of Toscanella where he meant to stay a day or two to see the two fine churches, and the Etruscan tombs. His conveyance was a primitive car little better than a coster-monger's cart, drawn by a weedy little horse, and driven by a hobbledehoy of a lad, the son of the proprietor. The road at first lay along the high plateau where the tombs were. In the country beyond there were no houses or villages to be seen, though the land was well cultivated, for the farmers and their men go in and out daily in carts from the town. The desolate country had been the scene of brigandage not long before, and the memory of Tiburzi and his nephew was not yet extinct. Giovanni amused Bryant with tales of this sordid hero, and of his escapes, and final capture, till their conversation was suddenly stopped by a lurch of the vehicle which threw them both into the ditch. On getting to their feet they found that beyond a few bruises and scratches, neither of them was hurt, but the cart had one wheel off, and the shaft broken. They were at least seven miles from Corneto, and more from Toscanella; there was no place nearer where help could be had, and they were in a bad case. At last they decided the only thing was to get back to Corneto. The ruined car they pulled into the ditch, and with cords from the harness secured Bryant's slender luggage on the back of the horse, and set off on foot to retrace their way to Corneto.

Their return caused no little surprise. It was too late to make a fresh start that day, and Bryant returned to his old quarters. As he was undressing his eye caught the ring. "Well," thought he, "if Antonietta knew of this accident it would give her a fine argument for her theory that the ring would bring me bad luck."

The loss of a day made Toscanella and Viterbo out of the question, for Bryant had to hurry back to London to complete a magazine article which was wanted by a certain date. Next day therefore, he took the train to Pisa and Genoa on his way home to England. He was curiously unlucky. His luggage was delayed at the frontier, and he arrived in Paris with nothing but a hand bag. This kept him three days more, till the missing portmanteau arrived, and he reached London nearly a week later than he had intended. Other little accidents of less consequence happened, and combined to cause him some uneasiness. His nights, moreover, were disturbed by dreams. He seemed always to be drawn towards that silent tomb, and to be face to face with the scowling monster on the pillar. A morbid feeling of terror slowly mastered him. He could not shake it off, and gradually the evil countenance began to intrude itself into his thoughts by day. It interrupted his work, and his writing which had been his greatest pleasure became a labour and a burden.

One day it occurred to him that he had not sent that Etruscan ring to the Museum, and he carefully packed it and sent it to the curator with a letter to say he had been fortunate enough to pick up a genuine piece of Etruscan goldsmith's work in Tuscany, and he would be glad if the Museum authorities would accept it for their collection. He took the packet to the post office himself, and on his return found a parcel on his table from his publisher. On opening it, he found it contained the manuscript of the article he had sent since his return from abroad, the one in fact for the sake of dispatching which, he had been so anxious to get home. A letter from the publisher accompanied it. It ran as follows:

> "Dear Sir,—I regret to say I am obliged to return your article which in its present shape is quite unsuitable for our pages. The subject on which we invited you to write was one on which we had reason to believe you were an authority, but what you send us seems unequal and largely irrelevant. In particular we fail to understand the allusions in which it abounds to Etruscan mythology.
>
> "I am, Sir,
> "Your obedient servant,
> "The Editor."

"What on earth does this mean," said Bryant to himself. "The man must have got hold of another paper, and confused it with mine."

The paper, however, was his, and on glancing over it he was aghast. "Is it possible I wrote this balderdash," thought he. "I must be going mad," and he pressed his hand to his brow. But there was no mistake about it being his writing, full of literary faults and widely incoherent as it was. The colour rushed to his cheeks as he tore the shameful pages up and tossed them into the paper basket. Etruscan mythology, too, what on earth could have made him drag that into an article on the "History of the Colony of New Zealand." Was he never to get out of his head the memory of that ill-omened visit? And as his mind reverted to the events of the night the scowling visage of the Typhon presented itself to his mental vision. "Is it possible," he thought, "that that ring has some potent force for evil. Well, anyhow, I am rid of it now; and no further harm can come of it."

He slept better that night, and next day decided to go for a long walk in the country in the hope of steadying his shaken nerves. He found an old college friend disposed for an outing, and they took the train to Clandon, and walked over Newlands Corner to St.

Martha's chapel, down to Shamley Green, Wonersh, and Bramley, and so home by rail. They dined together at the Oxford and Cambridge Club, and then parted, Bryant to his chambers in the Temple. On his table, he found a packet by registered post. It contained a letter from the Director of the museum, and a small parcel in cotton wool of which he guessed too well the contents. The letter ran thus:

> "Dear Sir,—We are much obliged to you for your kind offer of the enclosed ring, which we return with our thanks. It appears to us to be one of the clever copies made in Germany of Etruscan antiquities, by which many collectors have been taken in. We venture to express our hope that you were not too heavily mulcted in the purchase.
> "Your obedient servant,
> "—, Director."

"Much they know about it," said Bryant bitterly, as he unfolded the packet, and looked at his fatal possession with dismay. The window was open, and in a sudden rage he flung it far and wide into the court, and went to bed.

He felt better next morning, and after breakfast settled down to some literary work that had come in the day before. But it would not do. His mind was confused, and all power of clear expression seemed to have left him. As he was sitting in despair with his head on his hands there was a knock at the door, and Mrs. Filcher, the laundress, entered with something in her hand.

"Begging your pardon, Mr. Bryant," she began, "I picked up this 'ere little ring in the court, and seeing as I have noticed it on your finger, I know'd it to be yourn, and so I have brought it up. Thank you, sir, good-morning, sir.

And the good woman sidled out a shilling the richer, but leaving Bryant in an agony of despair. "Can I never shake off this strange oppression?" thought he, as he gazed on the fatal circlet of gold that lay on the table before him. The words of Antonietta came back to his memory: "it will never leave you till you restore it to the place you took it from." It seemed as if it were true. Twice he had tried in vain to get rid of it, and twice it had been restored; that night he would make sure of a riddance. He remained in his rooms till evening in a sort of mental torpor. He could neither eat nor drink. A creeping horror took possession of him; as he cast his eyes about in the dusk, innocent book-shelves seemed to resolve themselves into sepulchral forms, and in the midst appeared the scowling visage of the Typhon. At last when night fell he took the ring, descended his staircase, and found his way to the Embankment. The tide was up; with all his might he flung the ring into the river, and then sank down on one of the seats. Famished and exhausted he felt more dead than alive, and half fainting, and half asleep, he lost consciousness.

"Now then, wake up," said a gruff voice in his ear, some hours later, while a heavy hand on his shoulder gave him a good shake, and he woke to find the morning breaking, and a burly policeman standing over him. He roused himself, and stood up. "Beg pardon, sir," said the policeman, seeing he was a gentleman, "bit overcome, sir, was you? Hadn't you better get to your home, sir, 'stead o' lying here? Let me lend you a hand till you've steadied yourself."

Bryant thanked the man who went off contented with half-a-crown, and then tottered back to his chambers, and threw himself on his bed in a fever. As he sank on the pillow he happened to raise his hand. On his finger was the fatal ring. Was it then only a dream that he had flung it into the river? He could not tell. His brain was in a whirl; one thought only beat upon his mind, "it will never leave you till you restore it to the place you took it from." He rose from his bed resolved to act on the warning. Every attempt to part with it had failed; the Museum would not have it; and it came back mysteriously twice when he had hurled it away in desperation. Antonietta must be right. He would go to Corneto and find her, and she should guide him again to the fatal place which he now wished to heaven he had never seen.

In half an hour he had put up a small bag of his things, and was on his way to Cook's to secure a sleeping-berth in the St. Gothard express. The excitement he had gone through, his fasting the day before, and his sleepless night began to tell on him. He scarcely noticed anything on the journey, and lived as in a dream. At the frontiers he roused himself to pass the customs, and then sank again into a sort of stupor. At Chiasso he felt a thrill at the thought he was again in Italy, and nearing his point. At Milan there was a delay of some hours which put him in a fever of impatience. Another night in the train, and then, thank Heaven, in the early morning he alighted at Corneto. He was so weak he could hardly stand, but he managed to reach the omnibus, in which he climbed the hill to the city which is some two miles or so from the station.

He was greeted as an old acquaintance by the padrone of the inn where he and Morton had stayed before, to whom he had telegraphed for a room. Breakfast and a bath restored him a little, and then he set off to find Antonietta. He found his way to her house without difficulty, and saw the familiar figure standing at the door and spinning with distaff and spindle as of old.

"Antonietta," he cried, "I am here again, and want your help." The woman turned and faced him. It was not Antonietta. Bryant stood amazed and confounded; the disappointment was too great.

"The Signore asked for Antonietta," said she. "Perhaps the Signore knew Antonietta."

"Yes, yes," stammered he, "I knew her. Where is she? I am come from England expressly to see her."

"Ah! Signore, you have not heard. *La povera Antonietta è morta*. She is dead."

Bryant reeled as if he had been shot. His last hope was struck from under him. He staggered and would have fallen had not the contadina caught him, and put him into her seat.

"*Prego! S'accomodi?* the Signore seems ill. I will fetch a glass of water."

Bryant recovered himself a little, and said:

"And her daughter, Chiarina, is she dead too?"

"Oh, no! la Chiarina is well, but she is not here. She is with her friends at Montefiascone. I can give you her address if you like."

Bryant seized on this suggestion with the eagerness of a drowning man grasping at a floating spar, and after resting a little longer at the invitation of the good woman, he rose and managed to regain his hotel. He wrote at once to the address that had been given him, but he could not wait for the answer, and ill as he was he sallied forth to try and find that fatal tomb. All that afternoon he wandered like an unhappy spirit over the ground. He knew they had gone two miles or more from the town, and that they penetrated a wood. He searched every copse and thicket he could see, but in vain, He found nothing like the scene of their midnight adventure, and returned dispirited in the evening to his hotel. The next day he again sallied out and wandered to and fro in his quest, wearying himself in vain, for he could find nothing like the place he was looking for. A carabiniere saw him, and watched his devious movements with suspicion.

"The Signore seems to be seeking something," said he.

"I am looking for a tomb," said Bryant.

"The Signore should apply to the custode who will guide him. All the tombs are closed, and visits are not permitted without the custode."

Bryant murmured something in reply, and wandered on while the carabiniere kept the eye of suspicion upon him. In the evening he staggered home. No news had come from Chiarina, and in despair, utterly worn out, and broken down, he threw himself on his bed, and gave himself up for lost.

Dr. Morton was sitting in his rooms at Oxford after breakfast, smoking his morning pipe, and casting an eye occasionally at the notes of a lecture he was to give that morning on folk-lore. In writing it he had made use of his experiences in Tuscany during the late holiday. The thought of this brought Bryant to his recollection, and he drew from his pocket a letter received from him a few days back, which had puzzled him a good deal. It was very short, and consisted of a few broken sentences to which he could not attach much meaning. It said: "I am being bothered and pestered beyond all endurance in a way that drives me mad. I cannot part with that ring. You do not know what I am suffering. One thing is certain, I must obey Antonietta, and go back."

"But why," thought Morton, "does he bother himself about his ring? Why should he part with it, if he does not like to do so, and why does he let people pester him about it? Some dealer or other I expect who wants to buy it. But who's there? Come in," he said in reply to a knock at the door.

The new-comer was one of the Fellows who was a great friend of Bryant, and Morton after a few words on general matters asked him if he had heard anything of Bryant lately.

"Well, as you ask me," said Williamson, "I have, and I am uneasy about him. You know he wrote a great deal for the Piccadilly magazine, and in fact was one of their principal contributors. Well, I met Henderson, the editor, at the Athenæum the other day, and he said to me, 'What is the matter with your man, Bryant?' 'Nothing that I know of,' said I. 'Why do you ask?' 'I ask,' said he, 'because he sent us an article the other day for the Piccadilly that he could only have written if he were drunk or mad. It was rambling and illiterate, and of course, useless to us. But the curious thing was that it dragged in head and shoulders a lot about Etruscan tombs, and a fatal ring, that had nothing whatever to do with the subject.'"

"A ring you say," said Morton. "Now that is curious, for I was just reading when you came in, a letter from him that I received a few days ago, about a ring. I remember he did pick up a ring in an old Etruscan tomb we visited together, and one of those half necromantic women of the place prophesied it would bring him no good. He talks also of going back there. I remember the inn where we stayed, and I have a mind to wire out to find out if he is there."

Morton accordingly telegraphed to the padrone of the Stella d'Oro at Corneto to ask whether Signor Bryant was there, and he prepaid the answer. The answer did not come till the next day. It said:

"The Signore is here. Very ill. Prays you to come."

Morton was much concerned, for he had a great regard for Bryant. Something was evidently wrong, and the ring seemed to be at the bottom of it. Morton remembered saying to Bryant that he would have done better to leave it behind. His researches in folk-lore had revealed to him the superstitious belief of the peasantry in the old Etruscan mythology, and it had sometimes occurred to him, though he always dismissed the idea as absurd, that they might have some ground for their faith. And now here was Bryant evidently in some mysterious way or other in trouble about the ring he had picked up. Well, at all events, Morton resolved to go at once in answer to his friend's appeal.

In due time he arrived at the Stella d'Oro, and the padrone met him with a serious face. "I am glad you are come, Signore," said he. "Your poor friend has been raving and calling for you. He keeps crying out about a ring and a tomb, and we cannot tell what he means. The doctor shakes his head, and will not say what he thinks."

Morton was much concerned, and asked for particulars of his illness. The landlord said Signore Bryant had been very strange, very unlike what he was when Morton had been there with him; that he spent his days wandering about the country as if in search of something, so that the police had noticed it, and had been inquiring about him, as if they suspected him of some mischief. But that at last he had completely worn himself out, and had now been lying a week in a raging fever and delirium.

"You had better come and see him, Signore, though I doubt he will not know you." They mounted the stair silently, and stole quietly into the darkened room.

"He is very still now," said the padrone, as they approached the bed. "I hope he is sleeping; sleep will do him good."

But as Morton bent over his friend and called him by his name he realised that poor Bryant's troubles were over. He was dead.

MORTON WAS EXCESSIVELY SHOCKED, and quite overcome. Bryant had been his most intimate and congenial friend; he had watched with interest his literary career, which promised great things, and he grieved to think a life that had opened so well should be so prematurely cut short. He sat by his poor friend's bedside in sincere distress.

A message was brought to him a little later that a young woman, a *contadina*, was below, and asked for the English gentleman. Morton descended, and found himself face to face with Chiarina, who remembered him at once. She explained that she had come in reply to a letter from the English Signore, and would have come sooner had it been possible, but she had been from home for some days.

"And now, Chiarina," said Morton, "you come too late to see him. The poor Signore is no more."

Chiarina expressed her regret and sympathy, and asked what the poor Signore died of.

"He wore himself out," said Morton, "looking I imagine, for the tomb you showed us that night."

"Oh! Dio! Surely he did not venture to go there by himself," said Chiarina. "Is it that which has brought this illness on him?"

"No, I think not. He seems to have failed to find it. But he has been in trouble about a ring. You remember he picked one up in the tomb, and your mother told him it would bring him bad luck. What can you tell me about it?"

"Ah! Now I understand," said Chiarina. "Signore, that ring has killed him. Those you know of never forgive. You will remember my mother said 'the hand that took must be the hand to restore.' Till he restored it, he would have no peace, and now it has brought him to his death."

Now, thought Morton to himself, I understand his return to Corneto, his wild rambling about the place, and his anxiety to find Antonietta and Chiarina. He wanted, of course, to get them to guide him to the tomb and return the ring.

He stood a little while in thought, and then asking Chiarina to await his return, he went back to the chamber of death, and stood by the dead man's bedside. He took the cold hand in his; on the finger was the fatal ring.

"Humph!" said Morton, "There is no knowing what mischief it may do. Perhaps after all the ring had nothing to do with it, and poor Bryant's sufferings may have been imaginary so far as it was concerned. But anyhow, it seems to have plagued him in life, and I should be sorry to think it plagued him in death. On the whole, I had better draw it off from his finger, and give it to Chiarina to take it back to the place it came from."

A ROMANCE OF THE PICCADILLY TUBE

OLD MR. MARKHAM LAY DYING in an upper room of a fine mansion in a great London square. The house was plunged in that oppressive stillness which reigns when sickness is there and death is near. Footsteps were stealthy, and voices subdued, and the ticking of the clock was audible in the silent room. By the bedside of the old man was Mr. Harvey, his confidential solicitor and old friend, come to attend the execution of the sick man's last will and testament.

"You are quite resolved then," said Mr. Harvey, "to dispose of your property thus? I have drawn the will exactly to your instructions, but as an old friend of you and your sons, you will forgive my putting this question again for the last time."

"Yes," said a feeble voice, "that's what I mean."

"You cut off your elder son, George, with a thousand pounds, and leave all the rest, except some minor legacies, to James. The old will, you remember, left them equal shares."

"Yes, yes," said the old man peevishly, "I have paid George's debts over and over again till I am sick of it, and what I might give him now would only go the way of the rest. He has a little money of his own from his mother, if he hasn't spent it, and he must make that do. James is a careful lad and the estate will fare better in his hands."

"Well, I have no right to say more, though I'm sorry. But of course, you must do what you please with your own."

The old man was propped up in his bed, a pen was put into his feeble fingers, a servant was called in as a second witness, the deed was duly signed and attested, and Mr. Harvey took it away with him.

The two sons were waiting in the dining-room. They had finished a late luncheon and were standing by the fire. They knew of Mr. Harvey's visit, and guessed its purpose, and various thoughts were passing through their minds. George indeed did not trouble himself much about the will. In his careless way, he thought things would be all right, and he need not worry himself about them beforehand. He was concerned for his father, whom he really loved, though he knew how often he had plagued and offended him, almost beyond forgiveness. James, on the contrary, being of a cooler and more calculating temper, could not help wondering what was meant by a new will, and an altered disposition of the property. The estate was a large one, with lands in the country, beside the house in town, and large sums in the funds, and he wondered how his interests would be affected by what was going on upstairs.

The door opened and Mr. Harvey came in to bid them good-bye. He had known them since they were boys, and had a regard for both of them, though in his secret heart he preferred the scapegrace George to his more careful brother.

"Well, sir," said George advancing to meet him, "how did you leave my father? I am sorry to say the doctor gives us little hope. Do you think he would like to see me?"

"I doubt it, George; you must ask the doctor or the nurse. He is very feeble."

"Was he able to attend to the business you came about?" asked James.

Mr. Harvey thought the question rather ill-timed and unfeeling, and answered a little curtly, that there had been no difficulty. He then took leave of them. George accompanied him to the door, and as they were parting, Mr. Harvey putting his hand on his arm, said:

"Tell me, George. Have you any debts?"

"Not a penny," said he radiantly, "my dear old father paid them all off last week before he fell ill. It was awfully good of him. I know I have behaved badly, and did not deserve it from him."

"Well, George," said Mr. Harvey, "let me give you a hint. There must be no more debts in future. You will have to be careful. I speak seriously for your good. Farewell, and don't forget what I say."

Left to himself, George wondered what was meant by this hint, connected, he supposed, with the new will, if indeed a new will had really been executed, as he and his brother believed. Mr. Harvey's words seemed to convey a friendly warning that things had not been going favourably for him upstairs. He had always understood that he and his brother were to share equally in the estate; was this arrangement now to be disturbed? That would be awkward, for he had only small means of his own, and his way of living had always been after an opulent fashion.

"Hang it all," he said, "it will be deuced hard on me, if James gets more than his share. After all, I'm the eldest son, and he has no right to cut me out."

Like the two sons of the Patriarch, the two Markhams differed entirely in character and pursuits; but in the modern case, the parental preference had been reversed, for it was the mother who had loved the Esau of the family best, and the father who favoured the Jacob. George Markham was lively and adventurous, a lover of pleasure and selfish and self-indulgent in its pursuit; but he had a kindly and generous vein in his composition which in the view of his friends went far towards compensating his faults. James was of a cautious and calculating nature, who did everything with deliberation, looking carefully after his own interests, and fencing himself round with precautions. He was married, and had children, and a business in the City which was doing well. Since his mother's death, George's influence in the family steadily declined: Esau sank into disfavour and the star of Jacob ascended; till at last, as we have seen, their father resolved that by leaving George free of debt and with a thousand pounds in his pocket, he might wash his hands of further responsibility for him.

In this perturbed state of mind, after parting with Mr. Harvey, George avoided rejoining his brother, and taking his hat, sallied forth to go to his chambers in the Temple. The justification for these chambers was a shallow pretence he made of reading for the

Bar, though beyond eating his dinners he did little else to qualify himself for a forensic career. However, it served as a pretext for establishing himself in bachelor's quarters, which was convenient for his way of living, and his father had long given up in despair any inquiry after his legal studies.

It was growing dusk as he descended to a station of the Piccadilly tube. There was the congestion of would-be passengers usual at eventide when offices close and myriads of clerks and servants flock from the centre of London to the outskirts. Trains arrived crammed to suffocation, not a seat vacant, passages choked with strapholders, and entrance lobby solid with perspiring humanity. When the carriage doors were opened to discharge a few travellers, the mob surged desperately to force an entrance, half of them to be disappointed, and condemned to wait for another train, where they might be more fortunate. George was near one end of the platform where the crowd was a little less compact, though even there he had hardly room to move. A train was heard approaching and every head was turned in that direction. At that moment a gentleman in front of him dropped something, and stooped to recover it, though the crowd allowed him little room for movement. George saw it at his feet: it was a paper folded length-ways and lay more within his reach than that of the owner. "Let me get it for you, sir," he said, and stooped to pick it up and restore it. The roar of the train sounded close at hand; the crowd pressed on the stooping figures, as they rose together they were pushed violently against one another; the other man was close to the edge of the platform, and to his horror, George saw him lose his balance and fall over the edge. As he fell, George caught sight of his face; it was his old friend, Mr. Harvey. The train was upon him in a moment.

There was a shriek from the crowd, first a recoil and then a rush of agonised spectators; George was swept back to the far side of the platform and stood leaning against the wall, trembling and sick with horror. Officials arrived, the train was moved, and men went down on the line upon their ghastly errand. He could not bear to wait and see the recovery of the body, or witness the frightful details of the accident. Shaking in every limb, he found his way to the exit, half unconsciously; the lift was remote and news of the accident had not reached the attendant when George took his place, and there was no delay. As he reached the surface, he noticed that he had in his hand the fatal paper which had occasioned the disaster. It was too dark to see the address, and he put it in his pocket. It had belonged, he supposed, to his poor friend, and on the morrow he would forward it to the address it bore. It did not matter now, his only aim for the moment was to get to his quarters and try to recover his nerve. He called a cab and drove to the Temple.

Arrived at his rooms, he sank into an armchair and covered his face with his hands. The whole dreadful scene passed before him in imagination; the crush, the collision, the reeling back of his poor friend, the glimpse of his face and of the grey hair as his hat fell off, and then the train came upon him. It made him sick to think of it. By and by, as the first horror of the scene passed and left room for calmer reflection, he thought less of the accident, and more of the man. Harvey had long been his father's friend and adviser; he had always been kind to himself as a boy, and had often stood his friend when he had need of an advocate with his father. He thought of him with affection, and remembered how many times he had given him sound advice which had never been followed, but of which he now saw the value; and now that was all at an end, and what an end!

After a time he rose, and thought he would go and dine somewhere quietly. He could not bear to go to his club and face his friends with this horror fresh on his mind, and so he had a quiet chop at one of the old eating-houses in Fleet Street, where he knew he should meet no one of his acquaintance, and it was late when he came back to his chambers.

When he had turned on the light, his eye fell upon something that lay on the table. It was the fatal paper, which he had taken from his pocket before going out. He took it up listlessly, to see if it bore any address to which he should send it in the morning. But it bore no address, and when he had read the endorsement, he stood some minutes motionless with the paper in his hand, as if he were turned to stone. He saw it was a will, or rather a codicil to the last will and testament of Richard Markham, which had been executed that very afternoon. After a time, he laid the paper again on the table, and stood with his back to the fire thinking what he should do.

So there really had been a new will, or a codicil to alter the old one, and from the hint dropped by his poor friend, Mr. Harvey, he gathered that the alteration had not been in his favour. The temptation was strong to open the paper and see how he stood, but he was restrained by a scruple, and continued to stand by the fire looking at it as it lay on the table before him. He supposed that his loss would be James's gain. James had always been his lather's favourite, comparisons had been drawn between him and James, to James's advantage; James had been proposed to him as a pattern, though he hated James's cautious ways which seemed to him mere selfishness. The selfishness of his own idle extravagant life naturally did not occur to him. James, he thought, was a schemer, who had always got the better of him, and had robbed him of his birthright as eldest son. What would be the justice of James taking more than a fair share of his father's estate? The longer he thought about it the stronger grew the temptation to open the paper and see what provision it made for him. There it lay before him, as it were looking him in the face and inviting him to take it; a riddle awaiting solution, charged with fate and the whole current of his future life. He took it in his hand and weighed it: on this fatal sheet his fortunes depended. In a matter so vital it was folly to be over-scrupulous; as he gathered, he was the person most likely to be affected by its contents; surely he was entitled to know them, and it could not matter to anyone else whether he knew them or not.

He sat down and opened the paper. It was a codicil to the old will, very short, and it dealt almost entirely with the one subject of George's share in the disposition of the estate. He laid the paper down in dismay, and sat in silence looking into the fire.

"A thousand pounds and nothing more," he kept repeating to himself. "It is monstrous. What have I done to deserve to be treated thus?" Independently of the money, how was he to explain his position to the world, for his friends had always looked on him as his father's heir. How was he to live on the slender income inherited from his mother, which, luckily for him, she had so tied up that he could not touch the capital? All his habits and tastes were expensive; he constantly outran his father's liberal allowance, and as constantly had to appeal to him for money to clear his debts. There was no one now left to appeal to, for it would be idle to approach James, who he knew would stand on his rights and give him his thousand pounds and no more. Besides which, he could not bring himself to beg of his younger brother; no, that at all events was not to be thought of—and there lay the accursed paper in his lap. What was to be done with it? He supposed it ought to go to Messrs. Harvey & Moor, his father's lawyers. But that might wait till tomorrow. And poor Harvey was dead. That however did not affect the matter, for the firm was there. He must send it to them to-morrow, he supposed.

It was then that some pestilent devil at his elbow seemed to whisper in his ear, "Why send it at all?"

The idea covered him with shame and he scotched it at first, for reckless as his life had been he had never stooped to anything dishonourable. But it would not be so dismissed, and kept pestering him with suggestions of the ease with which the codicil might be suppressed. Putting things together he made out that Mr. Harvey had taken the codicil to Mr. Markham, who had signed it, the witnesses being Mr. Harvey himself and the footman, whose names appeared in the document; that Mr. Harvey had taken the paper away with him, and had arrived at the station on the Piccadilly tube at pretty nearly the same moment when he got there himself. The rest of the story we know.

"Then," thought George, "one of the witnesses was dead, and the footman could only testify that he signed a paper, not knowing what it was, which might have been something quite different." The lawyers, of course, had instructions for drawing the codicil, and probably a rough draft of its contents, but what evidence could they produce that it had ever been executed? The only proof of that was the codicil itself and that now lay in his lap; and the fire was burning opposite him. It would only be an affair of a moment, the

hateful deed would be reduced to a few ashes, and he would in-
herit the half of the estate to which he maintained he was entitled
by every consideration of justice and fair-play. James would have
the other half, which was his fairly enough, and he was already
doing well in business, and so would really be much better off than
his elder brother. The temptation was strong; almost irresistible;
the devil at his elbow kept urging him; and his very fingers itched
to twitch the fatal paper from his lap on to the glowing coals. But
his better self restrained him: he could not bring himself to do it,
and locking the deed up in his drawer he went to bed.

He was roused next morning by a messenger from his father's
house, with a letter from his brother James, enclosing another
addressed to himself.

> "Dear George," it began, "You will not be surprised
> to hear that all is over here. Our dear father died
> quietly last night. You will, no doubt, come at once
> to help me make the necessary arrangements. I
> enclose a letter for you from Messrs. Harvey & Moor,
> which, as it was marked 'immediate,' I ventured
> to open. You will be shocked at its contents. Your
> affectionate brother, James Markham."

Messrs. Harvey & Moor's letter announced the unfortunate death
of the elder partner from an accident on the railway. They thought,
as he was engaged in business for Mr. Markham at the time of his
decease, they ought to lose no time in communicating the sad intelligence to Mr. Markham's representative.

George had not expected his father's death so suddenly, and
was much affected. He wished he had been with him at the end.
Their relations had not always been friendly, but he admitted the
fault had been his own, though the punishment in the end was
unfairly severe, he went home therefore with mixed feelings of
sorrow and resentment.

He alighted at the same station on the tube railway which had
been the scene of the catastrophe the night before, and he looked

with horror at the fatal spot. As he made his way to the lift he had an uncomfortable feeling that he was being followed. To be sure a crowd was going with him, but it was not that; he saw no one especially noticing him, and could not account for the feeling. He had given up his ticket and entered the lift, when the attendant said "Ticket, please," to someone behind him. He turned but saw no one.

"Old gentleman with you, sir?" asked the attendant. "Why, what has become of him?" he continued, looking about him.

"No. There is no one with me," said George, much surprised.

"Well, I'm dashed," said the attendant, staring about. "He's gone, anyhow. That's rummy"; and then he attended to his duty and started the lift.

George found the great house with all the windows darkened: the straw with which the street had been strewn during the late owner's illness deadened all sound from outside, and within was the silence of death. James met him, already attired in funereal weeds, and his wife was there whom George disliked, for he thought her intriguing and meddlesome, and mistrusted her influence on James himself. He knew instinctively he had no friend in her should any question arise about the disposition of the estate. He went and saw his father; the tears stood in his eyes as he thought of the unkindness that had grown up between them year by year, and he was touched with remorse as he recalled the many occasions on which he had given cause for his father's displeasure. He even, at that moment, forgave him that fatal codicil, though the feeling of resentment returned as he sat at luncheon with James and his wife, and thought how unfairly they were to benefit at his expense. He took his part in the arrangements for the funeral and other matters, but would not stay in the house, and returned in the evening to his chambers in the Temple, anxious and dispirited, and with a sense of impending calamity. And then he remembered that he was to have sent that paper to the lawyers in the morning, and had not done so. Well, it was too late to-night; he would do it in the morning. He would be glad to be rid of it and be put out of his misery.

His sleep was not untroubled. He seemed to go back to the time when he was a boy, and his father a younger man, who had been kind to him and proud of his performances in his school games, at which James had always been a duffer; and then his father's face grew serious and displeased as it had become in later life; and then it melted away into another face, the face of his old friend Harvey, sad and warning, and oh, horror! there were streaks of blood, and with that he awoke. Morning was beginning, he could sleep no more; a cold bath restored his nerves, and a walk in the brisk morning air before breakfast braced him up somewhat for the coming day.

Days passed and the time came for the funeral, and after that he knew the executors would be moving in the matter of the will, and questions would arise about the codicil. It still lay in his drawer. He had put off from day to day taking the irrevocable step of sending it, which would deprive him at once of all claim to what he held was his rightful inheritance. He said to himself it was useless to put it oft; it could make no difference to him whether he sent it now, or kept it a few days longer: the result would be the same; and yet he had not the courage to do the fatal act. The pistol was at his head as it were, and his finger on the trigger, and he dared not pull it, though he knew he was doomed. He grew pale and anxious and avoided society. Of James he saw as little as possible, though family arrangements made it necessary they should meet sometimes. He fancied his sister-in-law looked at him with an air of subdued triumph, though what could she know about the codicil and its contents? It raised his bile and hardened his heart, and he thought how easily if he pleased he could defeat her.

Mr. Markham's executors were two, Mr. Winter, a City magnate, and Sir Charles Mallet, a retired Indian civilian, and they were already in communication with the solicitor firm of Harvey & Moor. The only will in evidence was that made some years before, which gave the two brothers an equal share in the estate. But Mr. Moor produced the draft of the codicil which upset this arrangement, and which he believed had been duly executed, though at present it could not be found.

"What makes you think it was executed?" asked Sir Charles.

"I think so," said Mr. Moor, "because we had Mr. Markham's instructions to send it to him for signature, he being then ill in bed. It was therefore copied out fairly, and my partner, Mr. Harvey, took it with him to Mr. Markham's house. He was seen there by both the sons, and we know that Mr. Markham signed something, for a servant, whom we can produce, witnessed it, and we presume it was the codicil. Mr. Harvey, as you know, was unhappily killed on his way home, and the document which he no doubt had with him was, we presume, lost or destroyed in the accident."

"What the servant witnessed," said Mr. Winter, "may have been only a transfer of stock or something of that kind."

"Perhaps, but we are not aware of any such transfer being made at that time."

"On the other hand," said Sir Charles, "Mr. Markham may have changed his mind and altered the codicil before signing it. I confess it seems to me it was a monstrous piece of injustice from first to last."

"Well, gentlemen, what do you suggest?" said Mr. Moor.

The executors debated about the matter a little longer and at last it was agreed to have another meeting at which the two Markham sons, who were principally concerned, should be present.

"What could induce my old friend Markham to make such a change in his will as that unhappy codicil was to have done?" said Sir Charles as the two executors walked away together.

"I know he was much put out by his elder son's extravagance," said the other, "and had paid a deal of money at times to get him out of debt. I suppose he thought that should be brought into the account."

"Well, I should be sorry if George lost his share. He is a good fellow at bottom," said Sir Charles, "and I dare say he has sown his wild oats by now. But what about this tiresome codicil? Do you think it was really executed, and if so, shall we ever find it?"

"Goodness knows," said Mr. Winter. "At all events I think it will give us a lot of trouble. Dear me! Who would be a trustee or executor?"

"I don't like James, the younger brother," said Sir Charles. "George is a much better fellow, though he has been playing the fool."

"And it is James," said Mr. Winter, "whose interest it is to put forward the codicil."

"You mean he will oppose the probate if we propound the old will without it?"

"Well," said Mr. Winter, "I know something of James in the City, and he is a good man of business."

"I see," said Sir Charles. "Good-bye; here I think our ways part." And then they shook hands and separated.

The proposed meeting at which the two brothers were to attend was fixed about a week later at Mr. Markham's house, where James Markham and his family were staying to see about the necessary domestic arrangements. Thither, at the time appointed, George Markham made his way, alighting at the tube station nearest the house as usual. He hated the sight of the place, which had such painful associations, and had he thought of it, he would have come another way, but from force of habit he had unconsciously followed the usual route. As he gave up his ticket at the lift the attendant looked hard at him, and then beyond him over his shoulder. The man's manner made George turn round to see what he was looking at. But he saw nothing.

"He's gone again," muttered the man. "I don't 'alf like it. Bill," said he to another attendant when he had discharged his living cargo at the top, "did ye see that grey-haired old gen'leman as come to the lift at the bottom, but didn't get in?"

"Not me," said Bill, who was not interested.

"Well, but look ye here! He follers that gen'leman as you see there walking away, up to the lift, and when I arst 'im for 'is ticket, why—he isn't there."

"Trying to bilk the company, very likely," said Bill. "If you can ketch 'im, p'rhaps you'll get a reward."

"Don't be a fool, Bill," said the other. "I tell you this has happened every time that same man comes 'ere. And I'll tell you another thing," said he, lowering his voice. "Do you remember that accident the other day when an old gentleman was killed?"

"Why, in course I do. What of that?"

"Why, as they carried 'im away, I see 'is face, and I see that face again just now at the foot of the lift."

"Oh, go along with you!" said Bill, as he walked away. "I don't believe in ghosties—you've been drinking and got the horrors."

The meeting took place in the dining-room. Both the executors were present with Mr. Moor, and George and James, by whose side his wife was sitting, with whom he frequently conferred in a whisper.

Both brothers had, of course, been formally made acquainted by the solicitor with the terms of the will, and also of the missing codicil.

But the solicitor stated the case afresh to make sure that it was understood in all its bearings by those concerned. The old will was obviously to be put forward for probate: about that there was no room for difference of opinion. The only difficulty was about the codicil. The codicil being missing, the question was one of proof that it had ever been executed.

Sir Charles Mallet said the whole thing was very uncertain. Even if the codicil had been duly executed, of which positive evidence seemed wanting, how were they to know whether it had been signed without alteration?

"It is not for me," he continued, "to criticise Mr. Markham's motive in making that codicil, but the effect of it, if I may be allowed to say so, is so unusual in the difference it makes between his sons, and so serious in the case of the elder brother, that it is quite conceivable that the testator may have changed his mind before signing. A stroke of the pen, for instance, might have converted Mr. George Markham's thousand pounds into ten or twenty thousand, or even more."

Mr. Winter, the other executor, seemed to concur with this view. He said he did not quite see his way to act on the draft codicil in the absence of the document itself. But, of course, he would be guided by the lawyers.

"I think," began James, "my dear father's last wishes—" but here he was stopped by marks of disapproval on the faces of his auditors.

"You were about to say something, Mr. Markham," said the solicitor. Mrs. James had been whispering to her husband, and obedient to her prompting he proceeded. "I was going to ask whether we should be doing right if we disregarded what we positively know to have been my father's last wishes as to the disposition of his estate."

"You mean that you should take my share as well as your own?" said George, who had not spoken before.

But James took no notice of this remark.

"Do I understand," said Mr. Moor, "that you will oppose the probate of the will without the codicil?

"Well, I am of course in a somewhat difficult position," said James, "being an interested party. But I have to consider others as well as myself, who would be affected; for myself, I might be disposed to waive any claim, but there is my wife, and there are my children, who would have rights in the matter, and so—well, gentlemen, you see the difficulty of my position."

His speech ended rather lamely, and it was received by the company in silence. Sir Charles looked at his colleague and raised his eyebrows. The other nodded, and the party broke up without any formal resolution, it being understood that the executors would be guided by legal advice in their procedure.

Sir Charles shook hands with George as they went out, and said it was an awkward business, and he was sorry for him if things went wrong. As for James, Sir Charles managed to avoid his parting salute.

"James showed very badly," he said to his colleague as they walked away. "He should have held his peace. That cant about his wife and children was in bad taste."

"You'll see James means to have his knife into his brother," said Mr. Winter. "We are in for a lawsuit over this business if I am not much mistaken."

Meanwhile the codicil still lay lurking in the drawer of George's writing-table in the Temple. The longer he deferred sending it, the harder it seemed to be to do so. He still said to himself he supposed it had to be done, but the more he thought about it the more cruel did the necessity appear. It was monstrous injustice to rob him of what his father had intended to give him by the will. Sir Charles Mallet had almost said as much at the meeting, and when he shook hands with him at parting. And James, with his hypocritical pretence of shielding himself behind the absurd rights of his wife and children! If anything would make him keep back the codicil it would be a desire to defeat James and his odious wife. James, with half the estate and a flourishing business in the City, was a rich man already, richer than he himself would be, even if he got his share. James ought to be satisfied with that, and not try to rob his elder brother of his rightful inheritance. With these thoughts George worked himself up into a passion of resentment against his brother, his sister-in-law, the codicil, the lawyers who drew it, and every one concerned about it, and persuaded himself that he was the injured victim of a conspiracy to defraud and beggar him. And all the while the same pestilent little devil at his elbow kept whispering, "Don't send it, don't send it; burn it, burn it."

And yet, when he got to his chambers, took it out of the drawer, and looked at it and at the fire, he could not do it.

"Not yet, not yet," he said to himself, and he put it back into the drawer and locked it up. But he had taken a step nearer the fatal act, and the next step would be a short one.

And James; he too was not quite happy. He had been greatly surprised to learn the contents of the codicil, which went far beyond any change he had imagined it would make in the disposition of the estate. He was not without affection for his brother, who had protected him at school, though he laughed at him and thought him a muff, and who had always acted generously to him as they grew up. Underneath a crust of cold selfishness still glowed the embers of their old friendship, and his first thought on reading the lawyer's communication had been: "It is very hard on poor George; what will he do?" It even occurred to him to let the matter of the codicil drop, especially as the document itself had been lost, and there was no positive proof of it ever having been executed. He was well off; the estate was a large one, and half of it with what he had would make him a rich man. He could afford to let George's half go as the old will had intended it should. But, unhappily, James consulted his wife, who overpersuaded him, and suggested the arguments which he had employed at the meeting, and by which, with her help, he at last succeeded in convincing himself. His father no doubt thought he was acting for the best, and his last wishes ought to be sacred; he had never cost his father a penny since he started in life, whereas George had bled his father's purse freely over and over again, and that surely ought to be taken into account. And then there were his wife and children—but here he paused: the faces of the executors at the meeting when he used that argument recurred to his memory, and he felt it would not do. He even blushed slightly at the recollection, and felt he had lowered himself by stooping to such a shallow pretence, which deceived nobody, not even himself.

Had James at this point been left alone he was not incapable of a generous decision. He had half a mind as he left the meeting and realised the unfavourable impression his claims had made on the executors, to write to the lawyer and say he waived any claims he might have arising from the codicil, and was content to abide by the original will; but he reckoned without his wife. Her tears and reproaches overcame his weak leaning to the generous side, and he resolved to claim his legal rights under the missing codicil, if his lawyers advised him that he had a good case.

The matter therefore had to be decided in a court of law, for the executors decided on ignoring the draft codicil, and propounded the original will. There was a special jury empanelled, and the highest talent of the Bar was employed on either side. James and his wife were there throughout the whole proceedings. George would not go near the place. In a manner he was relieved by the course things were taking. If the court decided that the codicil was to be upheld, why he had done no harm by keeping it hidden; the result would only be the same as if it had never been lost. If, on the other hand, the codicil should be negatived, he would take it as his justification in suppressing what he held to be an unfair invasion of his rights as the elder son. He was not really satisfied with these arguments; his conscience told him he was guilty of a dishonest act, and so far prevailed that he could not bring himself to show his face in court. He therefore spent the day in the country; the trial, he was told, would certainly take all day, and he would hear the result when he returned in the evening.

He had a long tramp over the Surrey hills, from Epsom race-course to Headley Common and Boxhill, returning by Mickleham and Leatherhead. The day was lovely, the larks singing in a sky of heavenly blue, the trees were still decked in the fresh virgin green of spring, and there was that delicious brisk buoyancy in the air that makes a man say life is worth living. But to George, at that time, it did not seem so. Life seemed to him a sordid affair. Take his own case; think of the choice before him: on one hand to be honest and a beggar, or on the other to be wealthy and a thief. Was such a life worth living in either case? Between the horns of this dilemma he was miserable. It haunted him as he walked, and as he ate his solitary luncheon at the wayside inn. His conscience troubled him; his honour in any case was smirched; whatever reparation he might make would not wipe off the stain; and that being so, that pestilent little tempter suggested, "Why worry about it? You have gone so far, you can't undo the fact that you have been guilty; it is too late to mend matters; go home and burn the deed. If the jury decide against you it won't be wanted, and if they decide for you it will be best in the fire to make things safe."

It was with this resolution finally fixed in his mind that George returned to town and sought his chambers. A telegram and some notes lay on his table, as he naturally supposed, containing a report of the result of the trial. He felt no impatience to learn what it was; he was disgusted with himself and the whole business.

The telegram was from the lawyers, and said:

"Will maintained, codicil upset." A later note from them confirmed this, and offered congratulations. Another note from Sir Charles Mallet, warmly expressed, said how glad he was of the result: that for his part he could not believe his old friend Mr. Markham really had signed a deed which was so obviously unjust.

"If he only knew," said George to himself, "that the codicil lies at this moment in the drawer under my hand, what would he think of me?"

He sat down to consider what he should do. He was now a rich man, but he felt no elation. It was however impossible to draw back. He must go on to the end. If ever the codicil were to be given up, it should have been done before the trial. The half of the estate was now legally his; to give it up would be quixotic. He half persuaded himself that his father, had he lived, would have reconsidered such an unfair division of the estate, and that the result of the trial, could he know it where he was, would not be displeasing to him.

He went to dine quietly at a City eating-house, not feeling fit for society, and unable to face the congratulations of his friends if he went to his club. He sat an hour over his port wine, making up his mind. He now had what he held to be his just rights, and it was necessary to make them secure. If he had made a bargain with the devil, at least he would have the fruits of it. The codicil should be destroyed that night, and James, with his odious wife, should be finally defeated for good and all.

Having made up his mind he went back to his chambers. His mind was in a strange confusion, a sort of nervous oppression weighed on him as he opened the door and entered. A fire was burning in the grate sending flickering gleams about the room. He turned on the lights; unlocked the drawer, and laid the fatal paper on the table. He stood a minute looking at it, and then he suddenly discovered he was not alone. Seated by the fire with his back to him was a man, whose grey head was visible over the top of the easy chair. George was on the point of asking who he was and what he wanted, when something seemed to arrest his speech, and he could only regard his strange visitor in silence. The figure rose slowly and turned to confront him across the table. The face was the face he had seen in his dream, the face of his old friend Harvey, and it regarded him with an earnestness that penetrated his very soul. George was unable to speak, to act, or even to move. He seemed fixed in a trance and could only look piteously at that serious face and wait in terror for what was to come. Still keeping its gaze fixed on him, the figure advanced to the table and laid its hand on the paper that lay there. Its regard was severe, but not unkindly; it seemed even to express pity and sorrow. Resting its hand on the fatal codicil it seemed to ask a question. George knew what it was, and the answer it wanted. Fierce debate raged within him, greed and passion on one side, shame and remorse on the other fought for supremacy, and still that steady gaze penetrated his inmost being. Gradually his evil passions seemed to melt before those calm searching eyes; his conscience awoke to better things; the resolution to do right prevailed. He knew the question that was put to him, and in a passion of tears he stammered out, "I will," and sinking into a chair he covered his face with his hands. When he removed them he was alone.

When he recovered himself he rose with a lightened heart, for a weight seemed to have been lifted from him. Reparation, that was the question that he had answered; reparation was what he had promised. It could not be made too soon. It should be made that very night. He put the codicil into an envelope and sealed it, and addressed it to Messrs. Harvey & Moor. They need not know whence it came, and so his shame need not be exposed. And yet without confession the reparation would not be complete. He would write to James and tell him all. And in order that James should learn it first from him, and not officially from the lawyers, he would take the letter himself and put it in the letter box after posting that for the lawyers.

As he walked through the streets in the cool night air he felt happier than he had ever felt in his life. He had done right at last, and had been mercifully saved from consummating his shameful offence. He now looked back on it with horror. What had possessed him to act as he had done? Thank God! he had been spared the worst. His heart was light and joyful, and he could even smile to think of the lawyers' surprise next morning.

He posted his letter and then walked on to his old home, and having dropped the letter for James in the letter box, found his way to the tube station, which had been the scene of poor Harvey's accident. Had he really seen his old friend that night, or was it a vision of his imagination? He could not tell; whichever it was, it was Harvey who had been his saviour; to Harvey he owed the recovery of his self-respect, the victory over his worse self. He thought of his old friend with love and gratitude, and thanked God for him.

The platform was congested with people from the theatres which had just closed. Never had he seen such a crowd. The train came up and George was carried in the rush to the entrance of the car. It was over full already; his foot was on the step when the gate was slammed in his face; he could not extricate himself from the crowd; the train began to move, his foot slipped, and was caught between the car and the platform; the train went faster and faster; he was dragged down and down, and he knew no more.

TWO MISSIVES were put into James Markham's hand early next morning. One was George's letter:

> "Dear James,
> "I have had the codicil all the time. It came into my hands by a mere accident, and at first I did not even know what it was. To-night I intended to destroy it, but I was prevented by my good angel. I have just posted it to Messrs. Harvey & Moor. They will not know whom it comes from. I ask you to keep my secret, to forgive me, and if you can to think kindly of your brother.
> "George."

The other letter was from St. George's Hospital, to say that a gentleman, named Markham, had been brought there with injuries received in a railway accident, which it was feared would be fatal, and that he wished to see his brother, Mr. James Markham, before he died.

James was shocked and deeply affected. The old fraternal affection, which had been buried under a load of selfishness and greed, awoke within him. George's noble renunciation of the advantage he had won, and candid confession of the wrong he had done, filled him with admiration. He could not help asking himself how he would have behaved had he been subjected to such a trial.

When he stood by George's bedside it was too late. He had died during the night. The tears stood in James Markham's eyes as he took the cold hand in his, and bending over his brother whispered, "George, I forgive you; your secret is safe with me."

THE EVE OF ST. JOHN

"HE WAS SITTING IN HIS LIBRARY . . ."

Simple words, which, if one comes upon them in the course of a story call up a pleasing picture of cultured ease, and literary leisure. One may lay down the book on one's knee, and shut one's eyes, and see in a vision the snug room, crimson-curtained; hear the gentle patter on the hearth of the ashes from the glowing fire, the only sound that breaks the silence, save perhaps the rustle of the leaves, as the occupant turns his page. On the walls, dimly seen by the light of the shaded lamp, are the well-stored shelves, volumes rich with the sombre splendour of morocco and gilding, folios in the wider shelves below, quartos and octavos above; the spacious leather covered table, with silver inkstand and ample room for atlas volumes, is drawn in front of the fire; along the walls are comfortable stuffed morocco seats, and by the corner of the table is the master's favourite easy chair, luxuriously padded, leather-clad, and well worn by constant use; before the shining brass fender lies the bearskin rug, beloved by Tim, the fox-terrier, sole sharer with his lord of this temple of study, and comfort, and not infrequently of repose.

It was summer, and the hearth was cold, but otherwise the library in which Cecil Maynard was sitting fully satisfied the conditions of this imaginary picture. It was a lofty and stately apartment with long windows and deep window seats, the fretted plaster ceiling, rich with interlacing ribs and floreated borders bore the arms of the Maynard who had restored and improved the old

70

building three hundred years before, altering it from the chateau fort of the middle ages into a habitation suitable to times when private wars had been suppressed, and a better administration of public justice had taken their place. Through the open casements came the soft summer air bringing in the scent of the hay-field, and in the gathering twilight could just be distinguished well-wooded slopes and green pastures falling rapidly to the river that brawled along its rocky bed, with many an eddy and stickle where the fisherman might look to tempt with his fly a lusty trout.

Cecil Maynard had only a short time before come into possession of the estate of Castle Maynard, which he inherited from an uncle who had died a widower and childless. He knew nothing of the history of his new home, and since taking possession, and settling down after the troublesome technicalities of succession, he had amused himself by hunting up information about it in county histories, and by diving into the materials afforded in plenty by family papers in the muniment-room, which had been well kept in orderly arrangement by his predecessors. He had read of Maynards who went to the crusades, selling half their estates to raise a contingent of their followers, and impoverishing their successors for several generations. He read of other Maynards who partly retrieved the family fortune only to lose it again in the Wars of the Roses. Recovering their estates under the Tudors, on whose side by a happy accident they had been engaged, they managed to struggle through the civil wars of Charles and the Parliament without much loss of goods, but some loss of credit, owing to the shifty policy of Sir Everard Maynard who then owned the estate, and who by crafty intrigue, and by judiciously trimming his sails to catch the breeze of prosperity that blew sometimes from one quarter and sometimes from another, managed never to compromise himself with the losing party and to turn up in the nick of time on the side of the winner.

At the moment when we are introduced to his successor, sitting in his library that summer evening, he was in fact reading in the county history the story of his ingenious ancestor, of whom he felt he had no particular reason to be proud. As he read on he began to think that political insincerity was not the worst fault that could be laid to Sir Everard's charge, and that there were passages in his life which bore a dubious, not to say a sinister character. Sir Everard lived to be an old man, and prospered exceedingly, leaving his estates in a more flourishing condition than they had been for a long while before. He died childless, and the estate passed to a distant kinsman.

"Well," said Cecil Maynard, as he closed the weighty folio of his county history, "I am glad at all events that the kinsman from whom I come was only a distant relative; for the less we and ours have of Sir Everard's blood in our veins the better."

The door opened as he spoke, and his young wife came into the room. Mrs. Maynard was a year or two younger than her husband. They had only been married a short time before they came to Castle Maynard, and she knew even less about the place than he did.

"Why, Cecil, whatever did you find to pore over in that dusty old volume?" said she as she seated herself on the elbow of his chair, and put an arm over his shoulder.

"To tell the truth," said he, "I have been reading the life of a very disreputable ancestor of mine. What is told of him for certain is bad enough, but I doubt whether there is not worse behind. There are many hints given of foul play that never came to light."

"A family romance," said she; "how interesting! How are we to find out more about this disreputable ancestor? I confess he interests me more than all the respectable ones. How long ago did he live?"

"Ah! you women," said Cecil, laughing, "you all of you, I believe, love the sinner rather than the saint."

"Now that's too bad of you," said she, as she kissed the top of his head, the spot which from her position was most accessible to caresses. "I don't love him at all, but I should love to find out what he did. Do go on, and learn more about him. I should dearly like to find that Castle Maynard was the scene of a real tragedy like Dunsinane, or the mystery of Udolpho, or the Castle of Otranto. As it is I have been bitterly disappointed that nobody has ever heard of a ghost in the house. It is hardly respectable in an old family to be without one."

"A defect no doubt," said Cecil, "of which we ought to be ashamed, and I don't know how we are to make it good. But listen, Alice, to what *Baker's Chronicle* tells of our disreputable ancestor. I won't bother you with all his political tricks and dishonest manoeuvres to keep in with the winning side. They are bad enough. But listen to this:

"'This Sir Everard was much respected during his life on account of his prosperity, and the favour in which he was held by the Court. He much increased the family estates, which had sunk to a low condition. He married twice, but left no issue by either marriage. His first wife was an heiress who died suddenly, and her inheritance passed to Sir Everard under a will executed shortly before her death. None of her family benefited thereby, though she had always professed attachment to them. His second wife was the daughter of Sir James Tiptoft, Knight and Baronet of that same, and was very beautiful. Sir Everard and his wife did not agree, and it is said she threatened to leave him and bestow her lands on another. Certain it is that she disappeared and was never again heard of. Sir Everard seized on her inheritance, and as the lady's family had sided with the Parliament in the late wicked rebellion which ended in the murder of that most Blessed Martyr, King Charles I, Sir Everard was confirmed in possession after the happy restoration of his Sacred Majesty King Charles II. Sir Everard lived to a good old age in much honour, and lies under a handsome monument with his effigy in alabaster in the parish church.'"

"How horrible," exclaimed Alice, "what a monster! both his wives!"

"You think he murdered them?" said Cecil.

"Why Cecil, of course he did! He was another Bluebeard. No doubt he poisoned the first and made away with the second. It is as plain as a pikestaff, and why couldn't that stupid musty old Chronicler say so outright instead of going twaddling on about his Blessed Martyr and his Sacred Majesty, as if they had anything to do with it."

"On the other hand," said Cecil, "the first wife may have died a natural death. People do so. And the next may have run away from her disagreeable husband, and lived happily ever afterwards."

"I don't believe it, Cecil," said she, "and I am sure you don't believe it either."

"Well," said he, "I confess there is not much to be said for Sir Everard's morals. But murder! No! that is a different thing altogether from politics, and I think even Sir Everard might have stuck at that. But what I don't like is to think we enjoy his ill-gotten wealth, whether your view should be the true one or not. It is a disagreeable reflection."

"But it's not our fault," said Alice; "how can we help it? Whom could we give it back to?"

"To be sure," said Cecil, "there's Harry Tiptoft living not ten miles off; but I doubt whether he would make any claim after a couple of centuries. And by the way, I remember now hearing of another shady ancestor who lost most of his fortune in play with Sandwich, and Dashwood, and Wilkes, and the Dilettanti lot, so let us hope Sir Everard's money went that way. Our present wealth comes from my great grandfather, the famous admiral, and that at all events is clean money, honestly earned in fighting the French."

"Let us get a candle and go and look at Sir Everard's portrait in the picture gallery," said she. "I shall regard him in future with increased interest, for a mystery attaches to him. I wonder what became of that poor second wife. I shall never rest till I find out."

Arm linked in arm they mounted the grand staircase and reached a long gallery at the top of the house where pictures of deceased Maynards hung in a long series, some by famous artists, some by indifferent hands of little merit. Sir Everard's picture was among the best works of Sir Peter Lely, who, though he generally devoted his art to what Walpole calls "the Court of Paphos," occasionally painted a man, in a style both graceful and masculine. The countenance riveted their attention. It was handsome and refined, and at first sight attractive; but the longer you looked at it the less you liked it. Behind its superficial beauty there seemed to be a certain craftiness, a slyness in the eye, a satiric curl in the mouth. The figure was draped in a rich coat of crimson velvet, with ruffles and lace cravat, and in the background was a rough perfunctory likeness of Castle Maynard.

"Well," said Cecil, "what do you think of him?"

"I think," said she, "he looks like a cruel man, and I could believe anything of him."

"Poor Sir Everard," said Cecil. "He won't get any favour from you. But it is very late and time we went to bed. So say good-bye to him and let us go."

Cecil resolved to search among the family papers on the morrow for more information about this uncomfortable member of his family; and it was agreed that they should go to the church and have a good look at the alabaster effigy which preserved the likeness of that shifty politician.

THE CHURCH OF CASTLE MAYNARD stood a little way from the house just outside the park gate and at the end of the village street. Long and low its walls of flint and stone, hoary with age, embosomed amid immemorial yews and shady elms, it was a typical example of an English village church. There are no such village churches in other countries as those of rural England; modest and yet comely, simple and yet refined, gems of homely art and beautiful restraint, rich in interest both historical and artistic, no two of them really alike, and each, unless it has been spoilt by later bad taste, generally possessing some special charm that distinguishes it from any other.

Cecil's ancestors were buried in an aisle or chapel belonging to the family. There were brasses inlaid in the floor with inscriptions in black letter; tablets on the walls, of more recent date, recording merits and virtues not perhaps remarkable during life, but discovered after the death of the person whom they commemorated; altar tombs with recumbent effigies, and knightly armour hanging above; and lastly Sir Everard's monument, the most sumptuous of them all, a Jacobean structure of marble, black, red, and white, against the wall, where under an arch Sir Everard in alabaster, painted and gilt, lay on his side raising himself on one elbow, and with a dog at his feet. A fullsome epitaph recorded his virtues with an unblushing assurance that made one think Sir Everard must have written it himself to forestall what his successor might perhaps say of him; and indeed it was said that the tomb was constructed in his lifetime, which accounted for its being in an earlier style than the date of his death warranted.

The morning sun was shining brightly through the window traceries, and flickering lights and shadows played over wall and monument, as the wind gently tossed the boughs of the trees and the trailing sprays of ivy that clung to the wall outside, when Cecil and his wife stood before the monument of the redoubtable Sir Everard. The old sexton and verger was with them listening as Cecil translated the cumbrous Latin for the benefit of his wife.

"Law, sir," said he, "do'ee reelly say arl that 'bout Sir Everard? I allus heer tell as he was a bad 'un, beggin' your parding, sir, you bein' a relation."

"Yes, Walter," said Cecil, "it does say all that. Whatever he may have been in life, you see that is what he would like us to think of him after he was gone."

"Then Mr. Maynard, sir, I suppose many of these 'ere writings is no better than so many lies?"

"So it is, I fear," said Cecil. "But tell me, is there any monument to either of Sir Everard's wives? I know he was married twice."

"The first wife, sir, lies buried among her own people at Chaldicote. They took her away, I've heerd tell, to spite Sir Everard."

"And the second wife, where does she lie?"

Old Walter looked uncomfortable, and shifted from one leg to the other and scratched his head before replying.

"That I can't tell 'ee, sir," said he. "They do say, but—well—I don't know nothing about it."

"But what do they say, Walter?" said Mrs. Maynard. "I am interested in that poor lady, and want to know all about her."

"Well, mum, when Squire arst me where she lie, I says I don't know. No more I don't, and wot's more, no more don't anybody know. But they do say," and here old Walter lowered his voice, "they do say she don't lie nowhere, and that she walks."

"And have you seen her, Walter?"

"No, no, mum, I never see her," he replied hastily. "Oh, no! I never see her. But beggin' your parding, it's time for me to ring the bell and I must go. Oh, no! I never see 'er."

And so saying the old man shuffled off, as if to avoid any more questions on the subject. "So you see, Cecil," said his wife, "we have a ghost in the family after all. Isn't it delicious?"

He laughed, and led her out into the sunshine. They wandered a little among the tombs, reading an inscription here and there. Many of the gravestones went back to the seventeenth century, and "if the dead who lie here could speak," said they, "we might learn a good deal about Sir Everard, for they must have known him."

"But look there," said Alice, pointing to a headstone covered with hoary lichen that almost obliterated the inscription, "is not that word, Everard?

"So it is," said Cecil, and he stooped down to read the epitaph. With some trouble he made it out as follows:

HERE LYETH
ROGER TRUMBALL GENT.
SOMETIME STEWARD TO THE NOBLE KNIGHT
SIR EVERARD MAYNARD. JUNE 24. 1662
THERE IS NO DEVICE IN THE GRAVE WHITHER THOU GOEST
ECCL. IX 10.

"Here is one, at all events, who knew him well," said Cecil, "but what a strange text to put on a man's grave! One would think it was chosen by some one who owed him a grudge, and was glad to get him buried."

"Sir Everard again no doubt," said Mrs. Maynard, "the words 'the noble knight,' betray him. It is just his style."

"Poor Sir Everard," said Cecil, "you believe he murdered his two wives, and now I suppose you will have it that he murdered his steward, Roger Trumball, gent., and put up the tombstone to show his malice."

"Well, I shouldn't wonder if it were so," said she.

Cecil burst out laughing, and said though Sir Everard was a trimmer and a time-server, and a grabber of inheritances, it was going a long way further to make him a three-folk murderer as well, and so they both laughed and strolled back towards the castle.

"I fancy we are getting Sir Everard on the brain," said Cecil as they wandered slowly over the pleasant green-sward. "Let us forget all about him; he is really not worth remembering, for though he may not be the blood-stained villain you would make him out, he was a mean trickster, and an unscrupulous and treacherous politician. Let us leave him there."

"Why no, my dear," said she. "I don't think we know the worst about him. That poor second wife dwells on my mind. I wish we could find out what became of her."

"That seems hopeless," said he. "I wonder by the way, whether the Tiptofts could tell you anything about her. Harry Tiptoft is an old college friend of mine. We were at Merton together. Suppose we ask him over to come and stay a day or two. He can bring his fly-rod and try for a trout, and there are lots of rabbits on the hill that want shooting."

The invitation was sent and accepted for the following week. Sir Henry Tiptoft, of Tiptoft Manor, Baronet and Justice of the Peace, was the Maynard's nearest neighbour and a young man a couple of years Cecil's senior, though they had been at Oxford together for more than a year. Any differences between the families arising from the unhappy marriage of the heiress of one branch of the Tiptofts with Sir Everard, and her mysterious fate, had long been forgotten and the Maynards and Tiptofts had for some generations been intimate friends. But as Cecil stood in his library with Harry Tiptoft's letter in his hand, and the memory of their morning walk and visit to the church fresh in his mind, he could not help recalling the ugly story of his crafty ancestor's marriage with poor Hilda Tiptoft, and of its mysterious sequel. From old Walter's hints he gathered that it had passed into the legendary stage among the villagers, and that a superstitious fear prevented their talking of it. But it all happened nearly three hundred years ago, and what, thought he, could they know about it? The truth must have come out long since, had there been anything in the story more than an ordinary parting of an uncongenial couple. And if she was never heard of again it might only be that she hid herself, so that her husband should never find her. And yet it was a queer story.

"Her disappearance," said Cecil to himself, "seems to have caused some excitement at the time. Sir Everard's successors must have troubled themselves a good deal about it. I wonder whether there is anything among the papers in the muniment-room to throw light upon it. I'll go and have a hunt."

The muniment-room was a small chamber in an angle turret secured with iron doors. Within, the deeds and parchments were arranged on shelves in tin boxes carefully labelled; and in pigeon holes and drawers, numbered and dated, were papers of all kinds, old letters, old accounts, various documents of more or less interest bearing on the family history. Cecil was by this time becoming pretty well acquainted with the collection, and readily put his hand on the papers relating to the latter part of the seventeenth century. There were farming accounts, notes of lawsuits in which Sir Everard apparently dabbled a good deal, for he seemed to have disagreed with most of his neighbours. There were letters, some of them written by him to his parents when a little boy at Westminster, full of innocent, school-boy prattle, and generally ending with a petition for money. Dr. Busby, that great man who had flogged Sir Roger de Coverley's grandfather, figured in them sometimes as an awful being, too great to be criticised. It was pathetic, in view of the writer's after career, to read these simple childish epistles, full of happy, youthful spirits and warm home affections. Cecil put them back with something like a sigh. Among the letters was a lock of fair curly hair tied with a faded blue ribbon, and wrapped in a paper on which was written in a woman's hand: "my dear boy's hair on his first going away to school."

It would have been better for poor Sir Everard, thought Cecil, had he died young, an innocent, warm-hearted school boy.

As he replaced the parcel of letters, he dislodged from a corner where it seemed to have been purposely concealed with some care, a small packet of papers in a sealed wrapper, endorsed in a clerkly hand on the outside. Roger Trumball, 1662.

"Oh!" said Cecil to himself, "Roger Trumball! That is the man whose tombstone had that queer text from Ecclesiastes upon it. If I remember, he is described as Sir Everard's steward. I dare say these are only bills, or accounts of rents, or sales of stock, of no particular interest." He was just going to put the parcel back where he found it, but on second thoughts he broke the seal and glanced at the contents. Something that caught his eye made him pause, and after a moment's reflection he locked up the muniment-room, and took Roger Trumball's packet with him back to the library.

The packet consisted only of about a dozen loose sheets of paper, written evidently at different times, and in a hand sometimes beautifully clear in the fine calligraphy of that age, and sometimes merely scribbled as if in haste or fear. On the inside of the wrapper were these words:

> "I, Roger Trumball, being in deadly fear for my lyfe,
> put these papers where perchance they will be found
> and ye truth known. Lord, how long shall ye wicked,
> how long shall ye wicked triumph."

This portends something serious, thought Cecil, as he drew his chair to the table, and spread the manuscripts before him. They were all dated, and he arranged and read them in order. The first one was imperfect, beginning in the middle of a sentence.

> " . . . . comyng home of my ladye. Would God thyngs
> were better ordered for her. I cannot but grieve."

The next paper was dated 1661, and seemed to be written after an interval.

> "Sept. 15, 1661.—Strange things have happened to-
> day. My duty calls me to continue this record for my
> dear ladye's sake. To-day my master called me to the

small parlour. There was a table set and my Ladye Hulda sat thereat, with a parchment before her and pen and ink. She looked pale, poore sowle. My master was walking up and downe the room seeminglie much distraught. 'Now, Hilda,' he said speaking as it were mildly, 'here is Roger come to witness your signature.' 'Roger,' he said to me, 'you will sign here as witness after my ladye.' But my ladye made no movement and sat with her pretty hands in her lap. 'Come, Hilda,' said he, 'we are waiting, what is wrong with you?' 'I will not sign this,' said she at last, speaking low. 'What,' said he in his softest manner, 'and why not, my dear?' My ladye cast on him a look of contempt, mistrusting his gentleness. 'You know why,' at last she said, 'you know my condition.' 'What, and let half your land go to your beggerly Roundhead Tiptoft cousins! By heaven! No!' said he. 'The land is mine,' said my ladye, 'and I love my cousins.' My master stamped on the floor. The evil look I know so well came into his face. 'By God!' he said furiously, 'sign it you shall; alive or dead, I'll have all the land from you.' 'You will never get it by frightening me,' said my dear ladye, who has a fine bold way with her when she is misspoken. My master, in a passion snatched ye parchment up. 'Go,' said he to me, and I left the room much concerned for my poore ladye, and doubting some mischance."

There was an interval of nearly two months between this paper and the following one, which was written less carefully.

"Nov. 5, 1661.—Truly I am grieved to the heart for my poore ladye. My master treateth her unkindly, for though he speak softly, his tongue deviseth mischiefs like a sharp razor, working deceitfully, as saith the Psalmist. This day I had occasion to speak with him on the matter of Bullfinch Acre, and I found him on the terrace with my ladye. As I came near I heard him say: 'To give your lands to those Tiptofts is but a kind of treason. They are Roundheads and enemies to the throne now so happily restored.' 'And so were you a Roundhead as you call them,' said my ladye, 'when Oliver ruled the roost. At all events my poor cousins have not ratted from a falling house.' 'Oh, my dear,' said he, 'I now know better. I have learned on which side the right lies.' 'I think,' said my ladye firing up, 'you are a better judge upon which side the might lies.' This roused my master's choler, and turning on his heel, he saw me. 'What, eavesdropping, Roger? I have a good mind—' said he, raising his cane as if to strike me. But I looked him in the face and he saw I was not one to take a beating quietly. 'What brings you here, listening to what concerns you not.' I told him my business, and he said I was to take it to him on the morrow, and I left them. Truly, my dear ladye hath a high spirit, and can give a shrewd answer, but what says the Proverb: 'A soft answer turneth away wrath, but grievous words stir up anger.'

"Nov. 12.—My master being away in London on some affairs, and my ladye biding at home alone, she sent the maid Madelon who waiteth on her, to say she would fain speak with me. This girl is not to my liking, for things are told of her and my master that are not seemly. So she said, smirking, and looking out of the corner of her eyes as is her way with mankind:

"'Master Roger, my ladye will have you to meet her on the terrace anon.'

"'Well, Madelon,' said I, 'I will do my ladye's bidding at once,' and I turned to go, for I liked not her company.

"'But why so hasty, Master Roger,' said she playing with her ribbons, 'May we not have a pleasant word together? we have not met for a long while. And what do you think my ladye wants you for?'

"'Nay, I know not,' said I, 'she will tell me herself and then I shall know.'

"She looked for a minute or so for a further answer, and as none came, she said:

"'Well then, go for a churl as you are. I am sorry I wasted words on you,' and so she went. She is a comely lass enough, but a bold one, and I mistrust her. Doth not the wise man, say 'As a jewel of gold in a swine's snout, so is a fair woman which is without discretion?'

"I found my dear ladye walking alone on the terrace. She was pale and the tears were in her eyes.

"'Roger, come here,' said she, 'I want a word with you. I think you are true and that I may trust you.'

"'Indeed you may, madam, I would serve you to the death,' said I, for I was sorely grieved to see how sad she was.

"'I believe you,' said she, 'and I will tell you what you can do for me. You have seen and heard enough, Roger, to know how things go with me.'

"'Alack! madam,' I said, 'and sore grieved I am that matters should be so between you and my master.'

"'You know, Roger, my people have fought on the losing side, and now they will be made to suffer for it, and I dare say are already in danger.'

"'Aye, madam, Sir Charles Tiptoft and your cousins fought for the good cause—I mean for Parliament,' said I correcting myself, for times are changed, and it is not prudent to speak well of the Commonwealth.

"'Yet you were right, Roger, to call it the good cause, for so I hold it myself. And now my uncle and cousins will be in trouble and lose their lands, if not their lives, and I want to save half of my estate to bestow on them in their need when it will be safe to do so. But Sir Everard prevents me and will have it all.'

"I told her that was what I understood from what I had witnessed; and further that I had heard the sequestrators were already at Tiptoft Manor taking a valuation of the estate.

"'I know nothing of it, Roger, and what I want you to do is to ride over and find out what has happened, and bring me word. They keep everything from me. My own waiting-maid, I believe is a spy upon me, for everything I do or say is reported to Sir Everard.'

"I told her on no account to trust Madelon, who I was sure would betray and ruin her if she could. My mistress was much startled at this, and thanked me for my warning. I promised to ride over to Tiptoft which is but 10 or 12 miles away, the next morning, and so left her—

"Nov. 14, 1661.—This morning, my master being still away, my ladye sent for me to meet her as before on the terrace. I had been to Tiptoft Manor, and I knew she was expecting me. As I appeared, she came anxiously to meet me, and asked what news I brought.

"'Alas! madam,' said I, 'I would I had better news for you, for I bring sad tidings. The Manor is in the hands of the sequestrators, and your uncle and cousins are not there.'

"I did not tell her that her uncle was in jail, as a supporter of the late Rebellion, and that her cousins were in London trying to get together interest among their friends to save his life, and also, if possible, his estate. She told me she was now at a loss what to do. That she hoped, if her family had been there to have escaped to them, for that her life here was not to be borne any longer. That she had hoped for my help, and that she was so watched and guarded that without aid, her escape was impossible.

"'But now,' said she, 'that hope is gone, and I am a wretched woman. I sometimes think he wishes me dead, and then he would have his way with my estate, for my uncle and cousins are in no case to resist him. There is nowhere now for me to fly to. But promise me one thing, Roger,' said she.

"I said I would faithfully promise to do all she asked me, even at the peril of my life if needs be.

"'Then promise me, Roger,' she said, 'that if anything should befall me, you will seek out my cousins and tell them all you know.'

"'And what but good should befall such a virtuous and obedient wife?' said a gentle voice behind us, and there stood my master with his evil smile that means mischief. He had come in time to hear my ladye's last words. I trust he did not hear what passed between us before.

"'I see, Madam,' he continued, 'you have chosen a confidant, and that you are enlisting my servant against me.'

"'You leave me no choice,' she said, 'when do you ever let me see a friend.'

"'That you may enlist him also I suppose,' said he, 'No, Hilda, I cannot have another enemy within my borders,' and then, turning sharply to me, 'and you, Master Steward, must be taught to know your place, and not to meddle with what concerns you not.'

"I had it in my mind to answer him, yet it might have made matters worse. For what saith the Psalmist?: 'I will keep my mouth with a bridle while the wicked is before me.' He gave me an ugly look, and led my ladye away into ye house. I much fear evil is intended against her, and what can I do to help her, poor sowle?"

"Well, upon my word," said Cecil to himself, laying down Roger's manuscript, and leaning back in his chair when he had read thus far. "My disreputable ancestor seems to have been a domestic tyrant of the worst kind. I wonder what comes next. I think I must call Alice, for the plot thickens, and she is interested in that 'poor sowle,' as Roger calls her. Roger, by the way, seems to have been an honest fellow, and I hope he stood by his 'dear ladye' to some purpose. I'll go and call Alice to hear the rest of the story."

Mrs. Maynard, however, saved him the trouble, by entering the room at that moment. She had her garden hat on.

"What are you doing, Cecil?" said she. "I want you to come out and see the roses. They are lovely."

"All right," said he, "we'll go by and by. I've something here that will interest you more. You remember that tombstone of Roger Trumball, steward to the noble knight, and so on, that we saw in the churchyard. I've found a sort of diary of his all about that poor second wife of his noble knight, whose fate interests you so much. You had better run your eye over the pages I have read, and then we will go on. There is more to come."

"Why, what a tyrant!" said she, when she had finished reading. "He is every bit as bad as I thought him. You won't defend him now, Cecil?"

"Well, we have not come to a murder yet," said Cecil, "and, according to you, he has three standing to his account."

"Three! I should not wonder if there were half a dozen," said she. "I think your Sir Everard was capable of anything. But do let us go on. I am dying to know what happened, and it makes it so real to have it all from the mouth of an actual eyewitness that it is almost as horrible as if it were happening now."

Cecil took up the manuscript again and cast his eye over the next page to that where he left off. "By heavens!" said he, "we seem coming to a crisis.

"March 5, 1662.—I, Roger Trumball, take up my pen after many months, being in some concern for my safety, but more for that of my dear ladye. For how shall I say it? She is gone, and I know not whither. It is a month now since she disappeared. My master hath made search for her, but he seemeth not to care to find her. Her own people at Tiptoft Manor are away, and I know not where to seek for them in order to discharge my promise to my dear ladye. The idle jade Madelon flaunteth in ribbons and gay attire and plays the mistress. She says forsooth she is housekeeper. I know not what to think.

"Mar. 10.—To-day happening to be in ye stone gallery, I picked up a glove. ''Tis my ladye's,' said I. 'What is that?' said my master, who was near by, 'give it to me'; and he turned it over and threw it on the fire. 'Maybe,' said I, 'she dropped it as she went away.' My master changed colour and looked hard at me without speaking. 'Went away,' said he. 'Perchance you know whither she went and where she is.'

"'No, sir,' said I, 'an I knew I would tell you, and if she were in trouble do my best to help her.'

"'I doubt you will never find her,' said he, looking sourly at me.

"'Maybe, sir,' said I, 'you have a better clue than I.'

"I know not what made me say that; but it had a queer effect. My master turned pale, looked hard at me for the space of a minute, and walked away without a word. I marvelled at his manner.

"Mar. 11.—I write this from my bed in ye steward's room, being hurt, though not badly. Last night, coming back to the Castle through the woods, I heard a shot, and felt a blow on my leg which brought me to the ground, where I lay till Giles the keeper came in sight, to whom I called for help.

'Why, Master Roger,' quoth he, as he lifted me up, 'what's wrong with you? Why, you bleed like a pig,' and, whipping off his handkerchief, he bound up my wound as well as he could, and then, leaning on his shoulder, I managed to get home and to bed, where good Mistress Margery, the still-room maid, tended me, and sent for the leech. I saw no man in the wood, and know not of any that beareth me an ill-will. My wound is only slight, but I shall be lame for a while. There is great talk of it among the servants.

"April 30.—This day I was summoned to the Hall, where sat my master and with him was Denis Cowley, the farmer of Hay-hill.

"'Roger,' said my master, speaking quite smooth and gently, 'I have been asking Denis for his quarter's rent, and he says he paid it to you.'

"'That is so, ain't it, Master Roger,' said Denis, 'and here is the receipt and your name to it.'

"'Quite right,' said I, 'and you will mind, sir, how I handed it on to you the next day.' 'Indeed,' said he, 'I do not mind it; but if so you will have my note of it in your book.'

'I will go this moment and fetch it,' said I, and I went to my room. My master was speaking so mildly and gently that I doubted he had some mischief in hand, for he is never so dangerous as when he is in that vein. However, I brought him the book and put it in his hand.

"'Well, Roger,' said he, turning over page after page, 'I don't find the note you speak of. You know you always take a note from me to show I have had the money.

"'That is true, sir,' said I. 'Denis's rent is the last entry in the book, and there you will find it. I mind well your writing it in the small parlour, and you putting the money away.'

"He looked at me queerly for a minute, and then said, 'Take your book, then, and find it for yourself.'

"But, when I looked, the page was gone. 'Have you found it?' he asked.

"'Sir, I know not who hath done it, but the page is gone.'

"'Indeed,' said he, 'that's odd, but I think it would have been still odder had you found it, for I don't believe it ever was there.'

"I was so taken aback that I could find no words for a moment.

"'It is not the first time, Roger, I have had my suspicion of you. And now here is honest Master Cowley to prove you had the money, and your book to show you never paid it to me.'

"'Sir,' said I, 'you know you had the money. But this seems a plot to ruin me. I'll make the money good if you wish, but I'll never submit to be called a thief.'

"'Denis,' said my master, 'you hear him. He admits he took it and will make it good. But,' said he, turning to me, 'that won't clear you. You are a thief, and by God it's a hanging matter if I give you up. If I spare you for a while you will owe it to my mercy. Now go.'

"I went slowly to my room, for my lameness still troubled me, and sat down to think it over. I examined the book, and saw how the page had been cut out with a sharp knife. There has been some foul treachery here. 'Deliver me, O Lord, from the evil man, and preserve me from the wicked man.' Truly David had his trouble from traitors when he wrote that. As I sat on my bed I thought of all that had befallen me of late: first the wound in my leg, and now this plot for my ruin. My life and my honour were both in danger, but who was my enemy, and who would be the better for my destruction? I knew my master misliked me for my confidence with his ladye, and then there came into my mind his strange behaviour when I found the glove and spoke with him of my ladye's loss. It was the very night after that that I was shot, and thoughts came into my mind that there might be some link between the two things. But I dare write no more of this. My master hath me in his power, for who will take my word against his as to this matter of the money?

"June 10.—Great to-do among the servants about Madelon, who is to go to her home. It seems the master has misused her, and she would have none of it, and so she is to leave. I fear I have misjudged the girl, and that she is better than I thought her. This day I happened on her coming out of my room. I was surprised, for she had no call to be there. She had been crying, and I spoke to her kindly.

"'Why, mistress Madelon,' said I, 'I hear you are going, but that should not grieve you; you will be well out of this house.'

"'Indeed I shall, Master Roger. I would I had never entered it. I have been made to do things I am ashamed of, and am sorry for now. And for some of them I cannot now make amends; it is too late.'

"'Why so, Madelon?' 'Nay, you know very well,' said she. 'I mean my mistress.'

"'I know,' said I, 'you were set to spy on her by my master.'

"'I was,' she said; 'he made me, and I am sorry I did it.'

"'And do you know where she is,' said I, 'and what has happened to her?'

"Madelon looked round and waited to know if any one were within hearing before she answered in a whisper:

"'Nay; I know not, though I can make guess, and I think he suspects me. I hate him, Roger, and will do him a mischief if I can, for he has treated me vilely.' Here we heard steps approaching, and the girl said in haste:

"'I know you love me not, Master Roger, but I have been a better friend to you than you wot of,' and with that she ran away.

"My master has said nothing more to me about the money, but I can see he views me with an evil eye. My leg troubles me sorely, and I doubt I am lamed for life, though I can ride, and get about with a stick well enough. I have no news yet of Sir Charles or his sons, and it vexes me that I cannot perform what I promised my dear ladye; but I have sworn on the Holy Bible that I will perform it, and that, alive or dead, I will make known unto them what she suffered before we lost her, and what has since befallen her should I find out."

"I wonder," said Alice, as Cecil laid down the manuscript for a minute, "whether poor Roger ever did find the Tiptofts and redeem his promise."

"We shall have Harry Tiptoft here in a day or two," said Cecil, "and he may be able to tell us something about it. But I fancy they know as little over there of the story of poor Hilda as I did till I happened on this account in the *County History* which set us all on this quest."

"Well, go on," said she. "I hope poor Roger came to no harm from that murderous master of his."

Cecil resumed the reading:

"June 15.—A strange thing happened to-day. I was receiving rents from two or three tenants for their farms, and giving them receipts. It was the first time this had happened since the affair of Master Denis

Cowley, and this time I resolved there should be no handle for my master's malice, and that in future the book in which he noted that I paid him the money should be kept in a more secure place under lock and key. So I put the money in a bag, and took down my notebook, and opened it, and a piece of paper flew out upon the floor. When I picked it up I saw it was the missing leaf, with my master's receipt on it. I was so taken aback that I sat down again to think it over, for I was fairly overcome. Then I bethought me of Madelon, and how I surprised her coming out of my room, and of her words at parting, and it was borne in upon me that she had cut the page out at her master's bidding, and had kept it for future service if needs should be, and had put it back when her master had offended her. I blessed the girl in my heart and forgave her for what she first did, and I rejoiced to feel that my master had no longer that hold over me. I saw plainly it had been a plot to get me into his power, so that I should not be able to stir hand or foot against him for fear of the gallows. But what had I against him? I bethought me of that I said to him about my ladye's loss when I found the glove, which might have made him think I suspected him of something wrong. But he had no reason, for I knew nothing then, and I know nothing now about my poore ladye's fate. And then it was borne in upon me that perhaps he knew more about it than he would have me suspect. I begin to fear that there has been some foul play, and I then remembered Madelon's last words. I must see her again.

"However, after a while I recovered myself and, taking my notebook and the money, I sought my master in the great library, where it was his pleasure to sit. I told him I had brought the rents and I laid them on the table that he might count them, and

I spread the note-book open before him that he might enter his receipt. When he had signed his name, he said:

"'This time you are right, Roger. Last time you made a little mistake, if I remember.'

"'Sir Everard,' said I, 'I know not what you mean. If there were a mistake 'twas not I that made it.'

"'A little mistake,' said he, smiling, 'that brought you within danger of the gallows, eh, Master Roger.'

"'Nay, sir,' I replied, quite coolly, ''twas not I that was in danger of the gallows. I mind me there is a law to punish those that plot to ruin their fellows by false charges.'

"He turned furiously on me. I wonder I had the courage to threaten him as I did. But I was mad with anger.

"'Plot and punishment,' cried he. 'You dare to accuse and threaten me, gallows-bird; to jail you shall go this day and stay there till the hangman is ready for you.'

"'You charge me with stealing the money, though you had it fairly from me, and gave me your receipt,' said I.

"'Show me the receipt, then,' cried he savagely. 'You know you have not got one.'

"I took from my pocket the loose leaf I found in my book and held it before him.

"'Give it me,' he cried.

"'Nay,' said I, 'it shall not leave me again.'

"He sank back in his seat. The blood rushed to his face, and he sat staring at me with his mouth open for the space of a minute. At last he began to stammer out a word or two of excuse, but he could hardly speak for shame and mortification. I gathered up my books and papers, but as I turned to go I heard him mutter to himself, 'the jade—played me false.'

"I fear I have angered my master beyond sufferance, and that he may take some vengeance upon me, for he is one that never forgives, though he smooths his anger over with fair pretence. I bethink me of that shot in the wood, and doubt I am in some danger of my life. I pray God I may live to find my ladye, and to fulfil the promise to which I have sworn. 'Deliver me from mine enemies, O God, defend me from them that rise up against me.'

"June 23.—This morning I found on my writing-desk a note written in a hand that I knew not, and none of the servants could say how it came there. It was written in a crabbed style by one who was no scribe.

'To Master Roger Trumball,
'Look to yourself; there is mischief determined against you. Where you found the glove you may find more. Sir Charles is home.—M.'

"I take it this comes from Madelon. It is a kind lass and I thank her. I must be careful.

"To-day I had occasion to speak with my master on business. Since the matter of the receipt note he hath avoided me, though when we meet he treateth me civilly. I found him to-day in the stone gallery. There were two masons there, and work going on. Some furniture had been moved, and I saw a hole in the wall, which was being built up. I had never noticed it before, and indeed a cabinet had stood in front, and I was curious to see what it was. My master seemed anxious to prevent me, and stood in my way. It was dark within, and I thought I saw a door some way back, but my master called me away with him to the other part of the room, and, as the cabinet that had been moved out stood across, I could see no more what was behind it. My master said he had long been troubled with a draught from that empty cupboard, and was having it walled up. When I had discharged my business I said to him:

"'Sir, they say Sir Charles Tiptoft hath made terms with the government, and is now at home. Would you that I ride and tell him of my ladye? I doubt he knows not of her loss, for he has been in jail till now.'

"'No!' said he, 'let him find it out by himself. I will have no dealings with malcontents and Roundheads.'

"This put me out, for I had hoped to have seen my ladye's family and to have discharged my trust. So I went about my business as usual till after noon. In the evening my master sent for me. I found him walking up and down the library, and he seemed in a good humour.

"'Roger,' he said, 'I think you were right this morning and I was wrong about Sir Charles. It is true we were on different sides in politics, and during the war, enemies, but that is all happily over, and we must now live in good fellowship as neighbours. He ought to know about my poore wyfe, which will grieve him as it grieves me, and you shall ride over to-morrow and tell him of her sad and strange departure, and of our failure to find out whither she has gone.'

"I was much surprised to hear him talk in this way, for he had never shown much love for my dear ladye while she was with him.

"'What time will you start?' asked he.

"I said I would start about ten o'clock next morning.

"'And which way will you go?'

"I said the nighest way would be by Langford and Chaldicote.

"'Aye, aye,' said he, 'that will take you through the woods, and be pleasant riding this summer weather. It is hot, and tomorrow you know is Midsummer Day. I would not ride fast if I were you, but take it slowly through the forest.'

"I said I took it kindly of him to think of me so, and that I was sure Sir Charles would be much grieved by my news.

"'Truly, I think so,' said he. 'You start, then, at ten o'clock to-morrow morning. Do not be later. And you go through Langford and Chaldicote, by way of the forest? I wish you a pleasant ride. Be sure and see me when you come back.' So I took my leave, marvelling much at his pleasant humour, and yet somehow mistrusting him, for I knew him to be treacherous. As I reached the door, I turned and saw him looking at me with a strange smile on his face that I did not like.

"So to-morrow I shall tell all I know to my ladye's kin, as I have sworne, and yet it cometh not to much, though I suspect a good deal. Alive or dead, I have sworne, and I know I shall keep my oath. Yet I like not my master's manner. Why so nice about my road and about the hour? The wood was where I was shot. I will be wary, and go armed. And as I shall be away it will be safer if I hide these records of my dealings with my master and my ladye in some place where they may not be found, should ought befall me, till this tyranny be overpast.

"To-morrow is Midsummer Day. Today is what the Papists called St. John's Eve, when all enchantments come undone, and the truth appears. Would that it might reveal the truth of what befell my deare Ladye."

Here Cecil stopped. "Well, go on," said his wife. "We can't stop here. I wonder how he fared on his ride."

"That's all," said Cecil. "There is no more."

They looked at one another. "Do you remember," said Cecil, "the date on poor Roger's tombstone?"

"Yes," said she, "I do. I remember it was June 24, 1662. I particularly remember noticing that it was Midsummer Day."

"And this last entry was written on Midsummer Eve," said Cecil, "so poor Roger never got to Tiptoft Manor, and has never yet been able to keep his promise."

FLAMING JUNE WAS MORE than half spent when Sir Henry Tiptoft drove up to Castle Maynard, and was welcomed in the hall by his host and hostess. The luncheon bell was ringing, and as soon as the visitor had been shown his room, and washed off the dust of travel, they sat down in the cool oak-panelled dining-room, overlooking the old-fashioned garden. It was the last addition to the house, built in the time of George II., with tall panels reaching up to the ceiling, and a wide marble chimneypiece placed cornerwise across one angle. A room stately and yet homely, not unlike a Common-room at Oxford.

The talk was such as was natural between old friends—Oxford memories, local gossip, speculations concerning the harvest and hay-crop—and after luncheon they adjourned to the garden, and had coffee on the terrace, with a lovely view of park and river, a real English landscape, green and lush. The old house, too, was typically English, and could have been in no other land, a mixture of splendour and homeliness, state and comfort. The main part was Jacobean, of red brick, mellowed by time, with many gables, mullioned windows and projecting bays. But at the end was a considerable part of the old castle of Plantagenet times, finished at the river brink with a huge round tower that rose above the highest roof, and was the most conspicuous feature in the structure. As the ground fell steeply towards the river, the tower descended some twenty feet below the ground floor level and the terrace in front of the rest of the house. The old part was built of flint and wrought stone, with windows enlarged to comfortable dimensions from the original arrow-slits.

Henry Tiptoft was as yet a bachelor, but was to be married shortly. He had passed through Oxford with distinction, and was already making his mark in the county as an able magistrate, and it was thought he meant to contest the seat in Parliament. His tastes, however, were rather literary and scientific than such as make the ardent politician. While an undergraduate at Merton, he had published at his own expense a small volume of poems, of which he was now heartily ashamed, and since then had made some more successful efforts in prose. He was a bit of an antiquary and a student of history. His poetical vein had not been dried up by his early failure; his imagination was strong and active, and not a little touched with sentiment. Castle Maynard appealed to him strongly and roused him to enthusiasm.

"I had not realised," said he, "what a wonderful old home you have. My old house is not bad, about the date of your Jacobean part, but your remains of the old chateau fort is beyond anything at Tiptoft."

"Yes; it's not a bad old place, is it," said Cecil. "I'm very fond of it, and have been amusing myself since I came here with trying to learn all about its history."

"That's well," said his friend; "it shows you deserve to own it. I can't understand how any man of intelligence can live in an old historical place without hunting up all that can be known about it. I've been doing a bit in that way at Tiptoft, but you have more ample material here and a longer history."

"We have only just discovered that we have a ghost," said Mrs. Maynard. "For a long time I thought there wasn't one, and I was quite disappointed."

"Really! And have you seen it? And, pray, whose ghost is it?"

"Why, it's rather funny, Sir Henry, that you should ask me that question, for the ghost is one of your own family."

"Indeed! You interest me greatly. I am a profound believer in ghosts, and never miss a meeting of the Psychical Society," said he, laughing. "But, tell me, who of my family is it that favours you with a visit, Mrs. Maynard?"

"Did you ever hear of a Hilda Tiptoft in the time of Charles II., who was married to Sir Everard Maynard?"

"Why, I think I have, now you mention it. Was there not some tragedy about it?"

"Quite right," said Cecil. "She was lost, or ran away, or at all events she disappeared, and my wife will have it her husband murdered her."

"Why, Cecil, you know he did," said she.

"I confess things look rather black against him," said Cecil. "But we haven't quite got to the bottom of that story. However, at all events, we have convicted him of murdering another person. I have evidence enough to hang my respectable ancestor if I had him here."

"Well, every family has its black sheep," said Sir Henry. "I dare say we Tiptofts have not always been angels. But where did you get all this story from? You speak as if you had made a discovery."

"So we have, Sir Henry," said Mrs. Maynard. "You must get Cecil to show you the papers we have found, written by an eyewitness of all Sir Everard's atrocities."

"Not quite that," said Cecil, laughing. "A man can hardly be summoned as an eyewitness of his own murder. And we are not quite sure yet that Sir Everard really murdered anyone else."

"I was in hope," said Mrs. Maynard, "that Sir Henry would have been able to help us to clear the matter up. But I fear he knows nothing about it."

"No! I am sorry to say that, beyond a vague idea that there was a mystery about poor Hilda Tiptoft, I know nothing more. But I should like, of all things, to see the papers you have found if I may be allowed to do so."

"By all means, my dear Henry," said Cecil. "In fact we have been looking forward to your doing so, in hope you may throw some light on the mystery. To speak seriously, it is really a gruesome story, and, told as it is at first hand, I confess it made an unpleasant impression on me, although it all happened so long ago. But you shall see the papers and judge for yourself."

They had tea under the trees by the river at the foot of the great tower, at which Tiptoft looked with interest.

"What is there in the lower part of this great tower?" said he. "It is a whole storey below the rest of the house."

"Nothing at all, so far as I know," said Cecil.

"That's disappointing," said Sir Henry. "I thought at least some crusading Maynard had a dungeon there where he kept captive Jews like Front-de-Boeuf, and drew their teeth in order to extract their gold."

"No. I fancy it is solid," said Cecil. "At all events, if there is anything inside there's no way of getting into it."

After tea some neighbours dropped in, and there was tennis, and then they dined, and after dinner they sat on the terrace, and the men smoked and talked till far into the pleasant summer night before they went to bed.

The next few days were spent in the way usual at a country house. There was fishing and a little rabbit shooting, and a villagers' cricket match, where under the captaincy of the blacksmith, Maynard and Tiptoft helped Castle Maynard to beat a rival eleven from Chaldicote. And it was not till the day before midsummer that Henry Tiptoft recollected the papers, of which he had been promised a view. It was a rainy morning, and he thought he could not spend the time more agreeably than in reading them. They were produced from the muniment-room and spread out in order on the table in the library, and Cecil, who had business to attend to, left his friend to amuse himself till the evening. Scarcely, however, had he settled himself comfortably at the table with the prospect of an interesting historical research, exactly to his taste, before Mrs. Maynard made demands on his company, and then after luncheon they went for a ride, and it was not till after tea that he at last sat down quietly to enjoy Roger Trumball's diary.

Cecil Maynard did not get back till just before dinner, and had only time to dress and join his wife and his friend in the great hall before they were marshalled by the butler into the dining-room. During dinner Henry was rather silent and abstracted, and left his host and hostess to carry on most of the conversation. Cecil had been at quarter sessions, and was full of stories and episodes of the proceedings, and Mrs. Maynard had much to say of village matters and local politics, and so they hardly noticed the change in their guest's manner. It was not till Mrs. Maynard had retired, leaving them on the terrace smoking, that Cecil was struck by Sir Henry's silence, and could not help asking him whether anything was amiss.

"I'm glad you asked me," said Tiptoft. "I've been longing to tell you, but I could not speak of it while Mrs. Maynard was here, for fear of frightening her."

"Why, what has happened?" said Cecil in some alarm.

"I've been reading those papers you showed me," said he. "They leave off abruptly, and there cannot be much doubt that he was in danger on that ride of his. Do you know anything further about it?"

"I do, indeed. You may have noticed that the last page was dated June 23, 1662, the date of his ride to your house. In our church-yard here we found Roger Trumball's tombstone with the date of his death, June 24, 1662, the day following."

"I see. You mean that he was murdered on his way. The ride was a plot of his master to get rid of him?"

"Just so. And the tombstone must have been put up by his murderer. He suspected Roger of scheming to expose him, and so sent him to his death and wrote on his tombstone 'There is no device in the grave whither thou goest.' Can you conceive a more ghastly piece of Satanic humour?"

"Devilish, indeed. But do you remember why Roger wanted to go to Tiptoft?"

"Yes," said Cecil. "It was to tell your people how his poor mistress had been treated, and had disappeared, and no doubt to hint at some foul play so as to put an inquiry on foot."

"He says he had promised his dear lady he would do this, living or dead, and that he had sworn it on the Holy Bible, if you remember."

"I remember," said Cecil. "But, poor fellow, he did not live to fulfil his promise."

"He says living or dead," replied Tiptoft.

"What do you mean?" said Cecil, looking at him after a pause.

"He has fulfilled it," said Henry.

There was silence for some minutes. At last, recovering his composure which had been much disturbed, Henry continued:

"I'll tell you exactly what happened. You know I was in the library? Well, as I read poor Roger Trumball's story I became more and more absorbed. It seemed to fascinate me in a way I never had experienced before. It was as if the scene were before me; as if it were being enacted now, and by living men and women, instead of having happened nearly three hundred years ago by those who are now dust and ashes. It laid hold of me in such a way that I seemed to lose my own identity, and to be a mere visionary spectator of a horrible drama; of scenes in which, though I was present, I was powerless to act. A sense of something supernatural overcame me, unseen influences seemed around me, and as I finished the last page I sat a few minutes trying in vain to collect my faculties. At last I rose from my chair, and, leaving the manuscript open upon the table, I walked to the fireplace. I looked round the room. This was the place, I said to myself, where the scene took place between Roger and his master, when he confounded him by producing the missing receipt. This was the room, too, where the last scene in the story was enacted, and I seemed to see Sir Everard with his devilish hypocritical bonhomie laying the trap for his victim's death, and poor Roger, loyal to his mistress, falling into the trap, not without some misgivings, but resolved at all hazards to fulfil his promise to tell all he knew to the Tiptofts. He had sworn he would do it, living or dead. I found myself saying aloud almost unconsciously, 'living or dead; living or dead.'

"At that moment I happened to turn my eye towards the place where I had been sitting. That part of the room was in shadow, and the evening was beginning to set in, but I saw at the table a figure standing and seeming to look at the papers that lay there. Thinking it was a servant come to arrange the room, for I did not see him very distinctly, I said, 'Please do not disturb those papers; I will attend to them.' As he took no notice, I repeated what I said.

The figure slowly turned and looked at me. Something seemed to seize me by the throat and stop my speech, and I could only look at him in silence. The face was grave, and the expression good and kindly. He seemed a man of middle age, strongly built, dressed in sober brown or grey, but I did not much notice his dress, for his face fascinated me. He took up the last page of the diary and put his finger on the bottom line, and then laid it down. A noise at the other end of the room startled me, and I looked round. When I turned my head again he was gone. I looked at the line to which he pointed. These were the words: 'Alive or dead, I have sworne, and I know I shall keep my oath.' And then I knew he had kept it to-night."

The two men sat silent for a while, and then Cecil said:

"A strange story. You, I know, are a believer in psychical phenomena. I am not. Forgive my asking, but are you quite sure it was not a dream? It is exactly what one might dream after having been excited as you were by this gruesome story. I felt something like you myself as I read it, and had to keep thinking and saying to myself this is all ancient history, the actors are gone and turned to dust, and the sinners have paid the penalty of their misdeeds, long long ago."

"I don't wonder at your doubt, my dear Cecil. In your place I might doubt too. But believe me, it was no dream, for there was no awaking. I remember walking out of the library to my bedroom quite distinctly, and I can recall all that passed till we met at dinner. No. Roger swore to take his message to a Tiptoft, and he has, I firmly believe, fulfilled his promise."

"Well, there are more things in heaven and earth—you know the rest," said Cecil. "And now, I see, you are shaken and want a good night's rest, so let us go."

But Tiptoft could not rest when he got to his bedroom. His nerves were shaken and still in a flutter. If it had really been a vision, and not, as Maynard supposed, a dream, what did it mean? What was to follow? It could hardly have been allowed without a purpose, and the matter could not end here. He walked to the window and leaned out. The moon was high in the clear summer sky, and touched the landscape with magic light. The old crusading

tower shone out white and brilliantly against the dark trees beyond the river, of which the gentle murmur as it broke over its
rocky bed, was the only sound audible. Henry thought of all those
ancient walls had witnessed, of good and evil, joy and sorrow, of
crime and mystery, of Sir Everard and poor Roger Trumball, and
of the pitiful lady whose fate was unknown, and whose blood ran
in his veins. A strange fancy possessed him that Roger had be-
queathed the quest to him, and that it was his part to solve the
mystery of Hilda Tiptoft. In vain did he pooh! pooh! the idea, and
say with Cecil, that it was all ancient history, that the actors, both
sinners and victims had long been dissolved into their native earth.

The narrative he had read made it all alive again. How was the
matter to be brought to light? And then there came into his mind
Roger's words about Midsummer Eve, and the Popish superstition
that all enchantments were dissolved and truth revealed on St.
John's Eve. And, by heavens, it was Midsummer Day to-morrow,
and this was St. John's Eve, the anniversary of poor Roger's last
entry in his diary before he went to his death. How strange the
coincidence. Could it be that to-night was to solve the mystery of
the past three hundred years? A desire seized him to read the words
again. The manuscript, he knew, was still lying on the library table;
it was near midnight and everybody would be asleep, and he could
get what he wanted without disturbing the house.

As he turned to leave the window his eye fell on the old Cru-
saders' tower, and in the lower part he saw a light glimmering from
a narrow slit where Cecil had said there was no room, but only
solid masonry. This surprised him, as he remembered afterwards,
but at the time his thoughts were elsewhere. The queer sense of a
supernatural presence that had weighed upon him in the afternoon
was upon him again. Unseen influences seemed again to surround
him and he was almost in a trance when he reached the library
door and laid his hand on the latch. He did not enter, for something moving a little way down the corridor caught his eye. It was
in the shadow now, but beyond was a patch of moonlight from a
window, and whatever it was, it was bound to cross it. Surprise

and alarm recalled some of his scattered wits, when he saw distinctly the figure of a man creeping stealthily with silent footfall along the wall. He seemed dressed in black and had something in his hand that for a moment caught the moonlight and glittered. There were some ancient weapons hanging on the walls, and Henry instinctively grasped an old pistol from among them, the first thing his hand fell upon, and then followed as quietly as he could. The man led him through several passages to an old part of the castle, where he had never been before. The moonlight that entered here and there only made the rest of the way darker by contrast, but Henry was able to keep the man in view. They were now in a long gallery, imperfectly lit, for it did not face the moon, and the man suddenly disappeared. Putting out his hand and feeling along the wall he found an opening, a doorway it seemed, low and narrow, and looking down he saw a faint light below and a narrow stairway descending. The man was before him, moving strangely quietly, for his footsteps were inaudible. Henry was drawn on by an irresistible impulse to follow. The man never looked round and was apparently quite unaware he was being followed. The stair ended in a room, round, low and vaulted. There was a table and a lamp on it, shedding a feeble light, and at the table, with her head on her hand and her face towards him, sat a beautiful woman. The man was hidden in the passage and she did not see him, but Henry could look clearly over his shoulder. They remained thus some minutes, and then the woman rose, fell on her knees at the table, her head sank on her clasped hands and she seemed in prayer. Her back was towards them. And now the man stole softly forward towards her and in his hand was the long dagger that had glittered in the moonlight. In another moment he would be upon her, his hand was raised, when some spell seemed to break. Henry found his tongue and cried aloud. The man turned and looked at him for a moment and Henry saw his face distinctly. It was not the face of a living man, but of a malevolent demon. The man said nothing, but advanced upon him with the dagger raised. Henry snapped the pistol at him, but of course in vain, for it was unloaded, a fact that in his dreamy state had not occurred to him. He flung the empty pistol at his assailant without effect, for he still came on; there was a chair close by, and hurling that in his enemy's path, Henry fled up the stair. He was pursued, but reaching the top found a door, which he slammed to behind him, and ran breathless till he reached the main staircase, on which he fell with a cry and remembered no more.

The cry brought out Cecil, who found his friend in a faint. Assistance was called, and Henry was put to bed. He was not in a condition to answer any questions, and indeed, seemed in such a state of terror that he could not be left alone. That diabolical face haunted him; he could not get it out of his mind; he raved in a semi-delirious state for some hours, while Cecil stood by him, wondering much what disaster had overtaken him, and when at last sleep came to him, he still seemed to find terror in his dreams.

IT WAS A WEEK AFTER THIS that the two friends were sitting in the garden, Henry Tiptoft, still somewhat pale and out of sorts, for he had suffered a severe shock. Mrs. Maynard was sitting with them, and Henry Tiptoft had for the first time found courage to tell his experience of that fateful night. They had listened with amazement and some incredulity.

"But, my dear Harry," said Cecil, "you must have dreamt it, for there is no place in the castle in the least like what you describe."

"Perhaps not now," said Tiptoft, "but there may have been. What I saw, remember, was an image of what took place nearly three hundred years ago. That at least, is how I understand it. It was borne in upon me, to use the expression poor Roger Trumball was so fond of, that I was destined to discover the fate of his poor lady, and that he came for that purpose to pass the quest on to my shoulders. I believe what I saw was what really happened: that the lady was imprisoned in some vault in the castle, and murdered there by her husband, in order to get possession of the whole of her estate it would seem."

"You saw the man's face, you say. Should you know it again?"

"Know it! I shall never forget it."

"Well then, you shall come to the picture gallery and see whether you can pick out Sir Everard from the rest, and identify him with your vision. That would be very interesting."

"Yes, but I see you are still incredulous and think I dreamed it all. The only thing to convince you will be to find the stair and the vault."

"Do you remember," said Mrs. Maynard, "Roger says he found Sir Everard with workmen engaged in walling up a doorway?"

"By Jove, Alice," said Cecil, "so he did. That seems to afford a clue. But he said it was in the stone gallery, and there is no place in the house known by that name, or answering to it."

"It comes back to me," said Henry, "that I saw a light glimmering from a slit in the lower part of the old tower which you said was solid with nothing inside. Now I think I can see something like an arrow slit there behind the ivy."

Some ivy was pulled down, and a narrow window was exposed and Cecil was obliged to confess that so far, at all events, he was wrong. There might be a vault then, if Sir Henry's vision was to be depended upon, in the old tower, of which the existence had been forgotten.

"The stone gallery must be that passage which leads to my boudoir on the ground floor of the old tower, and if there is a vault, my boudoir must be over it," said Mrs. Maynard, and she guided them to it. The boudoir was a round room with a lovely view, but Mrs. Maynard said if it was over any horror she should never like it again. The problem now, was to find the doorway which Roger saw being blocked. Workmen were sent for, and after careful examination a piece of walling was detected as an insertion, by the experienced eye of the clerk of works. Behind was found a doorway and a stair. Lights were brought and the two men descended. Henry went first. At the foot of the stair he uttered an exclamation:

"Don't let Mrs. Maynard come down, Cecil," said he, "I don't want her to see it." In the vault, among cobwebs and dust beside an old table, lay a heap of something indefinite, some remains of drapery and linen, yellow with age; and among them, all that was left of poor Hilda Tiptoft.

She was found at last.

It may be added in conclusion, that Sir Henry Tiptoft was taken to the gallery and unhesitatingly picked out the portrait of Sir Everard, though some might say he had the costume of the seventeenth century to help him.

"But the curious thing about it," said Maynard, "is that I picked up an old pistol in the vault just like one that hangs in the hall."

"Then," said Sir Henry, "perhaps now you will believe that my vision was not a dream."

But Cecil said, "I must first go and see if there is one missing from the hall."

PEPINA

THE ASSIZES WERE BEING HELD in the county town, and between the rising of the Court and the time for the Bar mess at the "Bull's Head" a few hours were available for a little pleasant exercise. The surrounding country was pretty and inviting, and offered many field-walks, and two members of the Bar, taking advantage of the summer evening, might have been seen strolling along a woodland path a mile or two from the town. Their demeanour, however, was not in keeping with the peaceful scenery, for there were angry words between them. The elder of the two was a man of fine presence, and a distinguished air. His countenance was expressive of power and determination. He seemed a man who would have his own way whatever it might cost others, but with due allowance for its selfishness, it was not altogether a bad face. He looked like a man easy to get on with if you did not cross him. His companion was a good deal younger, his countenance was frank and open, intelligent and kindly, though at this moment it was clouded with displeasure.

"But I don't understand you," said the elder. "What do you object to?"

"I've told you, Sir Edward," said the younger man, "that your addresses to my sister must be discontinued. I cannot consent to their going on."

"But, my dear Cranston, you are not your sister's keeper. I am, of course, very sorry you disapprove, but your sister, I am sanguine enough to think, does not agree with you. At all events, she has not discouraged me."

"She does not know all I do about you, or she would think as I do. I do not think you are fit for her, and as her brother, I object to the alliance."

"Indeed," said the other with some hauteur, "I should have thought an Attorney-General good enough for the sister of a junior barrister."

"You know very well that is not what I mean. Think of your past. Have you forgotten Naples and Pepina?"

"Oh!" said Sir Edward Wilson in some confusion, "you are going to rake up that story. Of course, I remember Pepina, though I dare say she has forgotten me. It must be three years ago—"

"Then you do not know what became of her? It was like you never to inquire."

"Well, no; we parted in a hurry, and—"

"And what? You meanly threw her off after ruining her, and broke her heart," said Cranston. "Shall I tell you the rest?"

"Well!" said Sir Edward. "What is it?"

"The morning after you brutally turned her adrift and left Naples, her body was found in the canal."

Sir Edward, much shocked, said nothing for a minute. Then recollecting himself, he stammered out:

"I am very sorry. I had no idea she—well—yes, I am really distressed, but—"

"But, you are going to say, it was not your fault. I tell you her blood lies at your door. I wonder her spirit does not haunt you. Let me tell you one thing more. The last thing she did before she threw herself into the water was to send me a note. I have it still. It only contained these words: '*Dica al traditore, ti rivedro all' ora giusta.*—Pepina.'"

"Cranston," said Sir Edward, recovering himself, "this is a sad story, but it is past and gone and cannot be helped. It is unkind of you to revive it."

"And do you think my sister would marry you if she knew it?"

"But she need never know it."

"That depends on you," said Cranston.

"What do you mean?"

"She shall know it if you continue your addresses."

"Do you mean you will tell her?" said he in rising passion.

"I do."

"By Heaven," said he, standing in front of him, "you shall not!"

"Then I understand you mean to persevere," said Cranston. "She shall know it this very night," and he turned on his heel to go homewards.

The other held him, and Cranston, unable to release himself, struck him; the blow was returned, and in a moment they were locked in a deadly struggle. They were not unequally matched, for if one were the stronger the other was younger and more active, but at last Cranston stumbled and fell, and the other, seizing a stick that lay handy, struck him on the head once and again, and then stood panting and looking at his fallen foe.

Cranston did not move. The victor grew anxious and bent over him. "Cranston, for God's sake, my dear fellow, speak to me. I did not mean it, speak to me," cried he in an agony.

The dying man opened his eyes and looked at him; in a whisper came the words, "I leave you to Pepina."

Sir Edward Wilson felt all the horror of his position. It had not been a fair fight; that last blow made it a murder. What was to be done? The wood was thick, and the body might be hidden for a time at all events. He dragged it into a thicket and hid it as well as he could, and then rearranging his disordered dress, returned to the town.

There was nothing noticeable in his manner as he sat at the Bar dinner except that he was more silent than usual, for generally his brilliant talk and caustic wit made him the arbiter of the conversation. It was thought he was fatigued, for he had conducted a very important case that day in court.

"What has become of Cranston?" said some one. "He'll get no dinner unless he looks sharp. Did he not go out with you, Sir Edward?"

"Yes," said he. "We started together, but he went beyond me and I came back alone."

"I'm told," said another, "it's not very safe just now to wander about in these woods. The miners are out on strike, and they say several people have been stopped and robbed—"

"Oh! Cranston's able to take care of himself," said a third. "I don't think he will come to any harm."

And then the matter was forgotten, and other topics came up. But next morning, when a cause came on in which Cranston was engaged, he was missing, and it was found on inquiry that he had not been at his lodgings. Telegrams were sent to his friends, who replied they knew nothing of his movements. People began to be alarmed, and search was made in the neighbourhood. It was not, however, till the third day that the Press was able to make the following announcement:—

"We regret to have to report that the mystery attaching to the disappearance of Mr. Philip Cranston, a barrister attending circuit in this town, has been solved in the most tragic manner. The body of that unfortunate gentleman was found yesterday in the neighbouring woods under circumstances indicating that a foul murder has been committed. Evidences were apparent of a struggle, and a bludgeon was discovered with blood and hair on it, evidently the instrument of this atrocious deed. The body had been rifled of all valuables, watch and chain were gone, and the pockets were turned out, showing that robbery was the motive for this dastardly crime. We take this opportunity of reminding our readers that several cases of robbery in the neighbourhood have occurred recently, and it would seem that the police have been singularly lax in their surveillance. We understand the inquest will be held on Tuesday."

The inquest was held, but there was little evidence to put before the jury. The policeman who found the body told his story, and Sir Edward was called as having been the last person in his company, but he only repeated what he had said before at dinner, and the jury returned a verdict of "Wilful murder against some person or persons unknown," accompanied with a recommendation to the police to be more careful. Many of Cranston's friends attended the inquest, including the judge himself, and there was much discussion about the matter afterwards, as they walked away.

"What puzzles me," said one, "is why Mr. Attorney and Cranston went out for a walk together. I know Cranston did not like him."

"Nonsense," said the other. "Everyone knows Wilson wants to marry Cranston's sister."

"I fancy that is not settled," replied his friend; "I know Cranston objected. He has never been friendly with Wilson since that time they went to Italy together three years ago. Something or other happened to make a breach between them, but I believe it was Cranston who took offence and not Wilson."

"However, they went out for a walk together that day anyhow, which looks friendly."

"Yes," said the other. "Wilson was the last man seen in his company."

"Why, you don't mean—" said the other laughing.

"No, no, I mean nothing, but it's rather funny, isn't it?"

The assizes were over. The judge was gone to the next county town, and the Bar was following. The Attorney-General returned to town to attend to his Parliamentary duties. As he sat alone in the railway carriage with nothing to occupy him, the full horror of what had happened rushed in upon him. The scene in the wood; the struggle; the fatal last blow. Would to God he had not yielded to that mad homicidal impulse. And Cranston had been his chosen friend and companion; he had in his selfish way loved him. To think he should have slain him! And Lucy Cranston. How could he face her with her brother's blood on his hands? That at all events was all over now. As to discovery, he felt safe. The robbery of the body diverted suspicion in a wrong direction, and the thief would be silent for his own sake. He had at first thought of telling the truth, and taking his chance; but then there was his position at the head of his profession, with the highest prize almost in his grasp, and to confess to a murderous brawl, and stand his trial for manslaughter meant ruin in any case, and was not to be thought of. At all events, it was too late now; things had gone too far. And then he thought of Pepina.

Her blood too, as Cranston said, lay at his door. Two deaths stood against him in the great account. He was a selfish, but not naturally a cruel man, and the horror of it almost stunned him.

"Good God!" he cried, "what have I done to bring all this upon me?" He thought of pretty Pepina, as he first saw her, an innocent and happy rustic beauty in the vineyards near Naples. Of her love and trust in him, and of his desertion of her. He hated himself as he thought of it, and would have made any conceivable atonement; but the time for that was past; she was dead, and he had to bear the guilt of her death. "What did her last message mean? He was to see her again at the right time. When would that be? Though a sceptic as to things supernatural, he felt afraid. And then Cranston's dying words recurred to him, "I leave you to Pepina." They fastened a creeping terror upon him, and seemed burned into his brain. He felt they would never leave him. That day and night the thought of Pepina would recur to him, and perhaps drive him mad.

But Sir Edward Wilson was a man of strong self-command; when the train drew into the terminus he was able to recover himself, and when he met his household he showed no traces of the ordeal he had gone through.

SIX MONTHS HAD SLIPPED AWAY, and few but those who loved him ever thought of the murder of Philip Cranston, though it made a stir at the time. Two ladies in deep mourning were sitting in a pleasant drawing-room in the West end of London, looking out on the Square garden, where the trees were just burgeoning into fresh life after their winter sleep.

"Lucy," said the elder lady, "did I tell you Sir Edward Wilson called about a fortnight ago for the first time after poor Philip's death. You will remember how kindly he wrote about it at the time. He asked about you, but I think you were out."

"No, I was not out. But I did not wish to see him."

Mrs. Cranston laid down her work and looked at her daughter in some surprise. After a pause she continued:

"I may be wrong, Lucy, but I fancied you did not discourage his addresses. All our friends seemed to think it would be a match."

"Oh, no, indeed, mother," said Lucy. "There is nothing between us. He has said nothing to me, and I hope he never will, for I could not listen to his proposals, and should be sorry to have to refuse him."

"And yet he has much to offer. He is at the head of his profession, with a brilliant career before him. But, of course, if you don't like him well enough to marry him, you are right to avoid him."

"No, mother, with all his brilliant career, and all that, I could never marry him. To tell you the truth, I am afraid of him. I think he is an idolater, and the idol he worships is himself, and he is prepared to sacrifice to his idol everything that stands in his way."

"You think him selfish and unscrupulous?"

"Yes. I think any woman who married him would have to be either his slave or his victim, and I have no wish to be either."

"And yet you remember he was dear Philip's most intimate friend at one time. They travelled together in Italy only three years ago."

"That is true, but I know Philip did not like him so well lately. Something or other happened on that tour that made Philip distrust him. He never said anything to me about it, but I could see that he did not like Sir Edward's coming here so often."

There was silence for a little while, and then Lucy said: "I have often wondered what it was that offended Philip, for I know he was attached to Sir Edward formerly, and had an unbounded admiration for his talents. You know I have been looking over his old letters and papers, and I thought I might find something there to throw light upon it, but I found nothing, unless one curious scrap, written in Italian, has anything to do with it. I did not destroy it with other papers that seemed not worth keeping and which I tore up, for it seemed rather curious. I will go and fetch it, for I should like you to see it.

She went to her room and came back with a piece of paper in her hand, and gave it to her mother. It had been folded as a note and sealed, and was addressed on the outside in an illiterate hand to Signor Filippo, Inglese. Mrs. Cranston read it thoughtfully, and laid it in her lap. After a while she said to her daughter:

"It is very curious, Lucy. '*Dica al traditore ti rivedro all' ora giusta.*' 'Tell the traitor I shall see him again at the right time.' It is signed 'Pepina.' What do you make of it? It sounds rather like a threat."

"What do you make of it, mother," said Lucy. "Why, the question is, who the traitor was to whom Philip was to give the message?"

"Well, you know who was with him."

"Yes. I suppose you are right. As usual, a woman in the case. It looks like some disgraceful intrigue. The writing is that of a peasant woman. I wonder who poor Pepina was?"

"I think," said Lucy, "this really does throw some light on the change in Philip's manner to Sir Edward."

"Very likely," said her mother. "He must have behaved badly to the girl, and Philip disapproved. I suppose we shall never know anything more about it. Some sad story, only too common a one, I am sorry to say."

At this moment the servant opened the door and announced Sir Edward Wilson. For some days after his return to town, Wilson had felt unable to renew his relations with the Cranstons. It was horrible to think of seeing them again. That he should write a letter of condolence was inevitable, considering their former intimacy. It would naturally be expected of him, and its omission might awake suspicion; but to write it cost him an agonising effort. The situation was appalling; to think of their reading expressions of sympathy written by the hand that had done the deed! But it had to be done, and he got through it somehow, though the letters seemed to him to be written in blood. And he pictured to himself Lucy reading it. If she only knew! It was dreadful to think of. She had attracted him as no other woman had ever done. In his selfish way he really loved her; he thought she was worthy to share his fortunes and would take her place with dignity and grace as his wife in the high position to which he aspired. But now, that, he thought, must all be at an end; he must think of her no more. To ask the hand of the sister of the man he had killed was too horrible to contemplate. Another trouble presented itself. He must meet Philip's mother and sister as soon as a decent time had elapsed since the funeral; he had been a constant visitor at the house, and to drop at once all intimacy would be dangerous. He would have to face them, but God alone knew how he could do it. How could he show his guilty face again in that familiar room associated with recollections of pleasant meetings and innocent intercourse?

But time went on. The murder was forgotten, no suspicion was ever directed against him, law and politics combined to absorb his attention more and more, and the first heat of his sell-reproach and remorse began to cool. He even succeeded in finding excuses for himself; after all, Cranston had struck the first blow; he only acted in sell-defence, and the quarrel ended unfortunately for poor Cranston, for whom he sincerely grieved. And then Pepina. He had almost forgotten that part of the business. Poor Pepina; it was very sad, but how could he have foreseen that she would take the matter so seriously. Those Italians were so very excitable. Still he blamed himself for not having provided somehow for her future. However, there was no help for that now.

He determined at last that the time had come when he must go and see the Cranstons, or his absence might be remarked upon. And now he did not somehow feel the same reluctance as at first. Having satisfied or rather blunted his own conscience, he had a feeling that what had been enough for himself might satisfy others as well, and that as he had brought himself to believe that he was rather the victim of circumstances in which by accident he had to his great regret injured others, the same view would be taken by the world at large should the matter ever come to light. He called then, as we have seen, on Mrs. Cranston, and managed to impress her with his sympathy. He was quieter and more subdued than usual, and Mrs. Cranston approved his manner, which seemed to show real feeling. Lucy, as we know, was not present, which was a disappointment, for he had looked forward to seeing her. If she could not now be his, still it would be pleasant to be with her again on something like the old friendly relations. Mrs. Cranston thought him improved; less masterful and self-assertive, and she was touched by his kindly words and manner.

He thought a good deal of Lucy as he walked away. To give her up cost him a pang. Every memory of her graceful ways, her bright intelligence, and her ready sympathy made it more difficult. After all, was it out of the question, he said to himself, that she should be his wife? And then the thought rushed upon him, "Suppose she found me out after we were married?"

That was horrible; too horrible. But was it at all possible that this should happen? The whole thing was sunk into oblivion, and unlikely ever to be heard of again. There could be no danger.

"I am sure," said he to himself, "I could make her a happy woman. I can offer her position, wealth, and influence; Lucy would make a grande dame of whom I should be proud."

It was then with a determination to persist in the course, to prevent which her brother had fallen by his hand, that Sir Edward Wilson knocked at the door a fortnight later, and asked whether Mrs. Cranston was at home. He was shown into the drawing-room, and there, as we know, he found Lucy as well as her mother.

They rose to meet him, Mrs. Cranston laying on the table the mysterious paper which Lucy had given her to read. They thought Sir Edward looking worn and aged, and he explained rather hurriedly that he had had a good deal to worry him of late. They talked of politics, and of a great speech he had made in the House which had been much praised, and he was pleased to hear that Lucy had read it in *The Times* and admired it. He talked well, and they were pleased with his manner, which was a good deal softened from its former style. He bore the inevitable allusions to poor Philip with more composure than he could have anticipated, and replied to their questions that no further clue had been found as to the author of the crime.

"For my part," said Mrs. Cranston, "I wish they would drop the inquiry, and let the whole sad affair be forgotten."

"So do I," said Lucy, "and so I am sure would poor Philip if he could speak. I am quite willing to leave the murderer to the torments of his own conscience."

Sir Edward said nothing, and soon after rose to take his leave. As he shook hands with Mrs. Cranston he was standing by the table, and his eye fell on the paper Mrs. Cranston had laid down as he entered the room. She felt him start; he dropped her hand, and, as she looked at him in surprise she saw he had turned ashy pale. He staggered for a moment and supported himself by the table, before recovering himself. To her expression of fear that he was not well, he explained rather incoherently that he felt a little dizzy for the moment; that he had been overworking himself, and supposed his doctor was right in telling him he wanted a rest. But he could not recover his wonted composure as he bowed himself out of the room, declining Mrs. Cranston's invitation to sit down and wait till he felt better. Lucy stood aloof, and avoiding shaking hands with him, dismissed him with a bow.

"There, mother," said she when the door closed, "you see we were right. If ever a guilty conscience could show itself it did so now. Depend upon it there is some tragedy connected with poor Pepina."

"It certainly was very odd," said her mother. "I thought he would have fainted. Are you sure it was the sight of that paper that upset him?"

"Quite sure. I saw his eye fall upon it; and I saw him read it, and then he changed colour at once, and staggered as if he would have fallen. Nobody but a man of his great self-command could have recovered himself as he did in a minute."

"I think, my dear," said Mrs. Cranston, "that paper should be taken care of. It is possible it may be wanted some day."

"I think so too. I will take it to my room and lock it up," said Lucy.

As Wilson walked away his head was in a whirl. He called a cab and went home, and shut himself up in his study. All the edifice of self-deception, exculpation, and complacency which he had built up around him had fallen to the ground at the sight of that fatal paper of which Philip told him before he died. He was left naked and exposed to all the tortures of an awakened conscience. He saw Cranston lying in his blood, Pepina in her watery grave, and himself their murderer. Where now were his shallow evasions; where were the vain pretences with which he had deceived himself. He saw himself as he was, a criminal, a double criminal, with blood on his hands of one who had loved him, and one who had been his trusted friend. It was too much; why not end it all with a dose or a pistol shot? Then at all events the secret would die with him, his fair fame would be saved, and it would never be known that the great lawyer, the brilliant politician should by right have been standing in the dock at the Old Bailey.

And that paper: *ti rivedro all' ora giusta*. When am I to see her again, and why would she come? In his present dejected state he never doubted that she would make her word good. A cold shudder ran through his frame. He was to see her again, but when and where! Philip's last words were "I leave you to Pepina." Pepina was to avenge them both. Well, let her come, things could not be worse than they were. He wished he were dead and all were over.

ANOTHER YEAR had slipped away, and Lucy and her mother were sitting as we last saw them in their pleasant room looking at the spring blossoms that were bursting in the garden of the Square. Lucy was engaged to be married shortly to Frederick Warren, a young barrister, rising into good practice, who had been a friend of her brother Philip, and was with him on that fatal circuit. He was one of the last to see him before he went on his last walk, and he had attended the inquest, which he thought very badly managed and too easily satisfied. Mrs. Cranston and Lucy were now expecting him to drop in to tea, as he usually did when his day's work was done. He came in radiant, for the case in which he was engaged under one of the big-wigs of the Bar had won the day, though the great Attorney-General had been opposed to them.

"I think he was rather sick about it, Lucy," said he, "for he cannot bear to be beaten. There never was a man more determined to have his own way in everything."

"Lucy says he is an idolater, and that the idol he worships is himself," said Mrs. Cranston.

"A very good description," said Warren. "He is an egoist, if ever there was one. I doubt if he would let anything stand between him and his pleasure if he could help it; and yet at bottom there is something good about him which comes out so long as you don't thwart him."

"He is a very masterful person," said Lucy, "and I think he would have made a very good tyrant in the Middle Ages, like

Sigismondo Malatesta, and Bernabo Visconti, and the rest of the Italian despots."

"By the way," said Warren, "that reminds me of your story about him and an Italian girl. Some paper you found that you showed him, and it upset him a good deal."

"Of course we know nothing more about it," said Mrs. Cranston, "but I fancy there is some tragedy in the case, and that Sir Edward was implicated in it, and to blame for it."

"Do you know," said Lucy, "I have been having some curious dreams about it, which made me rather uncomfortable, especially as they were followed by a reality. But you don't believe in dreams, Frederick, and will laugh at me if I tell you."

"Certainly not," said he, "especially since they have made you uncomfortable, and still more wonderful, were followed by a reality."

"There now," said she, "you are laughing at me already."

"No. I'll promise to be serious indeed," said he.

"Well then," said Lucy "you will remember the girl's name was Pepina and she was an Italian, and to judge by her writing a peasant woman. My dream was rather vague, but it has been repeated three times. I seemed to be in a vineyard; there were many figures there but all very indistinct, except one face which showed up clearly, a beautiful face, quite classical, like a Greek statue. I could not see what she was doing, for the whole scene was misty, only the face was clear; and then all seemed to fade away and change to a river side. It was nearly dark, but I saw something in the water, something white, and as I looked I saw it was the same beautiful face looking up at me out of the water. It troubled me a good deal and I awoke. But the dream was repeated twice more, just the same and no more of it. Do you think it was Pepina?"

"I think you had Pepina in your mind when you went to bed, and invented the pictures in your sleep."

"Well, but why three times? And I never thought of the river and poor Pepina in it. That at all events was no invention of mine. I think she drowned herself and that was the tragedy, and that the dream was sent to let me know."

"Well, perhaps so. But what of the reality that followed?"

"If you don't believe in dreams," said Lucy, "I suppose you won't believe in ghosts."

"Nay, I don't say that," said Frederick. "But what have you to say about ghosts?"

"Well, just this. Yesterday, as I was crossing the park to come home, I saw the same face as that in my dream."

"Indeed," said Frederick, "that is curious. What happened?"

"Nothing happened. It was getting dusk and I was rather late, when I saw a woman in black standing where I should pass her. As I came up, she turned and looked at me. It was the same lovely classical face that I had seen in my dream. I should know it again anywhere. It was very pale and sad. She said nothing but looked hard at me, and I was so frightened that I dared not speak to her. I heard steps approaching and looked round, and when I turned again she was gone."

"Didn't you see her figure moving away?"

"No. She had vanished utterly."

"That is a very curious story," said both of her listeners—and they sat for a few minutes in silence.

"Then you think," said Warren, "that poor Pepina, for I assume, of course, you dreamt of her, wishes to establish some communication with you."

"I do indeed, and I fancy it concerns Sir Edward Wilson."

"You know, Lucy," said he, "I am, or rather have been, a confirmed disbeliever in ghosts and spiritualism, but I am not such a prig as to believe myself infallible. Your experience is certainly very strange. I wonder whether anything more will come of it. I think you should write it all down at the time so as to be sure of the facts. They often get exaggerated by repetition of the story."

"There is another thing, however, that occurs to me. Do you remember what was on the paper that so upset Sir Edward?"

"No. I forget," said Warren.

"It said, 'I shall see you again at the right time.' Now do you think this figure has come to show itself to him?"

"Who knows. If we can guess the story right, Sir Edward betrayed poor Pepina and deserted her, and she went and drowned herself. But, of course, we have no proof of anything of the kind, except your dream and vision, and that, as we lawyers say, is not evidence."

"No, that is true. But I don't envy him his feelings if he is visited by his victim. It should be enough to make a man mad. Perhaps this is the right time—'*l'ora giusta*,' of the letter."

"But why should she come to you of all people in the world?"

"I think it is because I am Philip's sister, and it was to him her note was written, and I have the note itself in my keeping."

"And have you seen much of Sir Edward lately?"

"No, very little," said Mrs. Cranston. "I fancy he does not like the recollection of having, in a manner, betrayed himself when he saw that paper. He only comes now when he is pretty sure of finding company here."

"I'm glad of that," said Warren, who remembered the time when it was thought Sir Edward and Lucy were to make a match of it.

LONDON WAS AT THE HEIGHT of the season. Fashion and society were in full swing, Parliament was sitting and many measures of consequence were under debate. Sir Edward Wilson was conspicuous among the champions of the Government: never had he carried more weight in the councils of the nation, never had he shone more brilliantly in debate, never had he been so formidable to his opponents. It was thought the Chancellor wished to retire, and by common consent Sir Edward was regarded as the next custodian of the Great Seal. He had dropped in one evening at the Athenæum for a cup of tea before going down to the House, and as he stood talking and laughing amid a group of friends who were congratulating him on the part he had played in last night's debate, he felt he had touched the zenith of his fortune and that the great prize of his profession was almost within his grasp. When his friends left him he sat down to his tea and idly took up an evening paper that some one had left on the chair at his side. As he glanced over it, his eye fell on a paragraph that made his heart stand still.

"The Northborough Murder
"It will be remembered that about two years ago a shocking murder was committed near Northborough,

the author of which has till now escaped justice. The
victim was Mr. Philip Cranston, a rising barrister,
who was attending circuit in that town. The body was
found stripped of all articles of value and hidden in
a thick part of the wood. Hitherto the police have
had no clue to lead them to the discovery of the
criminal. Yesterday, however, the arrest was made
of a man of bad character, in whose possession some
of the property taken from the unfortunate gentleman was found. The capture reflects great credit on
the local police, and illustrates the old saying that
'murder will out.' The man is named Abel Sanders,
and we understand he will be brought before the
magistrates on Tuesday."

The blow for the moment stunned him. This was an eventual-
ity on which he had not counted. He saw at once how it affected
him. This wretched yokel would be tried for his life, and might be
convicted and hanged. He himself, and no other, could save the
poor wretch, but he could only do it at his own expense, by changing places with the prisoner. Had it come at last to this? He turned
the matter over this way and that, but saw no escape from the dilemma, if the man were convicted. It was, of course, possible that
he would be acquitted, and if so all would be well. At all events he
would wait and see the result of the inquiry before the magistrates,
and then decide what must be done.

When he got home he found, as he expected, a subpoena requiring him to appear as a witness before the bench of magistrates
at Northborough. The evidence at the inquest had been read over
and his presence was necessary, he having been the last person in
poor Philip's company.

He found the court crowded, for the arrest had made a great
stir in the county. There was a large attendance of the county magistrates on the bench, some of whom were known to him and
greeted him as a distinguished friend. Among the witnesses he was
surprised to see Lucy Cranston, who had been summoned to swear

to the property of her brother. Warren had come with her to see her through this disagreeable business, for which he thought, as did poor Lucy, a servant would have done as well. Sir Edward had heard of their engagement, but it distressed him less than it would have done twelve months before. He had long given up any pretensions in that quarter.

The prisoner was brought in, a shambling, ne'er-do-well sort of yokel, who stared stupidly about him, and did not seem to realise the seriousness of his position. The evidence was much the same as at the inquest, with the addition of the new matter connected with the arrest. The watch and chain, and various small articles that were found in the prisoner's possession were identified by Lucy as having belonged to her brother. The policeman who found the body told his tale over again, and Sir Edward repeated the evidence he had given before the coroner.

One of the magistrates, however, who had known Cranston, asked a question which caused some surprise in court.

"I believe, Sir Edward, if I am right, there had been some sort of quarrel between you and Mr. Cranston?"

"There certainly was at one time," replied Sir Edward, "a slight coolness on Mr. Cranston's part towards me, arising from a trifling family matter, but I am happy to think that that had passed and we were good friends again. In fact it was Mr. Cranston who proposed our going for a walk together on that fatal day."

This was confirmed by other witnesses who had been present and heard Cranston give the invitation, and nothing further was said. But Warren looked at Lucy and raised his eyebrows.

The prisoner's story was that he found the dead body in the wood, and he admitted taking from it the things found in his possession. He said also:

"I see two gents a walking into the wood, and after a bit only one of 'em come out. If you can spot that man I warrant he'll be the one as you want."

Asked if he could identify the man he saw come out of the wood he said, "No, he was too fur off. It was a biggish man, something of the size of the gen'lman a setting there," and he pointed to Sir Edward.

Sir Edward rose at once and said he had no doubt the man was speaking the truth. "Your worship will remember I said in my evidence that my poor friend Cranston and I entered the wood together, and that we parted, he continuing his walk further on, and I returning alone. I have no doubt it was I whom the prisoner saw leaving the wood."

There was no more evidence forthcoming, and the Justices, after conferring together, agreed that it was a case for further investigation, and the man was committed for trial at the forthcoming assizes on two counts, one of wilful murder, and the other of unlawful possession of the property found on him.

As they were leaving the court with the crowd that was pouring out, Lucy clutched Warren's arm.

"Look, look," said she.

He followed her gaze and just caught sight of a pale face, beautiful and sad, turned towards them for a moment, and then the figure was lost in the crowd. They sought to find her but in vain.

"It is she again," said Lucy. "Now you will know her. This cannot be the last time we shall see her. Depend on it she is not here for nothing."

Wilson's reflections as he went back to town were not agreeable. The man was not acquitted as he had hoped, and he did not like the question put to him by Mr. Turner from the bench. It might direct suspicion on him. Mr. Turner had, no doubt, been talking to his friends about the case, and may have made uncomfortable suggestions, which would be remembered when the matter came on for trial. As on the former occasion before the magisterial examination, he comforted himself by the thought that the trial might end in an acquittal, and that the whole matter would then sink again into the oblivion from which the arrest of Abel Sanders had lifted it. But on the other hand the man might be convicted and sentenced to death. What was he to do then? It rested with him and him alone to rescue an innocent man from the gallows, but at what a price! Could he afford to pay it? He was no coward. It was not the fear of punishment that weighed on him. But the shame, the disgrace of being dragged down from his splendid position to ignominy. He had so much to lose.

Wilson, though arbitrary and self-seeking, was not an entirely unscrupulous man. Self interest at times had driven him towards what he naturally disapproved, but he now felt there was a limit beyond which he could not go. Brought face to face with this tremendous problem, he felt that truth and justice left him no choice, and that there was nothing before him but ruin.

However, there was still the chance of the trial ending in an acquittal, and that would solve all his difficulties.

It was in the hopeful state of mind created by this last consideration that he entered his chambers in the Temple one morning a short time after the Northborough inquiry, and asked his clerk what had come in since yesterday.

The clerk ran through a list of matters, small and great, which had to be attended to, and then produced an official letter that had just been handed in.

"A brief for you, sir, from the Crown, for the prosecution, in the case of Rex. v. Abel Sanders. I think that was the murder down at Northborough. You will remember, sir, you had to attend the inquest. With you will be, let me see, Mr. Jones and Mr. Evans."

Sir Edward sank into his chair and said nothing. He dismissed his clerk and said he would call him when he wanted him later. For the moment the monstrous situation paralysed him. He felt that to hold his peace during the trial was bad enough, but it was impossible for him to stand up and prosecute an innocent man for the crime he himself had committed. He could not think of it without horror: at all events he must escape from that position, and he would, of course, decline the brief.

He wrote to that effect to the Home Secretary, returning the brief on the plea that his other engagements and his Parliamentary work, which just then was very arduous, obliged him, to his regret, to decline to act. He observed also that he had appeared as a witness in the case and might be called again.

The Secretary, however, was persistent. He said the matter was very important as complaints had come from that district of insufficient protection against the frequent robberies with violence that had been committed: that hitherto no criminals had been captured, and that should it prove that Abel Sanders was guilty the example of his punishment would be useful. For that reason it had been decided to employ the best talent at the bar, and to brief the Attorney-General.

Undaunted by this Sir Edward went to see the official, who received him rather coldly, and made light of the objection he raised on the ground that he had been called as a witness before the magistrates.

"Your evidence was not important, Sir Edward, and we can do without calling you at the trial very well."

As Sir Edward persisted, the Secretary said in some surprise, and with a little irritation, he could not see the difficulty.

"I do not understand what motive you can possibly have for declining, Sir Edward," said he. The word motive alarmed Sir Edward. It must not be supposed he had any motive beyond the difficulties he had mentioned. He hastened to plead again pressure of work as his reason.

The great man at once recovered his good temper.

"We all know the demand the public interest makes on Sir Edward's time," he said, smiling. "But this is a very simple case. The man is an old offender, and the property was found on him. It will not give you much trouble. So I conclude you will act, and am much obliged to you. Good day." And then, shaking hands, he accompanied him to the door and dismissed him. The week before the trial was spent by Sir Edward in a sort of ghastly dream, He lived, as it were, in hell, for hell itself could not be worse. Some deadly diabolical web seemed to him to be enveloping him and dragging him ever lower and lower into an abyss of crime. He could trace a horrible sequence in all that had befallen him; crime grew out of crime; the whole had hung together; he had been drawn step by step along the same dark path which was leading him to perdition. Till that fatal Italian tour his life had been clean and honourable. The tragedy of Pepina began it, and then the devil's toils began to close around him. Pepina's death led to the second tragedy, that fatal murderous blow in the forest at Northborough. And as if the devil had not got him already involved in his meshes, he was now forcing him to a worse sin still, to drag an innocent man to the gallows in order to conceal his own crime and save himself from shame and punishment. Worse, far worse this, he said, than the former crimes. Whatever palliation there might have been for them, this was deliberate cowardly murder.

For his victim, indeed, he felt no pity. He hated Abel Sanders with a bitter hatred as the author of his present misery. Why could not the scoundrel have hid his spoils better? He compared his own brilliant position with that of this ignorant clown. "What," he thought, "is that ignoble life worth in comparison with mine? What is the fairness of putting it in the balance against one of so much more value? The wretch was a mean thief; he bore a bad character, and had been in prison more than once. He would probably have come to the gallows anyhow, whereas I, whose life and honour he puts in jeopardy, can ill be spared. And yet," thought he, "a third death will lie at my door! My God! What have I done to bring all this upon me?" He was not convinced by his own excuses. His self-respect was gone; he knew he was sinking lower and lower into the abyss of guilt; that the toils spun about him by some devilish agency were dragging him down to perdition; but he had no power to resist. A fatal necessity was upon him, a spell enveloped him, and he knew that whatever happened he must now go through with this accursed business.

It was remarked, as the day of trial grew near, that he became haggard and depressed. His erect frame began to stoop, his step was languid and his eyes dull.

"Wilson is killing himself with overwork," said his friends. "If he does not look out, and take things more easily, he will not reach the Woolsack after all."

The court was crowded to suffocation on the day of the trial. All the county magnates attended, and several members of the circuit had been there at the time of Philip Cranston's disappearance two years before. The Lord Chief Justice was to preside, and it was known that the Attorney-General had been briefed for the prosecution. Among the members of the Bar who were present was Frederick Warren, who had promised to bring a report of the trial to Mrs. Cranston and Lucy. Their interest in the trial was not great, and they rather wished to know nothing about it, but Warren thought it necessary on their account to be present and take notes of what occurred.

It was late when he returned and sat down with them, and they could see by his manner that something unusual had happened. He was much agitated, and it was some minutes before he began his story.

"I've strange things to tell you," he said at last, "and I don't quite know myself what to make of it all. It is mostly about Wilson, and the trial is not finished yet. When he came into court I hardly knew him. You never saw a man so changed. His face was yellow, his lips dry and parched, his cheeks were sunk in, and he looked more dead than alive. Everyone was shocked, even the judge, who sent a message to ask whether Sir Edward Wilson was unwell. However, the trial began; the jury were sworn, and witnesses were called and examined, but it was all pretty much the same as when you and I were at the magistrates' court a month ago, Lucy. I need not bother you with that all over again. When Wilson got up the excitement became greater. Everybody was anxious to hear the great Attorney-General, whose reputation as a speaker and debater stood so high. I was pretty near him, and watched him closely. He spoke well, but I did not like the tone of his speech. He seemed inspired with a sort of venomous spite against the poor devil of a wretch in the dock, very different from his usual generous way of dealing with the evidence rather than with the criminal. I think it made the judge himself rather uncomfortable, for several times he was on the point of interposing a remark, but apparently altered his mind. I think, however, Wilson did himself harm with the jury, who, as all honest Englishmen do, like fair play, and don't like to see a man hit when he is down. This went on for some time, and I could see from looks that passed among us barristers that Wilson's speech was making a bad impression. Still he was speaking brilliantly and well, when an awful thing happened. He suddenly faltered and put his hand to his head. I looked up at him and saw him turn ashy pale, with his eyes fixed on a figure that had risen in the well of the court just in front of him. It was the figure of a woman in black, who looked him full in the face. She was not a yard from him. It was all a matter of less than a minute, and then, with a sort of sobbing gasp, Wilson covered his face with his hands. 'At last you are come,' he said, and then sank on his seat. There was a great commotion; ushers ran and brought him water. Every one was standing up, even the judge was leaning over his desk. Every eye was on Sir Edward, but I looked at the woman as she passed me to go out. She was close to me, and I saw her face, that beautiful sad face which you showed me at Northborough. Inquiry was made for her, but she had disappeared during the confusion, and no trace of her could be found. The ushers declared the doors were locked and no one had left the court since the trial began, to their certain knowledge. Now, what do you think of that?"

"I think," said Lucy, "the right hour, *l'ora giusta*, had struck, and she saw him again as she had promised."

"But what happened afterwards?" said Mrs. Cranston.

"Well, of course the trial was suspended, the prisoner was removed, and the court broke up in some confusion. Sir Edward, in a semiconscious state, was carried back to his hotel, where all sorts of inquiries were made after him, and then I came away to tell you all about it, just catching my train as it was on the point of starting."

"It is all so strange," said Mrs. Cranston, "that I don't know what to think. Is the trial to go on to-morrow?"

"I hardly know. The situation is so unusual. They may put it off till the next assizes. But it all depends on Sir Edward."

"Do you think that poor man is guilty?" asked Lucy.

The question seemed to disturb Warren, and he did not answer for some time. At last he said:

"Well, to tell the truth, I don't. But I have ideas about it that I hardly like to put into words. It is too serious a matter to speak of lightly, and I have little ground to go upon."

WILSON WAS LYING ON A SOFA in his room at the Bull's Head. The doctor had seen him and given him a sedative, and advised perfect rest and quiet. He was much shaken, and gladly acquiesced in the doctor's prescription, refusing to see any of the friends who came to inquire after him.

So he had seen Pepina at last. She had come as she promised, and it was at the right time that she came, for it was just in time to save him from a ghastly crime that now, in his weak and nervous state, seemed to show itself nakedly in all its enormity. He had been about to declare himself a convinced believer in the guilt of the wretch in the dock, whom he knew to be innocent, while he himself was the real culprit. His conscience awoke. He knew himself to have sunk to a level of infamy which he felt would make all men recoil from him in disgust were the truth known. It had come to that. He, the envied leader of his profession, the brilliant politician, who had the world at his feet, was in reality a sordid wretch of whose meanness and treachery Abel Sanders would have been ashamed. From the worst consequences of his guilt Pepina had come to save him. She had come not as the avenger, but as his good angel; not in anger, but in mercy. His heart went out to her in love and gratitude. In the gathering dusk he seemed to see her again before him. It was the face he had loved that was looking at him, sadly but not unkindly. The face that had been bright and happy till he came to blast her innocence and then betray her and leave her.

"Pepina," he cried, "do you forgive me, for I cannot forgive myself? You have saved me from another crime. I am not worthy of your forgiveness."

He seemed to feel her near him, to feel her breath on his face, her touch on his hands, and then he knew he was forgiven, and sank into a quiet slumber.

ALL ENGLAND WAS STARTLED next morning by a heading in large capitals on the newspaper posters—"Sudden death of the Attorney-General." The reports ran thus:

"We regret to announce the sudden death of Sir Edward Wilson, K.C., Attorney-General. The learned gentleman had apparently been ailing for some little time owing, in the opinion of his friends, to overwork. His appearance in court yesterday at Northborough caused general concern, which was changed to consternation when he suddenly broke down in his speech and had to be carried to his rooms in the Bull's Head Hotel. His condition when the doctors left him last night did not appear to be critical, but we regret to say the learned gentleman was found dead in his bed early this morning. He had apparently died in his sleep."

In another part of the paper was a long obituary notice of his career and distinctions. When the court met that morning nothing was talked of but the death of their great chief. The head of the Bar made a moving speech about the loss of their eminent and distinguished colleague, which was listened to by his audience, all standing. The judge followed with a few remarks, and was much affected, and it was some time before they proceeded to the business of the day. When the case of Rex v. Abel Sanders was called up, his lordship asked the junior counsel for the prosecution whether they were prepared to go on with the case, or whether, under these unhappy circumstances, they would prefer to let it stand over. But before they could answer, a letter was put in his hands by a messenger from the Bull's Head. It was in Sir Edward's writing, and the judge, after reading a few lines, changed countenance and retired to his private room. The counsel, both for the prosecution and defence, were shortly afterwards called to join him, and the letter was laid before them. The contents were never published, but it was understood by the few who were better informed that it contained a full and true account of the death of Philip Cranston, written by Sir Edward Wilson the evening before he died.

When they returned to court the judge asked, as he had done before, whether the remaining counsellors for the prosecution were prepared to go on with the case, and the senior of the two, Mr. Jones, rose and said that from instructions he had received he withdrew the charge on the first count, and was prepared to proceed with that on the second count only.

As the prisoner had confessed his guilt on this count, he was sentenced to a short imprisonment, and so ended the case.

Some years afterwards Lucy talked to her husband about the trial, and asked him what he thought was the real history of its sudden collapse after Sir Edward's death, which had always puzzled her.

"Do you remember, Lucy, at the magistrates' examination, a question being asked by Mr. Turner, one of the magistrates, who had been a friend of poor Philip?"

"Yes. He asked whether there had not been a quarrel between Sir Edward and Philip. But you surely don't mean—"

"Well," said Frederick, "let us leave it there. '*De mortuis nil nisi bonum*'—we have need to pray 'lead us not into temptation.'"

THE RED HOUSE

ON THE EDGE OF A GREAT COMMON, not many miles from London, there still stands an ancient red brick house with many gables, dating from the time of James I. Two wings of a later date have been added, but they do not interfere with the parent block. Standing originally as the principal house of a country village, it is now surrounded by modern villas, from which it courts seclusion within its high walls and gates, and the shady old-fashioned garden, into which, in summer at all events, the prying eyes of neighbours cannot penetrate. It seems to stand aloof from its modern surroundings, as a gentleman of the old school might shrink from the slang and vulgarity of the smart set of to-day. Within are stately rooms, loftier than usual for the date, some with old chimney-pieces and rich fretted plaster ceilings, in one of which appear the arms of the prosperous East Indian merchant who built the house when Shakespeare was still alive and Milton unborn. At the time of our story, however, it was still a country place. Here and there round the village green were a few comfortable houses where well-to-do London merchants sought repose after the turmoil of the City, and within a short mile was the stately home of the Lord of the Manor, with its wide-spread park stretching away towards London, and its great lake in the valley below the garden terraces.

In the reign of George III. this was the home of Sir Richard Hetherington, Baronet and Justice of the Peace, who was connected with the great family at the Manor House, and had considerable property also in Kent near Sevenoaks. He had ridden down in the afternoon from his town house in Queen's Square, Westminster, and was reading a note put into his hands just as he was starting:

> Mr. Dawes to Sr Richard sends compts begs Pardon for not meeting him at the Bedford according to appointment Did not Dine till Five & in such Company as pushed the Bottle about, marvellously quick that about 7-o'clock His Humble Servant was very unfit for St James's.
>
> Sunday Warwick Court.
>> To
>> Sr Richard Hetherington
>> Queen's Square.

"Dicky Dawes," said he to his wife, laughing, "is a bit too fond of the bottle, but is a good fellow at bottom. You know, my dear, he comes here to-morrow."

"I like Mr. Dawes well enough," said she, "when he is not in his cups."

"A plaguey rich fellow, Dawes, so they say," said William Hetherington, Sir Richard's nephew, who was in the room and listening to the conversation.

"Aye, he is well enough to do," said Sir Richard, who did not like the tone of the remark, "but what is that to you, William?"

"To me, uncle? Why, nothing at all. How do you suppose he will get here?"

"On horseback, I suppose, over the bridge and by the common. I have warned him not to ride late, for there are highwaymen about."

"Jerry Abershaw," said Lady Hetherington. "They say he is here again and has stopped the coach on the High Road."

"Oh! Jerry Abershaw!" said William, rather rudely. "Jerry Abershaw would have to be in a dozen places at once, if we were to believe all people say of him. Mr. Dawes will be safe enough on his ride, and there is no need to frighten him."

And so saying, William Hetherington swung out of the room.

"A young cub!" said Sir Richard, as the door closed behind him. "He grows more insufferable every day."

"I wish he would go away and do something for himself," said his wife.

"So do I, my dear, heartily. But my poor brother has left him in my charge, and as his guardian I must see him through his minority. However, in a few months he will be of age, and then our troubles will be over."

"But what will he do with himself when he is his own master? I fear he will go from bad to worse."

"I fear so too, but I see no way to do more for him than I have done," said Sir Richard. "He will have a decent patrimony if he does not fool it away when he has it, after he comes of age. I have nursed it carefully for him during his minority. But, from hints that have been given me, I fear he has got into bad company. I am glad my poor brother is not here to see it."

William Hetherington was a likely-looking lad, well-built and not ill-favoured, though there was a shifty glance of his eye, and a weak expression of the mouth, that were not encouraging. Losing his father early in life, he had been brought up by his uncle; but he learned little at school, and profited less by the severe discipline of those days. And when the time came for settling him in life, every attempt to establish him in any useful calling had been unsuccessful.

Mr. Richard Dawes, the expected visitor, was a middle-aged gentleman of moderate fortune, and a small estate in Kent near Sir Richard's property in that county. He was a jovial, easy-going man, fond of good living and good company, and very popular among his friends and acquaintances. If he sometimes overdid it, as on the occasion mentioned in his letter to Sir Richard, he generally managed to carry his liquor as well as any man living in that hard-drinking age, and seldom fuddled his wits with the fumes of his potations. He had a strong vein of native shrewdness in his composition, and a dry caustic humour that never failed him in an emergency; and nobody ever tried to score off him without coming out of the encounter badly.

But when Mr. Dawes arrived, in the evening of the day following that when the discussion we have reported between Sir Richard and his lady took place, his usual quiet humour was sadly upset. As he dismounted at the door, and gave his nag to the stableman, he was full of grunts and muttered growls, and when he shook hands with his host and hostess, his flushed face and perturbed expression made them both ask what was the matter.

"The matter!" quoth Mr. Dawes. "The matter is this, Sir Richard, that two rogues have waylaid me on your confounded common, and damme if they haven't robbed me of my purse, my watch, and whatever else they took a fancy to in my valise. What do you think of that my lady?"

They both exclaimed together that it was abominable, and that information should be sent at once to the magistrates, and men be set on the offenders' track.

"Much good will that do me," growled poor Mr. Dawes. "They may catch the thieves and hang them, but that won't give me my property back."

"And should you know the men again if you saw them?" asked my lady, while Sir Richard was gone to send messengers off at once to give the alarm.

"They were masked," replied he; "both were young men, the slighter of the two a mere lad, I fancy. I think I might know their voices if I heard them, for they were talking to one another while they rifled my unhappy valise."

"And whereabouts did it happen?

"About a mile from this house," said Mr. Dawes, "just where a cart-track turns off from the bridle-path to go to a windmill that stands in the waste. And when they had done they galloped off that way. The younger man guarded me with a pistol at my head, while the other plundered the valise that was strapped on to the saddle."

"How dreadful," said Lady Hetherington. "But it is well you came off with your life."

"I suppose, after all," said Mr. Dawes, "it is as well I was unarmed, for otherwise I could not have helped giving the rascals a shot, and then getting two back myself, for they were two to one, though one of them seemed only a lad."

"I suppose they knew you had no arms," said Lady Hetherington.

"I am not sure of that," said he, "for the younger man, as they galloped up and stopped me, cried, 'Hands up,' and with his confounded pistol at my head, I had to obey."

"They say Jerry Abershaw is at work here again," said my lady. "I doubt he was one of the two, but who could the other one be; a mere lad, you say?"

"Ay, ay, Jerry may have been the elder man very likely," said Mr. Dawes, "for they managed it cleverly enough, and he is a practiced hand. As for the youngster, the sooner he comes to the gallows the better, for he has taken to the trade betimes, and should be scotched before he does more mischief."

"Yes, I suppose so," said my lady, "and yet it is sad to think of one so young coming to such an end."

They were at supper when William, Sir Richard's nephew came in. He had been riding, and said he had been over to the town to get his whip mended, and that made him late home.

Mr. Dawes had seen him before and did not like him, for he thought him ill-mannered and empty-headed, and wondered how Sir Richard and his lady could put up with his idle ways.

They supped in the hall, and then adjourned to the great chamber above, with its fine plaster ceiling and walls hung with tapestry, for it was Sir Richard's fancy to keep the old place unaltered as it had come to him, in the mode of the preceding century, before the invasion of continental fashions from France and Holland.

The sun shone brightly the next morning, and after breakfast they sauntered about the garden. Like the house itself, the garden, which lay behind it, was kept in the style in which it had been laid out by Robert Bell, the founder in the days of James I. There were the straight paths and formal parterres where Mrs. Alice Bell used to grow her gilliflowers and roses, divided by miniature hedges of box or privet; there was the sun-dial with its motto:

AS THESE HOURS DOTH PASSE AWAY
SO DOTH THE LIFE OF MEN DECAY,

and beyond the spacious grass-plot was the raised terrace walk with seats overlooking the meadows, where were the cows.

Lady Hetherington observed with some surprise the pleasure Mr. Dawes seemed to take in her nephew William's company. Putting his arm through that of the seemingly unwilling lad, Mr. Dawes tried to get him to talk, William, awkward and embarrassed, tried to escape, and only answered in monosyllables or short sentences to Mr. Dawes's flow of conversation. He was giving William a full account of the disaster of the day before, and describing the persons of the two robbers as minutely as he could. But the story, far from interesting William, seemed to cause him much uneasiness. At last he was released, and, when he was out of earshot, Mr. Dawes, smiling to himself, muttered, "Very like. Very like. I think it will do."

From the flower garden they wandered into the kitchen gardens, where the fruit was ripening on the walls of mellow red brick. There were some tempting plums just out of reach of Lady Hetherington, and she called William to get them for her. He had both his arms stretched above his head when a loud voice behind exclaimed, "Hands up! as that young villain said yesterday." William spun round, as pale as ashes, and faced Mr. Dawes, who was looking at him with a sarcastic smile.

"Why, William," said his aunt, "what's the matter? You look as if you had seen a ghost."

"Perhaps he has, my lady," said Dawes, with a short laugh, as he turned away, and followed Sir Richard to another part of the garden. "I think he was pretty nigh making one yesterday," he continued to himself, "What is to be done now? Poor Sir Richard! He ought to know; but how am I ever to tell him?"

"What did Mr. Dawes mean, William?" asked his aunt, when Mr. Dawes was out of hearing.

"Some of his nonsense," said William. "He is always saying disagreeable things to me. I hate him."

But William was sadly discomposed, and had a scared look that Lady Hetherington could not help noticing.

They dined at the fashionable hour of five, and both Sir Richard and his lady could not help wondering at the unaccountable predilection Mr. Dawes showed for William's society and conversation. He placed himself by his side and plied him with questions, to which he only got short and sulky answers.

"We have spread the news of the robbery far and near," said Sir Richard, "but have as yet no clue to the culprits. We were right, I think, in saying they were young men, and one of them almost a lad."

"Yes, quite so," said Mr. Dawes. "The youngster was about the height and build of my friend William here, the other a little older." This directed all eyes on William, who looked sheepish and uncomfortable.

"And you said it was near by the turning up to the mill?"

"Yes, just by there; you know the place, William, I dare say," said Mr. Dawes.

"No, I don't," said William. "Why should I know it?"

"Oh!" said Mr. Dawes, "I thought I had once met you just there; but perhaps I am mistaken."

"You never were more mistaken in your life," said William sullenly, and he got up from the table and without further ceremony left the room.

"Whatever are you up to with William?" said Sir Richard, with some amusement. "He can't stand banter. But your questions were innocent enough."

"Well, I can't tell you now," said Dawes. "I hope I shall not have to tell you by-and-by."

LEAVING THE HOUSE the hopeful youth was striding across the wildest part of the common, through woods and bracken to the valley beyond. At the end of a lane that joined the high road leading to the county town five miles away, stood a humble hostelry, where, under the sign of the "Bald-faced Stag," good accommodation was promised for man and beast. It was a solitary house in a lonely part of the road, and bore a dubious reputation for the company it kept.

The bar was full of men, drinking and smoking, and exchanging banter with the bouncing red-cheeked barmaid, who received William as he entered with a smile and a nod of recognition.

Sitting rather alone in a corner, with a jorum of ale before him, was a man, well-dressed in a riding suit, with top boots and spurs, a lace cravat not over-clean, and a hat drawn rather over his brows so as partly to obscure his features. With his coarse affectation of fashion, this gentleman, like Gil Blas' acquaintance, Captain Rolando, *ne laissait pas d'avoir l'air d'un franc fripon.*

"Well, my buck," said he, as William made his way through the crowd and sat beside him, "and what brings you here to-day? Hi! Betsy, a tankard for this gentleman, and fill mine up again."

"Nay, nay," said William, "I dare not stay, I shall be missed and must get back. But, hark ye," and he whispered something in his companion's ear.

The other nodded, and going outside the house the two conferred together a few minutes in a low tone.

"I tell you he has found us out," said William.

"Us! you mean you," said the other sharply. "Why, you're not meaning to go back on me?" said William. "Remember it was I that put you up to this job; and you got most of the swag—"

"And earned it too," said the other. "What could you have done without me? You were in a funk all the while."

"Well, but Jerry, what am I to do? Dawes means to blow on me, and I'm not going to be hanged alone, you may be sure of that."

"Oh, that's the game, is it," said the other. "Why don't you knock him on the head before he peaches?"

"What, murder him?" said William uneasily.

"Your life or his," said Abershaw. "If he peaches, you'll shake hands with the hangman. I know how to take care of myself. So you can do as you please. And now I shall clear off for the scent grows too hot for me here."

He made his way to the stable, and as William started homewards he saw his confederate gallop away towards London.

Left to himself he began to feel very uncomfortable. That Mr. Dawes suspected him he felt sure. Though he had been inspired to deeds of daring by Abershaw, into whose company he had got by frequenting the Bald-faced Stag, and whose reputation as the most notorious highwayman of the day had made him a hero in his ill-regulated mind, William was at heart a coward. He feared detection and its consequences, and would prevent it at all costs. And then Jerry Abershaw's evil counsel recurred to him. To murder Mr. Dawes before he peached. That was horrible: though he hated the man, he could not go as far as that. And yet, if it would save his neck—why then! But there was hitherto only suspicion, and no proof. He need not decide yet, and would wait till Mr. Dawes made another move. At all events he would be safer away from home, and would make an excuse for going away for a while.

At supper, therefore, he announced his intention of going on a visit to some cousins he had in Essex.

"And when do you start?" asked his aunt. "And how long shall you be away?"

"I go to-morrow," said William, "and I dare say I shall be away some weeks."

"Do you ride there?" asked Sir Richard.

"Yes, uncle—I will ride Daisy, and take my valise with me on her back. There will be some hunting down there and she will carry me well."

Mr. Dawes was looking at William steadily all the while. "Do you ride alone," he asked, "or shall you have a companion with you?"

"No. I have no companion," said William sullenly.

"Why, that's a pity," said Mr. Dawes, "two is better than one on the highway nowadays."

"What do you mean by that?" asked William.

"Oh! nothing," said Mr. Dawes, while Sir Richard and my lady looked with some surprise from one speaker to the other.

"By the way, Sir Richard," said Mr. Dawes, "I have a clue to the scoundrels who robbed me, and I hope it will lead to their discovery."

"Indeed: that is good news," said his host.

"Yes. I can't tell you just yet, but the day after tomorrow I trust I shall have proof positive of one of the two at all events to lay before you."

William listened with growing terror. The net seemed closing round him. He had a day, however. Mr. Dawes was not going to tell Sir Richard till the day after his departure. Why was he waiting for that?

He had only to wait till the next morning for the explanation. He was in the stable yard seeing to the equipment of his mare, when Mr. Dawes found him, and putting his arm through William's led him, all reluctant, into the garden.

"So you are going into Essex, William," said he.

"Yes," said William, "I am. What is that to you?"

"Why, nothing at all to me," said Mr. Dawes. "But it may be convenient for you. Shall you be near Harwich?"

"Not very far from it," said William.

"Well, William, at Harwich you will find a packet two or three times a week for Antwerp or Rotterdam. Why not take a trip abroad for a few months, or perhaps longer?"

"Why should I?" said William.

"Why should you? Why, because this air does not suit your constitution. It is not wholesome for you."

William was silent for a few minutes. At last in a low voice he said, "What do you say that for?"

"Come, come, William," said Mr. Dawes, "you know that very well. I'm an old friend of your uncle and aunt, and do not wish to see them brought to shame. I shall not tell them what I know till I learn that you are safe out of the way; I'll give you a week's start, but then I must tell them what I know of their nephew. They ought to know whom they are harbouring under their roof. I have connections abroad in Holland who might befriend you and I will write to them on hearing you are landed safely. This will enable you to break with your old associates and reform your life. You will want some money; here are twenty guineas, and these with the ten or twelve I believe you already have of mine will give you a start. So now, farewell; think of what I have said, and resolve to lead a new life."

William, as he rode away, did indeed think of what he had just heard. "After all," he said to himself, "old Dawes had behaved handsomely to him." That he could not deny. But on the other hand he was sending him into exile, perhaps for life. What was twenty guineas to that? And he could not bear the thought that his uncle and aunt, for whom he felt as much affection as lay in his nature, should be made acquainted with his real character. And the old home too; was he never to see that again? In spite of the twenty guineas that jingled in his breeches pocket, he felt Mr. Dawes had done him an injury, and his old hatred revived with double force.

His good mare, Daisy, carried him briskly to London, and when there he repaired to a hostelry in the Borough with which he had been made acquainted by his evil genius, Abershaw, who, he supposed, would by this time be far away pursuing his trade in a new district. However, on entering the bar parlour the first person he saw was that worthy with a pot of ale before him. William did not want to meet him, and would have shirked away, but the other beckoned to him.

"And what evil wind blows you here," said he. "Why do you follow me?"

"I didn't know you were here," said William. "I am going away for a bit till I can go safely back."

"Has the old man peached?" asked the other.

"No, but he will in a few days' time," said William. "He told me so himself."

"And are you going to let him, you young fool?" said Abershaw. "I'm ashamed of you. Here, come, listen to me," and their further conversation was carried on in whispers. It was evening before William remounted his mare, Daisy, to continue his journey.

About a week later, when the family were at supper in the hall, Mr. Dawes being still with them, a figure approached through the darkness, and entered the house by a back way, with which it was evidently familiar. The servants were all engaged in the kitchen or in attendance in the hall, and no one saw the intruder creep silently up the fine old carved oak staircase to the top storey. On reaching the room occupied by Mr. Dawes, which looked backward into the garden, he struck a light, and opening a door entered a short dark passage. A narrow winding stair led thence to a turret on the roof of the house, but half-way up, a carefully concealed door admitted him to a small chamber artfully hidden in the hollow of the roof. It had been a hiding place in former days, such as were frequent in old houses during the times of civil commotions, and its existence had almost been forgotten.

An hour or two later Richard Dawes came to bed. He had been anxiously expecting a letter from Holland to report William's arrival, but in vain.

"I suppose the young fool has had sense enough to go. I have given him a week's law. He ought to be safe now," thought he. "So I will tell Sir Richard to-morrow what I know of his hopeful nephew. It will grieve him and my lady sadly, but it may save them future grief by and by, and may prevent that young rascal from continuing his career towards the gallows." With these reflections the worthy Richard Dawes went to bed and was soon snoring comfortably.

The door of the secret passage was silently opened, and a figure cautiously entered. Taking something from the dressing table, the intruder approached the bed. There was a slight struggle, a sickening sound, a gush of something, and then silence. The figure noiselessly crept downstairs the way it had come, and left the house. No one heard the sound of horse's hoofs as he rode away in the dead of night.

Next morning Sir Richard and Lady Hetherington were roused by shrieks, and servants bursting into their room told the dreadful news. Mr. Dawes had been found in his bed with his throat cut from ear to ear, and the room was deluged with blood. By the bedside was found one of Mr. Dawes's own razors, with which the deed had evidently been done, for it was covered with blood. The murderer had left no trace. A little later, however, it was observed that the back door was found unfastened. The door leading to the turret stair was ajar, and some one had evidently been in the secret chamber. Later still a groom reported that the gate of the stable yard stood open when he came to his work in the morning, so that the criminal had probably escaped that way.

"A rummy thing too," said the man to himself, "I see the marks of horse's hoofs in the yard, and if I didn't know Master William was away with Daisy, I could have sworn it was her footmarks, for her off hind foot is shod peculiar."

"Probably an old mark before she went away," said Sir Richard, when this was pointed out to him. But the old stableman did not seem convinced.

At the inquest a suggestion was made that it was a case of suicide. The razor, it was pointed out, was Mr. Dawes's own. But both Sir Richard and Lady Hetherington testified that Mr. Dawes had gone to bed in his usual spirits, after passing the evening agreeably in their company, and that he had no troubles of any kind to worry him. Besides which, there were obvious signs that some one had been hidden in the secret chamber and afterwards escaped by the back door. Mr. Dawes was not known to have any enemies, and yet, as nothing had been taken from his room, the motive of the crime did not seem to be robbery. The only verdict the coroner's jury could return was that of "Wilful murder by some person or persons unknown."

It was past midnight on the fatal evening of the murder when William rode into the yard of the hostelry in Southwark where we have seen him before. His mare had been ridden hard, and was covered with foam and sweat as he gave her to the stableman, but that was no unusual thing in that establishment, and it was the rule there to ask no questions about the going and coming of the customers.

Mounting hurriedly to his bedroom, William threw himself in his clothes on the bed. He thought with horror of what he had done. "It was all Abershaw's doing," he said to himself. Left alone he could never have brought himself to such a deed. He thought of Mr. Dawes's proposal that he should go abroad for a time and start a new and a better life, and he would have given worlds, now it was too late, to have listened to it. All the events of that horrible night recurred to his memory. He enacted the whole scene again. His ride to the house, his secret entry and climb to the fatal room, and then—oh, God! what had he done? He could not sleep, but got up, paced the room for hours and then sat desolately at the window till the morning light came and showed him some dark stains on his clothes, that made him shrink with horror. With soap and water he tried to wash them out, but in vain. There they were, evidences for his conviction. What was to be done? He changed his dress from his valise: the clothes with the tell-tale stains should be burned, and meanwhile he hid them carefully under the mattress.

And then, what was to be his course now? To return home, to that house on which he had brought the stain of guilt, where he had spent a childhood of innocency, where lived the uncle and aunt who had brought him up and been as parents to him, and which was the scene of that night's atrocity, was abhorrent to him. He felt he could never go back but must fly the country as he wished he had done when his victim had proposed it. Yes, he would get to Harwich again and hide himself from his family for ever in a strange land.

However, unstable and irresolute as ever, William put off his departure from day to day, and hung about London till his purse was nearly empty, and he found there was not enough left to do more than pay his passage. To land penniless in a foreign country, of which he did not even know the language, seemed impracticable. He began to think that after all he would have to face the return home which he still could not contemplate without terror. But some weeks had passed, his feelings were less alive than at first to rec-ollection of the past, and he had almost resolved to write to his uncle and announce his intended return, when, on coming down one morning, he met Abershaw.

His immediate impulse was to avoid him. Abershaw was the cause of all his crimes and all his misery. He would have no more to do with him. But Abershaw was not so easily got rid of, and, taking William by the arm, he led him to a quiet corner of the yard, where they were alone.

"Well," said he.

"Let me go," said William. "I'll have no more to do with you."

"Nay," said Abershaw with a sneer; "old friends don't part like that."

"You've brought a curse upon me," said the other. "I wish I had never seen you. I tell you again I have done with you."

"Aye, aye," said Abershaw, "but I've not done with you, my buck. Remember, I know your secret."

"Why, what do you mean? Do you mean to betray me?"

"That depends," said Abershaw, "on whether you do what I tell you or not."

"But who would believe you? You dare not appear, for you are in danger of arrest yourself, and the gallows if you are caught."

"That's well pleaded, Master William," said the other, "and true enough. But what is there to prevent my writing a letter to the magistrates without my name to it? I could tell them certain things about you that would put the halter round your neck. Eh? What do you say to that?"

William could find nothing to say to it, and stood aghast at the prospect before him. He felt himself in the power of this ruffian, and unable to escape.

"Come, come," said Abershaw, "don't be downhearted about what you did. Remember, it was your life or his. By this time he would have given information to your uncle, and you would have been in quod. Now you have made yourself safe like a brave fellow. Come, cheer up. I'll not be hard upon you."

"My uncle would never have prosecuted me," said William, "nor do I now believe Mr. Dawes would. He even offered to befriend me if I went abroad."

"Well, then," said Abershaw lightly, "I daresay they would not. But now you've cut his throat, and I know it, and if I am to hold my peace you'll have to do what I tell you."

"What do you want me to do?" said William sullenly.

"I'll tell you, then," said the other. "I've been unlucky of late, and the locker is empty and must be refilled. The high-roads are watched and there is little to be done there just now. I must crack a crib. Now they say your uncle has a fine lot of silver plate which he could very well spare to me, and you must help me to get it."

"I'll do nothing of the kind," said William indignantly.

"Oh, yes you will," said the scoundrel. "All I want you to do is to see that the back-door is open on the night I tell you, and I will see to the rest."

"I'll not do it. They have always been good to me, and I would not hurt them to save my life."

"Not even to save your life?" asked Jerry, with an ugly leer. "Just think," and with a significant motion of his hand to his neck and his cravat he suggested the fatal noose.

William turned pale. He was, as has been said, at heart a coward. His companion let the idea work, and watched the change in his countenance with attention. At last he said:

"There shall be no harm done to the old people, nor to anybody, nor do I want you to help. All I will have you do is to see that when the household is asleep the back-door shall be left open. I and my pals will do the rest. Come, that's little enough. And your uncle is rich, and can afford to let me have a share of his silver plate and be none the worse for it."

"Will you swear not to hurt anyone in the house?" asked William.

"I'll swear by all the gods," said Abershaw; "nobody shall come to harm. I only want the silver."

"And if I do this will you leave me alone in future?" asked William.

"Aye, that I will. I shall have done with you then, and you'll be no further use to me."

The wretched youth felt himself powerless, and in the end promised to do what was demanded of him. It was arranged that William should return home within three or four days, and that the robbery should be made on that day week.

As they parted a figure moved out from a corner close by, and walked slowly away. They only saw its back, the back of a well-dressed gentleman of middle age. Jerry laid his hand on his pistol, and William changed colour.

"Who's that?" whispered Abershaw. But William did not answer. The figure bore a dreadful likeness to one he dared not face.

"'Tis he!" whispered he after a minute or two, while the figure slowly retired up the yard. When it reached the house it turned and looked steadfastly at the pair, who stood spellbound. The face was that of Richard Dawes. In another moment it was gone.

For the rest of the day William had an uneasy feeling that he was watched. That someone was near him following his movements, whom he could not see. He dreaded the night, and feared to be alone. Even Abershaw's company would be better than none, but that worthy had gone off on business of his own, leaving William with final instructions, and an assurance that he would be as good as his word if William failed to obey him in the least particular. At night he was haunted by dreams of Richard Dawes, of his crime, and of the gallows. As the days passed he grew pale and thin, and trembled on the least suspicion that anyone looked at him with more than usual attention. He had written home to say he was returning from his visit to Essex, and Sir Richard and his aunt were expecting to see him ride in any day.

It was within three days of the time appointed by Abershaw for the robbery that William decided to go home. The feeling that all his movements were watched, and that some unseen presence was ever near him, had never left him, and it inspired him with a growing terror. As the fatal day drew closer this sensation grew stronger, and William constantly felt that at any moment the influence that haunted him might put on a visible form.

As he mounted his mare Daisy in the evening, when night was already closing in, the sky was lurid and threatening, and thunder was growling in the distance. There had been a sultry feeling in the air all day, and everything portended a storm of unusual violence. Before he had passed the last houses of the London suburbs a few large drops of rain began to fall, and the thunder grew louder and more frequent. He cared not; his mind was reduced to such a state of passive misery that external trouble did not affect it; there was even something in the turmoil of the elements congenial to his disordered temperament. The storm burst on him in full fury when he reached the outskirts of the wild common, across which the last few miles of his journey lay. His horse was fidgety and frightened by the lightning, which now became incessant, and it

was then that William first became aware that he was no longer
alone. By his side and within a yard of him rode another horse-
man, keeping exact pace with him as if he had been his shadow.
His face was hidden and his movements were silent. But although
they were on turf and heather and the footfall was soft, and, moreover, the storm was enough to deaden other sounds, still the noise-
less riding of his companion was unnatural. A dread fell upon him
of something unearthly. The figure kept exactly even with him,
riding faster or slower as he quickened or slackened his own pace.
Each flash of lightning showed him still by his side, silent and
mysterious, not to be shaken off. William realised in this ghostly
companion the hitherto unseen presence that had haunted him for
days. Horror seized him; he dared not take his eyes off from that
ghostly figure. A more vivid flash than usual showed him his companion with his face now turned to him, the face he dreaded of all
others, and oh, horror! across the throat a gory line. William
shrieked with terror. The horse, frightened to death by the flash
and the crash of thunder that followed instantaneously, bolted like
a mad thing across the common towards its well-known stable; the
stable-yard gates were shut, the horse, checked in its career,
slipped, fell, and threw the rider violently against the wall, where
he lay insensible, and as one dead.

The tempest gradually abated, the thunder rolled farther and
farther away, morning broke, and the men coming to work found
William still insensible lying in the road, and the mare Daisy standing trembling by him. They lifted him up and alarmed the household; he was put to bed in his own old room and messengers were
sent for the doctor.

After a time William was restored to consciousness, but his
mind wandered. He talked as if in his sleep; the watchers by his
bedside caught incoherent scraps of sentences. They heard the
name of Dawes frequently, with cries of "take him away, take him
away." His rambling about Jerry and a back-door puzzled them.
"Keep it locked," he would repeat over and over again, until at last
he sank into a troubled sleep.

He had been terribly injured in his fall, and the doctor held out no hope of saving his life. A few days at the longest must end it and his sufferings. As the end approached, his mind became more calm, and he was able to think and talk rationally. He still repeated, however, his warnings to keep the back-door locked, which they thought was a relic of his former delirium, but he never rested till he was assured that his warning had been attended to.

On the last day, when he knew he was near his end, he asked to see Sir Richard and his aunt alone. They remained with him some time, and when they came out the tears were in their eyes.

"Poor William!" said Lady Hetherington. "What a story! To think of all this going on while we knew nothing."

"He will die easier, now he has made a confession," said Sir Richard. "I see now what puzzled us in Richard Dawes's behavior to him. He recognised his voice, and led him to betray himself by his ingenious way of questioning."

"Poor Mr. Dawes!" said she. "He would have been a good friend to William, had not the other man got him into his power and persuaded him to his ruin."

"Yes—the scoundrel! I shall never rest till I hear he has come to the gallows that as sure as death awaits him."

The tragic events of the past few weeks gave Sir Richard a distaste for the old house of which he had been so fond, and before long he sold it. Since then it has passed through many hands; it has been occupied and visited by statesmen and heroes of victories by land and sea. Afterwards it was a school for eighty years before once more becoming a private residence. The tradition of a murder was kept alive; boys who slept near the fatal room felt a not disagreeable shudder when they remembered the legend, and former pupils who often come to see again the scene of their schooldays, invariably ask for the "murder chamber," and beg to be allowed to revisit it.

Jerry Abershaw, it may be mentioned in conclusion, was hanged on Kennington Common on August 3rd, 1795. He was arrested at the "Three Brewers" in Southwark—the inn he frequented, and he shot one of his captors dead, at the same time accidentally wounding the landlord in the head. He died a hardened ruffian at the age of twenty-two.

His mother, foreseeing in his youth the end to which he was bound to come, had prophesied he would, as the saying went, die in his shoes. To prove she was mistaken he kicked them off at the last moment. His body was gibbeted on the Portsmouth Road at the foot of Wimbledon Common, the scene of his most famous exploits, and Jerry Abershaw's gibbet lasted long enough to be mentioned in one of Captain Marryat's novels.

THE DEATH MASK
AND OTHER GHOSTS
Mrs. H. D. Everett

THE DEATH MASK

"Yes, that is a portrait of my wife. It is considered to be a good likeness. But of course she was older-looking towards the last."

Enderby and I were on our way to the smoking-room after dinner, and the picture hung on the staircase. We had been chums at school a quarter of a century ago, and later on at college; but I had spent the last decade out of England. I returned to find my friend a widower of four years' standing. And a good job too, I thought to myself when I heard of it, for I had no great liking for the late Gloriana. Probably the sentiment, or want of sentiment, had been mutual: she did not smile on me, but I doubt if she smiled on any of poor Tom Enderby's bachelor cronies. The picture was certainly like her. She was a fine woman, with aquiline features and a cold eye. The artist had done the features justice—and the eye, which seemed to keep a steely watch on all the comings and goings of the house out of which she had died.

We made only a brief pause before the portrait, and then went on. The smoking-room was an apartment built out at the back of the house by a former owner, and shut off by double doors to serve as a nursery. Mrs. Enderby had no family, and she disliked the smell of tobacco. So the big room was made over to Tom's pipes and cigars; and if Tom's friends wanted to smoke, they must smoke there or not at all. I remembered the room and the rule, but I was not prepared to find it still existing. I had expected to light my after dinner cigar over the dessert dishes, now there was no presiding lady to consider.

157

We were soon installed in a couple of deep-cushioned chairs before a good fire. I thought Enderby breathed more freely when he closed the double doors behind us, shutting off the dull formal house, and the staircase and the picture. But he was not looking well; there hung about him an unmistakable air of depression. Could he be fretting after Gloriana? Perhaps during their married years, he had fallen into the way of depending on a woman to care for him. It is pleasant enough when the woman is the right sort; but I shouldn't myself have fancied being cared for by the late Mrs. Enderby. And, if the fretting was a fact, it would be easy to find a remedy. Evelyn has a couple of pretty sisters, and we would have him over to stay at our place.

"You must run down and see us," I said presently, pursuing this idea. "I want to introduce you to my wife. Can you come next week?"

His face lit up with real pleasure.

"I should like it of all things," he said heartily. But a qualification came after. The cloud settled back over him and he sighed.

"That is, if I can get away."

"Why, what is to hinder you?

"It may not seem much to stay for, but I—I have got in the way of stopping here—to keep things together." He did not look at me, but leaned over to the fender to knock the ash off his cigar.

"Tell you what, Tom, you are getting hipped living by yourself. Why don't you sell the house, or let it off just as it is, and try a complete change?"

"I can't sell it. I'm only the tenant for life. It was my wife's."

"Well, I suppose there is nothing to prevent you letting it? Or if you can't let it, you might shut it up."

"There is nothing *legal* to prevent me—!" The emphasis was too fine to attract notice, but I remembered it after.

"Then, my dear fellow, why not? Knock about a bit, and see the world. But, to my thinking, the best thing you could do would be to marry again."

He shook his head drearily.

"Of course it is a delicate matter to urge upon a widower. But you have paid the utmost ceremonial respect. Four years, you know. The greatest stickler for propriety would deem it ample."

"It isn't that. Dick, I—I've a great mind to tell you rather a queer story." He puffed hard at his smoke, and stared into the red coals in the pauses. "But I don't know what you'd think of it. Or think of me."

"Try me," I said. "I'll give you my opinion after. And you know I'm safe to confide in."

"I sometimes think I should feel better if I told it. It's—it's queer enough to be laughable. But it hasn't been any laughing matter to me."

He threw the stump of his cigar into the fire, and turned to me. And then I saw how pale he was, and that a dew of perspiration was breaking out on his white face.

"I was very much of your opinion, Dick: I thought I should be happier if I married again. And I went so far as to get engaged. But the engagement was broken off, and I am going to tell you why.

"My wife was some time ailing before she died, and the doctors were in consultation. But I did not know how serious her complaint was till the last. Then they told me there was no hope, as coma had set in. But it was possible, even probable, that there would be a revival of consciousness before death, and for this I was to hold myself ready.

"I daresay you will write me down a coward, but I dreaded the revival: I was ready to pray that she might pass away in her sleep. I knew she held exalted views about the marriage tie, and I felt sure if there were any last words she would exact a pledge. I could not at such a moment refuse to promise, and I did not want to be tied. You will recollect that she was my senior. I was about to be left a widower in middle life, and in the natural course of things I had a good many years before me. You see?"

"My dear fellow, I don't think a promise so extorted ought to bind you. It isn't fair—!"

"Wait and hear me. I was sitting here, miserable enough, as you may suppose, when the doctor came to fetch me to her room.

Mrs. Enderby was conscious and had asked for me, but he particularly begged me not to agitate her in any way, lest pain should return. She was lying stretched out in the bed, looking already like a corpse.

"'Tom,' she said, 'they tell me I am dying, and there is something I want you to promise.'

"I groaned in spirit. It was all up with me, I thought. But she went on.

"'When I am dead and in my coffin, I want you to cover my face with your own hands. Promise me this.'

"It was not in the very least what I expected. Of course I promised.

"'I want you to cover my face with a particular handkerchief on which I set a value. When the time comes, open the cabinet to the right of the window, and you will find it in the third drawer from the top. You cannot mistake it, for it is the only thing in the drawer.'

"That was every word she said, if you believe me, Dick. She just sighed and shut her eyes as if she was going to sleep, and she never spoke again. Three or four days later they came again to ask me if I wished to take a last look, as the undertaker's men were about to close the coffin.

"I felt a great reluctance, but it was necessary I should go. She looked as if made of wax, and was colder than ice to touch. I opened the cabinet, and there, just as she said, was a large handkerchief of very fine cambric, lying by itself. It was embroidered with a monogram device in all four corners, and was not of a sort I had ever seen her use. I spread it out and laid it over the dead face; and then what happened was rather curious. It seemed to draw down over the features and cling to them, to nose and mouth and forehead and the shut eyes, till it became a perfect mask. My nerves were shaken, I suppose; I was seized with horror, and flung back the covering sheet, hastily quitting the room. And the coffin was closed that night.

"Well, she was buried, and I put up a monument which the neighbourhood considered handsome. As you see, I was bound by no pledge to abstain from marriage; and, though I knew what would have been her wish, I saw no reason why I should regard it. And, some months after, a family of the name of Ashcroft came to live at The Leasowes, and they had a pretty daughter.

"I took a fancy to Lucy Ashcroft the first time I saw her, and it was soon apparent that she was well inclined to me. She was a gentle, yielding little thing; not the superior style of woman. Not at all like—"

(I made no comment, but I could well understand that in his new matrimonial venture Tom would prefer a contrast.)

"—But I thought I had a very good chance of happiness with her; and I grew fond of her; very fond of her indeed. Her people were of the hospitable sort, and they encouraged me to go to The Leasowes, dropping in when I felt inclined: it did not seem as if they would be likely to put obstacles in our way. Matters progressed, and I made up my mind one evening to walk over there and declare myself. I had been up to town the day before, and came back with a ring in my pocket: rather a fanciful design of double hearts, but I thought Lucy would think it pretty, and would let me put it on her finger. I went up to change into dinner things, making myself as spruce as possible, and coming to the conclusion before the glass that I was not such a bad figure of a man after all, and that there was not much grey in my hair. Ay, Dick, you may smile: it is a good bit greyer now.

"I had taken out a clean handkerchief, and thrown the one carried through the day away crumpled on the floor. I don't know what made me turn to look at it as it lay there, but, once it caught my eye, I stood staring at it as if spell-bound. The handkerchief was moving—Dick, I swear it—rapidly altering in shape, puffing up here and there as if blown by wind, spreading and moulding itself into the features of a face. And what face should it be but that death-mask of Gloriana, which I had covered in the coffin eleven months before!

"To say I was horror-stricken conveys little of the feeling that possessed me. I snatched up the rag of cambric and flung it on the fire, and it was nothing but a rag in my hand, and in another moment no more than blackened tinder on the bar of the grate. There was no face below."

"Of course not," I said. "It was a mere hallucination. You were cheated by an excited fancy."

"You may be sure I told myself all that, and more; and I went downstairs and tried to pull myself together with a dram. But I was curiously upset, and, for that night at least, I found it impossible to play the wooer. The recollection of the death-mask was too vivid; it would have come between me and Lucy's lips.

"The effect wore off, however. In a day or two I was bold again, and as much disposed to smile at my folly as you are at this moment. I proposed, and Lucy accepted me; and I put on the ring. Ashcroft *père* was graciously pleased to approve of the settlements I offered, and Ashcroft *mère* promised to regard me as a son. And during the first forty-eight hours of our engagement, there was not a cloud to mar the blue.

"I proposed on a Monday, and on Wednesday I went again to dine and spend the evening with just their family party. Lucy and I found our way afterwards into the back drawing-room, which seemed to be made over to us by tacit understanding. Any way, we had it to ourselves; and as Lucy sat on the settee, busy with her work, I was privileged to sit beside her, close enough to watch the careful stitches she was setting, under which the pattern grew.

"She was embroidering a square of fine linen to serve as a tea-cloth, and it was intended for a present to a friend; she was anxious, she told me, to finish it in the next few days, ready for despatch. But I was somewhat impatient of her engrossment in the work; I wanted her to look at me while we talked, and to be permitted to hold her hand. I was making plans for a tour we would take together after Easter; arguing that eight weeks spent in preparation was enough for any reasonable bride. Lucy was easily entreated; she laid aside the linen square on the table at her elbow. I held her fingers captive, but her eyes wandered from my face, as she was still deliciously shy.

"All at once she exclaimed. Her work was moving, there was growing to be a face in it: did I not see?

"I saw, indeed. It was the Gloriana death-mask, forming there as it had formed in my handkerchief at home: the marked nose and chin, the severe mouth, the mould of fore-head, almost complete. I snatched it up and dropped it over the back of the couch. 'It did look like a face,' I allowed. 'But never mind it, darling; I want you to attend to me.' Something of this sort I said, I hardly know what, for my blood was running cold. Lucy pouted; she wanted to dwell on the marvel, and my impatient action had displeased her. I went on talking wildly, being afraid of pauses, but the psychological moment had gone by. I felt I did not carry her with me as before: she hesitated over my persuasions; the forecast of a Sicilian honeymoon had ceased to charm. By-and-bye she suggested that Mrs. Ashcroft would expect us to rejoin the circle in the other room. And perhaps I would pick up her work for her—still with a slight air of offence.

"I walked round the settee to recover the luckless piece of linen; but she turned also, looking over the back, so at the same instant we both saw.

"There again was the Face, rigid and severe; and now the corners of the cloth were tucked under, completing the form of the head. And that was not all. Some white drapery had been improvised and extended beyond it on the, floor, presenting the complete figure laid out straight and stiff, ready for the grave. Lucy's alarm was excusable. She shrieked aloud, shriek upon shriek, and immediately an indignant family of Ashcrofts rushed in through the half-drawn portières which divided the two rooms, demanding the cause of her distress.

"Meanwhile I had fallen upon the puffed-out form, and destroyed it. Lucy's embroidery composed the head; the figure was ingeniously contrived out of a large Turkish bath-sheet, brought in from one of the bedrooms, no one knew how or when. I held up the things protesting their innocence, while the family were stabbing me through and through with looks of indignation, and Lucy was sobbing in her mother's arms. She might have been foolish, she allowed; it did seem ridiculous now she saw what it was. But at the moment it was too dreadful: it looked so like—so like! And here a fresh sob choked her into silence.

"Peace was restored at last, but plainly the Ashcrofts doubted me. The genial father stiffened, and Mrs. Ashcroft administered indirect reproofs. She hated practical joking, so she informed me;

she might be wrong, and no doubt she was old-fashioned, but she had been brought up to consider it in the highest degree ill-bred. And perhaps I had not considered how sensitive Lucy was, and how easily alarmed. She hoped I would take warning for the future, and that nothing of this kind would occur again.

"Practical joking—oh, ye gods! As if it was likely that I, alone with the girl of my heart, would waste the precious hour in building up effigies of sham corpses on the floor! And Lucy ought to have known that the accusation was absurd, as I had never for a moment left her side. She did take my part when more composed; but the mystery remained, beyond explanation of hers or mine.

"As for the future, I could not think of that without a failing heart. If the Power arrayed against us were in truth what my superstition feared, I might as well give up hope at once, for I knew there would be no relenting. I could see the whole absurdity of the thing as well as you do now; but, if you put yourself in my place, Dick, you will be forced to confess that it was tragic too.

"I did not see Lucy the next day, as I was bound to go again to town; but we had planned to meet and ride together on the Friday morning. I was to be at The Leasowes at a certain hour, and you may be sure I was punctual. Her horse had already been brought round, and the groom was leading it up and down. I had hardly dismounted when she came down the steps of the porch; and I noticed at once a new look on her face, a harder set about that red mouth of hers which was so soft and kissable. But she let me put her up on the saddle and settle her foot in the stirrup, and she was the bearer of a gracious message from her mother. I was expected to return to lunch, and Mrs. Ashcroft begged us to be punctual, as a friend who had stayed the night with them, would be leaving immediately after.

"'You will be pleased to meet her, I think,' said Lucy, leaning forward to pat her horse. 'I find she knows you very well. It is Miss Kingsworthy.'

"Now Miss Kingsworthy was a schoolfriend of Gloriana's, who used now and then to visit us here. I was not aware that she and the Ashcrofts were acquainted; but, as I have said, they had only recently come into the neighbourhood as tenants of The Leasowes. I had no opportunity to express pleasure or the reverse, for Lucy was riding on, and putting her horse to a brisk pace. It was some time before she drew rein, and again admitted conversation. We were descending a steep hill, and the groom was following at a discreet distance behind, far enough to be out of earshot.

"Lucy looked very pretty on horseback; but this is by the way. The mannish hat suited her, and so did the habit fitting closely to her shape.

"'Tom,' she said; and again I noticed that new hardness in her face. 'Tom, Miss Kingsworthy tells me your wife did not wish you to marry again, and she made you promise her that you would not. Miss Kingsworthy was quite astonished to hear that you and I were engaged. Is this true?'

"I was able to tell her it was not: that my wife had never asked, and I had never given her, any such pledge. I allowed she disliked second marriages—in certain cases, and perhaps she had made some remark to that effect to Miss Kingsworthy; it was not unlikely. And then I appealed to her. Surely she would not let a mischief-maker's tittle-tattle come between her and me?

"I thought her profile looked less obdurate, but she would not let her eyes meet mine as she answered:

"'Of course not, if that was all. And I doubt if I would have heeded it, only that it seemed to fit in with—something else. Tom, it was very horrible, what we saw on Wednesday evening. And—and—don't be angry, but I asked Miss Kingsworthy what your wife was like. I did not tell her why I wanted to know.'

"'What has that to do with it?' I demanded—stoutly enough; but, alas! I was too well aware.

"'She told me Mrs. Enderby was handsome, but she had very marked features, and was severe-looking when she did not smile. A high forehead, a Roman nose, and a decided chin. Tom, the face in the cloth was just like that. Did you not see?'

"Of course I protested.

"'My darling, what nonsense! I saw it looked a little like a face, but I pulled it to pieces at once because you were frightened. Why,

Lucy, I shall have you turning into a spiritualist if you take up these fancies.'

"'No,' she said, 'I do not want to be anything foolish. I have thought it over, and if it happens only once I have made up my mind to believe it a mistake and to forget. But if it comes again—if it goes on coming!' Here she shuddered and turned white. 'Oh Tom, I could not—I could not!'

"That was the ultimatum. She liked me as much as ever; she even owned to a warmer feeling; but she was not going to marry a haunted man. Well, I suppose I cannot blame her. I might have given the same advice in another fellow's case, though in my own I felt it hard.

"I am close to the end now, so I shall need to tax your patience very little longer. A single chance remained. Gloriana's power, whatever its nature and however derived, might have been so spent in the previous efforts that she could effect no more. I clung to this shred of hope, and did my best to play the part of the light-hearted lover, the sort of companion Lucy expected, who would shape himself to her mood; but I was conscious that I played it ill.

"The ride was a lengthy business. Lucy's horse cast a shoe, and it was impossible to change the saddle on to the groom's hack or my own mare, as neither of them had been trained to the habit. We were bound to return at a foot-pace, and did not reach The Leasowes until two o'clock. Lunch was over: Mrs. Ashcroft had set out for the station driving Miss Kingsworthy; but some cutlets were keeping hot for us, so we were informed, and could be served immediately.

"We went at once into the dining-room, as Lucy was hungry; and she took off her hat and laid it on a side-table: she said the close fit of it made her head ache. The cutlets had been misrepresented: they were lukewarm; but Lucy made a good meal off them and the fruit-tart which followed, very much at her leisure. Heaven knows I would not have grudged her so much as a mouthful; but that luncheon was an ordeal I cannot readily forget.

"The servant absented himself, having seen us served; and then my troubles began. The tablecloth seemed alive at the corner which was between us; it rose in waves as if puffed up by wind, though the window was fast shut against any wandering airs. I tried to seem unconscious; tried to talk as if no horror of apprehension was filling all my mind, while I was flattening out the bewitched damask with a grasp I hardly dared relax. Lucy rose at last, saying she must change her dress. Occupied with the cloth, it had not occurred to me to look round, or keep watch on what might be going on in another part of the room. The hat on the side-table had been tilted over sideways, and in that position it was made to crown another presentation of the Face. What it was made of this time I cannot say; probably a serviette, as several lay about. The linen material, of whatever sort, was again moulded into the perfect form; but this time the mouth showed humour, and appeared to relax in a grim smile.

"Lucy shrieked, and dropped into my arms in a swoon: a real genuine fainting-fit, out of which she was brought round with difficulty, after summoned help of doctors.

"I hung about miserably till her safety was assured, and then went as miserably home. Next morning I received a cutting little note from my mother-in-law elect, in which she returned the ring, and informed me the engagement must be considered at an end.

"Well, Dick, you know now why I do not marry. And what have you to say?"

PARSON CLENCH

STOKE-ST. EDITH IS A SMALL and deeply rural parish, a complete back-water; at least it was so fifteen years ago, and changes move so slowly within its boundaries that I should doubt it being greatly altered, even now. It has been said about the Stoke-St. Edith people that they just begin to realise they are born when it is time for them to die, and that it takes at least as long to convince them they are dead. And by the latter proposition hangs a tale.

As sometimes happens, though the case is rare, this retired and unimportant parish has a fatly endowed living, such as was reck-oned in former times a suitable provision for younger sons. And some two-and-sixty years before the period of this story, the Albury younger son of that date not being of an age to take orders, the Reverend Augustus Clench was put in to keep the benefice warm for him.

But when the time came for Mr. Clench to surrender his cure, the younger son had developed other views, and the warmer was undisturbed. And so the long procession of years went on, and the old gentleman—whom none of us could picture as ever having been young—became more and more autocratic, more deeply conserva-tive, more blind to all advantage in change, even when change was plainly for the better. It seemed to us juniors that he must have been born in a black gown and bands, bald-headed and wearing spectacles—(no doubt the bald head was fact)—and that of all things at Stoke-St. Edith he was the least mutable. So it came as a shock to us all, then scattered far and wide, when among the newspaper announcements we read that the Reverend Augustus Clench was no more

I was not a resident in the parish when the following events took place, but I heard of them from a faithful correspondent, and later supplemented her account by personal inquiry on the spot.

The next presentation to the living was in the gift of the widowed Mrs. Albury at the Hall, who had long designed that fat provision for her nephew, the Reverend Basil Deane. He was working as curate in an East London parish, and when Mr. Clench's death took place he had his doubts whether he would be justified in exchanging strenuous duty so early in his career, for the soft cushion of rural ease. But it was now or never for his chance in life; his aunt Emmeline, good gentle soul, was a confirmed invalid, and at her death the Albury property, with the presentation right, would pass under her husband's will to a distant cousin, who would have no concern or care for any Deane.

Mr. Clench was only just buried when Mrs. Albury wrote: "I want you to come down for this next Sunday and take the services here, as the churchwardens are in a difficulty, and then we can arrange about your succession to the living. You know it is my earnest wish to have you settled at the Rectory. I cannot be thankful enough that I returned from France to be here at this time. I do not generally leave the Riviera so early in the spring, and it really was as if I had been led. But I caught a severe cold on the homeward journey, and am obliged to keep to my own two rooms, which I know you will excuse."

Mrs. Albury used to spend the greater part of the year abroad, and Basil's visits to her had hitherto been paid either at the Riviera villa or in London: he had not seen Stoke-St. Edith since his childhood. So he came with only the faintest recollection of what the place was like, and none of the old man it was proposed he should succeed.

He was unable to get away from his London duties till the Saturday, and his first appearance at the village church was shortly before the eleven o'clock service: there was, he had been told, no celebration, as that took place only once a month, and had been held the Sunday before, after the funeral sermon. Basil reflected that he would change all that, but it was too early yet to announce intentions: at the present moment he was called upon to do no more than carry on the services in the well worn rut of many previous years.

The clerk, an elderly man wedded to Stoke-St. Edith ways, awaited him in the vestry, ready with instructions, and looking somewhat askance at the coloured stole Basil took out of his vestment bag. "We aren't used to that sort of thing here," the official ventured to him; but Basil proceeded to assume it, despite the disapproval. It was likely to be a lengthy service. The Litany was expected of him, and also the ante-Communion office, but Basil reflected he might shorten his sermon, and took the opportunity to glance at the notes he had prepared. The choir were not surpliced, so he would have to go in alone; a final instruction from Aldridge dictated where he was to read the service.

"When you come to the chancel, sir, you'll see two reading-desks, one on the right hand side and one on the left. 'Twas the one on the left hand the old Rector always used, and that will be your place. We keep the other for a visiting parson when there is one, like as may be a missionary coming to preach for the Gospel in Foreign Parts collection. I think I mentioned there would be no collection to-day."

But when Basil marched into church, feebly accompanied by a voluntary on the wheezy old harmonium, he found the desk on the left of the chancel already occupied, so turned into the other. He felt some slight surprise, concluding he had mistaken Aldridge (who was frowning disapproval from one of the back pews at this insubordination on the part of his pupil). And, when the music ceased and he opened his book, he looked across at his *vis-a-vis*.

It was an elderly clergyman who was seated opposite, wearing a black skull-cap to cover his baldness, and spectacles over which a pair of very keen eyes critically regarded the younger man. He did not stand for the opening of the service, so Basil concluded he was infirm as well as aged; as old, or nearly so, as the nonogenarian priest who had officiated there for so many years. Probably he was a retired parson resident in the village, who came in to give assistance in some part of the service—a part he had not yet reached, but Aldridge ought to have told him.

He made a slight pause on arriving at the Lessons, both the first and the second, but the opposite parson did not budge; and again before the Litany, with the same absence of result. He did not rise for either of the Creeds, but was observed distinctly to frown when Basil turned to the East, which doubtless had not been Mr. Clench's practice. When it came to sermon time, however, he got up very alertly, and ascended the pulpit stairs just as Basil was approaching them. Then from that elevation he looked back at the younger priest with a distinctly malicious smile.

What was Basil to do? He could not challenge the usurper of his pulpit then and there, or drag him out in the face of the watching congregation and take his place. He went back to the reading-desk as if for a book; and then, the loudly shouted hymn having come to an end, he became aware that the man in the pulpit was not intending to preach, though he occupied the legitimate place of the preacher. There was an awkward—an extremely awkward—pause. Aldridge was fidgeting at the bottom of the church; the sparsely filled aisles displayed a vista of astonished faces. So in desperation Basil came forward to the chancel step, and from there delivered his address.

He had been in priests' orders close upon four years, and during that time had faced many congregations; the nervousness of the raw hand was no longer his, or so he flattered himself. Why should it be harder to speak to these country bumpkins than to the keener people of the towns? But on this occasion his nerve failed him, he stumbled over his words, lost the place in his notes, and recovered the thread of the argument with agonizing difficulty, while a cold perspiration broke out over him, and he turned from red to white, and then to red again. Yet, had he been cool enough to analyse his feelings, he would have discovered the disturbing element emanated from one only among his hearers, the strange old man who had mounted into the pulpit, and who now bent forward over the tasseled cushion, staring him in the face, and smiling with a sort of evil amusement and triumph.

He had intended to shorten his address, and short it was indeed, as he stumbled through it to a premature and pointless close. The blessing followed, the wheezy harmonium struck up with renewed spirit, and as he turned towards the vestry, the old man descended the pulpit stairs as if to follow him thither. But on reaching the door which Aldridge was holding open, there was no one to be seen.

Aldridge shook his head more in sorrow than in anger, as he prepared to help Basil off with his vestments.

"People here always make such a talk over any little difference. I'm afraid, sir, they won't half like you preaching to them from the floor, when they have been used to take their sermons out of the pulpit. Begging your pardon, sir, have you always been accustomed to preach so?

"I have often done so," Basil answered. "But to-day, as you would see, I had no choice. Who was the old clergyman who sat on the left side of the chancel, and then went up into the pulpit, though he did not preach? It was impossible for me to ask him to give place."

"Old clergyman, sir? I didn't see no old clergyman. Where was he, did you say?"

"In the reading-desk when I went in, and he went up before me into the pulpit. Where do you sit in the church, that you did not see—?"

"I could have seen right enough anything that was there," blurted out Aldridge, forgetful of his manners. "The pulpit was open to you the whole time, and the reading-desk as well, sure as I am here a living man. Begging your pardon, sir, for being positive." And then the clerk paled from his usually healthy colour, as a strange thought occurred to him. "Might I ask, sir, what the gentleman you saw was like?"

"An old clergyman in a surplice and a black stole. An Oxford hood he had too, for I saw the crimson silk as he went up the pulpit stairs. He had on a black skull-cap and spectacles, with sharp eyes looking over them. Bushy white eyebrows, and thin bony hands, with the veins standing out on them."

"The Lord have mercy upon us!" Aldridge was staring with his jaw dropped. "It was Parson Clench himself, and you not knowing! And him buried a fortnight come Wednesday! Lord save us: what is to be done?"

"Come, come, my good man, this is rank nonsense." But Basil was dismayed as well as angry, and a horrid creeping shiver about his scalp might verily have raised his hair had it not been so short-cut. "Mr. Clench is dead and buried. It could not have been Mr. Clench in church."

"It would be him if it was any one at all," the clerk said doggedly. "He was buried in his vestments just as you saw him. I went to the Rectory for a last look before the coffin was closed, so I know. And I daresay you've heard tell how bent he was on preaching to the last, even after he began to fail. He hated letting any one else up into his pulpit, and he wasn't one to change. I'd lay odds a feeling he had in life wouldn't be so much different now. Heaven itself would have a tough job to alter Parson Clench, where he had set his mind; begging your pardon, sir, for speaking free. But to think of him in the church, and seen by you!"

This was a last mutter, as Basil assumed his coat. He said no more to Aldridge in the way of assertion or contradiction, but he went out of the vestry utterly dazed. The church as he glanced round it was empty, except for a girl sorting music at the harmonium—no doubt the "organist" who had officiated at that wheezy instrument: she looked completely undisturbed. Had no one else shared his vision? Basil was of course aware that there were records of such happenings, and that popular interest in them (or curiosity?) had of late years greatly increased; but hitherto he had been indifferent if not sceptical; and utterly unexpectant of any such experience happening to himself. He would fain, even now, have withheld belief, but it was difficult to remain incredulous when he had seen, and had been able minutely to describe, a man who was a stranger to him, with whose appearance in life he was unacquainted, and of whom he had no thought other than indifference in coming to Stoke-St. Edith to fill his place.

He returned to the Hall and the waiting luncheon much perturbed in mind. It was not easy to face Aunt Emmeline and her affectionate interest: what did he think of the church, and was it easy to fill (a matter of voice)—also had he a full congregation, and did they appear attentive and interested? He hated himself for giving such half-hearted replies to her enquiries, and was sensitively aware of her disappointment in them; and yet how could he help it and what could he say, wishing as he did that he had never seen the Stoke-St. Edith church, and might never set foot in it again. And a renewal of his ordeal was before him as close at hand as three o'clock, the custom there dictating that the evening service should be read in the afternoon.

Mrs. Albury's catechism did not last long on this occasion, as the butler came to say luncheon awaited him in the dining-room; his aunt had her tiny invalid meal served to her upstairs. "I shall see you again this evening, my dear, and then we will have a *real talk*," she said as she dismissed him. Alas! a real talk must mean his acceptance of the Stoke-St. Edith living, or a confession of the barrier of the ghost.

As he walked across to the church, which was situated at no great distance from the Hall, he reflected that perception of this species of appearance, may happen to a man on some isolated occasion, once in a lifetime, never to be repeated again. He might take the duty at Stoke-St. Edith year in and year out, and never again encounter the wraith of the late incumbent, though the fact that he once had done so would be an unforgotten and unforgettable experience. But, despite all reasoning, the ordeal before him made heavy demands upon his courage, and it was a very dourlooking young man who walked into the vestry, and was assisted by Aldridge to robe.

"I can't make out that anybody else saw what you saw, sir, in the church this morning," that functionary whispered. "But I've been told since, there's a talk about in the village that the late rector *walks*. There are some who met him in the lane when he was on his death-bed, stricken so that he could not move; and one at least who saw him going by, out of her cottage window, the day after he was buried. People will tell such-like stories as you know, fancies running away with them; and there are few that heed."

The wheezy harmonium struck up a voluntary, and Basil went on into the church. Approaching the chancel, he saw that both reading-desks were vacant, and he fully purposed to take possession of the left hand one, which was his own. But he found himself powerless to carry intention into action. It was as if he was firmly seized by the shoulders, and pushed into the right-hand seat by a force he could not resist, or was unable to do so without a struggle, which would have been unseemly in the face of the congregation. What Aldridge was thinking in his place at the west end, Basil could only conjecture, but probably his guess only erred by falling short of the fact.

For the first part of the service the left-hand reading-desk remained empty, but on returning to his seat after the second Lesson, he found that it was filled by the same appearance as before, the old man in his vestments and skull-cap, peering at him over spectacles with unfriendly and defiant eyes. It was almost a relief when the presence externalised and became visible, instead of being merely felt in every fibre of his bodily frame.

What was to happen when sermon time arrived? The figure opposite made no movement when Basil was about to leave the desk, and yet in a moment, instantaneous as a flash of light, there it stood at the bottom of the pulpit stairs, barring his way, and facing him with a malignant smile.

Basil did not contest the passage. He delivered this second address from the chancel step, and when he turned at the conclusion, the figure had disappeared.

"Did you see him again, sir?" demanded Aldridge, who was waiting in the vestry, and Basil briefly assented: he was in no humour to discuss the marvel a second time, and Aldridge had no fresh explanation to advance.

There was nothing for it now but to be candid with Aunt Emmeline, and how she would take the communication he dreaded to think: women were always a mass of nerves, especially invalid women. But his aunt was more reasonable than he had ventured to expect, and was ready to respond to his wish that they should keep the matter to themselves.

"I do not want to be labeled as a man with a supernatural extra sense, or to give Stoke-St. Edith a bad name. I am afraid the matter may to some extent have gone abroad through Aldridge, but I'll try to see him, to-morrow, and give him an injunction not to talk."

"Yes, my dear," the aunt acquiesced. "It was wonderful, of course, that you should see, and be able to describe a perfect stranger. But it may never happen again, to you or to anybody else. And Basil, I hope, I do trust, that this will not set you against accepting the Living. We know it is likely—I suppose it is likely—that the spirits of the dead are about us always: you know it speaks in the Bible of the great cloud of witnesses. So surely we need not take it as extraordinary if we see one of them now and then. And Mr. Clench was a good man. He would do nobody any harm."

His aunt might have thought differently, Basil reflected, had she seen the malignant eyes of the apparition which barred his way.

"If it went on happening, I could not stay here. Better for someone to come who would not see."

"I don't want you to decide in a hurry; take a week or two to think it over. I will not have you give me a definite answer to-night. Things may look different on reflection. It is such a chance for you, my dear; and it would be so happy for me to know you were here looking after the people, when I am obliged to be so much away. And there is such an excellent rectory-house, quite a country gentleman's place, the best rectory in the county, so they say, and in very good repair. You need not open the whole of it, if you thought it too large for you alone. It could be made so nice. I was not going to tell you just at once, but I have five hundred pounds put aside to help you with the furnishing!"

What was he to say to all this kindness—how was he to repulse the soft entreating hands held out to him full of gifts? It would make no difference, of that he could be certain; but yes, if she wished he would take a longer time to think the matter over, and he would see the Rectory on the following morning, as he need not take train for London till the afternoon. And then he endeavoured to tell her how deeply he felt her kindness, and what a disappointment it would be to him too, so to put the great chance of his life away.

That ended the Sunday evening, and after Monday's breakfast he went across to the Rectory, in fulfilment of the promise given over night.

The red-brick Georgian mansion, with its stone pediments and cornice, and formal garden-court, was surely an attractive dwelling, cheerful to look at in the Spring sunshine, a home of which any young divine might well be proud. Probably Parson Clench had some such thoughts of it, when he came into possession at Stoke-St. Edith two-and-sixty years before. But he would not have had the same shrinking from the habitation in which his predecessor lived and died, that now disquieted Basil Deane.

Mr. Clench's housekeeper opened to him. She was staying on as caretaker, so she told him, until Mr. Clench's relatives decided what would be done about the sale. Nothing had been disturbed as yet, she was waiting instructions; and it was what the poor old gentleman had wished, that everything should be kept on just the same. He had spoken of it when he was wandering at the last, thinking he had a journey to go, but that he was coming back.

"Yes, sir, they are handsome rooms, both upstairs and down. A fine old house, just right for a family, but rather large and lonesome for one alone. The dining-room is on this side as you see, with a small breakfast-parlour behind, though it never was used for breakfasting, not in my time. May be you are the gentleman who is to succeed Mr. Clench, and who preached yesterday up at the church?

Basil told her that he took the services only as a visitor, and that nothing was decided yet about the living: the last not quite the truth, for in his own mind the decision against taking it was already made.

"Most gentlemen admire the staircase, which is oak as you see, and real old. And here is the drawing-room, but not in order, as we put up the bed you see for Mr. Clench when he got feeble at the last, and it was here that he died. It was convenient, being next to the study. A fine room the study is, and looks handsome lined with bookcases. It was a lot of books Mr. Clench had, and he was *that* particular over them. We have put a fire in here to keep away the damp, as I know he would have wished."

She was opening the door as she spoke, and holding it for Basil to enter. Yes, there was a fire on the hearth, and in a chair drawn near it was seated an old man, a man in a black cassock and skull-cap, with sharp eyes peering over spectacles: the old man of the church, though the white surplice was no longer worn. And there was the same hostility in the silent gaze which met and held his own.

Basil drew back.

"Who is the old gentleman who is using the room?" he asked in a low voice of the housekeeper.

"No one is using the room, sir. There is nobody in the house but myself."

"Why there he is, just before you, sitting by the fire."

The woman looked round in a scared way, and then shut the door again.

"Are you meaning to put a fright upon me, sir?" she said as they stood together in the hall; she seemed both indignant and alarmed.

Basil disclaimed any such intention.

"I am perfectly serious. I would be the last to wish to frighten you. I saw him so plainly sitting there, that I thought you must see him too. An old man in a skull-cap."

The housekeeper wrung her hands.

"If I was to see him I could not stay here, no, not for double the wage. People in the village make a talk about the old parson *walking*, but I never heed such tales. I saw him die, and I saw him buried. It is altogether past belief."

Basil declined to visit the upper floors: What was the use? It should never be his house; upon that he had now unalterably determined. It remained only to break the decision to *aunt* Emmeline, and then to return to the mill-horse grind of the East London toil.

Some ten days later he received the following letter:—

"My dear Nephew,—I have had you much in mind since we parted, and yesterday our solicitor, Mr. Kempson, came down to see me. I wanted to consult him what I could best do in your interests about the vacancy at Stoke-St. Edith. He thinks it will be quite possible to arrange an exchange of this benefice now vacant for the right to present to another one likely to fall vacant before long, of the same, or nearly equal value.

"Of course I did not tell him why you had refused Stoke-St. Edith; I left him to suppose you were too much engrossed in your present work to wish to give it up just at once. But, oh my dear Basil, it is indeed a cruel disappointment to me not to have you here.

Your affectionate Aunt,
Emmeline Albury.

"P.S.—The £500 for Rectory furniture will now be invested in your name, ready for you when the time comes, whether I live or die."

THE WIND OF DUNOWE

IT WAS GROWING LATE, the Autumn evening was advanced out of the long northern twilight to be on the edge of dark, when Reginald Noyes left the Dunowe smoking-room where he had been chatting to his host, and dashed upstairs, two steps at a stride, to dress for dinner. The warning bell had rung some time before, so he was not surprised to find his wife already attired in her evening gown. She was seated with her back to him, warming her toes at the wide and glowing fire of peat.

Noyes would have been just as well-pleased not to find her there—a moderate statement of his sentiments. It was a case of the grey mare being the better horse, and the young man had not always an easy time with his chosen partner. To one sensitive to such indications, the psychic atmosphere of the big state bedroom was charged with displeasure, and this was accentuated by a shrug of an averted shoulder. Surely something more was wrong than the mere fact that Noyes was behind time.

"Why, Flossie, what's the matter?"

The frivolous nickname ill-fitted Mrs. Noyes, at least in her present mood. And at all times she was rather of the severe type of beauty, even when the sun shone—the metaphorical sun.

"Matter? Matter enough! It's no use: I can't stick it out here for another ten days, to the limit of our invitation. I'm bored to death. Coming to Dunowe has been altogether a mistake. You must make some excuse for a change of plan, and take me back to town."

"Why—you wanted to cultivate the MacIvors: you even schemed to be invited. You were as pleased as I was when we were both asked—every bit. The shooting is excellent, and MacIvor such a good fellow. And I'm sure his mother received us with every kindness. Have you and she fallen out?"

"Do I ever fall out with any one? I've no patience with you when you are absurd. Of course there has been no quarrel. But I'm sick to death of this ghostly old barrack. There isn't the least chance here of bringing off any *coup*. And, as you know very well, if we don't between now and Christmas—!"

Here there was an effective pause. Noyes winced. Probably he did know what was meant. But he put up a further objection.

"You said, with a view to *coups*, that this visit was the very thing you wanted—to get into a house-party with Mrs. Noel MacIvor, and have a chance to draw the feather over her. By George, Noel was a lucky man when he married her, in spite of the snub nose and the American accent. A girl with two millions to her fortune, and likely to have as much again when Poppa dies. And when all the MacIvors are as poor as rats, and he the second son!"

"Two millions—yes. But it seems they were dollars, not pounds sterling, as we heard. And the girl is as sharp and as well able to take care of herself and her money as—as the paternal Yankee himself."

"Well—she can be fairly generous when she likes. MacIvor tells me she offered to restore Dunowe for him,—put the Castle in complete repair. That was pretty well for a sister-in-law. But of course he wouldn't consent."

"More fool he to refuse such an offer. But in other ways she is downright stingy: dresses herself like a schoolgirl of seventeen, sweet simplicity unadorned. Not a jewel, even. And she should have had plenty of toilets and jewels in those Saratoga trunks we saw carried in!"

"I daresay you would have liked to have the ransacking of them!"

"I thought of that. But the Noels are far off in the other wing, and she has a dragon of a maid who seems always to be on guard."

"Good heavens, Flossie! I hope you won't do more than think of it. That sort of thing never pays. And we should be marked for ever!"

"Nonsense. What marks one is not the doing, but being found out. I don't mean to run risks. I said, there is the maid. And I doubt if the jewels are there, though they ought to be. It isn't worthwhile. But we are bound to get hold of the money—or money's worth—by Christmas."

Probably Noyes winced for the second time at this renewed reminder, but he was at the moment out of sight. He had plunged into the dressing-room, and was throwing things about there in the course of a hurried toilet. The door between the two rooms was set wide, and now and then he came to the opening to speak.

"I thought you were depending on your bridge. You wanted to play Auction with Mrs. Noel—that was the tale in London. You never said a word about her jewels."

"Right: I meant to play here, and win from her. But the little fool hates cards. And the old lady is puritanical, and hates them too. They are practically barred, or allowed with a limit of sixpenny stakes."

"Can't you work it some other way? Flatter the heiress, and creep up her sleeve. Get her to restore us, as MacIvor won't let her do up the Castle!"—a laugh here, which was presently extinguished in the folds of a towel.

"I can get round most girls, but she doesn't take to me. She's like a—a glacis with no vantage for the foot. The only human bit about her is that she's curious. She's curious about the ghost here, and wants to find out. I told her I would try to help her—"

"*You* would help her! Why doesn't she question the family? They would know if there is anything in it. But of course there isn't."

"It is the solitary point on which we touch. A sympathetic interest in ghosts is better than no fellow-interest at all. I've given myself out as psychical—save the mark!"—and here the lady laughed. "I might personate the ghost, and get at the boxes that way. But the clue of how to make up is still to seek. We do not know what sort of figure is seen."

"Surely she could ask her husband!"

"Noel told her something, and then he shut up, and would say no more. Lady MacIvor can't bear the subject mentioned, and Sir Ian is just as bad. And she thinks Noel must have been laughing at her. He said the ghost was a gale of wind: a gale which blows inside the castle when the real weather is still. Now a gale of wind won't help me to the boxes. But it is mixed up somehow with an ancestress. I can't find out which, though I asked all the questions I could, quite innocently, about the pictures. Ghosts apart, I tell you there is no chance here, and the sooner we get out of this the better. I wrote to-day to Juliet in Hampshire: you know she wanted me for her bridge parties, though she says I must not sweep the board as I did last winter. But of course that was only her joke. Gracious, there's the second gong. I must go down at once, and leave you to follow."

Dinner was served in the hall at Dunowe Castle, a noble but somewhat bare room, stone-floored, and so lofty as to be open to the rafters. The diners were, however, well protected from any chill; a great fire blazed, and the table was set within folding screens of Spanish leather, while a thick carpet was spread under foot. Dunowe knew nothing of the modern luxury of electric light, and the moderate illumination of the table was effected by candles in tall silver holders. This was all very well within the screens, but the corners of the big room were abandoned to gloom, and only a single lamp burned overhead in the gallery. The piquante little American bride looked round her with a shiver as she descended the staircase. Here was hiding more than ample for dozens of ghosts, and that shrewd draught from the gallery which blew on her uncovered shoulders might be the precursor of the supernatural wind which was supposed to be the MacIvor family omen.

It was not a numerous party which assembled at the table. A married pair with a couple of clever daughters had quitted the Castle that morning, frigid old people, and the girls plain and elderly: impecunious also, and of no account from the point of view of Mrs. Noyes. There were Noel MacIvor and Reginald Noyes, and four other men who were "guns," seven in all with the host; but the American bride and Mrs. Noyes were the only ladies remaining, with the exception of the stately old dame who sat at the head of the table, and was Sir Ian MacIvor's mother. Sir Ian had placed the lady guest on his right hand, and his sister-in-law opposite. Mrs. Noyes was still in a clouded humour and had little to say, but she must have been well entertained by the pretty American's lively chatter. Ian MacIvor was a handsomer man than his more fortunate brother, but the family honours seemed to have brought with them a weight of care, not to say melancholy, and he looked old beyond his years.

"I went over to Eagles' Cairn to-day with the mater," said the bride, whose Christian name was Caryl. "You know they are all coming to Dunowe for the dance next week, and Mollie Campbell sent you a very particular message. She says they are going to put on fancy dress, as it makes it just twice the fun, and she hopes all the women you expect will do the same. Of course you men will wear the tartan. The mater did not seem to mind. I said I'd be delighted, and I thought Mrs. Noyes would dress up too." Then, with an appeal also to her *vis-à-vis*: "Say, that was right, was it not?"

"Quite right, if you ladies do not mind the trouble for such a small impromptu affair. It was just like Mollie Campbell to propose it. She is a child still about what you call dressing up!"

"Perhaps we all are. I can answer for one, at least. What do you say, Mrs. Noyes?"

"Certainly, if we are still here—I am not sure—"

"Oh, you must stay for it. We cannot let you off. And about costumes: the dear mater and I talked it over in the carriage coming home. She is going to wear a great-grandmother dress that she has stowed away with a lot of others in those chests on the gallery, and I am to try on a particular one that she thinks will suit me. It is like the dress Lady Sibell wears in the picture, where she has on the heirloom pearls and that queer harp-shaped brooch. Oh, Ian,"—with a sudden thought, and striking together the pink palms of her pretty hands. "It would be just splendid if you'd lend me the pearls for that one night! Say, will you? I'd take the greatest care of them.

That is, if you keep them here, and not lodged at the bank. Are they here at Dunowe?"

"Yes," he said, "I have them here." He did not refuse the request, but he met it gravely, and might have been divined unwilling by one less eager.

"Then you'll let me have them, won't you?"—the piquante little face eloquent with appeal, and the clasped hands held out.

"I'd like—oh, I would like to be Lady Sibell, just for the one night. I'd say I was Lady Sibell come alive out of the picture, if they can't guess who I am. I might even pretend to be the ghost!"

"A good idea," he admitted, but still there was that air of a reluctance he would not put into words. "But I wouldn't call myself Lady Sibell, if I were you. She mightn't like it. Couldn't you for the same period find a different name?"

"Why, is Lady Sibell the—! But I must not ask you that! It's charming of you, Ian. I must tell Noel. I feel as if I could hardly wait for Wednesday. If they are here in the house, could you show them me to-night?"

"I have them here—yes. In fact, they are in the built-in safe in my den, for they are not allowed to leave Dunowe. They don't often see the light. But you may be disappointed in them. They are not pure white, and some of them are irregular. No doubt they are Scotch river pearls, not oriental."

The description, though depreciatory, seemed to excite interest in both his hearers. Mrs. Noyes was also listening.

"Tinted pearls, are they? I wonder what colour?"

"Pinkish—to the best of my recollection."

"*Pink* pearls!" Caryl clasped her hands again. "They must be lovely. And I may wear them, may I not? Just for the one night!"

He smiled now in giving consent; she looked so pretty and childish in her eagerness.

"Yes, you shall have them for the dance. They may only be worn by a MacIvor. An odd provision, is it not; but it is in the deed, which also says they must not be taken out of the castle. But now you are married, you are a MacIvor, Caryl. So that will be all right."

It is said that lookers on see most of the game. Mrs. Noyes, looking and listening, was aware that Noel, who also listened, was rendered uneasy by his wife's request. He was on the edge of a protest, Mrs. Noyes thought, but Sir Ian made a slight repressive sign. Caryl the bride was to have her way. Other MacIvor brides had worn the pearls, but they were wedded to the head of the house, and not to a younger son. Noel was aware that Ian thought himself too poor to marry: was it in the elder brother's mind that Caryl in the future would have the right to the pearls as the reigning lady of Dunowe.

"Could you let me see them to-night?" Caryl persisted.

"And may I see them too?" put in Mrs. Noyes. "I admire pearls, and I may not be here when Mrs. MacIvor wears them at the dance. Our plans are uncertain. I daresay Reginald told you—?"

No, Noyes had said nothing: in fact he had had no opportunity since the conversation in the bedroom. Sir Ian hoped, conventionally, that nothing would hurry them away so soon. In the husband's case, it would be with him a genuine matter of regret, but he would be able to spare Mrs. Flossie with perfect equanimity. He had no great liking for the lady: the surface of her was smooth enough, but he had an instinctive feeling that something unpleasant might be encountered underneath. He would be happy, he said, to show the pearls to both ladies, if they would honour him by paying a visit to his "den."

While dinner was in progress the wind was rising, buffeting round the many angles and turrets of the house; and now and then there was a roar in the wide chimney of the hall. It was evident that Lady MacIvor was listening, and listening with apprehension, though was it not the saying that when the ghost wind blew in the castle, the outer and mundane weather was wont to be a dead calm? The old dame was never high-coloured—(old she was, to be the mother of those two stalwart sons). Hers was the ivory pallor of age, but a change of tint might have been noted on her cheek and lips, as she sat at the head of the table trying spasmodically to converse. On observing this, Sir Ian remarked, in a voice so far raised as to be sure to catch her ear:

"We are going to have a wild night of it. I could have forecasted as much when we were out to-day. The equinoctial gales have given us the go-by this year, but now it seems as if one of them was setting in in earnest."

Only an equinoctial gale, a natural feature, and Ian cheerful in the forecast. Surely that should have set her mind at rest, and she contrived to smile back at him down the length of the table. But there was still a quiver about the proud old head, and as she smoothed her lace mittens it was palpable that the thin hands they covered trembled. And when she heard of the display about to be made in the "den," it seemed as if her uneasiness increased. She said, however, no word to oppose. Lady Sibell's pearls must be shown and worn, as Ian had given his word. She was a fatalist in her way: what must be, must be: but Heaven grant showing and wearing might bring no evil on the house, which in the past had been stricken enough and to spare.

It was in truth a stormy evening, a gale sweeping over from the western ocean, and buffeting the old castle as it had been smitten many times before during its centuries of existence. But the wind was external, not within the walls, except for such natural draughts as found their way through undefended chinks and crannies. There was a huge fire in the castle drawing-room of logs and peat, but despite of it Lady MacIvor shivered, and drew a voluminous white cloud of Shetland knitting close about her shoulders as she sat alone.

The two younger women had betaken themselves to Sir Ian's den, and there he had the safe set open, and was displaying the contents of an antique casket made of some dark foreign wood, cornered and clamped with steel. Within, on a velvet bed, lay the pearls of Dunowe.

Both ladies admired the string, which was just long enough to encircle a slender throat, and had a ruby clasp. Caryl declared that the faint rosy flush upon the pearls was even more exquisite than the purity of white. She took them out of the case for closer view, and then passed the necklace over for Mrs. Noyes also to examine. But when they came into unrelated handling, a queer thing happened.

The room was lighted by four candles in tall holders, two on the table, and two set high on the mantel-shelf. These lights were not extinguished nor did they flicker, but the illuminating power of them died down till each showed only a faint point of bluish flame. The room was almost in darkness, and the three persons grouped at the table could scarcely distinguish each the face of the other in the sudden gloom.

"What is the matter with the candles?" Mrs. Noyes exclaimed: *esprit fort* as she considered herself, she was for the moment appalled.

Sir Ian took the pearls from her hand and replaced them in their case, and, as he did so, the lights gradually brightened until they burned as before. He did not answer the question or give any explanation: he appeared not to have noticed the darkness and the return of illumination.

"You shall have them on Wednesday evening," he said to Caryl as he turned the key. "I am glad they come up to your expectation."

"I think they are exquisite," she said, "but I am almost frightened of them now. Ian, I know you won't tell me, but is it that Lady Sibell does not want them worn? Was it her doing to put out the candles, and make them burn again when you took back the necklace? No, you needn't answer, for I have found out! You may keep it as secret as you like, but I am certain now she is the ghost!"

Mrs. Noyes was awake that night when her husband came up to their rooms; she had also something to say.

"You need not be in too great haste over arranging our departure. The fourteenth will do for me. I have made up my mind to stay over the dance."

"You will stay for the dance, and leave the day after: is that it? Rather a mistake if anything should happen to be missing, and there is a hue and cry. Better make it the end of the week, the day set for us, and let me have another good shoot."

"You think of nothing but your shooting, Reginald. I never knew any one so selfish."

"This time, my dear, I am thinking of something quite other than myself. I am thinking of you, and the risk you are running, or are about to run. For of course this change of plan is because you have seen the pearls."

"Don't speak so loud. Heaven knows who maybe outside the door."

"I am speaking with all discretion, and I want to know. You were there when MacIvor took them out of the safe. What are they like?"

"I had no time to look them over—of course, and there may be flaws. I had them in my own hands less than a minute. But I should say there were twenty at least the size of a large pea, and a dozen that would double that, all faintly tinted pink. The back of the string seemed made up of small ones, an odd and end lot, quite negligible. Whether those at the back were pink I could not see: there was a very bad light. But the middle ones would sell for a fortune in New York, if we can get them there. The latest craze of the Five Hundred is for pearls, and pink pearls head the market."

"You'll never get them out of this house without detection and exposure, let alone across the Atlantic. Give it up, Flossie: your scheme is a bad egg. I'm off on Monday, and I shall take you with me. That's my last word."

It might be Reginald Noyes's last word, but it was not Flossie's. Many words followed on the lady's part: indeed discussions and recriminations raged till the small hours, of which the result only need be noted. The couple would remain over the dance and until the following Saturday, and Mrs. Noyes held herself at liberty to pursue the course she had planned, and possess herself (if she could) of the pearls. And the following instructions were issued to the obedient Reginald, a little later on.

"Look here. I want you to engage Mrs. Noel for the fourth dance: it is a valse. No, I know you don't valse well, but that does not matter. The big saloon is cleared for dancing on account of the oak floor, but the flirtation nooks and refreshments will be in the hall. Get her to sit out with you, and take her to the nook right in the corner, left of fireplace, the one from which you see the stairs. It is shut in at the back with palms and evergreens, and there is a high-backed seat. Take her there while the dancing is still going on, and the hall is empty: tell her you want to confide in her: keep her engrossed."

"I can take her there—good: but as to confiding! What the devil am I to confide? She's the last sort of girl to stand lovemaking, and we haven't an idea in common. As you said once before."

"Talk to her about the ghost. Tell her you've seen it, with the tallest story you can make up—sulphur and brimstone, horns and hoofs, and all the diabolical horrors. She'll believe you, for on that subject she would swallow anything. If you do that, you'll have her fixed—for as long as will suit my purpose. You understand?"

The morning of Wednesday, Mrs. Noyes developed a headache. It was most tiresome of it to come when it did, and she accepted sympathy freely, and swallowed the offered remedies, which was heroic. To lose the dance would disappoint her, more acutely than words could say. No, not the actual dance; she must give up that in any case, for it would be impossible with such a giddy head. But if she could get better—ever such a little better—she would still hope to watch the spectacle from some quiet corner, where she would not be in the way. She was sure dear Lady MacIvor would excuse her arraying herself in the elaborate costume which had been arranged, and in which she was to be a *poudré*. But she happened to have with her a dark domino and half-mask, which would do well enough, and this she could throw on at the last moment if she felt able to come down. She would be inconspicuous so attired, and could slip away when fatigued.

So, when the evening came, she assumed a close-fitting sheath-like dress of black satin, in which her spare figure would occupy the least possible space, even when covered by the domino. She would not venture down till the dancing was well begun, but the right moment would find her ready and the headache cured.

Noyes hated the whole business, but had so far fallen under his wife's domination that he was prepared to play his part in the drama. He took the opportunity to acquaint himself with the special flirtation nook she had indicated, to which he was expected to lead his partner. It could not have been better arranged for Flossie's purpose. A large Chesterfield settee was placed across the corner, backed by an apparent grove of tall palms and evergreens, which masked the door into a side-passage. This door was not to be used

in the service of the night, as the passage did not lead to the kitch-
ens, and indeed communicated only with the gun-room and a side
staircase. Flossie would do her part, there was no doubt of that: it
only remained for him to act up to the role for which he was cast,
and whisper to a lady psychically interested some thrilling particulars about an imagined ghost.

He foresaw difficulty. The American bride was curious, but she
was also an indefatigable dancer, and determined to enjoy herself
to the full. Would she be tempted into that retirement, even by a
hinted confidence as to ghosts seen at Dunowe?

Caryl was in wild spirits when the hour arrived, enchanted with
the effect of her old-world costume, now completed with the heirloom pearls, and a quaint harp-shaped brooch which also figured
in the picture. Her hair was dressed after the fashion of Lady
Sibell's portrait, and Caryl made the painted lady a mock courtesy
as she passed her in the gallery.

"No, you mustn't say you know me," she said laughing to her
intimates. "I'm not Caryl MacIvor to-night, or Noel's wife. I'm his
lady-ancestress instead." And then, in a following whisper: "I doubt
if the dear old mater really approves of the travesty, though she
would not interfere to spoil my fun. You know she's very superstitious, and in dressing up as Lady Sibell I strongly suspect I'm also
impersonating the ghost."

The Dunowe dance being an impromptu, there were no printed
programmes; but those who had pockets—only the men had pockets—carried cards in them, and little stubs of pencils. In this way
Noyes had Caryl's name down for Number Four, but when he came
to claim it, that young person seemed to be deeply engaged with
another partner.

"Do you really want to dance with me?" she queried. "Because
I'm enjoying myself very much with Freddy." (Freddy was one of
the "guns.")

"I do really want this dance, and you know you promised. If
you wish, I'll let you off the other; but do try me first."

She yielded, and they swung off together on the well-waxed
floor.

"I know I valse badly," he said presently, "and I am unprac-
ticed in the new steps. What I really want is to get you to sit out
with me. I have something to tell you: it's—it's about a ghost. I
have just had a horrible experience, and you'll be the first to hear
of it: I have told nobody else. We shall get the hall to ourselves—
for five minutes—if you don't mind coming this way."

"About the ghost?" There was quickened interest in her repetition of his words: his fish was rising to the fly. And perhaps she
was not wholly unwilling to cut short her gyrations with an un-
skilled partner.

"You'll be comfortable sitting here, and that other fellow won't
think of looking for you behind this screen. I really want to consult you—ask your advice. For I've had the fright of my life this
afternoon."

She sank down on the soft cushions, leaning well back, which
was what Flossie wished. As he took his seat beside her, he heard a
slight rustle in the bower of foliage at the back of the couch, and it
did not help to steady his nerves.

"I suppose it would not do to say anything to Sir Ian. My first
idea, of course, was that it was a real man. A fellow with bad intentions, and no business where he was. In short, a burglar."

"A burglar—in broad daylight!"

"Ghosts are not supposed to like daylight, are they, any more
than burglars? Though I know next to nothing of the habits of
ghosts. But the daylight wasn't—wasn't broad."

Noyes felt he was floundering, and wondered what Flossie
would think of his efforts at narration, in her hiding-place at the
back.

"I mean it was getting dark—dusk, you know. If it hadn't been,
I could not have seen the flame so distinctly. Yes, there seemed to
be a flame about him, or at least a light. It came out of his eyes, I
think, but really I don't know. You see, I've had no experience."

"You thought it was a man first, and then you saw it was a ghost?
No, I wouldn't tell Ian: he does not care for these things, and I
think they make him uncomfortable. But I would like to hear more
about it. Ah-h-h, what's that?"

"Did you see anything?"

"No, but I thought something touched me—at the back of my neck—like a finger!"

Noyes noticed that her hand went up at once to feel for the safety of the pearls.

Flossie's first attempt had been a failure, and he was nearly at the end of ghost-invention. Flames out of the eyes: he had better say next that his apparition breathed them out of its mouth.

"What touched you was a camellia leaf: see, I have broken it off. What were you asking me?"

"Was it the flame made you think the appearance supernatural? Or was there anything else?"

"Well—you see a real man couldn't be on fire, and yet be still and give no sign of pain. But a ghost might look like that, if—if it came from the wrong place. But what made me sure in the end, was that it vanished. It just went right out—while I stood there."

Noyes was facing sideways as he sat, and, with attention apparently riveted on his companion, he saw with half an eye the two hands again come forward out of the bower of greenery to attack the clasp of the necklace—this time with a lighter and defter touch, which did not alarm the victim. The string of pearls dropped one dangling end, and then was cautiously withdrawn. He made a desperate effort after self-control, continuing to look his partner steadily in the face, as if absorbed in their conversation. The scheme had worked well, Flossie had secured her prize, and now the best thing he could do was to lead Caryl back without delay into the thick of the throng. It would not do for her to recognise too precisely when and where the heirloom disappeared.

"If you'll come a little further out into the room, I can show you whereabouts in the gallery the ghost stood. You never heard of anything like it haunting Dunowe? But you see, they will not speak of the Dunowe ghosts, so whether familiar or not we cannot tell. There is the music ending, and I suppose I must take you back to the dancing-room. Thank you for giving me a hearing. Think it over, and tell me what conclusion you come to. At supper, perhaps; or to-morrow."

He offered his arm, and at the same moment a slight click of the concealed door informed him Flossie had escaped from her hiding-place. Caryl rose, and presently he was pointing out to her an imaginary spot on the gallery above the hall.

"I was just turning out of the corridor on my way down, when there he was straight before me. I give you my word it was horrible. And then to go like that, snuffed out in a moment!"

He had not told his story well; he was conscious of its lack of *vraisemblance*. And it left on the listener's mind an impression of insincerity, eager as she was to believe. Yet there was about Noyes a kind of subdued agitation which was curious: he would hardly have been so moved, she thought, by what was exaggerated or untrue. Yes, they would take an opportunity to speak of it again, and he might tell her husband if he liked, but no word must be said before Ian.

As they crossed the hall, a car drove up with late arriving guests, and now the double doors of the entrance were being set wide. Servants came hurrying forward, and Lady MacIvor at the entrance of the ballroom was ready to receive her guests. Noyes and Caryl passed her going in, and but for the expectation and look beyond, probably she would at once have noticed the disappearance of the pearls. But the moment following a strange thing happened; one likely to be memorable ever after in the annals of Dunowe.

Did the gust of air rush in from those opened doors, or whence did it originate? A whirlwind blast tore through the house, extinguishing lights, swaying the pictures on the walls, tearing down wreaths of evergreens with which the saloon had been decked for the festal night. A wind which blew upstairs as well as down, shrieking through corridor and gallery, bursting open doors and whirling into closed rooms, so that no portion of the house escaped. There were cries of terror from the women-guests, but the blast ceased as suddenly as it began, and Sir Ian's voice was heard above the din, begging everybody to be calm. The room would be quickly re-lighted, and the dancing would go on.

But the lights when they were brought, revealed pale faces which looked questioningly one to another. This was a strange thing which had happened, and beyond nature. The ghostly wind of Dunowe had hitherto been a joke in the neighbourhood: after the experience of that night it would take rank as an article of faith.

The renewed illumination, however, brought with it a diversion. Caryl's loss was noted. Mollie Campbell exclaimed: "My dear, where are your pearls?" and the bride put both hands to her neck in uttermost dismay.

Had they been torn off and whirled from her by the ghost-wind—the act of an affronted ghost? But common sense suggested they had dropped to the floor, and had been swept away into some corner by a trailing skirt: this was advanced as the most likely explanation, though in these days all dancing gowns are sufficiently abbreviated. The necklace must be close at hand—Caryl was positive she had it in safety not ten minutes before—her dancing-partners could testify they had noticed it about her throat. The idea of theft occurred to nobody: theft was impossible in that secure house, and in the midst of friends.

"Oh, Ian, I am sorry: I am miserable to have lost it," she said, almost in tears. "I had no notion that the snap was weak: had I thought of it, I would have tied it on. I ought to have taken more care."

"You must not let that trouble you," he said to her kindly. "It will not be lost—it will come back to us": the last words *sotto voce* to Noel, who was as distressed as his wife. But what he meant by them he did not explain.

Noyes was among the searchers, round the floor and beyond, though well aware it could not be there. The ghostly wind, the darkness, had not helped to steady his shaken nerves, but in a way he welcomed the diversion. Every one was talking and thinking of the strange event, and if Caryl had been robbed, that darkness would be held thieves' opportunity. No suspicion could rest on Flossie, sick in her room.

But some half-hour later Sir Ian came to him.

"Noyes, I am sorry to tell you your wife is ill. We have a doctor here among our guests, and, if you are willing, I think it might be as well for him to see her. The matter? Oh, only a fainting-fit, but it seems to be obstinate. Some of the women found her lying in the corridor after the rush of wind, and I fear she may have been frightened. She was carried to bed, and the housekeeper and my mother's maid are both with her. If you will go up, I'll send Rawlins. He will know what to do."

Noyes went upstairs at once, his heart heavy with apprehension. Not so much on account of possible danger, though he was honestly fond of his wife, despite her outbreaks of temper, and the domination of the grey mare. What he dreaded was, discovery of what she had done. She must have fainted on her way back to their room, with the pearls upon her. And these women who found her in the corridor, who carried her to bed, would be certain to unfasten her dress in trying to recover her, and there would be the fatal necklace—doubtless well-known to both of them, housekeeper and maid. Neither would suppose it a guest's possession, even if unaware of Caryl's loss, and the search going on below. As he hurried upstairs, he felt like a man under sentence, who has just been informed that his hour has come.

He found Flossie laid upon the bed, moaning faintly.

"Madam is coming round nicely now, sir," said the housekeeper. "It was the faint going on so long that frightened us. I don't think she will be the worse."

The woman spoke cordially, not as if she knew them for discovered criminals; but there could be no further interchange, as the doctor was at the door.

While Dr. Rawlins examined the patient, Noyes looked round the room. Flossie's dress had been undone as a matter of course, and her few ornaments were unpinned and laid on the dressing-table, but the pearls were not among them. When he drew near the bed on the opposite side to the doctor, Mrs. Noyes turned her head on the pillow and looked at him. That she recognised her husband there could be no doubt, but there was a dreadful apprehension in her eyes. No word, however, could then be interchanged.

"Your wife has had a shock of some kind, and collapse has followed. Most likely the wind frightened her. I understand the people here consider it supernatural, and I am ready to confess it was *odd*, though I don't give in to spooks. You had better let the maid settle Mrs. Noyes comfortably for the night, and I daresay Mrs. Holbrook, the housekeeper, will sit up."

"No, no," Noyes objected. "Nobody need sit up. I can look after her: the women need not stay. You think there is no danger?"

"No danger that I foresee: she is reviving quite satisfactorily. But I will come up again before I leave. I shall find you here?"

Noyes assented, and expressed his thanks. Then, when he had shut the door upon the doctor, he went back to the bed. His wife's eyes met his, filled with the same agony of fear.

"Are—the women—gone?" she panted.

"Yes for the moment, but they are coming back. Where are the pearls?"

"I don't know—I don't know!"

"You had them. Where did you put them when you left the hall?"

"Inside the bosom of my dress—within everything—next to the skin. When I came to myself, all my clothing had been opened. They must have found—! Unless, indeed, the pearls were taken—when—!"

Speech failed, a violent shudder convulsed her, the apprehension in her face deepened into horror. The hand he had taken in his clutched him hard.

"Why—what—?"

"The wind came: it was more than wind—it was anger, fury. It seems, when I look back, there was a face with it; or I dreamed the face after. A face that was terrible. I was so near safety when it came: a few more steps: and I was full of triumph. The wind struck me down. I knew no more till I found myself in here, and the women with me. Do you think the pearls—were taken—when I fell?"

After the fateful interruption of the wind, and a general dismay over Caryl's loss, the dance was not kept up late. The first gay frolic of it was only half-heartedly renewed, and the guests did not find much appetite for the excellent supper. It was but little after one o'clock when Sir Ian closed the great doors upon the last departure, and retreated to his den. Caryl had put in his hands the quaint antique brooch worn to fasten her dress as Lady Sibell, and again she made tearful expression of her sorrow over the loss of the pearls.

"I think they will be given back," he said this and no more.

His errand to the den was to replace the brooch. He unlocked the safe with his own key, a key that had no duplicate, and never left his possession. He opened the steel-clamped casket to lay the brooch within, and there, safe and unharmed, was the gleaming roseate string, the heirloom pearls of Dunowe.

A few minutes later he knocked at his brother's door.

"Noel! it is I, Ian, I want to speak to you."

Noel opened at once: he was in pyjamas, and had been on the point of getting into bed. "What is it, old fellow?"

"Only to tell you that the pearls are found. Let Caryl know. She will sleep all the better."

"By George, I should think she will, and I, too! Where did they turn up?"

"In their place, in my locked safe. I unlocked it to put the brooch away, and they were there."

"In your locked safe! Did you leave it undone?"

"No. And I had the key."

"Then how—who—?"

"No mortal hand, I think. You know, there is a saying—! I tell you, but I shall slur it over to the others. Better so. Goodnight."

NEVILL NUGENT'S LEGACY
FROM MRS. MARGARET CAMPBELL TO A FRIEND

I

YES, YOU ARE RIGHT; the legacy was a great surprise to us—the surprise of our lives, in fact; and we were ready to bless Cousin Nevill in the beginning—at least I was. Kenneth now says he always had his doubts. But I do not think he had many when he came in to me after the post delivery—just one step from the bedroom to the sitting-room of our flat, with that look upon his face, and the open letter shaking in his hand.

It seemed to have come to us straight from heaven, Cousin Nevill's bequest. For you must know we were at that time very hard up; almost, as the saying is, "stony-broke." Kenneth giving up his profession to join the army made a great change in our circumstances. We could not keep on our pretty house, of which I used to be so proud; and, as soon as I was alone, I moved into a tiny flat in town, and got work to do. But when Ken came out of hospital last January so ill and broken, my work had to stop, for I was needed to nurse him. Ever since then the money has been flowing out, with only a little—so little—trickling in: I cried over it only the night before, of course when Ken did not see. For it seemed as if even the wretched flat was more than we could afford, and I did not know where Tom's school-fees were to come from for another term—all important as his education is, the chance of life for such a clever boy.

You will judge what a breaking of sunlight into darkness was the great surprise. Ken's voice had a choke in it as he said: "I saw

Nevill's death in the obituary, but I never dreamed it would benefit us."

"He was a rich man, was he not?" (I crowded my questions.) "Has he left us much money? *All* his money? What does the letter say?"

"All?—no, indeed! But a fair amount of property. It is a Mr. Bayliss who writes, an Edinburgh lawyer; and he would like to see me, as soon as I can make it convenient. Here, you can read for yourself."

He sank into the nearest chair, while I stood, devouring the communication; and now my hands were shaking too. Mr. Bayliss wrote that his client, Mr. Nevill Nugent, in a Will made the week before his death; devised the bulk of his property to Nugent relatives. To Kenneth, as representing his mother's side of the family, he gave the small estate of Mirk Muir, four miles distant from the manufacturing town of R—. It comprised the farms of South Muir, Bull Knowe, and Blackwater, and the residential property of Mirk Muir Grange, generally known as the Chapel House, and let off furnished, but now vacant. There was in addition a street of artisans' dwellings in R—, and most of these were in occupation. If well let, the entire property should bring in about £1200 per annum.

"Twelve hundred a year! Oh, Ken! That will be riches indeed—for us!"

"I wish indeed it was likely. It isn't as good as that. Go on, and you'll see."

The drawbacks followed, and they were considerable. The rents received the previous year barely amounted to £600. An action at law was pending, which the new owner would do well to compromise even at a loss. There was also an annuity charge for an old servant, passed on to us. And finally Ken was reminded that the death duties would be heavy. My first enthusiasm of greed was somewhat quenched.

"But, even so, there will be enough to make things better for us," I said more soberly. "Very—very much better. You can have the change you need so much—Tom's schooling can go on. And—"

"Yes, it will do all that, and more. It will be a change to go to Edinburgh. That is the first thing we must do, Maggie; you and I."

Two days later we set out on our journey. Tom was left at school, as he was in the middle of a term; and though part of my rejoicing was that his lessons need not be disturbed by our failure to pay, I was irrational enough to regret that he could not be with us. He would have enjoyed the adventure of new scenes and new hopes; and I set out with the thought of my one boy very much in mind—which may have had its share in attuning me to what followed.

We had not exhausted our wonderment during those days of hasty preparation. Ken remarked more than once:

"I'd give a good deal to know what made Nevill think of me at the last. Since he had that row with my dear old dad, we haven't been on speaking terms. And it must be a dozen years since last we met. If I am right in remembering, it was just before Tom was born."

"I never saw him," I chimed in. We were now in the great express on our way to Edinburgh—third-class travelers in spite of our accession of fortune. "Tell me what he was like."

"Oh—Nevill was a fellow with a crook in him, and looked it all over. He was always queer—about religion, as well as in other matters. Didn't hold with any of the recognised forms, and used to preach as a free lance when he could get anybody to listen. I've no doubt he meant well. I believe he built a chapel for himself."

"Is that why Mirk Muir Grange is called the Chapel House?

"I daresay it is. I'm glad he did not saddle his bequest with the provision I should do parson. There are disadvantages enough without that."

We were to hear more of the disadvantages from Mr. Bayliss in Edinburgh. He was a stiff, dry sort of man, but he became slightly more genial on finding Ken willing to take his advice about compounding the action, and selling a portion of the property to meet charges and duty, instead of putting a mortgage on the farms. He thought Ken would be wise to keep on a certain McGregor as his factor, as he had served Nevill Nugent for half a lifetime, and knew the place and the people. We might expect to get something like £300 in the course of the first year, but it was not likely to be more, unless a tenant could be found for the Chapel House: he called it that, I noticed, rather than the Grange. But we had better not be sanguine, as the house was not an easy one to let.

Ken asked why—a question on the tip of my tongue too, though it got no further.

Mr. Bayliss did not seem very ready with his answer. It was a good deal out of the way, he said at last. "Drains bad?" Ken suggested, but was answered no; all the sanitary arrangements had been put in complete order for the last tenant. Of course something might be done by advertising, as the autumn season was coming on; and Mrs. Wilding, who was left in charge, was said to be an excellent cook.

Ken turned to me.

"I don't see why we shouldn't go there ourselves, as it is standing vacant. For a few weeks at any rate, until a tenant offers. What would you say to the plan? It would give us the opportunity of looking round."

I caught at the idea.

"I shall like it of all things," I exclaimed. "And you can settle everything else from there."

It struck me Mr. Bayliss looked relieved.

"Yes, you would do well to go, Mr. Campbell," he said. "You will understand better about the property after seeing over it, and consulting with the factor. I think I told you the Chapel House cannot be alienated so long as Mrs. Wilding lives. You are bound to keep it up to afford a home for her, though she works there as a servant. The Will provides for that, as well as for the annuity charge of which I spoke."

A curious provision this, if you come to think of it; and it will be an odd position for us—for me—with a servant in the house over whom I can have no authority, as it is her home by as clear a right as it will be my own. I cannot bid her go, however much she may transgress. But I said nothing of this to Ken, for I did not want to make difficulty; and if it is true we cannot let the Grange, it will be cheaper to live in it ourselves than to pay rent elsewhere. Then the query came up, why could not the Grange be let?—this after we had left Mr. Bayliss, and were discussing the matter between ourselves.

"Do you think it can be haunted?" I suggested, but Ken laughed aloud in scorn of the idea.

"What are you fancying about it, Maggie? It isn't an ancestral castle, hundreds of years old, but just an ugly modern house, without a scrap of romance. Ghost, indeed! It's too far from a station, or up and down too many hills on a bad road. Those are the reasons that keep houses vacant, not humbug about ghosts."

II

KEN WAS RIGHT in part of his description. Mirk Muir *was* a long way out from R—, and on a hilly road; and the Grange certainly was an ugly house. Indeed it could hardly have been plainer, or presented a more dismal exterior, than it did when we turned in through the open gate, one wet cloudy evening on the edge of dusk. The walls were faced with stucco and painted drab, the windows flat, and the slate roof dark with rain. The house itself looked square and compact as it fronted us and the gate; but to the left was a long annex of one storey only, which appeared to be built of wood. "By George, that must be Nevill's chapel," Ken exclaimed. And then our "machine" drew up at the door.

It was opened to us by Mrs. Wilding, a tall gaunt woman, with quite the saddest face I ever saw. She made me think of those people who after a great grief are said never to have smiled again. But she was quite civil, even anxiously so; hoped we should not be inconvenienced because only two rooms had been made ready, but the notice was short, and she could only get in a girl to help. The dining-room was open, and presently there would be the service of a meal; the bedroom we were to occupy looked to the front immediately above. On the morrow, any changes we desired should of course be made.

It would do very well, we told her; and while Ken directed the driver about carrying up our luggage, I turned into the dining-room and sat down. There a lamp was lighted, and the table ready spread with a white cloth; there was even the cheer of a glowing fire which smelt delightfully of peat, and which the chill of the wet evening made welcome, summer as it was. I recognised comfort; but somehow, I knew not why, my spirits had sunk down to zero. There was no visible cause, but I seemed, on entering the house, to have stepped into a cloud of depression which engulfed and swallowed me up. I felt properly ashamed of myself when Ken came in, rubbing his hands.

"Really, this is very snug," he said. "And you will be pleased with the room above, for it has three windows, and a view each way. Early Victorian, of course, and a four-post bed with curtains at every corner, but nothing missed out that we can want. The luggage has been taken up, so you can go there when you like."

To have Ken pleased and cheerful—what more could I desire? I roused myself with an effort, and departed to unpack and make ready. Through the hall window I saw our driver climbing to the box of his vehicle, preparatory to driving away; and a boy was going out and closing the door behind him—a boy of about Tom's age; no doubt he had been got in to assist with the luggage.

I did not give him a second thought, but lighted the two candles which stood ready on the toilet-table, and prepared to change from my traveling-dress. Presently Mrs. Wilding brought me a jug of hot water. She seemed anxious to be attentive, and I was ready to like her, only that it gave me a chill at heart to see her face, from which all hope seemed to have gone out.

She served our meal, but not quite in the ordinary way, putting it on the table for us to help ourselves. She was alone in the house, she said, except for the girl who came in, and her husband, who was paralysed and a cripple. She thought she could manage for us with the girl's help; that is, if we were satisfied with what she could do. We might find it difficult to get a regular servant to stay. Here again there was reticence and no reason given; and something seemed to tie my tongue from asking why.

I broke Ken's rest that night by an outcry in my sleep, and when he roused me to know what was the matter, I was weeping and trembling, and at first beyond speech. I had heard Tom calling for me, that was my dream; his voice screaming "Mother—mother!" as if in awful trouble or unbearable pain. I woke with the cry still ringing in my ears, and it needed all Ken's common sense to console me. Even then I could not forget. Something terrible had happened to our child: that was my fear, but what I could not tell. I did not see him in the dream; it was a dream of sound and not of sight; the cries seemed to break out of some strange place which was his prison. Ken talked to me and comforted me till the grey morning light stole into the room, and after that he slept again, but I could not sleep. It was true what he said. Tom had always seemed perfectly happy at school, and the house-master and his wife were our friends, and would let us know at once if any ill befell the boy. And, as he reminded me, they knew of our changed address, as I had written from Edinburgh to say we were going on to Mirk Muir.

The post of that morning brought no ill news; in fact no news of any kind. After breakfast, Mrs. Wilding suggested I might like to see the house, and I went alone with her, as Ken had gone to call on McGregor the factor.

There was not a great deal to see: upstairs our bedroom was the only apartment of any size, though there were a number of smaller rooms. One of these I fixed on as a dressing-room for Ken, and another (in my own mind) as just right for Tom, if we stayed on at Mirk Muir and he came for the holidays. On the ground-floor there was a drawing-room, and a small nondescript third sitting-room. The drawing-room, a drab little place, was to the left of the entrance hall; it had only a single window, but on one side of the fireplace was another door, which Mrs. Wilding unlocked with a key taken from the pocket of her apron.

"This is the room Mr. Nugent built on to serve as a chapel," she said, drawing back to allow me to look in.

I found myself at the head of about six steps, leading down into an interior chill as a vault. It was a spacious place, bare of furniture, but with a sort of dais at the further end. It was lighted by four windows high in the wall, bordered by ugly strips of blue glass;

and a large stove for heating purposes had a black chimney-pipe carried up into the roof. There was also an outer door, which Mrs. Wilding said led into the garden.

"McGregor keeps the outer key, but of course he will give it up to Mr. Campbell; and I will now leave this one, so that you can enter when you like from the drawing-room. Yes, the chapel-room does strike cold, in spite of the wooden floor having been put in when it was used as a schoolroom. It was all stone flags to begin with, and the stones are still there underneath. Mr. Nugent did not use it many times, after going to all the expense of the build-ing. He took a dislike to Mirk Muir and went away; and the tenant next after kept a school for boys, and made it into a class-room— the house has been through many hands in the last eight years."

"And you have been here with all the changes?

"Yes, for that was Mr. Nugent's wish. I was matron when it was the school; but with the others I have cooked and kept house. Will you like to see the kitchen side?"

I was willing to see all she cared to show; but understood by a slightly hinted reserve, that the back premises were her own pecu-liar domain, on which I was not to intrude except by invitation. And I did not wonder when I discovered what was there.

The best kitchen is a spacious apartment, where, I imagine, cooking is rarely done, as there is another and more modern range in the second kitchen behind. There was a fire, however, and set beside it in an elbow chair was the helpless figure of a man.

He was paralysed below the waist, having sustained some in-jury to the spine, and the malady was creeping upwards; but he must once have been of uncommon strength, with a large and pow-erful frame. He still had the use of one hand; and he kept a stick beside him. At first he did not appear to notice my entrance, as he kept his eye on a collie-dog, a nice creature, which was sidling round to find a resting-place within the radius of warmth. I shall not soon forget the murderous look on his face, as he struck at the animal with his stick—missing it, happily, for the blow fell harm-less on the floor.

"Leave the dog alone," his wife commanded sharply. And then: "This is the new mistress, Mrs. Campbell," she said as we passed through.

The man then made some sort of civil salutation, but I could not bring myself to speak to him, except with the merest good-day. If from a man's countenance you may judge the quality of his soul, in this afflicted body must have dwelt a very demon. In the work-a-day kitchen beyond, a stout servant-lass was busy washing dishes at the sink: she had heard what passed, and the blow of the stick on the floor.

"Bassett'll be the death of that dog, missis, just as he was of the other," she remarked as she bent over her task.

"Who is Bassett?" I asked, though feeling sure what would be the answer.

"The man you have just seen—Thomas Bassett, my husband."

"But you are Mrs. Wilding?" I exclaimed, perhaps unwisely.

"I have taken back my former name, because I will not any longer be called by his. Did not Mr. Bayliss tell you?" was her counter-question, to which I answered No.

The tour of inspection ended, I wandered out into the garden, for it was now fine overhead, though everything was still drenched by yesterday's rain. Presently I discovered I had dropped my handkerchief, and as I knew I had it when Mrs. Wilding was showing me the drawing-room, I turned in there on reentering. There it lay on the drab carpet; but I was surprised to come upon the boy who—as I believed—helped over night with our luggage. Certainly he could have had no business there, in a room I was likely to occupy. Again he was in the act of slipping through a door: it was the front door the night before, and now he was disappearing into the chapel by the entrance Mrs. Wilding had left partly open. This time I followed, as I was curious to find out who he was and what was his errand; but the chapel-room was empty.

I shut the door upon the steps and turned the key, though I left it standing in the lock. Then I went back to the dining-parlor and sat down, for I felt suddenly weak.

The surprise of that complete disappearance was something of a shock to me, but not such as I would have supposed must be the effect on a living person of seeing what is called a ghost. Indeed I hardly admitted the haunting possibility to myself, even then: my mind was running on the fear of something having happened to Tom. I had heard of doppelgangers and apparitions of the living, and this boy was about Tom's size and age, though I could not say the figure was in his likeness: the face I did not see.

I said nothing to Ken when he came in, full of his business with the factor, and wanting me to walk over to South Muir with him in the afternoon, where he had an appointment to view the farm. Nothing then, or through the evening; and I rested quietly that night with no recurrence of my dream. But the next morning I saw the boy again.

I was about to cross the hall, and there he was on the staircase, mounting quickly, but full in view. I called to Mrs. Wilding, who was in the room behind me, collecting our breakfast-china on a tray.

"Who is the boy who has just gone upstairs, and what does he want?" I asked.

Mrs. Wilding put down the cloth she was folding; she did not seem surprised.

"I do not know, ma'am; but I'll see,"— and she ran up, while I waited below. I heard her pass from room to room, and then she came down to me. "There is nobody there," she said.

"Then what is it? You must tell me. I have seen this figure twice before. Is it a ghost?"

"Mr. Bayliss wrote that we were not to name it to you, but now you have seen for yourself I have no choice. People say it is a ghost, and some see it and some don't. I have never seen it for my part, though I have lived at Mirk Muir for years, and been through the house at all hours, day and night. I doubt if it is a ghost myself. There is no reason for a ghost to be here."

She looked strangely agitated, as she stood plucking at her apron with nervous hands, while two spots of feverish colour burned on her tragic face. The apparition seemed in some way to concern her nearly, though she professed to disbelieve.

"What do you think it is?"

"I have come to fancy—it is like to be—something made up out of my thoughts, which shows to others, though not to me—never to me. I'm always dwelling on my great trouble, that my son has gone away."

Here a sort of dry sob choked her voice, but presently she went on.

"He was but a slip of a lad, much like the figure they talk about, when he ran away to sea because his stepfather was cruel. I knew it was in his mind to go. 'Mother,' he says to me, 'I can't bear it any longer, and don't you fret. Whatever hard usage I get on board ship, it can't be as bad as what I've had here; and I shan't write, for I won't be sought for and brought back. But when I've got to an age and a weight so that Bassett can't touch me, then I'll come again to you, and we'll go away together.' Bassett had beaten him cruel, not once but hundreds of times. And the next day he was gone."

"And that is—how long ago?"

"Eight years and two months. It was when the chapel room was building. And within a year after that, Bassett fell off a ladder and was fixed helpless. Martin need not have feared him then, but I could not tell where my boy was, to let him know. I did put an advertisement in papers I thought he might see, but no notice came. Ma'am, they say that marriage is an honourable estate, and a married woman is respectable. I thought it would be good for me to be married; but I say now that the worst day's work that ever I did, and the wickedest, was when I married Bassett. To give him power over myself, body and soul, was bad enough, he being what he was; but the sin was to give him power over my child. I haven't said it out so plain to any one else; but I believe it is my thoughts dwelling on Martin that make the ghost, and not anything real."

KEN LOOKED WORRIED when he came in to lunch, after another confabulation with McGregor.

"I doubt more and more whether Nevill meant well to us when he left us Mirk Muir," he said when we were alone. "He has had no end of trouble with the tenants—money going out for repairs and claims, and precious little coming in. And this house won't let at any price; nobody will look at it. There is some confounded story which has got about—"

"The story of a ghost: is that what you mean? The ghost of a boy?"

"Who has been telling you about it?" he asked, frowning.

"I have seen it for myself, three times since we came. I saw it again this morning by broad daylight, and then I asked Mrs. Wilding. She says it is seen by some people, and always the same; but she thinks it is a sort of thought-shape, and not a ghost. I am not afraid of it, so you need not mind. What did McGregor tell you?"

"He appears to believe in it, unless he was pulling my leg. He says it has played all manner of what he calls 'pliskies,' and it began to be active when Grant took the house and brought his school. He was the next here after Nevill. McGregor has a notion Nevill saw it himself, and that was why he gave up living here, after going to the expense of building on that outside room. McGregor says the ghost was never heard of till after the chapel room was built; the house was quiet up till then, and of good reputation. It was as if the building disturbed something; though that, of course, is absurd. Now tell me what you saw, and what Mrs. Wilding said."

I HAD THE OPPORTUNITY of questioning McGregor myself that evening, as he came round to see Ken. He is a pawky old Scot, with a twinkle of humour in his eye, but I believe he was sincere in what he told me. Oddly enough, his errand was to ask Ken if he would be willing to sell the chapel room. He had just received an offer for it from a certain contractor, who would take it down at his own expense, to re-erect for some purpose connected with the war. The contractor would bind himself to take away the brick foundation and stone flagging, as well as the wooden part, and smooth the garden over to be as it was before. The price offered was less than a third of what it cost Nevill to erect, although all materials have gone up in value; but Ken was glad to realise even so much money, and well inclined to consent.

"I didn't tell him he might be buying the ghost along with it," said the factor with a wag of his head and a smile. "The ghost came with the chapel room, and maybe the ghost will go with it. And if it does, so much the better for the Grange."

"I wish you would tell me what you know about the ghost, Mr. McGregor. I'm very interested and not nervous, and my husband will not mind. It seems a very harmless sort of apparition, and I do not see why anybody should be afraid."

"Just so, ma'am, and I don't know that ever it did harm but once, and that most likely was accident and not intent. We first began to hear about it when Mr. Grant was here with his school of twenty boys, and we thought of it at the first as nothing but the young lads' mischief and a tale. To look at, it was much the same as one of them, and they got into scrapes being supposed to go up to the dormitories at wrong hours, and that. Then the dominie, counting heads, would find too many boys in class, and when he counted again they were right: he could not make it out. But the thing that began the trouble was a scribbling on the exercise-books and writing copies and that, scribbling done in pencil, not real writing, but W.W. or M.M., like this"—tracing with his finger on the table—"the same over and over again. I saw some of it myself. Nobody could make out who did it; and at last Mr. Grant locked the books in his own desk, but they were scribbled on even there. He got very angry, and vowed he would flog the whole school, from the senior lad down to the youngest, unless the one that played the trick would come forward and confess. And then there started up a boy who was a stranger and not one of the scholars, and went up to the master's desk with a copy-book in his hand. The dominie was about to take it from him; but no sooner were they face to face than Mr. Grant fell down in a fit, and that before ever he touched the book. And in the confusion that followed, the stranger boy disappeared, and no one could say where he came from or how he went. That was the biggest pliskie that was played. Those who came here after, have just seen him going through the rooms to vanish in some shut up place, and sometimes they have heard cries and knockings, but all the appearances have been much the same."

III

MY LAST LETTER ENDED with McGregor's narrative, did it not, dear
Susan?—and now you write to say you are interested, and ask me
what more has happened. No more apparitions have happened. I
have not seen the boy again, nor has Kenneth seen him: he says he
shall not, he is not so made; and, if a healthy scepticism is any
safeguard, I imagine he will not. But on the other hand, no eager
credulity could in my case have made visible that of which I did
not know.

I believe I told you Ken decided to sell the chapel room, and
have it taken away. It is needed for some War object, I am not sure
what; so for every reason we are glad to have it go. The contractor's
men have been busy all this week taking the timbers to pieces as if
it were a child's puzzle, and putting it, not in a box, but on a couple
of big lorries. Now they are at work upon the brick foundations
and the floor; and the door which led into it from the drawing-
room is to have glass panels, and be our way out into the garden.

Only one other event is worth naming since I wrote. That horrible old husband of poor Mrs. Wilding's has been taken ill, and I
believe the doctor thinks seriously of his state. He hates any sort
of change, Mrs. Wilding says, and he excited himself over hearing
the chapel room was to be taken away. Imagine this: the first night
after the work began, he crawled, nobody knows how, out of the
kitchen and through the hall and drawing-room, and himself un-
did that door. Then I suppose he fell down the six steps, for he was
found at the foot of them in the morning, only half alive. It is almost incredible that he could have done it without help. Since then
he has had two epileptic fits, and talks the strangest nonsense, so
his wife tells us. I wish he could be taken to a hospital—for her
sake, poor thing, as well as ours. Ken is going to speak to the doctor, and see what can be arranged.

You ask about Tom. We have had good news of him; two cheery
letters, all about cricket, and having got into the first eleven, the
height of his ambition. My dream could have meant nothing wrong
with him; and now I begin to think it must have been what
McGregor calls a "pliskie" of the ghost's.

I WAS INTERRUPTED YESTERDAY; but now in continuing I can tell you I have seen the boy again. I went out through the drawing-room to look how the work was getting on. The wooden floor has been removed, and now the men are taking up the stone slabs which were underneath, with care not to break them, as they are to be used elsewhere. There were two men at work over this, and the boy was talking to one of them. He seemed to be speaking very earnestly, and pointing to a part of the floor a yard or two away; and the man looked up in his face, and said something (I thought) in answer. I felt a cold shiver pass over me, but in spite of this I walked down the steps into the wrecked place, and, as I approached the group, the boy's figure seemed to slip behind the man with the pickaxe, and so was gone.

"What was that boy doing here, and what did he say to you?" I asked, though my breath almost failed me over the words.

I fancy the workers knew about the ghost, but both of them shook their heads. They had seen no boy, but something was a-whispering in the place—always a-whispering behind them, but they could not make out what it said.

I HAD BUT JUST WRITTEN that down, when there was a stir outside, of men calling and shouting. Mr. Campbell was wanted, and somebody else was bidden to run for the police. I did not know what was the matter, but Ken now tells me "human remains" have been found under that stone floor. It is very horrible. We have no notion how they came there, but there will, of course be an investigation. Don't you think we may have happened on a reason for the ghost?

I must post this letter now, if it is to go to night. I will write again when we know more.

(*FIVE DAYS LATER.*) Oh Susan, this has been a terrible business, and Mrs. Wilding is almost out of her mind with grief. The body was that of a boy twelve or fourteen years of age, and from the clothing and certain things found with it, there can be no doubt that it was Martin Wilding, her son. Bassett must have caught him about to run away, and either have killed him on purpose in a homicidal outbreak, or so beaten him that he died; and then buried his body under the floor of the chapel room, the flags of which were being laid down at the time. Mrs. Wilding has charged her husband, and will give evidence against him; and the wretch has been taken away. She says she hopes he will be hanged, but Ken thinks it is not likely the law will go to that extreme, as he is not in his right mind. But he will be shut up as a criminal lunatic for what is left to him of life.

I wonder whether Nevill Nugent foresaw the troubles that would come upon us when he left us the ghost as his legacy! Martin Wilding's remains have been coffined, and will be buried tomorrow. Ken got me some flowers, and I have made a cross of white lilies for Mrs. Wilding to lay on the grave. Is it not strange to think I should have seen him four times, looking as he must have done in life, when all the while his body was lying there? Poor, poor boy, to think what he must have suffered, not able to let his mother know! Now the mystery is cleared up, I don't suppose Mirk Muir Grange will be haunted any more, and Ken may succeed in letting it. As for ourselves, I do not think it likely we shall remain here. Ken says he would rather not, as the associations are too painful: odd that the objection should come from him, the one who saw nothing, and not from me!

THE CRIMSON BLIND

I

Ronald McEwan, aged sixteen, was invited to spend a vacation fortnight at his uncle's rectory. Possibly some qualms of conscience had tardily spurred the Rev. Sylvanus Applegarth to offer this hospitality, aware that he had in the past neglected his dead sister's son. Also, with a view to the future, it might be well for Ronald to make acquaintance with his own two lads, now holidaying from English public schools.

Mr. Applegarth was a gentleman and a scholar, one who loved above all things leisure and a quiet house: he retained a curate at his own expense to run matters parochial in Swanmere, and buried himself among his books. The holidays were seasons of trial to him on each of the three yearly occasions, and it would not be much worse, so he reflected, to have three hobbledehoy lads ramping about the place, and clumping up and down stairs with heavy boots, when it was inevitable he must have two.

The young Applegarths were not ill-natured, lads, but they were somewhat disposed to make a butt of the shy Scottish cousin, who was midway between them in age, and had had a different upbringing and schooling from themselves. Ronald found it advisable to listen much and say little, not airing his own opinions unless they were directly challenged. But in one direction he had been outspoken, afterwards wishing devoutly he had held his tongue. Spooks were under discussion, and it was discovered—a source of fiendish glee to the allied brothers—that Ronald believed in ghosts, as

215

he preferred more respectfully to term them, and also in such marvels as death-warnings, wraiths, and second-sight.

"That comes of being a Highlander," said Jack the elder. "Superstition is a taint that gets into the blood, and so is born with you. But I'll wager anything you have no valid reason for believing. The best evidence is only second-hand; most of it third or fourth hand, if as near. You have never seen a ghost yourself?"

"No," acknowledged Ronald somewhat sourly, for he had been more than sufficiently badgered. "But I've spoken with those that have."

"Would you like to see one? Now give a straight answer for once,"—and Jack winked at his brother.

"I wouldn't mind." Then, more stoutly, "Yes, I would like—if I'd the chance."

"I think we can give you a chance of seeing something, if not exactly a ghost. We've got no Highland castles to trot out, but there's a house here in Swanmere that is said to be haunted. Just the thing for you to investigate, now you are on the spot. Will you take it on?"

It would have been fatal to say no, and give these cousins the opening to post him as a coward. Ronald gave again the grudging admission that he "wouldn't mind." An then, being Sunday morning, the lads said they would take him round that way after church, and he should have a look at the window which had earned a bad repute. Then they might find out who had the keys in charge, if he felt inclined to pass a night within.

"I suppose, as neither of you believe, you would not be afraid to sleep there?" said Ronald, addressing the two.

"Certainly we would not be *afraid.*" Jack was speech-valiant at least. "As we believe there is nothing in it but a sham, like all the other tales."

Alfred, the younger boy, did not contradict his brother, but it might have been noticed that he kept silence.

"Then I'll do what you do." This was Ronald's ultimatum. "If you two choose to sleep in the haunted house, I'll sleep there too."

But, as the event fell out, the Applegarths did not push matters to the point of borrowing keys from the house-agent and camping out rolled in blankets on the bare floors—an attractive picture Jack went on to draw of the venture to which Ronald stood committed. After the morning service, the three lads walked some half mile beyond the village in the direction of the sea shore. Here the houses were few and far between, but two or three villas were in course of building, and other plots beyond them were placarded as for sale. Swanmere was "rising"—in other words, in process of being spoiled. Niched in between two of these plots was an empty house to let, well placed in being set some way back from the high road, within the privacy of thick shrubberies, and screened at the back by a belt of forest trees.

A desirable residence, one would have said at a first glance, but closer acquaintance was apt to induce a change of mind. The iron gates of the drive were fastened with padlock and chain, but the young Applegarths effected an entrance by vaulting over the palings at the side. Everywhere was to be seen the encroachment and overgrowth of long neglect: weeds knee high, and branches pushing themselves across the side-paths, though the carriage approach had been kept clear. The main entrance was at the side, and in front bowed windows, on two floors, were closely shuttered within, and grimed with dirt without.

The boys pushed their way round to the back, where the kitchen offices were enclosed by a yard. But midway between the better and the inferior part of the house, a large flat window on the first floor overlooked the flower-garden and shrubbery. This window was not shuttered, but was completely screened by a wide blind of faded red, drawn down to meet the sill. Jack pointed to it.

"That is where the ghost shows—not every night, but sometimes. Maybe you'll have to watch for a whole week before there is anything to see. But, if rumour says true, you will be repaid in the end. Whatever the appearance may be."

Ronald thought he saw a wink pass between the brothers. He was to be hoaxed in some way; of that he felt assured.

"I'll go, if we three go together, you and Alfred and I. If there is a real ghost to be seen, you shall see it too. What is it said to be like?"

"A light comes behind the red blind, and some people see a figure, or the shadow of a figure, in the room. Perhaps it is according to the open eye, some less and some more. You may see more still, being Highland born and bred. Very well, as you make it a condition, we will go together."

"To-night?

"Better not to-night. There's evening church and supper, and the governor might not like it, being Sunday. We will go tomorrow. That will serve as well for you."

The fake, whatever it might be, could not be prepared in time for that first evening, Ronald reflected. He was quite unbelieving about the red blind and the light, but firm in his resolve. If he was to be trotted out to see a ghost, the Applegarth cousins should go too. It was a matter of indifference to him which night as chosen for the expedition, so Monday was agreed upon, the trio to set out at midnight, when all respectable inhabitants of Swanmere should be in their beds.

When Monday night came, the sky was clear and starlit, but it was the dark of the moon. One of the lads possessed an electric torch, which Jack put in his pocket. And when it came to the point, it appeared that only Jack was going with him. Alfred, according to his brother, had developed a sore throat, and Mrs. Dawson the housekeeper, was putting him on a poultice which had to be applied in bed.

So it was the younger Applegarth who had been chosen to play the ghost, Ronald instantly concluded: he had no faith at all in the poultice, or in Mrs. Dawson's application of it, though he remembered Alfred had complained of the soreness of his throat more than once during the day.

There was little interchange of words between the two lads as they went. Ronald was inwardly resentful, and Jack seemed to have some private thoughts which amused him, for he smiled to himself in the darkness. Arrived at the Portsmouth road, they got over the fence at the same place as before; and now Jack's torch was of use, as they pushed their way through the tangled garden to the spot determined on as likely to afford the best view of the window with the crimson blind. Neither blind nor window could now be distinguished; the house reared itself before them a silhouette of blacker darkness, against that other darkness of the night.

"We can sit on this bench while we wait," and young Applegarth flashed his torch on a rustic structure, set beneath overshadowing trees. "I propose to time ourselves and give an hour to the watch. Then, if you have seen nothing, we can come away and return another night. For myself, sceptic as I am, I don't expect to see."

He could hardly be more sceptical than Ronald felt at the moment. Certain that a trick was about to be played on him, all his senses had been on the alert from the moment they left the road, and he felt sure that as they plunged through the wilderness of shrubbery, he had heard another footstep following. He did not refuse to seat himself on the bench, but he took care to have the bole of the tree immediately at his back, as some protection from assault in the rear.

Some five or six minutes went by, and he was paying little attention to the house, but much to certain rustling noises in the shrubbery behind them, when Jack Applegarth exclaimed in an altered voice: "By Jove, there is a light there after all!" and he became aware that the broad parallelogram of the window was now faintly illuminated behind the crimson blind, sufficiently to show its shape and size, and also the colour of the screen. Could young Alfred have found some means of entrance, and set up a lighted candle in the room?—but somehow he doubted whether, without his brother to back him, the boy would have ventured into the ghostly house alone. The fake he anticipated was of a different sort to this.

As the boys watched, the light grew stronger, glowing through the blind; the lamp within that room must have been a strong one of many candle-power. Then a shadow became visible, as if cast by some person moving to and fro in front of the light; this was faint at first, but gradually it increased in intensity, and presently came close to the window, pulling the blind aside to look out.

This was so ordinary an action that it did not suggest the supernatural. A moment later, however, the whole framework of the window seemed to give way and fall outwards with a crash of breaking glass. The figure now showed clearly defined, standing outside on the sill with the red illumination behind; but its pause there was one only of seconds before it leaped to the ground and came rushing towards them; a figure so far in ghostly likeness that it appeared to be clad in white. Following the crash of glass came other sounds, a pistol-shot and a scream, but the rush of the flying figure was unaccompanied by noise. It passed close to the bench where they were seated, and young Applegarth grasped Ronald's arm in a terror well acted if unreal.

"Come away," he said thickly. "I've had enough of this. Come away."

The light behind the blind was dying out, and presently the window was again in darkness, but these spectators did not stay to see. Jack Applegarth dragged Ronald back towards the road, and the younger lad broke from the bushes and followed them, sobbing in what seemed to be real affright, and with a white bundle hugged in his arms. They climbed the palings and went pelting home, and not till the distance was half accomplished did any one of them speak. Then Ronald had the first word.

"Why Alfred, I thought you were in bed. I hope your throat will not suffer through coming out to trick me with a sham ghost. I made sure all along that was what you and Jack would do."

Alfred hugged tighter the bundle he was carrying: did he fear it would be snatched off him and displayed?—it looked exceedingly like a white sheet.

"I had nothing to do with *that thing*," he blurted out between chattering teeth. "I don't know what it was, or where it came from. But I swear I'll never go near the blamed place again, either by night or by day!"

II

WHETHER THERE WAS ANY NATURAL EXPLANATION of what they had seen, Ronald never knew. His visit to his Applegarth relatives was drawing to a close, and, shortly after, the old Rector died suddenly during the service in church. The home was broken up, the two schoolboy cousins had their way to make in the world, and, whether ill or well made, this history knows them no more. And between the just concluded chapter, and this which is now begun, must be set an interval of twenty years.

Ronald had done well for himself in the meantime. He had become an alert hardheaded business man, a good deal detached from the softer side of life, for which, he told himself, there would be time and to spare by-and-bye. But now, at thirty-six, there began to be a different telling. He could afford to keep a wife in comfort, and it seemed to him that the time for choice had come.

This does not pretend to be a love-story, so it will only briefly chronicle that it was the business of wife-selection which took Ronald again to Swanmere. He happened to act as best man at his friend Parkinson's wedding, and one of the bridesmaids seemed to him an unusually attractive girl, happy herself, and likely to make others happy, which is better than mere beauty. Probably he let fall a wish that he might see Lilian again; any way, some time later, he was invited to run down and pay a week-end visit to the newly-married pair, when Lilian was at the same time expected to stay. And, as it happened, the Peregrine Parkinsons had settled at Swanmere.

"Do you know this place at all?" queried Mrs. Parkinson, who was meeting him at the station with the small pony-carriage, of which, and of her skill as a whip, she was inordinately proud.

"I was here once before, many years ago," was Ronald's answer. "I was only a schoolboy in those days, visiting an old uncle, who then was rector of the parish. Swanmere seems to have grown a good deal bigger than I remember it, or else my recollection is at fault."

"Oh yes, it has grown; places do grow, don't they? There was a great deal of new building before the war; villas you know, and that style; but 1914 stopped everything. Peregrine and I were fortunate in meeting with an older house, in a quite delightful well-grown garden. Oh no, not old enough to be inconvenient, and it has been brought up-to-date for us. We were lucky to get it, I can assure you: it is so difficult in these days to find anything moderate-sized. They are snapped up directly they are vacant, the demand is so much in excess of the supply."

Ronald did not recognise the direction taken, even when the pony willingly turned in at an open pair of iron gates, which he had last seen chained and padlocked—or if not these gates, their predecessors, as gates have a way of perishing in untended years. All was trim within, pruned and swept and graveled, and the garden a riot of colour with its summer flowers. But the front of the house, with double bows carried up to the first floor, did strike a chord of association.

"I wonder!" he said to himself, and then the wonder was negatived. "No, it isn't possible; it would be too odd a coincidence." And upon this he dismissed the thought from mind.

It did not return during the evening, not even when he went up—in a hurry, and at the last moment—to dress for dinner in the bedroom allotted to him; a spacious and well-appointed one, where his portmanteau had been unpacked and habiliments laid out. After dinner there was the diversion of some good music; Mrs. Parkinson played and Lilian sang. The Swanmere experience of twenty years ago was quite out of mind when he retired for the night; pleasanter thoughts had pushed it into the background and held the stage. But the recollection was vaguely renewed last thing, when he drew aside the curtains and opened the window, noting its unusual square shape, divided into three uprights, two of which opened casement fashion.

It was the only window in the room, but so wide that it nearly filled the outer wall. Certainly its shape recalled the window of twenty years ago which was screened by a crimson blind, and his watch in the garden with Jack Applegarth. He was never likely to forget that night, though he was far from sure whether the ghost was ghost indeed, or a sham faked by the Applegarth boys for his discomfiture. Probably these suburban villas were built all upon one plan, and an older foundation had set the note of fashion for those that followed. He never knew the name or number of the haunted house, or locality, except that it was entered from the

Portsmouth road; so in that way he could not identify it. And again he dismissed the idea, and addressed himself to sleep.

Neither this recollection nor the dawning love-interest was potent to keep him awake. He slept well the early part of the night, and did not wake till morning was brightening in the east. Then, as he opened his eyes and turned to face the light, he saw, and was astonished seeing, that the window was covered with a crimson blind, drawn down from top to sill.

He could have declared that nothing of the sort was in place there over night. The drawn-back curtains had revealed a quite ordinary green venetian, which he had raised till it clicked into stoppage at its height. To all outward seeming this was a material blind, swaying in the air of the open casement, and with no light behind it but that of the summer dawn. And yet, for all that, he lay staring at it with nerves on edge, and hammering pulses which beat thickly in his ears and throat: something within him recognised the nature of the appearance and responded with agitation, despite the scepticism of the outward man. That was a bird's song vocal outside, wheels went by in the road, the ordinary world was astir. He would rise and assure himself that the blind was a mundane affair, palpable to touch—it had of course slipped down in the night owing to a loosened cord, and was hung within the other.

And then he discovered that his limbs were powerless: it was as if invisible bands restrained him. He writhed against them in vain, and in the end, despite those rapid pulses of the affrighted heart, he fell suddenly into trance or sleep.

He had had a seizure of nightmare, he concluded when he awoke later, with the servant knocking at the door to bring in tea and shaving-water, and the open window cheerful and unscreened, letting in the summer air.

His first act was to examine the window-frame, but—of course, as he told himself—there was no crimson blind, nothing but the green venetian, and the curtains drawing on their rod. He had dreamt the whole thing, on the suggestion of that memory of a school-boy visit long ago.

He was well assured of the folly of it all, and yet he had again and again to reason the thing out, and repeat that it was folly—himself in colloquy with himself. This was still more necessary when in the course of the morning he strolled out into the garden and round the shrubbery paths. Though the wild growth of long ago had been pruned back and certain changes made, he had no difficulty in finding the spot—what he thought the spot—where he and Jack Applegarth had watched. There was still a rustic seat under the trees, full in view of the square window of his room where the red blind no longer was displayed. He sat down to light a cigarette, and presently his host appeared, pipe in mouth, and joined him on the bench in the shade.

"You have a nice place here," Ronald said, by way of opening conversation.

"Yes," Parkinson agreed. "I like it, and Cecilia likes it, and in every way it suits us well. Convenient for business you know, and not too pretentious for young beginners. We both fell in love with it at first sight. But I heard something the other day" (poking with his knife at a pipe which declined to draw) "something that rather disturbed me. Not that I believe it, you know; I'm not that sort. I only hope and trust that no busybody will consider it his, or her, duty to inform Cecilia."

"What did you hear?"

"Why, some fools were saying the house used to be haunted, and that was the reason why it stood long unlet, and fell into bad repair. Stories of that sort are always put about when a place happens to be nobody's fancy, whether the real drawback is rats or drains, or somebody wanting to keep it vacant for interests of their own. As you know. In this case I should say it was the latter. Because the man told me lights were seen when the place was shut up and empty. A thieves' dumping ground, no doubt. Or possibly coiners."

This in pauses, between whiffs of the pipe. Parkinson ended:

"I don't want Cecilia to know. She is fond of the place, and I wouldn't like her to be nervous or upset."

"Couldn't you warn the man?"

"I did that. But there are other men who know. And, what is worse, women. You know what women's tongues are. Especially when they think they have got hold of something spicy. Or what will annoy somebody else!"

"Why not tell your wife yourself, and trust to her good sense not to mind. Better for her to learn it so, than by chance whispers from a stranger. She won't like it if she thinks you were aware, and kept it up your sleeve."

But Parkinson shook his head. Fond as he was of his Cecilia, perhaps his opinion of her good sense had not been heightened by the experience of four or five months of marriage. And Ronald checked his own impulse to communicate the history of that former episode, together with the odd dream—if it was a dream—which visited him the night before. But he had found out one thing: now it was beyond doubt. This smartly done-up villa with its modern improvements, was identical with the closed and neglected house of long ago.

That day was Saturday. He had been invited to stay over the week-end, so there were two more nights that he was bound to spend at the villa. He did not enjoy the anticipation of those nights, though some slight uneasiness would cheaply purchase the intermediate day to be spent with Lilian. And what harm could any ghost do him, and what did it matter whether the window was covered with a crimson blind, or a white or a green!

It mattered little when regarded in the day, but during the watches of the night such affairs take on a different complexion, though Ronald McEwan was no coward. He woke earlier on this second night: woke to be aware of a faint illumination in the room, and of—he thought after, though it was hardly realised at the time—the instantaneous glimpse of a figure crossing from wall to wall. One thing he did distinctly see: over the window there hung again—the crimson blind! Then in the space of half a dozen heart-beats, the faint light, faded out, and the room was left in darkness.

This time the paralysis of the night before did not recur. He had been careful to place within reach at the bedside the means of striking a light, and presently his candle showed the window unscreened and open, and the door locked as he left it over night. He did not extinguish that candle, but let it burn down in the socket; and he was not again disturbed.

During Sunday he debated with himself the question to speak or not to speak. That spare room might next be occupied by some one to whom the terror of such a-visitation would be harmful; and yet, he supposed, all turned on whether or not the occupier was gifted (or shall we say cursed?) with the open eye. He felt thankful he had been quartered there and not Lilian. Finally he resolved that Parkinson must be warned, but not till he himself was on the point of leaving—not till he had passed a third night in the haunted room, disturbed or not disturbed. And, after all, what had he to allege against it in this later time? Could a room be haunted by the apparition of a crimson blind?

Saturday had been brilliantly fine throughout, but Sunday dawned upon unsettled weather, and a wet gale rushing over from the not distant sea. He went to rest that night resolved to keep a light burning through the dark hours, but found it necessary to shut the window on account of the driven storm. He strove to reason himself into indifference and so prepare for sleep, which visited him sooner than he expected, and for a while was profound. It was somewhere between two and three o'clock when he started up, broad awake on the instant, with the consciousness of something wrong.

It was not the moderate light of his candle which now illuminated the room, but the fierce glow of mounting flames, though he could not see whence they proceeded. The red blind hung again over the window, but that was a negligible matter: some carelessness of his had set the Parkinsons' house on fire, and he must give the alarm. He struggled up in bed, only to find he was not alone. There at the bed-foot stood gazing at him a man, a stranger, plainly seen in the glare of light. A man haggard of countenance, with the look of a soul that despaired; clad in white or light-coloured garments; possibly a sleeping-suit.

Ronald believed he made an attempt to speak to this creature, to ask who he was and what doing there, but whether he really achieved articulate words he does not know. For the space of perhaps a minute the two stared at each other, the man in the flesh and he who was flesh no more; then the latter sprang to the window, standing on the low sill, and tore aside the crimson blind. There was a great crash of glass like that other crash he remembered, a cry from below in the garden, and a report like a pistol-shot; the figure had disappeared, leaping through the broken gap. Then all was still and the room in darkness; those fierce flames were suddenly extinguished, and his own candle had gone out.

He groped for the matches and struck a light. The red blind had disappeared from the window, there was no broken glass and no fire, and everything remained as he had left it over night.

No one else appeared to have heard that shot and cry in the dead middle of the night. After breakfast he took Parkinson into confidence, who heard the story gloomily enough, plainly discomforted though unwilling to believe.

"You have been right to tell me, my dear fellow, and I am sure you think you experienced all these impossible things. But look at probability. Those Applegarth boys hoaxed you years ago, the impression dwelt on your mind, and was revived by discovering this house to be the same. Such was the simple cause of your visions; any doctor would tell you so. As for my own action, I don't see clear. It is a horribly awkward affair, and we have been to no end of expense settling in. Cecilia likes the place, and it suits her. So long as she does not know—!"

"Look here, Parkinson. There is one thing I think I may ask—suggest, at least. You have another spare bedroom. Don't put any other guest where I have been sleeping. Couldn't you make it a storeroom—box-room—anything that is not used at night?"

Parkinson still was doubtful: he shook his head.

"Not without an explanation to Cecilia. She happens to be particularly *gone* on that room on account of the big window. It was just a toss-up that she didn't put Lilian there, and you in the other. And—if in time to come a nursery should be needed, that is the room on which she has her eye. She would never consent to give it up for a glory-hole or a store-room without a strong reason. A very strong reason indeed."

Ronald could do no more: his friend was warned, the responsibility was no longer his. It was some comfort to know that Lilian was leaving two days later, going on to another visit, and the fatal house did not seem to have affected her up to now.

After this, a couple of months went by, during which the Parkinsons made no sign, and he for his part kept his lips entirely sealed about his experiences at Swanmere. It might be, as Jack Applegarth said long before, his Highland blood which rendered him vulnerable to uncanny influences, and the Parkinsons and their Southron friends might remain entirely immune. But at the end of two months he received the following letter:

"Dear Old Chum,—It is all up with us here, and I think you will wish to know how it came about. I am trying to sub-let Ashcroft, and hope to find somebody fool enough to take it. I haven't a fault to find with the place, neither of us have seen or heard a thing, and really it seems absurd. The servants picked up some gossip about the haunting, and then one of them was scared—by her own shadow, I expect, and promptly had hysterics. After that, all three of them went to Cecilia in a body, and said they were willing to forfeit their wages, and sorry to cause us inconvenience, but nothing would induce them to stop on in a haunted house—not if we paid them hundreds—and they must leave at once. Then I had to have it out with Cecilia, and she was not pleased to have been kept in the dark. She says I hoodwinked her—but if I did, it was for her own good; and when we took the place, I had not the least idea. Of course she could not stay when the servants cleared out—and nor could I; so she has gone to her mother's, and I am at the hotel— with every one asking questions, which I can assure you is not pleasant. I shall take jolly good care not to be trapped a second time into a place where ghosts are on the loose.

"There is one thing that may interest you, as it seems to throw light on your experience. The house was built by a doctor who took in lunatic patients—harmless ones they were supposed to be, and he was properly certificated and all that: there was no humbug about it that I know. One man who was thought quite a mild case suddenly became violent. He locked himself into his room and set it on fire, and then smashed a window—I believe it was *that* window—and jumped out. It was only from the first floor, but he was so badly injured that he died: a good riddance of bad rubbish, I should say. I don't know anything about a red blind or a pistol-shot: those matters seem to have been embroidered on. But the coincidence is an odd one, I allow.

"We were pleased to hear of your engagement to Lilian, and I send you both congratulations and good wishes, in which Cecilia would join if here. I suppose you will soon be Benedick the married man.

Yours ever,
Peregrine Parkinson."

FINGERS OF A HAND

"In the same hour came forth the fingers of a man's hand and wrote . . . . and the king saw the part of the hand that wrote."

THE CHILDREN WERE SUPPOSED to need a seaside change, and I daresay they did, poor wee things, as they had had whooping-cough in the spring, and measles to follow. As you know, we are taking care of them for Bernard, who is in India with his wife, and so we are even more anxious about them than if they were our own. That is one great use of unmarried aunts—to shoulder other people's responsibilities; and I, for one, think the world would be a poorer place if the "million of unwanted women" were, by some convulsion of nature, to be swept away. I only mention the children's measles as the reason why we took those lodgings at Cove at the beginning of July, for, now one has to economise, we should not have gone in for a seaside change as a luxury for ourselves.

The lodgings were clean and fairly comfortable, and we took them for two months certain, letting our own pretty cottage in the midlands for a similar term. And that was why we had no home of our own to retreat to when— But I am telling my story upside down, as Sara says I always do. You would not be likely to understand, if I did not begin in the right place, with what went before.

The house was Number Seven, Cliff Terrace, a row of detached villas above the road, on the other side of which was the esplanade and the sea. There were no other lodgers, as we took both Mrs.

Mills's "sets"; nobody in the house but ourselves and the bairns, and that important person Nurse, except Mrs. Mills herself, and her daughter who waited on us. So you see there was no one who could have played tricks— But again I am getting on too fast.

We had never been to Cove before, or to St. Eanswyth either, the larger watering-place which lies to the east of Cove; but we thought our choice of place for a summer holiday was amply justified by the pretty inland neighbourhood and the sweet air, and a safe beach close at hand, where the children could be out playing early and late under the guardian wing of Nurse. For the first fortnight we were all satisfied and happy, and, both in metaphor and actually, there was not a cloud in the sky.

Then the rain began, not brief summer showers and sunshine in between, but the worst weather of a wet July—a continuous downpour with hardly ten minutes intermission, and going on for days: such rain as Noah must have witnessed before the beginning of the Flood.

Of course the poor children had to keep the house, and, though they and Nurse had the dining-room set to themselves, there was but little space for them to play about. Sara and I occupied the drawing-room, and she had been sketching from the window—not that there was much visible to make into a picture: a leaden sea and slanting lines of rain, and boats drawn up on the beach. At last she pushed away colour-box and pencils.

"I can't stand this any longer," she said. "Rain or no rain, I am going out. It will be a good opportunity to test the resisting powers of my new cloak. You must stay in to-day, as I believe you have caught cold."

I did not dispute her fiat. Sara always decides what is, or what is not to be done, and I, who am a biddable person, submit to be ruled. And, to say the truth, I was not particularly anxious to get wet. I went on with my sewing till it was nearly time for Miss Mills to appear with the luncheon-tray, and then I began to clear the table of Sara's scattered possessions.

Some blank sheets of paper were lying about, besides the one pinned to her board with the half-finished sketch; and on one of these I noticed some large scrawled writing. Not Sara's writing, which is particularly small and neat; not the writing of any one I knew. The words were quite legible, but they were very odd. GO— by itself at the top of the sheet; and the same word repeated twice below, followed by GET OUT AT ONCE.

Of course I showed Sara this when she came in to luncheon, and she could not account for it any more than I. The sheets were unmarked when she took them out of her portfolio; of that she seemed to be certain.

"Some one hag been playing a trick on us," she said. "If it is Mrs. Mills, it is an odd sort of notice"; and at this very mild witticism both of as laughed.

But the idea of a trick being played was absurd: I had been in the room the whole time, as I said.

"Unless you think I dozed off while you were out, and did it in my sleep!"

Sara laughed again, and began to sort the loose papers back into place.

"Why, here is more of it," she exclaimed; and I saw on the sheet she held out, in the same large scrawl, a repetition of the words— GET OUT—GET OUT AT ONCE.

Now I could have sworn—had swearing been of any use—that I had looked those papers over on both sides after finding the first writing, and with that sole exception they bore no mark whatever. So these last words must have been written after my discovery and before Sara's return, and while I was beside them in the room. Surely they had been traced by no mortal hand!

You will not wonder that such a curious happening was the subject of discussion between us during the rest of that wet day. "I'd give anything to know who did it," Sara was saying, while I added: "I should like better still to know what it means." I am more credulous than Sara, and it seemed to me there must be some meaning in anything so unaccountable. I had this feeling from the very first, and, as you will see, both the conviction and the reason for it grew.

I pass on to the following Sunday. The weather was still wet, and the children were kept mainly to the house. For the sake of variety for them, Sara had little Dick and Nancy upstairs in our sitting-room for their Sunday lessons, which as a rule devolve on her to give, as she is a cleverer teacher than I. Lessons of the simplest, as they generally consist of showing pictures and giving explanations; and to be allowed to look at Sara's illustrated Bible is a frequent Sabbath treat. The children had gone down again to Nurse, and Sara was about to tidy the book away, when she gave a sharp exclamation.

"Grace, look here. Who can have done this?"

The volume was lying open at the nineteenth chapter of Genesis, and these words in the twenty-second verse were scored under blackly in pencil—*Haste thee: escape.*

Now Sara, who is particular in everything, is especially so about her books. She hates any soil or mark upon them, and nothing irritates her more than to have a lent volume returned with "purple passages" scored beside in the margin, whether in approval or otherwise. "Tut-tut," she was saying, at the usual pitch of exasperation. "It is really unpardonable. *Where* is my india-rubber? I must see if I can take it out. It could not have been the children. And the Millses would never—! But there is nobody else."

"You would have seen, had it been the children. They are good little things, and would not: besides, they had not a pencil" (thus I weakened an argument based on their righteousness). "And what odd words to have chosen to mark, when you think of the other scrawls. I wonder if this is all. It is possible there may be more."

"I shall look the book right through and see, and then I shall lock it in my box."

Sara sat down to her task armed with the piece of rubber, and by no means in a Sabbath spirit of peace and good-will. She did find two other texts scored under, and these were the marked words:

2 Kings, ninth chapter and third verse. *Open the door and flee and tarry not.*

St. Matthew, seventh chapter and twenty-seventh verse. *The . . . house . . . fell, and great was the fall thereof.*

I was superstitious, because disturbed by these happenings. So I was told, yet who would not have been affected in my place? I believe Sara too was disquieted in her secret mind, though she would not allow it. But then she was used to pride herself on being an *esprit fort.*

I kept saying to myself, What next?—and the next came quickly. I did not tell Sara what I purposed doing, but I left a couple of sheets of paper and a freshly-cut pencil displayed on the table when we were going out. More writing might be done with the opportunity given, and "it" might vouchsafe to make clear "its" meaning. I could not then have analysed what I meant by the convenient impersonal pronoun, nor am I clear of the exact meaning now.

We were about to do some shopping in the town, and I had stupidly left my purse on the mantel-shelf in the sitting-room, so I was obliged to turn back to get it. As I opened the door, my eyes fell at once upon the papers, and I saw some dark object moving across the white surface, and then quickly disappearing over the table edge. It was too big for a mouse; could it have been a rat? The thought of a rat gave me a nervous shiver; I think I would have a greater terror of rats than of ghosts. I looked at the papers though I did not touch them; yes, a vague scrawl was begun upon the upper one, not developed into legible words. I had disturbed the writer too soon. But what could the writer be, coming in the form of a rat, or the shadow of a rat, and yet able to write words which appeared to convey a message? I left the papers as they were, but the scrawl was not continued; no doubt that unexpected first return had scared away the writer.

I said nothing to Sara of my failed experiment; but next day about the same time I laid my trap again, this time staying in the room, but retired into a distant corner, where I set myself to watch.

For a long while there was nothing. Then an object ill-defined and shadowy crept across the paper, stealing towards the pencil as it lay. I hardly dared breathe, the excitement was so tense. Over the pencil this shadow paused, and now became denser, taking solid form. It was not the whole of a hand, but a thumb and two fingers, forming something like a claw. But, if you consider, a thumb and two fingers are all a hand needs to manipulate a pencil, and "it" may not have cared to materialise anything superfluous. The pencil now slanted upwards between these fingers and the thumb, and—yes, no doubt remained—the claw was writing. Now we would know all, such was my sanguine thought, not forecasting how deep the mystery would remain.

It was Sara this time who interrupted, coming in. The pencil dropped, the claw from a solid form became a shadow, and slipped away over the edge of the table, as I had seen it vanish before. Sara noticed nothing; she was too full of her news, and of the letter open in her hand.

"Look at this. We ought to have had it two days ago, but there was a mistake in the address. It is from Mrs. Bernard's mother" (Mrs. Bernard is our brother's wife). "She is at Diplake for ten days before they go to Scotland, and she wants one of us to bring the children there just for the time they stay. She says she is sorry she cannot have us both, but it is a case of single room, as the house is full. She is expecting us to-morrow, so I shall have to wire, and tell Nurse to get ready. Will you go, Grace, or shall I?"

"Of course you must be the one. I should never get on at Diplake, and with a large, gay party. You must go, Sara, and put your best foot foremost, for Bernard's sake. And— I'm glad you have to take the children. For look what is written here!"

I showed her the paper on which the claw had scrawled. Over and over again the word DANGER, as if it could not be too often insisted on. Then, also repeated: GO. GET OUT. Then an attempt at *children*, afterwards clearly written: DANGER. CHILDREN MUST GO.

I think Sara was impressed at last, though she hardly believed in the claw I had seen writing. As to that, I must—she said—have been hallucinated, or else slept and dreamed. But little time remained for argument, as all was in a hurry of preparation—boxes to be packed, and the children to be consoled, for their enjoyment of the seaside pleasures was very keen, and the attraction small of going to stay with an almost unknown grandmother.

"But we are coming back?" said little Nancy. "We are coming back again here?"

I believe I told her yes, but as to what will happen in the future, who can say?

They set out early next morning, Sara and the three children and Nurse, and I saw them off at the station. Sara said almost at the last:

"I don't half like leaving you alone here, Grace. If you find the lodgings too solitary, why not take a room at the hotel for the days I am away?"

I said I would think of it, but in truth I felt no special nervousness or concern, only an intense curiosity to see what would happen now we had (by pure accident) obeyed the dictation of the writing, and sent the children away.

The lonely evening passed for me without disturbance; Miss Mills came at the usual time to carry down my supper tray, and wished me good-night, and shortly after this I went to bed.

I slept, and do not remember any warning dreams. But in the very early daylight I was suddenly startled broad awake—not I think by any noise, but by an alteration in the level of my bed. My head was low, almost on the floor, and my feet were high in air. Everything in the room was sliding and altering; basin and ewer slipped from the washstand, crashed and broke, and pictures flapped from the wall. Then came a greater crash like the jolting of a thunderclap, and it was close at hand; chimney-pots falling, walls and roofs collapsing: was it an earthquake that had happened? I heard screams and shouts, but the sliding movement had stopped.

I struggled up and to my feet, for I had been half buried by the bedclothes falling back upon me; and there opposite was a great crack or rent in the outer wall, wide enough to admit my arm, with the new morning looking through, and a waft of air blowing in keenly from the sea. It was as if the house had broken in two. What but an earthquake could have caused such a disaster?—and again

I heard people screaming. The often repeated warning, the scored words in the Bible ran in my head. I could be thankful indeed that Sara and the children were safe at Diplake out of the way: what an agony had they been still here, and those screams possibly theirs!

I do not know how long it took me to scramble up the slanting floor, to find my clothes, my shoes, where all was confusion, so that if it were possible to get out of the house I might go forth clad. Then I tried the door.

It was in some way jammed, and it seemed as if ages passed before I could wrench it open. When at last it gave way, the wreck revealed without was worse than the wreck within. The staircase was a heap of broken wood, and the back wall had fallen inwards; there was no getting down that way. What had become, I wondered, of Mrs. Mills and her daughter, and was it their screams that I heard? I called to them by name, but there was no answer.

Baffled so, I looked from the window, which had hardly a whole pane left. It was as if the terrace had disappeared: the road was broken up, and the house had been carried down with the sliding earth, many yards nearer the sea. A crowd had assembled, staring at this phenomenon, but at a safe distance. I shouted to them, and a man called up to me instructions to stay where I was, as a ladder would presently be brought.

I knew later that they feared at first to touch the house, lest it should collapse in total ruin like the one next on the terrace, where, alas! two people had been killed, overwhelmed and buried in their sleep.

This was a danger indeed, about which that warning came. The part of our house which fell, was where the children would have been sleeping. I was told that tons and tons of masonry had crushed in their little beds; even now it makes me sick to think of what we so narrowly escaped. The Millses, mother and daughter, were dug out of the basement quite unharmed, but I am afraid, poor people, they are heavy losers. I myself had not a scratch.

The great landslip at Cove, with all its damage and disaster, will surely pass into history: the slide of the undercliff down into the sea, the gaping fissure torn above, hundreds of feet in length—

the alteration of the ground below, heaped into mounds and bil-
lows like the waves of the sea, while the buildings in the course of
the slide are broken up and displaced like a set of children's toys,
playthings in the hands of a giant. People who are wise about the
geological formation, talk of a bed of slippery clay underlying the
upper strata, and say water had percolated down to it owing to the
wet spring, and, following upon that, the heavy rains of that dismal week in July. But they are wise after the event and did not
forecast it: indeed it was anticipated by no one other than the writer
of those mysterious words.

THE NEXT HEIR

I

FRYER AND FRYER, SOLICITORS, of Lincoln's Inn, the original firm and their successors, have for the past hundred years acted as guardians of the interests of the landed gentry, buying and selling portions of estates, proving wills, drawing up marriage settlements and the like. And a glance at the japanned deed-boxes in their somewhat shabby office would discover among the inscriptions sundry names of note.

The original Fryers have long been dead and gone, but there is still a Fryer at the head of the firm. And on a certain day of spring, this ruling Fryer was alone in his private office-room, when his clerk brought in a message.

"Mr. Richard Quinton to see you, sir. He has no card to send up, but he says you will know his name and his business, as he has called to answer an advertisement."

Without doubt Mr. Fryer did know the name of Quinton, as it was legibly painted on a deed-box full in view, but something in his countenance expressed surprise. He signified his willingness to see Mr. Richard Quinton, and presently the visitor entered, a pleasant-faced youngish man, brown of attire, and indeed altogether a brown man, except for the whitish patch where his forehead had been screened from, the sun. Bronzed of skin, brown of short cut hair, and opening on the world a frank pair of hazel eyes, which looked as if they had been used to regard the wide spaces of waste lands, and were not fully used to the pressure and hurry and strenuousness of our over-civilised older world.

"I have called, sir, about an advertisement inserted by Fryer and Fryer in a Montreal paper. I have it here to show you. It was posted to me at the London hospital, where I have been since my wound. I see that the representative of Richard Morley Quinton, who emigrated to Canada in 1827, will hear on applying to you of something to his advantage."

"*May* hear of something," corrected the man of law. "Are you the representative in this generation?

"I am, sir. Richard Morley Quinton was my grandfather."

"Great-grandfather, surely? You are under thirty, and he was twenty-six years old when he left England."

"No: grandfather. He had a hard struggle in his first years on the other side. His English brother was not the sort to help him, and he never asked for help: he would not. He did not marry until late in life, and my old dad was the only son who survived infancy. There was a daughter who married and had children. But I don't suppose you want to know about her."

"We want the male heir. Or at least to know where he might be found."

"My dad married earlier, but he had no children by his first wife. He was well over fifty when he married my mother, and I am their only child. I can put you in the way of getting all the certificates you want, and vouchers from responsible people who have known the family. And now, tell me. Why am I advertised for? Is it an inheritance?"

"Not at the present moment, but it may be."

"Of Quinton and Quinton Verney—is that so? My dad would have been pleased. He thought much of Quinton, hearing about it from his father, who was born at the Court."

"If the present Mr. Quinton, your second cousin, makes no will, the Quinton property goes to the heir-male of your mutual great-grandfather. But he has the power of willing the whole where he pleases—to a hospital, or to a beggar in the street. You can count on no certain inheritance. You understand?"

"Then why—?

"We advertised because Mr. Quinton wished to ascertain who represented the Canadian branch of the family, and also to make your personal acquaintance. We can give you no certainty, but I gather from what he has written, that, if your cousin likes you, and if you agree to certain stipulations respecting the property, he intends to make you his heir. When the particulars you give me are verified, you will have to go down to Quinton, but he will reimburse any expense you may be put to, through loss of time and detention in England. You can hold yourself at our disposal?"

"If military orders do not interfere—yes, gladly, for the sake of a look at old Quinton Court, even with nothing to come after. But perhaps Mr. Quinton may prefer to meet me in London."

"You will have to go down there. Mr. Quinton is a complete invalid, and keeps a resident doctor: he is still under sixty, but most unlikely, I should say, to marry. His father was killed in the hunting-field; he had not been long married, but his wife, who was one of the Pengwyns, gave birth to twin sons, posthumous children. This Clement was the younger of the two, but his elder brother died at nineteen, also from an accident. There you have the family history in a nutshell. Give me an address, where a letter will certainly find you when I have looked into this."

RICHARD HAD NOT LONG TO WAIT for the expected letter. Mr. Clement Quinton seemed disposed to take his young kinsman on trust, without holding aloof till his story was verified. Mr. Fryer was still in correspondence with Canada when the summons came for Richard to present himself at Quinton Verney. The young Canadian was prompt in obeying, and on the day following he took train for the nearest railway point. No day or time had been named for arrival, so, after changing at the junction and alighting at a small wayside station, no conveyance was there to meet him. Nor, on enquiry, was any trap to be hired. His portmanteau could be sent by a returning cart in the course of a couple of hours, but for himself there was no alternative. He would have to walk the four miles, or rather more, which separated the station from Mount Verney.

Mount Verney, these people styled Mr. Quinton's dwelling, and not Quinton Court as he expected; the Quinton Court his old father used to talk of, told by the grandfather reminiscent of his youth. Why had the original name been changed?—that should be a first question when the time for putting questions came. Meanwhile he was not ill-pleased to be approaching Quinton on foot and alone, and a walk of four miles and over was but a light matter.

Four miles of lovely country verdant with the early green of spring, hill and dale unfolding wooded glimpses here and there, and the ancient Roman road stretching its white line before him, enduring still after all these centuries. He could hardly mistake the way, but after a while he thought it better to ask direction. There were iron gates and an avenue leading to Mount Verney, so he was told, and when he came to the iron gates he must turn in.

Gates and an avenue! His father had spoken of no such append- age to Quinton Court, but no doubt they were additions of a later time. He had his father much in mind during that walk, and the interest he would have felt in this possible—nay, probable—inher- itance for his son. His grandfather too; the grandfather who died before his birth: it was as if the two old men went beside him along the green-fenced way, made fair by the sunshine of late April. And he had another person in mind, one who up to now has not been named. Nan, his girl, who waited for him far off across the Atlan- tic, full of love and faith. If this succession truly came to pass, if it were even an assured future to him and to his heirs, marriage would be no longer an imprudence, it might be entered into at once on his return, released from war-service. That hope was enough to gild the sunshine, and spread the pastures with a brighter green. And then he came to the gates, and they stood open.

Mount Verney did not boast a lodge, though the drive was a long one. The avenue had been closely planted with ilex and pine, too closely for the good of the trees, and it was consequently dark in shadow: as he turned in he was conscious of a certain chill.

The open gates were hung on stone pillars, and the ornamen- tation of these uprights caught his eye. On either side, inwards and outwards, a face was carved in relief, but a face that was not human:

the mask of a satyr, with pricked animal ears and sprouting horns, and an evil leering grin. Richard had seen nothing of this sort in his backwoods experience, though possibly other things that were starker and grimmer. The leering faces filled him with repugnance; they should not remain there, he thought, to watch over the comings and goings of the house, did ever that house become his own.

The dark avenue had a bend in it; he could not see to the end, but he thought he knew well what he would find there, the old Quinton homestead had been so often described to him. The grey stone house, with its gables and mullioned windows, diamond-paned; the steep roof, up and down which the pigeons strutted and plumed themselves; the paved courtyard with its breast-high wall and mounted urns. He had a clear picture of it in his mind, and this was what at the turn of the avenue he expected to see. But when the turn was reached, his joyful anticipations fell dead. This was quite another place. Had he been misdirected after all?

What lay before him was a white stuccoed villa, spreading over much ground, but so pierced with big window-spaces that it presented to the beholder scant solidity of wall. This was the entrance side; towards the valley the walls rounded themselves into two semicircles with a flat central division, and here again were the big sash windows of plate-glass, overlooking the view. But there was no mistake. This was Mount Verney.

A grave-looking elderly manservant answered the bell, and it became evident the Canadian visitor had arrived too soon. Mr. Richard Quinton was expected, yes certainly, but the day had not been named, and Mr. Quinton was at present out in the car, and Dr. Lindsay with him. If Mr. Richard would step into the library, tea should be brought to him—unless he preferred sherry. His room had been so far prepared that it could be quickly made ready; he, Peters, would tell the housekeeper. And would Mr. Richard come this way?

So tea was served to Richard in the library, and his first meal under the Mount Verney roof was taken in solitude, as the master of the house did not return. The library possessed one of the wide bows overlooking the valley, but in spite of the tall sash windows the room was a dark one. They were, it is true, heavily draped with crimson curtains, and the furniture was also heavy, and of an inartistic period. He tried to picture Nan in these surroundings, sitting in the opposite big chair (it would have swallowed her up entirely unless she perched on the arm) and pouring out for him from the huge old teapot, but the effort was in vain. The fancy portrait of his little love would not fit into this frame, but doubtless the frame could be altered: like the grinning masks on the gates, there was much it would be possible to change. Meanwhile hurrying footsteps were heard on the floor overhead, housemaids were busy there; and presently Peters came again to ask if he should conduct the guest to his room.

Richard left the dull library with a sensation of relief. The chamber immediately above had been prepared for him, of equal size, and with windows commanding the view. Richard made some appreciative comment, which seemed to please the old servant.

"Yes, sir," he said, "this is the best bedroom, it has the finest look-out. Mr. Quinton himself gave orders for it to be yours. It used to be Lady Anna Quinton's."

"Lady Anna Quinton!" Richard repeated the name in his surprise. "I did not know Mr. Quinton had ever been married."

"No, sir, and he never was. Her ladyship was his mother. She went away to France and died there; it is getting on for thirty years ago, but Mr. Quinton couldn't bear to take the room to be his, though it is the best in the house. I'll send up your portmanteau, sir, directly it arrives." And with that, Peters withdrew.

Here Richard was certainly well lodged. He stood at the middle window which had been set open, and looked out over a wide prospect. The sun was now beginning to decline, and the first flush of rosy cloud was reflected in the chain of pools which filled the valley to the right, widened out almost to the dimensions of a lake— no doubt artificially formed by damning up the natural stream, which rushed over a weir out of sight. In the middle distance, between the house and the water, was a grove of young oaks, not thickly set like the planting of the avenue, but high-trimmed and rising tall and bare-stemmed out of evergreen undergrowth. The shimmer of water was visible through them in the background, not wholly concealed—though it might be when leafage was full.

The name of Quinton Verney was familiar, cherished among those legends of the importance of the family which the Canadian branch had preserved and handed down; but the lake was to Richard another innovation and surprise. Was it good fishing water, he wondered, and would rainbow trout flourish and breed there? As he stood looking, a boat shot out from the headland to the right, and, crossing the field of view, was lost behind the grove: it was only after it had disappeared that Richard began to wonder what had been the motive power. He could not recall any flash of oars or figures of rowers, or indeed any occupier of the boat.

This might have puzzled him still more, but his attention was diverted by the sound of an arrival below. A car had drawn up at the entrance, voices were now heard in the hall, footsteps on the stairs. After a brief interval, a sharp, rather authoritative knock came at his door and a man entered, a man still on the younger side of middle-age, reddish-haired and short of stature, with a close-trimmed bristly moustache.

"Mr. Quinton?" Richard exclaimed, coming forward. If this was his host, he was quite unlike the fancy picture he had formed. But then at Mount Verney everything was unlike and unexpected.

"No—my name's Lindsay—I'm the doctor. Mr. Quinton is sorry you were not met, but he had not understood you were arriving to-day."

"I hope my coming has not been inconvenient?"

"Not at all—not at all, unless to yourself. But I do not suppose you minded the walk from the station; it is pretty country, and you came here especially to acquaint yourself with the place and its surroundings. One thing more. I have to ask you to excuse Mr. Quinton for this evening, and put up with my company only. Mr. Quinton is, as you know, an invalid, and I have been with him to-day to his dentist for some extractions under an anæsthetic. He is a wreck in consequence"—here the little reddish man shrugged his shoulders—"and will not leave his own rooms again to-night. You are comfortable here, I hope?"—this after Richard had expressed concern at his host's condition. Now it was necessary he should praise his quarters, which he did without stint.

"Mr. Quinton would have it that Lady Anna's room should be made ready for the heir, and we were all surprised, as it has been long out of use. Well, adieu for the present: come down as soon as you are ready. Dinner is at seven: we keep early hours here in the country. What! your portmanteau not come? Then never mind about dressing; we will not stand on ceremony for to-night."

With that, Lindsay the doctor took himself off. But, after he had closed the door, some of his last words kept repeating in Richard's mind. *Made ready for the heir!* That was taking intention for granted in a way for which he was not prepared; and, suddenly, he felt strangely doubtful of his own wish in the matter. Did he really desire to be the owner of the Quinton property, and, if not, from what hidden root did disinclination spring?

Presently a gong sounded from below, and he went down to find the dining-room lighted up, though it was scarcely more than dusk without, and the window-screens were still undrawn. The table was set out with some fine old silver and an abundance of flowers, the service of the meal was faultless, and Lindsay made an excellent deputy host. Good food has a cheering influence, and the causeless depression which had threatened to engulf Richard's spirit was lifted, at least for the time.

"I hope you will like Quinton Verney," Lindsay was saying with apparent heartiness. "Mr. Quinton is particularly anxious that you should like the place, and take an interest in his hobbies. He will explain better than I can what they are. But be prepared to hear a great deal about Roman remains in Britain, and to be cross-questioned about your knowledge."

"Then I can only avow ignorance. It is a study that has not come in my way, but I am at least ready to be interested."

"Ah, well, interest won't be difficult in what has been discovered on your own land, for that is his especial pride. A fine tessalated pavement down there by the pools, and an altar in what is now the grove. I am a duffer myself in these matters, but Mr. Quinton is a downright enthusiast about the old pagans and their times. It was he who replanted the grove where it is supposed that a sacred one existed, and set up in the midst of it a statue of Pan copied from the antique. I chaff him sometimes about it, and tell him I believe there is nothing he would like better than to revive the Lupercalia, and convert the entire neighbourhood. That's an exaggeration, of course, but the element of mystery appeals to him. As you will discover."

Following this touch of personal revelation, Richard remarked:

"You know Mr. Quinton very well. I suppose you have been with him a long time?"

"Eighteen months—no less, no more. But you can get to know a man pretty well in that time, especially when you happen to be his doctor as well as his house-mate. He has been an invalid for many years—since boyhood in fact: a sad case: you'll know more about it after a while. I was at the war before that: got knocked out, and when free of hospital could only take on a soft job, and fate or luck sent me here. Quinton and I have got on well together. Indeed I may tell you in confidence that he offered to leave me all he possessed, provided I would bind myself by his conditions."

So the Quinton inheritance had been offered and refused elsewhere. Here was a matter that might well give Richard food for thought.

"And why did you not—?" he began impulsively.

"Why didn't I grasp at such a chance? Well, I allow it was tempting enough, to a man who is a damaged article—a damage that will be life-long. But I couldn't consent to bind myself as he would have me bound; and there was another reason. I would have been suspected of using my position here to exercise undue influence, and that I couldn't stomach. It was I who suggested to Mr. Quinton that he should seek out his next of kin—eh, what; what is the matter?"

The query was to Peters, who was whispering at his elbow.

"Pray excuse me. I am sorry, but my patient is not so well." And the little doctor hurried away.

Peters brought in the next course.

"Dr. Lindsay hopes you will go on with the dinner, sir, and not wait for him. He may be detained some time."

For the rest of the meal Richard was solitary. He declined after dinner wine and dessert, so Peters, who felt himself responsible towards the guest, suggested that he might like to smoke in the library, and coffee would be brought to him there. Richard rose from the table, and, as he did so, turned towards the unscreened window behind his chair, and experienced the shock of a surprise. There stood a strange-looking figure, gazing in at him and at the room, with face pressed against the glass. His exclamation recalled Peters, who was in the act of carrying out a tray; but by the time the old butler returned, the figure had disappeared. Who, or what was it? But Peters could not tell.

"I'll have it inquired into, sir. No one had any call to be there. These windows look into the enclosed garden, that is always kept private. A man, did you say, sir? Like a tramp?"

"A man," Richard assented, but he did not add in what likeness. Surely it must have been some freak of fancy that suggested those lineaments, the white leering face which resembled the bestial masks at the gate of the avenue, with their pricked ears and budding horns; and suggested also the naked torso, of which a glimpse was afforded by the light.

Peters brought word with the coffee that no one was found in the garden, but he meant to be extra careful in locking up, "lest it should be somebody after the plate." And indeed, were ill characters about, the unscreened window was likely to bring danger, as the display of silver on sideboard and table might well excite the cupidity of a looker-in.

Dr. Lindsay came down an hour later, but it was only to ask whether Richard had all he wanted for comfort and for the night.

"I shall be sitting up with Mr. Quinton," he explained. "Unluckily, hœmorrhage has followed these extractions, and he is morbidly affected by the sight and taste of blood. No, not a sufficient loss to be alarming: it will be subdued by to-morrow I don't doubt: it is serious only as it affects his special case. You'll give Peters your orders, will you not, and tell him when you wish to be called, and all that. I understand your portmanteau has arrived."

So Richard found himself back again in the best bedroom at an early hour, with the night before him, and his luggage unpacked, and despatch-case set on the writing-table. Now was the time for the letter he had promised Nan, with his first impressions of Quinton Verney, about which she was naturally curious; the old homestead he had described to her, which might some day be his home and hers. But when he spread paper before him, he felt an overmastering reluctance to write that letter. What could he say if he told her the truth—and surely nothing less than the truth and the whole truth was due to Nan, however much it might disappoint and puzzle her. Could he tell her, with no reason to allege, of the distaste he felt for this place, for the house and all that it contained?—a distaste which began with the first sight of those leering masks at the avenue gate: how tell her of that other living face which resembled them, seen peering into the lighted dining-room, pressed against the glass of the shut window a couple of hours ago? Better delay, than that he should fill a letter with maunderings such as these, when another day's experience, or a personal interview with the invisible cousin, might bring about an altered mind.

He was tired and out of spirits, and though he rejected with scorn the suggestion that a walk of less than five miles could have fatigued him, he was only lately out of hospital, and it was long since so much pedestrian exercise had come his way. And there had been throughout a certain excitement of highly strung expectation, from which no doubt reaction played its part. No, he would not attempt to write to Nan; the letter should be postponed until the morrow. And he would betake himself at once to bed.

II

IT HAS BEEN SAID that the chamber allotted to him was spacious and well-appointed, a private bathroom opened from it, and with one notable exception, it fulfilled every modern requirement. The rest of the house had been wired, and electric light installed, but here there were no means of illumination but candles, and, though these had been abundantly supplied on toilet and mantelpiece, and also at the bedside, the result was curiously dull. It was as if the walls and hangings of the apartment absorbed and did not reflect the light; a room of ordinary size would have been as well illuminated by a farthing dip. One of the windows was opened down a hand's breadth behind the curtains, and they stirred faintly in the air. Richard drew them apart to push up the lower sash, and then was struck by the beauty of the scene below. The valley had put on a veil of silvery mist, so delicate as hardly to obscure, and away to the left the moon was rising, a full yellow moon, magnified by its nearness to the horizon.

How still it all was. He had been used of late to the roar of a great city, audible even through hospital walls; before that to the thudding of great guns, and the scream of shell. How silent, and how peaceful: but presently not completely silent, for music broke into the stillness.

Somebody down below was playing on the flute, long-drawn notes and a simple air, but of enthralling sweetness. The music was difficult to locate; sometimes it seemed to come from near the house, sometimes from the grove of trees, and now to be a mere echo from a greater distance still. Could some rustic lover be serenading a housemaid? but no, that seemed impossible. Richard was himself no musician, but he knew enough to appreciate the rare quality of the performer. And then the final notes died away, and silence reigned under the rising moon.

He dropped the curtain over the window, leaving it open, and now applied himself quickly to prepare for bed. Tired as he was, he expected to sleep as soon as his head touched the pillow: such was his custom in high health, and the habit had served him in good stead when recruiting strength. But on this first night at Mount Verney sleep and he were to be strangers. No doubt there was some excitement of nerve or brain, the cause of which might be looked for entirely in himself. This at first; but by-and-bye there was something external, something more, though it was nameless and undefined.

A change had set in: this was no restlessness of his own that he was suffering, it was the misery and torture of another; a misery all the greater that it could not be expressed. It seemed to him that he was divided; he recognised that he was lying on the bed, but he was also walking the room from wall to wall, with tossed arms, with hands clenched and threatening, and then spread open; gestures foreign to his nature under an extreme of passion. He, or the entity which absorbed him, did not weep: no tears came to the relief of this distress, and his own voice was dumb in his throat; there could be no cry of appeal. Whether the passion which tore him was fury solely, or grief solely, he could not tell; or whether in its extreme anguish it combined the two.

For a while he was completely paralysed by this strange experience: he was walking the room with the sufferer; he *was* the sufferer: and then again he knew the personality and the agony were not his own; that his real self was stretched upon the bed, though he could neither lift a finger nor move a limb. How long did this endure in its alternations? Keen as was his after memory, he could not tell: moments count as hours when under torture, and in an experience so abnormal time does not exist, even as we are told it will be effaced for us hereafter. One fragment of knowledge informed his brain; how he knew cannot be told, for no voice spoke. The entity was a woman. It was no man's agony into the vortex of which he had been drawn; this was a woman who knew both love and hate, a mother who had possessed and also lost.

Then, in a moment, the strain upon him snapped: he could move again, he had the government of his limbs, he was in his own body and not that other, if the other was a body indeed. Candles— the means of striking a light—were at his hand; in less time than it takes to write, both flames were kindled: the whole room was plain to see, and there was nothing, nothing but empty air. And yet he knew, he knew that the woman was still there—that she was pacing up and down from wall to wall—that she was still torn with fury, from the vortex of which his own spirit was scarcely yet set free, as consciousness of it remained.

This would have been a staggering experience, even to one versed in psychic marvels, but of such matters Richard Quinton was completely ignorant. To him the ordeal he had passed through was as unique as it was unaccountable—a horror to have so penetrated another's being, and also in a way a thing of shame, to be covered up shuddering from the light of day, He leapt out of bed; he must seek the window, the free air, if he would not choke and die. In his rush forward it seemed as if he encountered and passed through the frantic figure that yet was invisible and disembodied; but the collision, if it was collision, affected neither: roused as he was, the grip of individuality was too strong. He tore the curtains apart, and there at last was the cool night, the serene moon, the wafting of free air, in which, behind him in the room, the lighted candles flared.

The moon was now high in heaven, the scene was bathed in white light, the shadows, where shadows fell, were black and sharply defined. The silvery mist of the earlier evening had disappeared, the light veil of it withdrawn, rolled up and swept away before that stirring of air. There was a path of reflected light across the quiet water of the pool, the headland stood out dark. And, strange to relate, from behind it again shot out the mysterious boat, the boat he had seen before, but now there were two men on board. He saw, or thought he saw, one man attack the other; for a dozen seconds they were locked together struggling. Then the rocking boat capsized and sank, and the men also disappeared.

Richard saw this, and yet in some dim way he realised that he had witnessed no actual disaster for which he need give the alarm: it was a scene projected into his mind from the mind of another. It did not even occur to him that there, within a bowshot of the house, were men drowning who might be saved. The moon-path on the water was smooth again now, undisturbed by even a ripple, the night utterly still. But a moment later the silence was broken by the same flute music which had discoursed so sweetly earlier in the night. It was, however, tuned to a livelier measure this second time, one that might accompany dancing feet. It sounded from the grove, and underneath the clear light Richard could distinguish moving figures, leaping among the trees.

There were five or six of them apparently, men or boys, and the figures looked as if naked above the waist. And the dance was not solely a dance, for they seemed to be chasing, or driving before them, some large animal which fled with leaps through the undergrowth, a goat possibly, or a sheep. The animal and the pursuing figures disappeared among the trees, and then appeared again as if they had made a circuit of the grove; the goat (if it was a goat) leaping in front, and the others pursuing. This was the end; a cloud drifted over the moon, and when it passed there was no more sign of movement in the grove, and the jocund fluting had ceased.

Richard turned back into the room, and now his perception of that fury and distress, if not wholly effaced, was dulled as if here, too, was the shadowing of a merciful cloud. But stretch himself on that bed he could not, nor address himself to sleep, lest it should be renewed with all the former horror. He would keep the lights burning, if only he had a book he would occupy himself with reading, but literature had formed no part of his light luggage.

He might seek one in the library below, treading softly in stocking-soles so as not to disturb the sleeping house.

But as he issued forth, candle in hand, he found a burner switched on on the landing, and the dressing-gowned small doctor crossing over from an opposite door. Lindsay at once accosted him.

"Can I do anything: what is the matter?—oh, can't sleep, and want a book: is that it? I can find you one close at hand, and mine are livelier than the fossils in the library. Come this way."

Lindsay's room opened over the entrance, next to Mr. Quinton's bedchamber. A set of bookshelves filled a recess.

"Help yourself. The yellow-backs on the top shelf are French—I daresay you read French. But you'll find English ones below, and perhaps they are more likely to put you asleep." He snapped on an extra light, and then turned for a fuller scrutiny of his companion. "You look pretty bad," was his remark. "Does a sleepless night always knock you up like this? I'm doctor to the establishment you know, and I prescribe a peg. Whisky or brandy will you have? Both of them are here, and so is a syphon. Sit down while I get it ready.

Three fingers—two—one? Good: you do well to be moderate. Get outside that, and you'll feel better. And then you can pick your book."

Lindsay did not question further as to the cause of disturbance, though he looked inquisitive, as if suspicions were aroused. Richard for his part remained tongue-tied, time was needed to digest and try to understand his experience: he might speak of it later on, but not now, while still his nerves were vibrating from the strain. The human companionship was, however, reassuring, and by the time the prescribed dose was swallowed, he felt altogether more normal. He inquired for Mr. Quinton, sat for a while conversing on indifferent subjects, and then departed with a book.

He did not venture again to lie down, but installed himself in a deep chair, the candles burning at his elbow. The effect of the novel may have been soporific, though he was an inattentive reader. After a long interval he fell asleep, and waked to find morning already brightening in the east.

The night was over, its perplexities and distresses had sunk into the past, and a new day had begun. It was refreshing to spirit as well as body to wash and re-clothe, to undo the bolts and chains which guarded the front door, and find himself in the free air. Though it was still the air which breathed over Mount Verney, he was delivered from the evil shadow of that roof. He retraced his steps of the day before, down the dark curving drive, out through the satyr-headed gates, to the highroad which was free to all, the road traversed by Roman legions in centuries that were past. He turned to the right, with the eastern sky behind him, and walked on, without object, but steeping himself in the freshness of the newly awakened world.

At first he appeared to be the only person astir and observant, but presently an old man of the labouring class pushed open a gate some way ahead and came towards him, a shepherd accompanied by his dog. Richard would have liked to exchange ideas with an English working man, but felt too suddenly shy to venture on more than a good-morning as they drew abreast. The man, however, stopped and accosted him.

"Beg pardon, master, but as you came along, did you mebbe happen on a straying sheep? A ewe she is, and has taken her lamb with her, one getting on in size, as it was dropped early. Me and the dog have been after her since first it was light."

Richard had no information to give; he had not seen the ewe and her lamb. And then he bethought him.

"I stayed last night at Mount Verney, and, looking out in the moonlight, I saw a sheep leaping about in the grove, the coppice of oaks by the water. Would that be the one you have lost?"

The man shook his head.

"No, sir, that would be Mr. Quinton's sheep. I drove it down myself, a prime wether, only a day ago; and my heart was sore for the poor thing. It seemed as if the dog here was sorry too, for he didna like the job. Mr. Quinton he buys one at the spring full moon, and again at harvest, of my master or one of the other breeders, always to be driven into the coppice and left there, and I doubt if ever the creatures live as much as two days. What he wants them for 'tis beyond me to say. Seems a waste of good meat and good wool, for it is just a hole in the field and dig them under, so I am told, and not a soul the better. Some folks will eat braxy mutton, meat being dear as it is; but not one of them would touch a sheep that had died up there in the wood, poisoned as like as not. 'Tis just a mystery to all of us. But I've no call to be passing remarks, seeing you know Mr. Quinton, and are staying at Mount Verney."

Richard might have replied with truth that he did not know Mr. Quinton, their acquaintance was still to make. But he asked instead for direction, and was told to cross a stile to the right into a certain field-path, which would bring him out opposite the house, by the bridge over the water.

The bridge was a rustic affair of planks and a hand-rail, and beyond it the way diverged to right and left, the path on the left entering the grove, barred only by a light iron turnstile. Was it curiosity, or another sort of attraction which drew Richard thither, to see by daylight the spot on which he had looked down under the moon the night before? Now it seemed ordinary enough; the paths cut through it were grassed over and green, but here and there, where the turf was soft, he noticed they were trampled by divided hoofs, larger than those of sheep. The trees, young and slender, shorn of their lower branches, were now faintly green with unexpanded leafage; the undergrowth, which was chiefly rhododendron, was here and there breaking into purple and pinkish flower.

While still some way from it, he could distinguish among the trees the statue of which Lindsay had spoken. It was mounted on a pedestal, and was, as he said, a modern copy of the antique. Pan with his pipes in bronze, an abhorrent half-animal figure; the brooding face less repulsive perhaps than those of the satyrs at the gate, but the regard it appeared to bend on the observer who approached, had a keener expression of intelligence and evil power. Richard as he drew near, his attention riveted on that face and crouching figure, almost stumbled over an object lying at the foot of the column.

It was the dead sheep. Had it been dragged thither with a purpose, or hunted till it fell exhausted where it lay? There was no mark upon it that he could see, of the knife of the executioner, but the swollen tongue protruded from the half open jaws, and thick blood had flowed from both nostrils, staining the ground.

Truly Mount Verney was a spot where there were strange happenings. The shudder of the night again passed over Richard, and he had now no least desire to linger in the grove, or to make further discoveries. Passing through another gate he gained a steep slope of lawn, leading up to the graveled terrace on which the windows of the library opened. His approach had been observed, and here was Lindsay waving him a cheerful greeting, with the intelligence of waiting breakfast.

III

"Been for an early ramble?—that was well done. Mr. Quinton wants you to see as much as possible of the place before he speaks to you of the future. A lovely morning. And this house stands well, does it not, above the valley? Gives you a first rate view."

Richard assented. And then put the question he had been meditating.

"Was this house built on the site of another, do you know? The house my father used to speak about was called Quinton Court. It was built long before his father's time, and was of stone; it had a walled courtyard and mullioned windows. I don't suppose it was ever a grand mansion. But that was what I expected to find in coming down here."

"Quinton Court is still in existence; the man lives there who has the farm. It is a fine-looking old place, but I expect it has gone a long way down hill since it was given up as the family residence. You will find it about a mile from here, on the other side of the hill."

"I should like to see it. I should greatly like to see it—!"

"Make it the object of your next walk. Go the length of the lake to the head water, and through the field beyond, and you will come upon a cart-road. I would show you the way, but I may have difficulty in leaving. And perhaps you would rather go alone."

That he would prefer to make the visit alone was so true that Richard left the suggestion uncontested. Lindsay passed lightly to another subject; one on which he was not improbably curious.

"I hope the novel and the 'peg' helped you to sleep? I hate to lie awake myself, but sometimes a strange bed—! There is fish, I think, under that cover. Or do you prefer bacon?"

"I am a good sleeper usually, in any sort of bed, strange or familiar. Dr. Lindsay, I am sorry to be a troublesome guest, but can I change my room? And, if you will allow me, I will do so before to-night."

"You can, without doubt. There are other guest-rooms, though with fewer advantages than the bow-room, as we call it. I will see about the exchange. But—may I be so indiscreet as to ask why? Because Mr. Quinton will put the question to me, and I had better be prepared to answer him."

"Then perhaps I may put a question on my side. I understand that bedroom has been long out of use. I know nothing about ghosts, and have never believed in them, but—it is not like other rooms. Is it supposed to be haunted? And, if so, why was it chosen for me?"

"I can't tell you much about it; remember I only came here eighteen months ago. As for why it was chosen, you must ask Mr.

Quinton: it was his doing, not mine. I never heard of any ghost being seen there. The only queer thing said about the room sounds like illusion, and could not disturb a sleeper. Nor would it, I suppose, be visible at night. But perhaps you, as a Quinton, would be more sensitive than a stranger."

"What is the queer thing?"

"Why it seems absurd, but they say whoever looks through that window sees a boat on the lake. I saw something like it myself on one occasion, but I expect it is a flaw in the glass. Was there a ghost last night?"

"No ghost in the sense you mean, but such an impression of misery—and not misery only, anger—that I found sleep impossible. That is all I have to tell. If Mr. Quinton is affronted by my wish to change, I must find quarters elsewhere till he is ready to speak to me."

"Nonsense: he won't be affronted, it would be absurd. I doubt if you will see him to-day, but he is decidedly better, and I shall not need to sit up another night. You'll like him, I think. He has his eccentricities, that must be allowed. But you would be sorry for him from your heart if you knew all."

"He is eccentric? I heard a strange story about him this morning, from an old shepherd I met in the road. Is it true that he purchases a sheep twice a year, and that it is driven into the grove to die? There is one lying dead there now, at the foot of the statue of Pan."

Lindsay shrugged his shoulders.

"I told you he was half a pagan, and I don't defend the sheep business. That sacrifice is one of the things he wants continued, and makes a condition; but I told him straight out that no successor would pledge himself to a thing so out of reason, and you had better be firm about it when he speaks. Of course it is natural he should wish Mount Verney kept up as the residence of the owner; there one can be in sympathy. His grandfather built it, and his father planned the grounds, and the ornamental water and all that. Odd about the lake, seeing what happened after. Why, don't you know. The elder, son was drowned there. Mr. Quinton's twin brother. Archibald, his name was. He was the Quinton heir."

Richard saw again, in a flash of memory, the two figures struggling in the boat and disappearing under water; but where was the good of taking Lindsay into confidence? He had said enough, and made it plain he would occupy the room no more, nor look from it over the lake: he did not care to what sort of apartment he was transferred; it would serve him for the time, however mean.

The doctor hurried away as soon as they had breakfasted, apologising for his enforced absence, but Richard was well content to be alone. He wanted to think out the warning again given about conditions. That which concerned the sheep was unthinkable, and could hardly be pressed; but evidently there were others, by reason of which Lindsay had refused the offered heirship. If he was required to live at Mount Verney in the future, and make it his home and his wife's home—what then? In one way the prospect of the inheritance was tempting enough to him, and would be to any man—an inheritance that would at once convert him into a person of importance, with a stake in the country as the saying is; a good position to offer his wife, ample means, provision for the children that might be born to them.

But if what he began dimly to suspect was fact; if the place had somehow fallen under a curse, in pagan times or now—such a curse as affected inanimate building, and tainted the very ground—it would be no fit home for her. And Nan was not covetous of riches— she would not mind struggling on with him and being poor; she would approve, so he justly thought, of a refusal made for the sake of right.

There was nothing to detain him indoors, so with these cogitations in mind, he set out in the direction Lindsay had indicated, following the north shore of the artificial lake, and crossing the headland which, viewed from above, had been the departure point of the mysterious boat. On the western side of the headland, furthest from the house and half hidden by the bank, were the remains of what certainly had been a boathouse; but in these days no boat sheltered there, and the timbers of the roof had rotted and fallen in decay. He passed through the gate by the headwater, a clear and fast running stream; found and followed the cart-road,

which after a while was merged in a superior approach, now well
nigh as worn and deeply rutted as the other.

He came upon the old Court suddenly, round a fold of the hill,
and there he stood for a while, his heart moved by a mysterious
feeling of kinship—if not utterly fantastic to suppose flesh and
blood can feel itself akin to walls of stone. The old homestead had
fallen from its first estate, but there was a dignity about it still, the
dignity of fine proportion and high quality, differing widely from
the jerry building of to-day. The grey gables were there as of old,
the roof of slabbed stone, the panes of diamond lattice; there the
flagged courtyard with its breast-high boundary wall, and five of
the six urns mounted in place; the sixth had fallen, and lay broken
at the foot.

The front door was fast shut, an oak door studded with iron,
but Richard drew near and knocked, treading the very stones the
footsteps of the dead had worn. Why, why had the later degener-
ates forsaken this dear place, and fixed their abode at Mount
Verney?

A neatly-dressed young woman opened to him, and looked in-
quiringly at the stranger.

"I'm sorry, sir, my father is not in, if so be as you come seeking
him."

No, Richard said, that was not his errand; but might he be allowed to see inside the house, if only a couple of the rooms?

"Why certainly, if you are thinking of taking the place. I didn't
know as it had got about that we are leaving, but news do fly apace.
But we shall not be out until September."

"My name is Quinton, and I am from Canada. My great-grandfather lived here, and it was here that my grandfather was born. I
am anxious to see the Court now I am in England. If you would be
so good as to allow—"

"Come in, sir, and look where you like; you are kindly welcome.
My father would make you so I know, for he is the oldest tenant on
the estate. We have no fault to find with the place, but the farm is
too big for father now he has no son with him, and the house too
large for us too. I am the only one at home, and mother is laid by

with the rheumatics. These long stone passages take a lot of clean-
ing, to say nothing of the many rooms, though more than half of
them we shut away."

So upon this invitation Richard had his wish, and saw over the
house upstairs and down. In some of the rooms put out of use there
were still pieces of old furniture, Quinton property, his guide told
him: an oak chest or two, corner cupboards with carven doors, a
worm-eaten dresser, chairs in the last stage of decrepitude. They
were let with the house, having been thought unworthy of removal
to Mount Verney. In the best parlour sacks of grain were stored,
and on the threshold of two of the empty bedrooms he was warned
to step warily, as the floors were thought to be unsafe.

Quinton Court had fallen from its first estate, but it was still
lovely in the eyes of this late descended son. It had been cleanly
kept, however roughly, and there was an air of purity about its
homeliness, of open casements and scents of lavender and apples.
He could picture his Nan here, a happy house-mistress under the
ancient roof of his forefathers; but not as the chatelaine of Mount
Verney with all its wealth: never at Mount Verney. Ah, if only Mr.
Quinton would make this place his bequest to the next heir, the
old Court and the surrounding farm which he might work for a
living; and leave Quinton Verney and his accumulated thousands,
where else and to whom else he pleased!

IV

SUCH WERE RICHARD'S THOUGHTS as he walked back along the green
shores of the lake, and under the mid-day sun. He and the doctor
were again tête-a-tête at luncheon; but he was told Mr. Quinton
desired to see him that afternoon in his private room above stairs;
also that he intended to dine with them, being greatly better than
the day before. So the first interview with his host came about earlier than he had been led to expect.

The appearance of his elderly cousin took him by surprise. Mr.
Clement Quinton was strikingly handsome, though older-looking
than his two and fifty years. He might have been taken for a man
advanced in the seventies, though his tall thin figure was still

upright. He owned a thick thatch of grey hair, a close-cut white beard, and bushy grey eyebrows above eyes of steely blue, rather unnaturally wide open. He welcomed Richard cordially, shaking him by the hand: a cold hand, his was, and yet the younger man felt uncomfortably, the instant they were palm to palm, that he touched something sticky and moist. Mr. Quinton's left hand was gloved, and Richard remembered after that he held a dark silk handkerchief in the other while they talked together.

There was nothing embarrassing or note-worthy about the earlier conversation. Mr. Quinton appeared kindly interested in Richard's past history, asking about his father and home, how he had been educated and where, and also the details of his military service. They had been talking together for half an hour, before any reference was made to the future.

"I want you to be interested in this place," he said with emphasis. "I want you to be particularly interested. For there are various things I am bound to leave to the doing of others, and much will depend on their punctual carrying on. It will smooth my pillow—as the saying is—if I may be assured of the co-operation of my successor."

This was not very easy to answer, as Richard could not assume successorship on a hint so vague. So he struck out into an account of his visit to Quinton Court, and pleasure over the discovery that the old house of which his grandfather had spoken with affection, was still solidly existent.

"I was afraid it had been pulled down, and Mount Verney built on its site."

"No, we destroyed nothing. My respect for antiquity is too great. As I will show you later, it has been my great desire to—call back into life, I may say—associations from the dead past of an earlier period still. Traces of what had been, were thick on the ground hereabouts: you shall have the complete history of how, and why, and what. You will find it remarkable indeed. I will tell you frankly, my young cousin, it is here and on Mount Verney I want your interest focused. This place dates back to the Roman occupation of Britain, and in comparison with the relics here, Quinton Court is but a thing of yesterday."

"Dr. Lindsay told me Roman remains had been unearthed. I think he said some portions of a pavement."

"There was a villa here, on this very spot; baths in the valley, with the water running through them; and an altar where you see the grove, which was once a dense thicket of wood. I have other means of knowing, besides conclusions drawn from the fragments that remain, and these communications the excavations have strikingly confirmed. I was directed where to dig. There was a special cult connected with this place. The worship of Pan."

"I observed the statue in the grove."

"It marks the site of the old altar. Pan is a deity about whom little has been known and much mistaken. From the sources of information at my command, I have compiled a treatise. And that is one thing I require of my successor. If unpublished at the time of my decease, I wish it given to the world."

The posthumous publication of a treatise! It would be well if other conditions were no more formidable than this.

"Some writers have made the mistake of confounding Pan with Faunus; surely an extraordinary error. My theory is entirely different. Cain was his prototype. Cain."

Here the recluse seemed to be stirred by some inward excitement, and he got up to pace the room.

"Cain!" he repeated. "Of course you know the scriptural narrative, and probably little else about that founder of an early race. There are mistakes in that account—it is libelous, the fabrication of an enemy. Eve put about unworthy slanders. If Cain did truly kill his brother, it was in self-defence, or in a fury of panic anger: I say if, for I do not allow it to be the truth. Abel, the favorite, was a sneak and a coward, and he knew whatever lie he set up, so long as it was against the other, would stand as unassailable truth. He was better blotted out, than left to be the father of a degenerate race. Cain was at least a man— And it is said the Lord put a mark on him. What did that mean, think you?"

"I have not the least idea. Does anybody know?"

"I know this much, that it was the curse of the partly animal form. Cain was crippled into that likeness, and some of his sons

took after him. Not the daughters, for they were in the likeness of
Eve. And it is on record that they were beautiful. The sons of God
saw the daughters of men that they were fair. But that does not
come into the argument, nor concern us now. It was because of
the mark set on him that Pan loved solitary places, the cool depths
of caves and the shadow of woods. It was he in the beginning, and not
Abel, who was the keeper of flocks. Abel did nothing but laze in the
sun and watch the fruits ripen, and then gather them for an offering. I
told you that the record lied. Do you wonder how I know all this?"

Richard could do nothing but assent.

"I will tell you—show you. I wish to instruct you in my methods, that they may be yours hereafter. It is not all who have the
gift of sight. Lindsay is psychically blind. But something tells me
you have it, or will have it. Come here with me."

He opened a door and showed an inner, smaller room, probably intended as a dressing-closet in the original design of the
house. There was a writing-table and chair in the sole window, but
the only other furniture was a high stand, on which was some object covered over with black velvet drapery. Mr. Quinton turned
back part of the covering, and directed, Richard to seat himself
before it. The lifted flap revealed the smooth and shining surface
of a large crystal, or ball of glass, set into a frame.

"You know what this is, and what its use? I want to test whether
I can make a scryer of you. The black cloth is used only to prevent
confusing lights. Now look steadily into the crystal, and tell me
what you see."

Richard looked, in some amusement and complete incredulity.

"I see the reflection of my own face," he said presently. "Nothing more. Except—yes—something which looks like smoke."

"Go on looking, and be patient. There will be more."

As Richard gazed, his own reflection disappeared, the smoke
cleared away, and there were the gates of the avenue with the leering faces, exactly as he saw them the day before. Then the cloud of
smoke returned, blotting them out; cleared again, and showed the
spy of the evening, peering in at the window of the dining-room.

Succeeding this, came the scene of the grove by moonlight, with the figures leaping among the trees, and driving the doomed sheep.

"I am seeing a procession of scenes," he replied to a further question. "But only what are in my mind and memory. Nothing new."

"Go on looking," was again the command. What is new will come."

The next scene was, as Richard half expected, the grove as he entered it that morning, with the statue of Pan on its pedestal, and the sheep before it lying dead. This persisted, not small as dwarfed within the limits of the ball, but now as if a window opened before him on the actual scene. But a change was taking place in the figure of the sod. The bronze seemed to soften and warm into flesh, the terrible, wise face was no longer serene and meditative, the eyes looked into his, and now there was mockery in them, reveling in his surprise. The thing was alive, moving, surely about to descend.

But no. The figure, without leaving its pedestal, stretched out one hairy ape-like arm, and clutched the body of the sheep, drawing it up to rest on his crossed hocks, while the mocking face bent closer, as if to snuff or lick the blood. Was the monstrous creature about to tear the victim open, ready to devour? The action of the hands looked like it.

Richard could look no longer. A sweat of horror broke out over him, and stood in beads on his forehead; he started up gasping for air.

"Let me go," he cried out wildly: "let me go!"

Mr. Quinton replaced the velvet covering.

"That is enough for to-day," he said. "I am sufficiently answered. You can see."

Richard hardly knew how he got out of the room, whether it was by Mr. Quinton's dismissal or his own will. Or how long a time elapsed before, finding himself alone, he happened to look at the palm of his right hand, which had felt curiously sticky after contact with Mr. Quinton's. The smear on it was dry and easily effaced by washing, but without doubt what he had touched was blood.

Mr. Quinton seemed to have been in no way affronted by Richard's abrupt withdrawal. He was in a genial mood when he joined the two younger men at dinner, now with his loose wrapping gown put off, and faultlessly attired in evening dress. A handsome man; and Richard noticed that his hands were beautifully shaped and white. But, to the guest's vision, there was one striking peculiarity about his appearance, a peculiarity which seemed to increase as the meal went forward. Perhaps the opening of Richard's clairvoyance, artificially induced some hours before, had not wholly closed. For doubtless what he now perceived, would not have been visible to ordinary sight.

Most of us in these later days have heard of the existence of auras, a species of halo which is supposed to emanate from every mortal, indicative of spiritual values and degrees of power; but it is doubtful whether our backwoodsman was aware. What he saw, however, was an aura, though formed of shadow and not light. It encompassed the seated figure of his host with a surrounding of grey haze, spreading to a yard or more from either shoulder, and equally above the head; not obstructing the view of the room behind him, but dimming it, as might a stretched veil of grey crepe. It was curious to see Peters waiting on him and passing through this, evidently unaware; his hand and the bottle advancing into the full light as he filled Mr. Quinton's glass, and then withdrawing to leave the veil as perfect as before.

Mr. Quinton made an excellent dinner, and chaffed Richard on his want of appetite; he also drank freely of the wines Peters was handing round, and pressed them on his guests. The glasses were particularly elegant, of Venetian pattern, slender stemmed and fragile. Peters had just replenished his master's glass, when Mr. Quinton in the course of argument, lifted and brought it down sharply on the table with the result of breakage. The accident attracted little notice; Peters cleared away the fragments and mopped up the spilt wine, and another glass was set in its place and filled. But as Mr. Quinton raised the fresh glass to his lips, Richard noticed that blood was dripping from his right hand in heavy spots, staining his shirt-cuff and the cloth.

"I am afraid, sir, you have cut yourself," he exclaimed impulsively; and almost at the same instant Peters appeared at his master's elbow offering a dark silk handkerchief.

Mr. Quinton did not answer, but uttered an exclamation of annoyance, and abruptly rose from table and left the room. Lindsay followed him, but presently returned, looking unusually grave. Richard inquired if the out was serious.

"Mr. Quinton did not cut his hand," Lindsay answered. "I am charged to tell you what is the matter. Though it is as far as possible kept secret, he thinks it better you should know."

The gravity of Lindsay's countenance did not relax. He poured out half a glass of wine and drank it, as if to nerve himself for the telling of the tale.

"When I came here as resident doctor eighteen months ago, I heard the story: it was, of course, necessary I should be informed as I had to treat his case. I shall have to go a long way back to make you understand. Lady Anna, Quinton's mother, had twin sons, born shortly after her husband's death. She must have been a strange woman. They were her only children, but almost from infancy she made a difference between them, setting all her affection on Archibald, the elder, and treating the other, Clement, with coldness and every evidence of dislike. Quinton says he can never remember his mother caressing him, or even speaking kindly. He was always the one held to blame for any childish fault or mischief, and pushed into the background, while everything was for Archibald the heir. We cannot wonder that this folly of hers led to bad feeling between the lads. It was active in their school days, though they were educated at different schools, and met only in the holidays. Whenever they met they fought. What the last quarrel was about cannot say, but Archibald was entering an expensive regiment, and the army could not be afforded for Clement, though it was his great desire: he owns to having been very sore. They were in a boat on the lake, and they fought there, and the boat capsized.

"It was said that Archibald hadn't a chance; he had been stunned by a blow on the head, or else had struck his head in falling. They both could swim a little, but he went down like a stone, and Clement reached the shore: the distance could not have been great, nor could one have expected such an accident to result in anything worse than a ducking. The horrible part of it was that Lady Anna saw what happened from her window in the bow room."

"Ah—!"

"Yes, the room you had, and where you were disturbed last night. She saw the fight and, the struggle, and was convinced of Clement's guilt: that he had plotted the occasion and killed Archibald, so that he might take his place. She wanted to have the boy tried for murder; ay, and would have had her way, had it not been for her brother, Lord Pengwyn, who was guardian to both the lads. He got the thing passed over as an accident, as no doubt it was. But the point I am coming to, though I've been long about it, is this. When Clement was drawn from the water, and brought in, sick and dazed, Lady Anna met him in a fury of passion. He was Cain over again, the first murderer who slew his brother: I wonder, did Eve do the like! 'Your brother's blood,' she said, 'will be upon your hands forever.' Quinton says he would not have cared, after that, if they had hung him then and there. He had an illness, and the palms of his hands began to bleed—from the pores as it were, without a wound—and they have continued to bleed at intervals from that day to this. You saw what happened to-night."

"It sounds like a miracle. Is there no cure?"

"Everything has been tried—styptics, hypnotism even. Sometimes the symptom remits for two or three weeks, and the bleeding is generally early in the day; he thought himself safe this evening. Miracle? no, unless the power of the mind over the body is held to be miraculous. You have read of the stigmatists—women, ay and men too—on whom the wounds of Christ have broken out, to bleed always on Fridays?"

"I have heard of them—certainly. But I set it down as a fraud— a monkish trick."

"It is as well vouched for as any other physical phenomenon. And this case of Quinton's is nearly allied, though horror created it in his case, and not saintly adoration. It has spoiled his life; for over thirty years he has been an invalid, and will so continue to the end. His aberration of mind has all arisen from this root: his queer fancies about Cain and Pan, blood-sacrifices to Pagan gods— satyrs and fauns and hobgoblins, and I know not what!"

"You speak of aberration, and yet assert that he is sane?

"He is sane enough for all practical purposes—a good man of business even, with a sharp eye to the main chance. Take him apart from these cranks of his, I like him—I can't help liking him. You'll like him too, when you know him better. You have seen the least attractive side of him, coming down like this, with the misgiving he is driving you into a corner. I'd have you stand up to him and speak your mind about what you will and will not do. And I believe he will hear reason in the end."

NEXT MORNING'S POST brought Richard a letter, forwarded on from London: a notice requiring his appearance before a certain Medical Board, and obliging his return to town. He sent a message to Mr. Quinton by Lindsay, explaining his abrupt departure, but saying he was willing to return if desired. The reply message requested an interview, in the same upstairs room as before.

It proved to be a long one. Lindsay, waiting in the hall for the car to come round, wondered what was the delay, and what was passing between the two. At last a door in the upper regions opened and shut, and Richard came down the stairs. He was white as chalk, staggering like a man dizzy or blind, and a cold sweat stood in beads on his forehead, as happened after the scrying of the day before. Lindsay sprang forward to meet him, and propped him with a hand under his arm. He leaned against the wall, and gasped out:

"It's all over—I've refused—you were right to refuse too. The thing he asks is impossible. This house is full of devils—of devils, I tell you—and they come out of Quinton's crystal. He made me look again—against my will, and I saw—what I can't speak of—what I never can forget—!"

"Come into the dining-room with me, and I'll give you a dram. You have been upset; you may think differently when you are calm."

"No—no. Never this place for me. He is beyond reason: he is given over to the fiend. I told him I would thank him for ever for just Quinton Court and a farm, but he would not part the property. It had to be all or nothing. And not even to gain Quinton Court would I be owner here. No, I'll have no dram. I want to get away."

The car was now heard coming round, and drawing up at the door.

"Goodbye, Lindsay, and thank you for your kindness. We may never meet again, but I shall not forget."

These were last words, and the next moment he was shut in and speeding away, the open gates with their watchful faces left behind.

V

RICHARD REACHED LONDON only to fall ill. The doctor diagnosed influenza, but seemed to think his system had received a shock: as to this he was not communicative. He had a week in bed, and another of tardy convalescence, a prey to depression and all the ills resulting from exhaustion. A fortnight had gone by in he left Mount Verney, when he received a communication from Fryer and Fryer asking for an interview. Mr. Fryer wished to see Mr. Richard Quinton on a matter of business, and would be obliged if he could make it convenient to call.

"I ought to have written to the old bird, to tell him I am out of the running," was Richard's comment, spoken to himself. "But, as I have been remiss, I had better go and hear what he has to say. I shall have to take a taxi."

He had no strength left for the walking distance, and even the office stairs were something of a trial. He was shown in at once to Mr. Fryer, and began with an apology.

"I have only just ascertained your address," said the man of law. "Are you aware, Mr. Quinton, that your cousin and late host is dead?"

"Indeed no, sir, I was not aware." And that Richard was shocked by the intelligence was plain to see.

"He died suddenly of heart-failure the night after you left. And, so far as Dr. Lindsay and I can ascertain after a careful search through all his papers, he has left no will."

This communication did not seem to inform Richard; he was still too dazed by what he had just heard.

Mr. Fryer tapped the blotting-pad before him, which was a way he had when irritated.

"You don't realise what that means? The whole property goes to you, both real estate and personal. Mount Verney, and all that it contains."

Richard gave a cry, which sounded more like horror than elation.

"You are telling me—that I am the owner of Mount Verney?"

"If no will is discovered later, certainly you are the owner."

"And does this bind me to live there? Because I cannot—I will not. I told Mr. Quinton so before leaving, and, as he made it a condition, I refused the inheritance."

"So I understand from Dr. Lindsay. No, you are bound to nothing. You can live where you please. And, as soon as the legal processes of succession are gone through, you can sell the property, should you prefer investment abroad."

Richard still sat half-stunned, slowly taking it in. He could rid himself of Mount Verney and all that it contained, and Quinton Court, the home of his desire, would be his own.

"You would have wished, of course, to attend your cousin's funeral, but you had quitted the address left with me, and we were unable to let you know in time. He was cremated, according to his own often expressed desire. There is one thing, Mr. Quinton, I would like to say to you—to suggest, though you may think I am exceeding my province. Your cousin's intestacy benefits you, but there are others who suffer by it. Old Peters, a servant who had been with him from boyhood: he would have been provided for without doubt. Probably there would have been gratuities to the other domestics, according to their length of service; and his resident doctor, Lindsay, would have come in for a legacy. Of course it is quite at your option what to do."

"I will thank you, sir, to put down what you would have advised Mr. Quinton in all these cases, had you prepared his will, and I will make it good."

It was not always easy to divine Mr. Fryer's sentiments, but he seemed to receive the instruction with pleasure. Lawyer and client shook hands, and then Richard was in the street again, hurrying away. O, what a letter—what a letter he would have to write to Nan!

LEGAL PROCESSES TAKE TIME, and summer was waning into autumn before Richard was fully established as owner of the Quinton property. Up to now he had sedulously avoided Mount Verney, though he had been in the near neighbourhood, and had several times visited Quinton Court. He knew only by the agent's report that his orders were carried out, the heads removed from the gate-pillars and the statue from the grove, which was a grove no longer, as the young oaks had been felled and carted away. The Roman relics had been presented to a local museum, and the house was now shut up, and emptied of most of its furniture. Lindsay, at Richard's desire, had chosen such of the plenishings as he cared for and could make useful, receiving these in addition to the money gift advised by Mr. Fryer.

All this was accomplished, the last load removed, and now the big white villa was shut up and vacant, and Clement Quinton's heir was about to enter for the first time as its possessor. But, strange to say, he had elected to make the visit late at night and in secret, so planning his approach across country that his coming and going might be unnoticed and unknown. A thief's visit, one would have said, rather than that of the lawful owner, who could have commanded all.

The latter part of the journey was made on foot, and throughout he carried with him, under his own eye and hand, a large and heavy gladstone-bag. He had studied incendiary methods when serving in France, and materials for swift destruction were contained within.

It was a wild evening; a gale, forestalling the equinox, hurtled overhead, tearing the clouds into shreds as they flew before it, and making clear spaces for some shining of stars. Rain was not yet, though doubtless it would fall presently. The wind would help Richard's purpose, rain would not, though he thought it could hardly defeat it. That intermittent shining of the stars gave little light. The night was very nearly "as dark as hell's mouth," and Richard had much the feeling that he was venturing into the mouth of hell.

It had needed the mustering of a desperate courage, this expedition on which he was bent, but he could entrust his purpose to no other hand. Purification by fire: there could be, it seemed to him, no other cleansing. He intended no oblation to the infernal gods, that was far from his thought: what he dimly designed was a final breaking of their power.

With this purpose in mind he turned into the dark avenue, the shut gates yielding to his hand, between the pillars from which the satyrs' heads were gone. Did faces pry on him from between the close-ranked trees? He would not think of it: and for this night at least he would shut the eyes of his soul, the eyes with which he had perceived before, or he might happen upon something which would make him altogether a coward. In the darkness he left the road more than once, and blundered into the plantation, needing to have recourse to the electric torch in his pocket before he could find the way. But at last he came upon the open sweep of drive, and there was the villa before him, stark and white, eyeless and shuttered, the corpse of a house from which the soul had gone out.

This new owner had been careful to carry with him the keys which admitted. He unlocked a side door and entered, and now the torch was a necessity in the pitch darkness which prevailed within. His first act was to go through the lower rooms, unshuttering and opening everywhere, so as to let in a free draught of air. Here a certain amount of the heavier furniture still remained: Lindsay had been moderate in his selection, though he might, with Richard's approval, have grasped at all. Then he mounted to the attics, opening as he went, and here the incendiary work started. The flames were beginning to creep over the floors and about the back staircase, when he turned his attention to the better apartments on the first floor, entering and igniting one after another. He left Mr. Quinton's private rooms until the last; the rooms where those momentous interviews had taken place, and where the devils had issued from the glass.

The private den had been wholly stripped, both of furniture and books; no doubt Lindsay, who was free to take what he pleased, had valued these mementoes of a patient who was also a friend. Richard was glad to find the apartment empty; there was less to recall the past. But as he moved the illuminating torch from left to right in his survey, it seemed to him for an instant that a tall figure stood before him—long enough to realise its presence, though gone in the space of a couple of agitated heart-beats. He never doubted that it was Quinton, present to reproach him, to arrest the course of destruction if that were possible. But in spite of what he had seen—if indeed he did see—he gritted his teeth and went on.

The inner cabinet was next to enter. Here nothing had been removed or changed; the writing-table in the window still had its equipment of inkpot and blotting-pad, and on the latter, Richard noticed, a sheet of blank paper was spread out. The velvet cover thrown over the high stand, no doubt concealed the uncanny crystal into which he had been forced to look. No one would look into it again after the destruction of this night! And then somehow, he knew not how, his attention was drawn to the white paper on the table.

Most of us have seen the development of a photographic plate, and how magically the image starts into view on a surface which before was blank. That was what appeared to happen under his eyes upon the paper, and the image was the imprint of a large hand, a man's hand, red as if dipped in blood.

The same awful sensation of sick faintness experienced before with the crystal, overcame him once again. It was a marvel to him afterwards that he did not fall unconscious, to perish in the burning house. He saved himself by a desperate effort of will, flinging what was left of his incendiary material behind him on the floor. As he gained the staircase, a rush of air met him from below, and this was perhaps his salvation. But the house was now filling with smoke, and from the upper regions came already the crackle of spreading flame.

The crackle of flame, and something more. Something which sounded like the clatter of hoofs over bare floors, and a cackle of hellish laughter; unless his senses were by this time wholly dazed and confused, hearing bewitched as well as sight. He found the door by which he entered, locked it behind him and fled into the night, now no longer bewilderingly dark, but faintly illuminated by the rising moon.

He did not take the direction of the avenue and the road, but climbed fences and made his way up the hill behind; and when on the wind-swept summit he turned to look back. He had done his work effectually; the white villa was alight in all its windows, fiercely ablaze within, and, as he still lingered and watched, a portion of the roof fell in, and flame and smoke shot up into the sky.

FROM THE LOCAL PAPER of the following Saturday.

> We regret to state that the mansion of Mount Verney, recently the residence of the late Clement Quinton, Esquire, and now the property of Mr. Richard Quinton, was destroyed by fire on Tuesday night. The origin of the fire is wrapped in mystery, as the house was unoccupied and shut up, and the electric light disconnected, so there could have been no fusion of wires. Much valuable property is destroyed, and part of the building is completely gutted. The blaze was first noticed between twelve and one o'clock, by a man driving home late from market. He gave notice to the police, but by the time the fire-engines arrived, the conflagration had taken such hold that it could not be checked, though abundant water was at hand in the Mount Verney lake. The loss to Mr. Richard Quinton will be very considerable, as we understand no part of it is covered by insurance.

FROM THE SAME-PAPER in the following December.

> We understand that a gift has been made to our hospital fund, of the shell of the Mount Verney house with the grounds that surround it, to be converted into a sanatorium for the treatment of tuberculosis, and Mr. Richard Quinton also adds to the subscription list the sum of £1,000. This munificent donation of

money and a site, will enable the work to be put in hand at once; and it is believed that what is left of the original mansion can be incorporated in the scheme.

The Mount Verney house, which, as will be remembered, was destroyed by a disastrous fire about three months ago, was not insured, and Mr. Richard Quinton had no wish to rebuild for his own occupation. He will, we understand, make his future residence at Quinton Court, the ancestral home of his family, so soon as he returns from Canada with his bride.

ANNE'S LITTLE GHOST

WE HAD PLANNED to take a holiday as soon as I was demobilised, and I claim that we had abundantly earned it, Anne and I. She had been a war worker all the time I was serving abroad—(for there were, alas! no children to tie her to the duties of home)—and she needed relief and change as much as I. It was to be a real holiday and in full measure—no wretched scrap measured by days, but lasting several weeks, and at our own option to extend into months if we so pleased. This gave a peculiar feeling of wealth and spaciousness; for once we were to be millionaires in the holiday line. But from the £.s.d. point of view, a quite separate matter, the holiday was bound to be cheap. So Anne decreed, and I left it to her to arrange what it should be, and where.

She was in high spirits the last time she came to see me in hospital, about a week before my discharge. She had heard of the very place for us, if I agreed—and of course I was ready to agree. Her friend Adelaide Sherwood recommended Deepdene, but there was no time to be lost; we must write or wire at once if we wanted to secure the rooms. Farmhouse lodgings in Devonshire; would not that be delightful?—with trout-fishing for me thrown in, and the sea not many miles away. It was really half a house, and the farm-mistress would board and cook for us: we could either bring a servant (we did not possess one) or a day-woman would come in from the village to order the rooms. Some friends of Miss Sherwood's had stayed there the previous autumn, and were abundantly satisfied

277

with everything, cleanliness included; the charge was, besides, astonishingly low.

"Just think, Godfrey, of getting the farm produce fresh on the spot—eggs and vegetables, to say nothing of dairy luxuries beyond. And in such pretty country as they say it is. I cannot fancy getting tired of the quiet, but perhaps you may feel differently. A large sitting-room with glass doors on to a verandah, and such a view from it; the farm-buildings quite away on the other side. The bed-room is on the same floor: that will be right for your lame leg, will it not? And then upstairs two more bedrooms, roomy attics. We shall not need to use these, but they are part of the half house, and are let with it. What do you say?"

A prompt telegram secured us the tenancy of the half-house, and a week later Anne and I were *en route* for our new abode. We took the journey leisurely—a fit prelude to a holiday which was to be all leisure—and stayed a couple of nights at Exeter on our way. So the journey of the last morning was a short one. We arrived at our destination soon after noon, to find all gilded with the cheer of mid-day sunshine, and a white-aproned landlady hospitably welcoming us at the door.

The house was neither picturesque nor old, but it promised comfort, and seemed likely to justify the encomiums of Anne's friend and correspondent. Mrs. Stokes the landlady was openly proud of it, and showed us round expecting appreciation. The kitchen and offices occupied the lower floor, but we had a separate entrance through the garden wicket up steps to the verandah, our private portion of it, which was cut off from the other set of lodgings by a light railing thrown across. This second set was at present vacant, but would be occupied in another fortnight by two ladies, sisters, who came always at this time of year, bringing with them their own maid.

The attic rooms were also shown, though we were not intending to occupy them. My lame leg excused me from a further mounting of stairs, but Anne accompanied Mrs. Stokes aloft. The occupiers of both sets had an equal right to these stairs, and the attic accommodation was impartially divided, two falling to our lot, and two to that of the sisters and their servant.

They were airy rooms, Anne told me, and would make pleasant bedrooms, looking out through smaller windows on the same lovely view that we commanded on the lower floor. This was all that was said at the time, but later, when tea was spread and we were partaking of it, she told me more.

"People must have been here with children," she said presently in an interval of filling my cup. "The attic over our bedroom has evidently been used as a nursery, for there are coloured pictures pasted on the wall, and a child's bed is pushed into one corner. Mrs. Stokes said she would take it out if it was in our way."

There was just the slightest sigh with this communication, and the least possible droop at the corners of Anne's sensitive mouth, but enough to give me a clue to what was in her mind. I can often read Anne's mind as plainly as the page of a book—though I do not tell her so; perhaps because of long association, to say nothing of affection. We two are singularly alone in the world, and so are drawn all the closer, each to each. We have been married rather more than eight years, and in our second year together we possessed, for a brief space of only weeks, a baby daughter. So brief a space that one might suppose both joy and grief would be easily forgotten; but those who so think, know little of a mother's heart— at least, little of Anne's. From the dear memory of that joy and that grief (the sword piercing her soul, as was foretold of another mother) comes the wistful interest she takes in all children. And I could divine her thought: "If only little Clarice had lived and had been with us here, the pictured attic would have been her nursery, and the little bed in the corner would have been ready made for her." But of this I said nothing.

"Perhaps Mrs. Stokes's own children sleep there when they are without lodgers," I suggested, but Anne shook her head.

"No, for I asked the question. They have only three big boys, all in their teens. The eldest works on the farm, and the other two are away at school. None of the Stokes family sleep under this roof;

a stable is converted into quarters for them, so that the house may be set apart as lodgings"; and again there came the slight and smothered sigh.

I should be giving a false impression if it were thought from this that there is anything dreary about Anne. No one is more resolutely cheerful, or more keenly and alertly practical, than this wife of mine. These inner feelings of hers, tender regrets and constant thoughts, have their own secret chamber in her mind, the door of which is shut and barred; a sacred threshold, which even I dare not openly approach. No more was said about the empty cot and the pictures, and that first evening of our stay at Deepdene passed delightfully amid country sights and sounds, and the sweet Devonshire air. Miss Sherwood's recommendation was, we thought, justifying itself to the full.

And at night, when the veil of dimness, not quite darkness, was drawn over the garden and the hills, what a healing silence prevailed: bird notes stilled, and at last even the plaintive cry of a lamb which had wandered from its mother, satisfied and at rest. I slept profoundly, but presently what was this? Anne's voice: Anne shaking me awake.

"Godfrey! Godfrey, listen! Do you hear?"

I was for the moment deaf and dazed with sleep.

"No," I said. "What is it? What is the matter?"

"It is a child sobbing. A little child in trouble. A child that has been shut out. I cannot hear it and do nothing. Can you?" Anne was thrusting her feet into slippers, and was already arrayed in her dressing-gown—blue and white, the colours of the Virgin Mother. "I can't make out where the sound comes from—whether it is overhead or out of doors. Listen, and you will hear it too. There are no words, only cries and sobs. I heard it again the instant before you awoke."

I was out of bed by this time and broad awake. I heard no crying, but I did hear footsteps: a child's pattering run across the floor overhead, once from end to end of the room, and then again in return.

"Now I know," said Anne, quite composedly, proceeding to light a candle. "It is upstairs in the attic I told you of; the room like a nursery, which is over ours. I wonder what child it can be. Mrs. Stokes should have let us know. I am going up to see."

That was so entirely Anne-like I was not surprised. She went out carrying the light, and I followed on to the landing in case I should be wanted. As I went, I heard again the pattering feet overhead, and I think Anne heard them too. I waited at, the foot of the stairs, not wishing to affright the child by the sight of a grim soldier-man in pyjamas. No child, not even the most nervous, could be frightened at the sight of Anne.

Waiting there, I could be certain that no living soul came down the stairs. I heard Anne pass from room to room, and then she called to me.

"Godfrey, I wish you would come up here."

I went up in the soft twilight that was not wholly dark, even in that enclosed place, entering where I saw her candle shine. She was in the attic with the pictured walls, sitting on the little bed, and her face was white and awe-stricken.

"I can't find anything," she said. "The rooms are all empty, and there is no place in which a child could be shut. I wish you would look too."

Of course I looked with her, and, equally of course, our search was fruitless. Then I persuaded her to go back to our room and listen there, while I hurried on some clothes and made search round the house outside. I talked some nonsense about the way in which sounds reflect and echo, and the difficulty there is about locating their direction, especially at night; but I do not think she believed me: unconvinced myself, I could hardly expect to convince another. And I was privately certain I had heard the footsteps of a child, not echoed, over floors from a distance, but distinctly overhead. There must be some way of getting up to those attics, and down from them, that we did not know.

But in the morning Mrs. Stokes could tell us nothing, and had no explanation to offer. No child could have got in without her knowledge. It must have been one out of the village wandering round outside, scared by the darkness, and afraid to go home because it had been threatened with the stick. That was how the good dame dismissed the matter, and we might have been satisfied about the crying, but not as to those footsteps overhead.

It will be well believed that I was eager to sample the fishing, and the next day saw us on the banks of the stream, Anne sitting near me with a book. But somehow in the week following she managed to catch cold, and after that I had for a while to pursue my sport alone, and she spent solitary hours at the Deepdene farm.

I think it was on the second day of her seclusion that she said to me when I came back in the evening: "I have seen the child."

I had better mention here that in the interval we had heard no more of the sobbing voice at night, nor of the footsteps overhead. Anne looked as if something had moved her profoundly, even to the shedding of tears.

"Did you find out whose child it is, and why it is here?"

"No. She did not speak, and it seems so odd that Mrs. Stokes does not know. I was on the landing when I saw her first, and she was running upstairs. There is no carpet on those stairs, and I heard quite plainly the patter of her feet. A little girl. I went up after her, and she ran straight into that room which was a nursery, the room with the pictures."

"And you followed?"

"Yes, I followed, but she was not there. I was puzzled—almost frightened, and went back again to the sitting-room. I think it must have been half an hour later when I saw her again. If you remember, it began to rain. It was so chilly, I was obliged to shut the glass doors."

"Yes?" I said. Anne had paused again, with that odd breathlessness which was new.

"She was out there on the verandah, and the rain was slanting in upon her. Such a pretty little girl, and about the age—" (I knew what Anne so nearly said, and why she checked herself and altered the phrase to "about six years old." Clarice would have been six years old had she lived.) "Not a poor woman's child. She had a pretty white frock on, worked cambric and lace, and a silk sash of a sort of geranium red. No cottagers child would be dressed so. And she had such an appealing little face, as if she was longing to be sheltered and comforted. It was raining, you know, all the time."

"And what did you do?"

"Why of course I opened the window. I said, 'Come in my dear, you will get wet.' I held out my hand and she put hers into it—oh, such a cold little hand, as cold and soft as snow. I can feel the touch of it still. I drew her into the room. 'We should be warm in here,' I said. No, I'm not crying, Godfrey; not really crying; but there was something in her face that touched me: a sort of surprise, as if no one had ever welcomed or been kind to her before. I asked her where she lived, but she only made a sign and put a finger to her lips. She heard me—I am sure she heard me, but I cannot help fancying the poor child is dumb.

"She heard me, for when I said, 'My darling, will you give me a kiss?' she put up both her little arms, and her face was close to mine. I would have had that kiss, only just then that tiresome Mrs. Stokes knocked at the door; the butcher, it seemed, had called, and she wanted to know if we would take a joint. The instant there came the knock, the child slipped away out of my arms. I had left the window open behind us, and she was gone."

"Mrs. Stokes did not see her?"

"No. She saw nothing, and could tell nothing; only I thought she looked a little odd when I was putting questions. I couldn't help wondering if there was any secret about it which she was bound to keep."

As the days went on, I began also to wonder this, and after a while that wonder shaped itself into action. But I anticipate.

That night we heard again the footsteps overhead, both of us heard them. It was still completely dark, and the rain, driven against our windows, was mixed with hail. The pattering steps crossed the floor above once, twice, and after an interval a third time. I was still awake, holding my breath to listen should they come again, when I heard another sound beside me. Anne was crying, very quietly, her face buried in the pillow so that all sound should be hushed. I put out my hand to touch her.

"What is the matter?"

"Oh Godfrey—oh Godfrey, that poor child," she sobbed. "It is so sad for her to be up there all alone in the cold and darkness, and only six years old. Six years old! Clarice would have been just that age. Can it be Clarice trying to come back to us? I felt as if she were Clarice when I held her in my arms."

I was not surprised. It was as if I had seen the thought taking shape, somehow as crystals form. But what could I do but dub it foolishness, born out of the sweet fond folly of a mother's love?

We heard no more that night. Next morning, without telling Anne of my intention, I went up to examine the attics for the first time by daylight. The rooms over ours were vacant, and in the one with pictured walls the little bed was gaunt and undraped, with its stripped mattress and uncovered pillow. There was no closet or recess in which it was possible for even the smallest child to hide, and as the walls were of thin modern building, secret entrances and passages were out of the question here.

I was to hear again later of that little bed. Nothing more passed between us touching that strange fancy of Anne's, the confession I had surprised from her in the night, until she said in a sort of shamefaced fashion (but again there were tears in her eyes)

"I made a pretence to Mrs. Stokes to-day; I hope it was not untrue enough to be wrong. I said we might be expecting a child visitor: we might expect any visitors you know, and some of our friends have children. And I asked her to have the pictured attic put ready, and the bed made up—in case. She did it this morning, and I did not want you to go up there and be surprised. It does not look nearly so miserable now the furniture is in order, and sheets and blankets are on the little bed. Any one who was up there in the night, and who was cold and tired, could lie down."

What was I to say to this, but again that it was folly?—but I could not charge Anne with folly when she looked as she did then. And hardly a night passed without the pattering footsteps overhead.

The parish to which Deepdene belonged was a scattered one; the church was a long half-mile away, and a mere cluster of cottages called itself the village. That cluster, however, contained the post-office, and the inevitable general shop, which included among its wares a few toys of the simpler sort. One day Anne returned from a post-office errand the purchaser of a doll, pretty of head and face, but with its nudity barely covered by a scant chemise of waxed muslin. She said nothing of her intention, but for a day or two that doll lay about in our sitting-room, while her skilful fingers were busied shaping for it more befitting garments—pink and frilly, and with a pinafore of lace. Then it disappeared, but I did not remark, nor for a while did she explain, not until I asked her a week later if she had seen the child again.

"She often comes when I am alone, peeping in at me from the verandah," was the answer. "And she was pleased when I gave her the doll. She took it from me and kissed me, but still she does not speak."

She took the doll! With this the mystery grew. How could an immaterial creature, one we dimly guessed to be spirit and not flesh; accept a material gift, removing it when she withdrew? Yet, Anne had given her the toy in exchange for a kiss, and the doll was certainly gone.

Next day when I came in from the stream, Anne was out, and some impulse urged me to go up again to the attic, the attic prepared for our supposed guests, which no one had arrived to occupy. It was vacant as before, but a couple of small vases held fresh flowers, of Anne's filling doubtless, and on the white pillow of the little bed there lay the pink-frocked doll.

I was beginning to be anxious about Anne. There was a change in her I did not like to see; a feverish spot on her cheek, and, slight as she was before, she had fallen away in the few weeks of our sojourn to be very thin. She laughed over it herself, and said her gowns must be taken in; but to me it seemed no laughing matter. Was vitality being drawn from her for the shaping of the child apparition in material form; and, if so, what would be the effect upon her health? I am not instructed in such matters, but I vaguely recalled some of the explanations put forward—material forms built up from the medium, and life-substance drawn away. Ought I to make some excuse, and cut short our stay at Deepdene? That was one question, but another followed it. Now that she fancied the appearance might be that of her dead baby, our little Clarice, would Anne be content to go?

Our little Clarice! Mine as well as hers; the father's tie as valid surely as the mother's, if not so close and fond. If to one of us, why not to both? But in the end I could no longer say this. Though only once, she was visible to me too.

Was it a projection from Anne's mind influencing mine? I have wondered since; but these are questions I can only indicate: they are beyond my power to answer.

We were sitting in the early twilight, the lamp unlit, as Anne had a headache: her head often ached in these days. The glass doors were open, and I dimly saw, first a glimpse of white on the verandah, misty and indefinite, which presently resolved itself into the figure Anne had described to me—the dainty figure of a girl-child in white frock and red silk sash, a cloud of dusky hair hanging about her little head. She was peeping in at me and drawing back; then with more confidence peeping again. Anne took no notice; she was, I think, asleep. I remained motionless, scarcely daring to breathe, lest I should startle this exquisite small creature, as one might fear to affright a bird. Presently she ventured as far into the room as where Anne was sitting, and stood resting her little elbows on her friend's knee, and looking me straight in the face.

I was able now to understand Anne's meaning about the child's pathetic eyes with their wistfulness of appeal, and also to appreciate something more: something that Anne herself had not noticed, was not likely to notice, as people seldom see likenesses to themselves. It was very marked—the eyes, the brow, the hair: here was Anne as she must have been a quarter of a century ago. Could I doubt that it was our child; and did a longing for the earthly parents' love draw her down to us, away from her safe and happy cradling in the satisfaction of Heaven?

I was still gazing when my wife moved and sighed, waking from her sleep; and the childish figure was gone in a flash, too abrupt for any real withdrawal. In spite of the evidence of those material-sounding footsteps—in spite of the handling of the doll—I never again thought of her as compacted of ordinary mundane flesh and blood.

I had seen her with my own eyes, and I could no longer doubt. But there was a point which I still desired to probe, despite that evidence of the resemblance. I wanted to find out whether the half-house we were renting could be haunted, and whether the child-ghost had been seen or heard by other people than ourselves.

It would be a difficult matter to ascertain, for in defence of their property against depreciation, very good people have before now thought it hardly a sin to pervert the truth. But I reflected that the clergyman of the parish had no interest in letting Deepdene. I would go in the first place to him, and then see what I could make of sounding Mrs. Stokes.

My errand to Mr. Fielding bore only negative fruit. He was a man advanced in years, a gentleman and a scholar, and he received me with suave politeness; if he could serve me in any way he would be glad. But when I put my question, I could see that a faint flicker of amusement underlay his grave attention; he, the minister of the Unseen, was wholly sceptical as to its demonstration. I said very little, merely asking did the house where we were lodging bear the reputation of being haunted? We—I, that is, for I left Anne out of it—had heard sounds that could not be explained, and seen a small figure that appeared to vanish. I should like to know whether it was a matter of common report.

The answer to this was No. There might be some vulgar story of the sort, it was just possible, but it had never reached his ears. Had it done so, he would have discredited it. I would readily see on reflection how easy it was to mistake sounds and their origin; and not only did our ears trick us in such matters, but also our vision. A supposed phantom generally meant that the percipient would do well to resort to an oculist.

I did not argue the point. As I told him, I only wished to ascertain whether there was, or was not, any local tradition. I wished him good morning, and my next resort was to Mrs. Stokes.

Here I was met by indignation, and the good woman was not easy to appease. I was interested, I told her, I was not objecting; rather than otherwise, it increased my interest in Deepdene. I only wished to know if any of the other lodgers—and doubtless in the course of the year she would have many—had mentioned to her any similar sights or sounds.

Her first answer was a flat negative; but there was, I thought, an uneasy consciousness in the eye that did not meet mine as before, and presently modification came. For her own part she knew nothing, as she never slept in the house herself, nor did Stokes *père*, nor the boys—(was this, it occurred to me to wonder, a suspicious circumstance?) She had never seen or heard anything "worse than herself," and I might take that as on her Bible oath; but, now she came to think, some of the lodgers had mentioned a running about on those upper floors, happening when they had the rats in at threshing time. They got some virus when they heard of it, and there were no more complaints after that was put down. If I had been disturbed, no doubt the rats were getting in again. But, certain sure, there were no ghosts.

I wondered, and I wonder still, whether some houses have a psychical atmosphere which can be variously moulded and used; the child employing it to approach us, and the spiritual environment of others putting it to a quite separate use. I think this is not impossible, but as to the truth of the matter, who can say?

As I have shown, I gained nothing by my inquiries, and this is nearly all I have to tell. The end of our sojourn followed quickly. I remember once discussing psychical matters with a friend. He was a believer, and he said to me: "I always know how to distinguish a true ghost-story from a faked one. The true ghost-story never has any point, and the faked one dare not leave it out." This ghost-story of mine, though not faked, has a point, but it is one the ordinary reader would overlook, and I do not insist on it. I am abundantly content to be disbelieved, and Anne is content too.

It was Anne's health which brought our stay at Deepdene to an abrupt close. I think I have said that for some time I had noticed she was looking ill, and wondered vaguely whether her vitality could be drained away to supply material for those manifestations we had witnessed and heard. It was, however, no case of gradually lessened strength, but a threatened crisis which demanded prompt attention—surgeon's investigation and a nursing-home. So, in figurative language, we struck our tents, seeking another encampment, and Deepdene knew us no more.

OVER THE WIRES

ERNEST CARRINGTON, captain in the "Old Contemptibles," was in England on his first leave from the front. There he had a special errand, hoping to trace a family of the name of Regnier, which had been swept away in the exodus from Belgium, then of recent date. Two old people, brother and sister, harmless folk who had shown him the kindest hospitality before their home was wrecked and burned; and with them their niece Isabeau, who was his chosen love and his betrothed wife. He had endured agonies in these last weeks, receiving no news of them, though he fully believed they had escaped to England: it was more than strange that Isabeau did not write, as she knew his address, though he was ignorant of hers.

A friend in London had made inquiry for him where the thronging refugees were registered and their needs dealt with, but nothing seemed to be known of the Regniers. Now he would be on the spot, and could himself besiege the authorities. Hay might have been lukewarm over the quest, but it seemed impossible that he, Carrington, could fail. His friend Hay, with whom he was to have stayed, had just been transferred from Middlesex to the coast defence of Scotland, but had placed at Carrington's disposal his small flat, and the old family servant who was caretaker.

The flat was a plain little place, but it seemed luxurious indeed to Carrington that first evening, in sharp contrast to his recent experiences roughing it in the campaign. His brain was still in a whirl after the hurried journey, and it was too late to embark upon his quest that night; but the next morning, the very next morning, he would begin the search for Isabeau.

Only one item in Hay's room demands description. There was telephone installation in one corner; and twice while Carrington's dinner was being served, there came upon it a sharp summons, answered first by the servant, and secondly by himself. Major Hay was wanted, and it had to be detailed how Major Hay had departed upon sudden orders for Scotland only that morning.

Now the meal was over and cleared away, and the outer door closed, shutting Carrington in for the night. Left alone, his thoughts returned to the channel in which they had flowed for many days and nights. Isabeau—his Isabeau: did the living world still hold his lost treasure, and under what conditions and where? And— maddening reflection—what might she not have suffered of privation, outrage, while he was held apart by his soldier's duty, ignorant, impotent to succour! He could picture her as at their last meeting when they exchanged tokens, the light in her eyes, the sweetness of her lips: the image was perfect before him, down to every fold of her white dress, and every ripple of her hair. His own then, pledged to him, and now vanished into blank invisibility and silence. What could have happened: what dread calamity had torn her from him? Terrible as knowledge might be when gained, it was his earnest prayer that he might know.

A groan burst from his lips, and he cried out her name in a passion of appeal.

"Isabeau, where are you? Speak to me, dead or alive!"

Was it in answer that the telephone call began to ring?—not sharply and loudly, like those demands for Major Hay, but thin and faint like their echo. But without doubt it rang, and Carrington turned to the instrument and took down the receiver.

"Yes," he called back. "What is it?"

Great Heaven! it was Isabeau's voice that answered, a voice he could but just hear, as it seemed to be speaking from far away.

"Ernest—Ernest," she cried, "have you forgotten me? I have forgotten many things since I was tortured, but not you—never you."

"I am here, my darling. I have come to England seeking you, with no other thought in mind. Tell me, for God's sake, where I can find you. Can I come to-night?"

There was a pause, and then the remote voice began again, now a little stronger and clearer.

"Ernest—is it really you? I can die happy, now you tell me that you love me still. That is all I wanted, just the assurance. All I may have in this world—now."

"Darling, of course I love you: you are all in all to me. Where are you speaking from? Tell me, and I will come?"

"No, no: it is all I wanted, what you have just said. It will be easy now to die. I could never have looked you in the face again—after— I am not fit. But soon I shall be washed clean. What does it say—washed? And they gave them white robes—!"

The voice failed, dying away, and when Carrington spoke there was no answer. He called to her by name, begging her to say if she was in London or where, but either the connection had been cut off, or she did not hear. Then after an interval he rang up the exchange. Who was it who had just used the line? But the clerk was stupid or sleepy, thought there had been no call, but was only just on after the shift, and could not say.

It was extraordinary, that she could know where he was to be found that night, and call to him. And how was it that the voice had ceased without giving him a clue? But surely, surely, it would come again.

To seek his bed, tired as he was, seemed now to be impossible. He waited in the living-room, sometimes pacing up and down, sometimes sitting moodily, his head bent on his hands: could he rest or sleep when a further call might come, and, if unheard, a chance be lost. And a call did come a couple of hours later; the same thin reedy vibration of the wire. In a moment he was at the instrument, the receiver at his ear, and again it was Isabeau's voice that spoke.

"Ernest, can you hear me? Will you say it over again: say that you love me still, in spite of all?"

"Dearest, I love you with all my heart and soul. And I entreat you to tell me where you are, so that I can find you."

"You will be told—quite soon. They are so kind—the people here, but they want to know my name. I cannot tell them any more than Isabeau; I have forgotten what name came after. What was my name when you knew me?"

"My darling, you were Isabeau Regnier. And you were living at Martel, with your old uncle Antoine Regnier, and his sister, Mademoiselle Elise. Surely you remember!"

"Yes; yes. I remember now. I remember all. I was Isabeau Regnier then, and now I am lost—lost—lost! Poor old uncle Antoine! They set him up against the wall and shot him, because they said he resisted; and they dragged the Tante and me away. But the Tante could not go fast enough to please them. They stabbed her in the back with their bayonets, and left her bleeding and moaning, lying in the road to die. Oh, if only they had killed me too. Don't ask me—never ask me—what they did to me!"

"Do not think of it, Isabeau dearest. Think only that I have come to seek you, and that you are safe in England and will be my wife. But I must know where you are, and when I can come to see you."

"I will tell you some time, but not now. The nurse says I must not go on talking; that I am making myself more ill. She's wrong, for it cannot make me ill to speak to you; but I must do as I am bidden. Tell me that you love me; just once again. That you love what I was: you cannot love what I have become."

"Darling, I loved you then, I love you now, and shall love you always. But tell me—you must tell me where—"

She did not answer. This seemed to be the end, for, though he still watched and listened, the wire did not vibrate again that night, nor for many following hours.

He did not spend those hours in inaction. He was early at the London office, and then took the express to Folkestone, but at neither place was there knowledge of the name of Regnier. Nor had he better fortune at the other seaports, which he visited the day following. But where there had been such thronging numbers, despite the organisation vigilance, was it wonderful that a single name had dropped unnoted? And if what had been told him was correct, about the murder of her uncle and aunt, she must have reached England alone.

His next resort was to a private inquiry office, and there an appointment was arranged for him at three o'clock on Friday afternoon.

He had arrived in London on the Monday, and it was on Monday evening and night that those communications from Isabeau came over the wire. Each of the following nights, Tuesday, Wednesday and Thursday, he had spent in Hay's rooms, but from the installed telephone there was no sound or sign.

No sign came until mid-day on Friday, when he was just debating whether to go out to lunch, or have it brought to him from the service down below. The thin, echo-like call sounded again, and he was at once at the receiver.

"Isabeau! Is it you? Speak!"

"Yes, it is I." It was Isabeau's voice that answered, and yet her voice with a difference: it was firmer and clearer than on Monday night, although remote—so remote!

"Where are you? Tell me, that I may come to you. I am seeking you everywhere."

"I do not know where I am. It is all strange and new. But I rejoice in this: I have left behind what was soiled. I would tell you more, but something stops the words. I want you to do something for me: I have a fancy. You have done much, dear Ernest, but this is one thing more."

"What is it, dearest? You have only to ask."

"Go to the end of this street at two o'clock. That is in an hour from now; and wait there till I pass by. I shall not look as I used to do, but I will give you a flower—"

Here the voice failed; he could scarcely distinguish the last words. Strange, that one thing could be said and not another, never what he craved to know. But in an hour he would see her—speak to her, and their separation would be at an end. Not as she used to look! Did she mean changed by what she had suffered? But not so changed, surely, that he would not know, that she would need to identify herself by the gift of a flower. And was the change she spoke of, of the body or the mind? A chill doubt as to the latter, which had assailed him before, crept over him again. But even if it were so, there would be means of healing. She was ill now, shaken by what she had suffered: with love and care, and returning health, all would be well.

He was punctual at the place of appointment. A draughty corner this street-end; but what did he, campaign-hardened, care for chill winds, or for the flying gusts of rain? The passers-by were few for a London street; but each one was carefully scrutinized and each umbrella looked under—that is, if a woman carried it. There was not one, however, that remotely resembled Isabeau. Taxis went by, now and then horse-drawn vehicles; presently a funeral came up the crossing street. A glass hearse with a coffin in it, probably a woman's coffin by its size. A cross of violets lay upon it within, but a couple of white wreaths had been placed outside, next to the driver's seat. A hired brougham was the only following.

They had done better to put the wreaths under shelter, but perhaps no one was in charge who greatly cared. As the cortege came level with the corner, a sharper gust than before, tore a white spray from the exposed wreath, and whirled it over towards him; it struck him on the chest, and fell on the wet pavement at his feet. He stooped to pick it up: he loved flowers too well to see it trodden in the mud: and as he did so, a great fear for the first time pierced him through. What might it not signify, this funeral flower? But no, death was not possible: scarcely an hour ago he had heard her living voice.

He waited long at the rendezvous, the flower held in his hand, but no one resembling her came by. Then, chilled and dispirited, but still holding the flower, he turned back to his lodging. It was time and over for his appointment at the inquiry office, but the rain had soaked him through, and he must change to a dry coat.

The servant met him as he came in.

"A letter for you, sir. I am sorry for the delay. You should have had it before, but it must have been brushed off the table and not seen. I found it just now on the floor."

Could it be from Isabeau?—but no, the address was not in her writing. Carrington tore it open: it was from the Belgian central office, and bore date two days back.

"We have at last received information respecting Mademoiselle Regnier. A young woman who appeared to have lost her memory, was charitably taken in by Mrs. Duckworth, in whose house she has remained through a recent serious illness, the hospitals being over full. She recovered memory last night, and now declares her name to be Isabeau Regnier, formerly of Martel. Mrs. Duckworth's address is 18, Silkmore Gardens, S. Kensington, and you will doubtless communicate with her."

Here at last was the information so long vainly sought, and it must have been from the Kensington house that Isabeau telephoned, though her voice sounded like a long-distance call. He would go thither at once; his application to the inquiry office was no longer needed: but still there was a chill at his heart as he looked at the white flower. Was some deep-down consciousness aware, in spite of his surface ignorance; and had it begun to whisper of the greater barrier which lay between?

As he approached the house in Silkmore Gardens, he might have noticed that a servant was going from room to room, drawing up blinds that had been lowered. At the door he asked for Mrs. Duckworth.

"I am not sure if my mistress can see you, sir;" was the maid's answer. "She has been very much upset."

"Will you take in my card, and say my business is urgent. I shall be grateful if she will spare me even five minutes. I am a friend of Mademoiselle Regnier's."

Carrington was shown into a sitting-room at the back of the house, with windows to the ground and a vision of greenery beyond. It was not long before Mrs. Duckworth came to him; she wore a black gown, and looked as if she had been weeping.

"You knew Isabeau Regnier," she began with a certain abruptness. "Are you the Ernest of whom she used to speak?"

"I am. She is my affianced wife, so you see I inquire for her by right. I have been searching for her in the utmost distress, and until now in vain. I have but just heard that you out of your charity took her in, also that she has been ill. May I see her now, to-day?"

The lady's eyes filled again with tears, and she shrank back.

"Ah, you do not know what has happened. O, how sad, how dreadful to have to tell you! Isabeau is dead."

"What, just now, within this hour? She was speaking to me on the telephone only at mid-day."

"No—there is some mistake. That is impossible. She died last Tuesday, and was buried this afternoon. Her coffin left the house at a quarter before two, and my husband went with it to the cemetery. I would have gone too, only that I have been ill."

At first he could only repeat her words: "Dead—Tuesday—Isabeau dead!" She was frightened by the look of his face—the look of a man who is in close touch with despair.

"Oh, I'm so sorry. Oh do sit down, Mr. Carrington. This has been too much for you."

He sank into a chair, and she went hurriedly out, and returned with a glass in her hand.

"Drink this: nay, you must. I am sorry; oh, I am sorry. I wish my husband were here; he would tell you all about it better than I. It has been a grief to us all, to every one in the house; we all grew fond of her. And we began quite to hope she would get well. When she came to us her memory was a blank, except for the wrong that had been done her. That seemed to have blotted out all that was behind, except her love for Ernest—you. But she said she could never look Ernest in the face again, and she wanted to be lost. She took an interest in things here after a while, and she was kind and helpful, like a daughter in the house—we have no children. And then her illness came on again; it was something the matter with the brain, caused by the shock she had sustained. She was very ill, but we could not get her into any hospital, all were too full. But she had every care with us, you may be sure of that, and I think she was happier to be here to the last. So it went on, up and down, sometimes a little better, sometimes worse. Last Monday evening delirium set in. She fancied Ernest was here—you—and she was talking to you all the time. It was as if she heard you answering."

"Have you a telephone installed? Could she get up and go to the telephone?"

"We have a telephone—yes, certainly. But she had not strength enough to leave her bed, and the installation is downstairs in the study."

"I declare to you on my most solemn word that she spoke to me over the telephone—twice on Monday night, and once to-day. It is beyond comprehension. Can you tell me what she said, speaking as she thought to Ernest?"

"She asked you to remind her of her forgotten name. We did not get Regnier till then, nor Martel where she lived; it was as if she heard the words spoken by you. I wrote at once to the organising people to say we had found out: I had no idea then that her death was so near. With the recollection of her name came back—horrors, and she was telling them to you. It seems she lived with an old uncle and aunt: would that be right for the girl you knew? They shot her uncle, the Germans did, when they burnt the house, and stabbed her poor old aunt and left her to die. I can show you a photograph of Isabeau, if that will help to identify. It is only an amateur snapshot, taken in our garden, at the time she was so much better, and, we hoped, recovering. It is very like her as she was then."

Mrs. Duckworth opened the drawer of a cabinet, and took out a small square photograph of a girl in a white dress sitting under a tree, and looking out of the picture with sad appealing eyes.

Carrington looked at it, and at first he could not speak. Presently he said, answering a question of Mrs. Duckworth's:

"Yes, there can be no doubt."

He had heard enough. Mrs. Duckworth would fain have asked further about the marvel of the voice, but he got up to take leave.

"I will come again if you will permit," he said. "Another day I shall be able to thank you better for all you did for her—for all your kindness. You will then tell me where she is laid, and let me take on myself—all expense. Now I must be alone."

There was ready sympathy in the little woman's face; tears were running down, though her words of response were few. Carrington still held the photograph.

"May I take this?" he said, and she gave an immediate assent. Then he pressed the hand she held out in farewell, and in another moment was gone.

THE SEQUEL TO THIS EPISODE is unknown. Carrington sat long that night with the picture before him, the pathetic little picture of his lost love; and cried aloud to her in his solitude: "Isabeau, speak to me, come to me. Death did not make it impossible before: why should it now? Do not think I would shrink from you or fear you. Nothing is in my heart but a great longing—a great love—a great pity. Speak again—speak!"

But no answer came. The telephone in the corner remained silent, and that curious far-off tremor of the wire sounded for him no more.

A WATER WITCH

I

WE WERE DISAPPOINTED when Robert married. We had for long wanted him to marry, as he is our only brother and head of the family since my father died, as well as of the business firm; but we should have liked his wife to be a different sort of person. We, his sisters, could have chosen much better for him than he did for himself. Indeed we had our eye on just the right girl—bright-tempered and sensibly brought up, who would not have said No: of that I am assured, had Robert on his side shown signs of liking. But he took a holiday abroad the spring of 1912, and the next thing we heard was that he had made up his mind to marry Frederica. Frederica, indeed! We Larcombs have been plain Susans and Annes and Marys and Elizabeths for generations (I am Mary), and the fantastic name was an annoyance. The wedding took place at Mentone in a great hurry, because the stepmother was marrying again, and Frederica was unhappy: Was not that weak of Robert?—he did not give himself time to think. We may perhaps take that as some excuse for a departure from Larcomb traditions: on consideration, the match would very likely have been broken off.

Frederica had some money of her own, though not much: all the Larcomb brides have had money up to now. And her dead father was a General and a K.C.B., which did not look amiss in the announcement; but there our satisfaction ended. He brought her to make our acquaintance three weeks after the marriage, a delicate little shrinking thing well matched to her fanciful name, and

300

desperately afraid of mother and of us girls, so the introductory visit was hardly a success. Then Robert took her off to London, and when the baby was born—a son, but too weakly to live beyond a day or two—she had a severe illness, and was slow in recovering strength. And there is little doubt that by this time he was conscious of having made a mistake.

I used to be his favourite sister, being next to him in age, and when he found himself in a difficulty at Roscawen he appealed to me. Roscawen was a moor Robert had lately rented on the Scotch side of the Border, and we were given to understand that a bracing air, and the complete change of scene, were expected to benefit Frederica, who was pleased by the arrangement. So his letter took me by surprise.

"Dear Mary," he wrote, and, characteristically, he did not beat about the bush. "Pack up your things as soon as you get this, and come off here the day after to-morrow. You will have to travel via York, and I will meet you at Draycott Halt, where the afternoon train stops by signal. Freda is a bit nervous, and doesn't like staying alone here, so I am in a fix. I want you to keep her company the weeks I am at Shepstow. I know you'll do as much as this for— Your affectionate brother, Robert Larcomb."

This abrupt call upon me, making sure of response and help, recalled bygone times when we were much to each other, and Frederica still in the unknown. A bit nervous, was she, and Robert in a fix because of it: here again was evidence of the mistake. It was not very easy then to break off from works and for an indefinite time; but I resolved to satisfy the family curiosity, to say nothing of my own, by doing as I was bid.

When I got out of the train at Draycott Halt, Robert was waiting for me with his car. My luggage was put in at the back, and I mounted to the seat beside him; and again it reminded me of old times, for he seemed genuinely pleased to see me.

"Good girl," he said, "to make no fuss, and come at once."

"We Larcombs are not apt to fuss, are we?"—and as I said this, it occurred, to me that probably he was in these days well acquainted with fuss—Frederica's fuss. Then I asked: "What is the matter?"

I only had a sideways glimpse of him as he answered, for he was busy with the driving-gear.

"Why, I told you, didn't I, that it was arranged for me to be here and at Shepstow week and week about, Falkner and I together, for it is better than taking either moor with a single gun. And I can't take Freda there, for the Shepstow cottage has no accommodation for a lady—only the one room that Falkner and I share. Freda is nervous, poor girl, since her illness, and somehow she has taken a dislike to Roscawen. It is nothing but a fancy, of course, but something had to be done."

"Why, you wrote to mother that you had both fallen in love with the place, and thought it quite ideal."

"Oh, the place is right enough, it is just my poor girl's fancy. She'll tell you I daresay, but don't let her dwell on it more than you can help. You will have Falkner's room, and the week he is over here I've arranged for Vickers to put him up, though I daresay he will come in to meals. Vickers?—oh, he's a neighbour on the opposite side of the water, Roscawen Water, the stream that overflows from the lake in the hills. He's a doctor of science as well as medicine, and has written some awfully clever books. I understand he's at work on another, and comes here for the sake of quiet. But he's a very good sort though not a sportsman, does not mind taking in Falkner, and he is by way of being a friend of Freda's—they read Italian together. No, he isn't married, neither is the parson, worse luck; and there isn't another woman of her own sort within miles. It's desperately lonely for her, I allow, when I'm not here. So there was no help for it. I was bound to send for you or for the mater, and I thought you would be best!"

We were passing through wild scenery of barren broken hills, following the course of the river up-stream. It came racing down a rocky course, full and turbulent from recent rains. Presently the road divided, crossing a narrow bridge; and there we came in sight of the leap the water makes over a shelf of rock, plunging into a deep pool below with a swirl of foam and spray. I would have liked to linger and look, but the car carried us forward quickly, allowing only a glimpse in passing. And, directly after, Robert called my attention to a stone-built small house high up on the hill-side—a bare place it looked, flanked by a clump of firs, but with no surrounding garden-ground; the wild moor and the heather came close under the windows.

"That's Roscawen," he said. "Just a shooting-box, you see. A new-built place, raw, with no history behind it later than yesterday. I was in treaty for Corby, seventeenth century that was, with a ghost in the gallery, but the arrangement fell through. And I'm jolly glad it did"—and here he laughed; an uncomfortable laugh, not of the Larcomb sort, or like himself. And in another minute we were at the door.

Freda welcomed me, and I thought her improved; she was indeed pretty—as pretty as such a frail little thing could be, who looked as if a pull of wind would blow her away. She was very well dressed—of course Robert would take care of that—and her one thought appeared to be of him. She was constantly turning to him with appeal of one sort or another, and seemed nervous and ill at ease when he was out of her sight. "Must you really go to-morrow?" I caught her whisper later, and heard his answer: "Needs must, but you will not mind now you have Mary." I could plainly see that she did mind, and that my companionship was no fair exchange for the loss of his. But was not all this exaction the very way to tire out love?

The ground-floor of the house was divided into a sitting-hall, upon which the front door opened without division, and to the right you entered a fair-sized dining-room. Each of these apartments had the offshoot of a smaller room, one being Freda's snuggery, and the other the gun-room where the gentlemen smoked. Above there were two good bedrooms, a dressing-room and a bathroom, but no higher floor: the gable-space was not utilised, and the servants slept over the kitchen at the back. The room allotted to me, from which Captain Falkner had been ejected, had a wide window and a pleasant aspect. As I was hurriedly dressing for dinner, I could hear the murmur of the river close at hand, but the actual water was not visible, as it flowed too far below the overhanging bank.

I could not see the flowing water, but as I glanced from the window, a wreath of white mist or spray floated up from it, stretched itself out before the wind, and disappeared after the fashion of a puff of steam. Probably there was at that point another fall (so I thought) churning the river into foam. But I had no time to waste in speculation, for we Larcombs adhere to the good ways of punctuality. I fastened a final hook and eye, and ran downstairs.

Captain Falkner came to dinner and made a fourth at table, but the fifth place which had been laid remained vacant. The two men were full of plans for the morrow, and there was to be an early setting out: Shepstow, the other moor, was some thirty miles away.

"I am afraid you will be dull, Mary," Robert said to me in a sort of apology. "I am forced to keep the car at Shepstow, as I am my own chauffeur. But you and Freda will have her cart to jog about in, so you will be able to look round the nearer country while I am away. You will have to put up with the old mare. I know you like spirit in a horse, but this quiet gee suits Freda, as she can drive her going alone. Then Vickers will look in on you most days. I do not know what is keeping him away to-night."

Freda was in low spirits next morning, and she hung about Robert up to the time of his departure, in a way that I should have found supremely irritating had I been her husband. And I will not be sure that she did not beg him again not to leave her—to my tender mercies I supposed—though I did not hear the request. When the two men had set out with their guns and baggage, the cart was ordered round, and my sister-in-law took me for a drive.

Robert had done well to prepare me for the "quiet gee": a meek old creature named Grey Madam, that had whitened in the snows of many winters, and expected to progress at a walk whenever the road inclined uphill. And all the roads inclined uphill or down about Roscawen; I do not remember anywhere a level quarter of a mile. It was truly a dull progress, and Freda did not find much to say; perhaps she still was fretting after Robert. But the moors and the swelling hills were beautiful to look at in their crimson flush of heather. "I think Roscawen is lovely," I was prompted to exclaim;

and when she agreed in my admiration I added: "You liked it when you first came here, did you not?"

"Yes, I liked it when first I came," she assented, repeating my words, but did not go on to say why she disliked Roscawen now.

She had an errand to discharge at one of the upland farms which supplied them with milk and butter. She drew rein at the gate, and was about to alight, but the woman of the house came forward, and so I heard what passed. Freda gave her order, and then made an inquiry.

"I hope you have found your young cow, Mrs. Elliott! I was sorry to hear it had strayed."

"We've found her, ma'am, but she was dead in the river, and a sad loss it has been to us. A fine young beast as ever we reared, and coming on with her second calf. My husband has been rarely put about, and I'll own I was fit to cry over her myself. This is the fifth loss we have had within the year—a sheep and two lambs in March, and the cart-foal in July."

Freda expressed sympathy.

"You need better fences, is that it, to keep your cattle from the river?"

Mrs. Elliott pursed up her lips and shook her head.

"I won't say, ma'am, but that our fences might be bettered if the landlord would give us material; as it is, we do our best. But when the creatures take that madness for the water, nought but deer-palings would keep them in. I've seen enough in my time here to be sure of that. What makes it come over them I don't take upon myself to say. They make up fine tales in the district about the white woman, but I know nothing of any white women. I only know that when the madness takes them they make for the river, and then they get swept into the deeps."

When we were driving away, I asked Freda what the farmer's wife meant about a white woman and the drowning of her stock.

"I believe there is some story about a woman who was drowned, whose spirit calls the creatures to the river. If you ask Dr. Vickers he will tell you. He makes a study of folk-lore and local superstitions, and—and that sort of thing. Robert thinks it is all nonsense, and no doubt you will think it nonsense too."

What her own opinion was, Freda did not say. She had a transparent complexion, and a trifling matter made her change colour; a blush rose unaccountably as she answered me, and for a full minute her cheek burned. Why should she blush about Roscawen superstitions and a drowned cow? Then the attention of both of us was suddenly diverted, because Grey Madam took it into her head to shy.

She had mended her pace appreciably since Freda turned her head towards home, trotting now without needing to be urged. We were close upon a cross-roads where three ways met, a triangular green centred by a finger-post. There was in our direction a bank and hedge (hedges here and there replaced the stone walls of the district) and the right wheel went up that bank, giving the cart a dangerous tilt; it recovered balance, however, and went on. Freda, a timid driver, was holding on desperately to the reins.

"Does she often do this sort of thing?" I asked. "I thought Robert said she was quiet."

"So she is—so we thought her. I never knew her do it before," gasped my sister-in-law, still out of breath with her fright.

"And I cannot think what made her shy. There was nothing—absolutely nothing; not even a heap of stones."

Freda did not answer, but I was to hear more about that cross-roads in the course of the day.

II

AFTER LUNCH FREDA DID NOT SEEM willing to go out again, so, as I was there to companion her, we both settled down to needlework and a book for alternate reading aloud. The reading, however, languished; when it came to Freda's turn she tired quickly, lost her place twice and again, and seemed unable to fix her attention on the printed page. Was she listening, I wondered later. When silence fell between us, I became aware of a sound recurring at irregular intervals, the sound of water dropping. I looked up at the ceiling expecting to see a stain of wet, for the drop seemed to fall within the room, and close beside me.

"Do you hear that?" I asked. "Has anything gone wrong in the bathroom, do you think?" For we were in Freda's snuggery, and the bathroom was overhead.

But my suggestion of overflowing taps and broken water-pipes left her cold.

"I don't think it is from the bathroom," she replied. "I hear it often. We cannot find out what it is."

Directly she ceased speaking the drop fell again, apparently between us as we sat, and plump upon the carpet. I looked up at the ceiling again, but Freda did not raise her eyes from her embroidery.

"It is very odd," I remarked, and this time she assented, repeating my words, and I saw a shiver pass over her. "I shall go upstairs to the bathroom," I said decidedly, putting down my work. "I am sure those taps must be wrong."

She did not object, or offer to accompany me, she only shivered again.

"Don't be long away, Mary," she said; and I noticed she had grown pale.

There was nothing wrong with the bathroom, or with any part of the water supply; and when I returned to the snuggery the drip had ceased. The next event was a ring at the door bell, and again Freda changed colour, much as she had done when we were driving. In that quiet place, where corners and goers are few, a visitor is an event. But I think this visitor must have been expected. The servant announced Dr. Vickers.

Freda gave him her hand, and made the necessary introduction. This was the friend Robert said would come often to see us, but he was not at all the snuffy old scientist my fancy had pictured. He was old certainly, if it is a sign of age to be grey-haired, and I daresay there were crowsfeet about those piercing eyes of his; but when you met the eyes, the wrinkles were forgotten. They, at least, were full of youth and fire, and his figure was still upright and flat-shouldered.

We exchanged a few remarks; he asked me if I was familiar with that part of Scotland; and when I answered that I was making its acquaintance for the first time, he praised Roscawen and its neighbourhood. It suited him well, he said, when his object was to seek quiet; and I should find, as he did, that it possessed many attractions. Then he asked me if I was an Italian scholar, and showed a book in his hand, the *Vita Nuova*. Mrs. Larcomb was forgetting her Italian, and he had promised to brush it up for her. So, if I did not find it to great a bore to sit by, he proposed to read aloud. And, should I not know the book, he would give me a sketch of its purport, so that I could follow.

I had, of course, heard of the *Vita Nuova*, who has not! but my knowledge of the language in which it was written went no further than a few modern phrases, of use to a traveler. I disclaimed my ability to follow, and I imagine Dr. Vickers was not ill-pleased to find me ignorant. He took his seat at one end of the Chesterfield sofa, Freda occupying the other, still with that flush on her cheek; and after an observation or two in Italian, he opened his book and began to read.

I imagine he read well. The crisp, flowing syllables sounded very foreign to my ear, and he gave his author the advantage of dramatic expression and emphasis. Now and then he remarked in English on some difficulty in the text, or slipped in a question in Italian which Freda answered, usually by a monosyllable. She kept her eyes fixed upon her work. It was as if she would not look at him, even when he was most impassioned; but I was watching them both, although I never thought—but of course I never thought!

Presently I remembered how time was passing, and the place where letters should be laid ready for the post-bag going out. I had left an unfinished one upstairs, so I slipped away to complete and seal. This done, I re-entered softly (the entrance was behind a screen) and found the Italian lesson over, and a conversation going on in English. Freda was speaking with some animation.

"It cannot any more be called my fancy, for Mary heard it too."

"And you had not told her beforehand? There was no suggestion?"

"I had not said a word to her. Had I, Mary?"—appealing to me as I advanced into sight.

"About what?" I asked, for I had forgotten the water incident.

"About the drops falling. You remarked on them first: I had told you nothing. And you went to look at the taps."

"No, certainly you had not told me. What is the matter? Is there any mystery?"

Dr. Vickers answered:

"The mystery is that Mrs. Larcomb heard these droppings when everyone else was deaf to them. It was supposed to be autosuggestion on her part. You have disproved that, Miss Larcomb, as your ears are open to them too. That will go far to convince your brother; and now we must seriously seek for cause. This Roscawen district has many legends of strange happenings. We do not want to add one more to the list, and give this modern shooting-box the reputation of a haunted house."

"And it would be an odd sort of ghost, would it not—the sound of dropping water! But—you speak of legends of the district; do you know anything of a white woman who is said to drown cattle? Mrs. Elliott mentioned her this morning at the farm, when she told us she had lost her cow in the river."

"Ay, I heard a cow had been found floating dead in the Pool. I am sorry it belonged to the Elliotts. Nobody lives here for long without hearing that story, and, though the wrath of Roscawen is roused against her, I cannot help being sorry for the white woman. She was young and beautiful once, and well-to-do, for she owned land in her own right, and flocks and herds. But she became very unhappy—"

He was speaking to me, but he looked at Freda. She had taken up her work again, but with inexpert hands, dropping first cotton, and then her thimble.

"She was unhappy, because her husband neglected her. He had—other things to attend to, and the charm she once possessed for him was lost and gone. He left her too much alone. She lost her health, they say, through fretting, and so fell into a melancholy way, spending her time in weeping, and in wandering up and down on the banks of Roscawen Water. She may have fallen in by accident, it was not exactly known; but her death was thought to be suicide, and she was buried at the cross-roads."

"That was where Grey Madam shied this morning," Freda put in.

"And—people suppose—that on the other side of death, finding herself lonely, (too guilty, perhaps, for Heaven, but at the same time too innocent for Hell) she wants companions to join her; wants sheep and cows and horses such as used to stock her farms. So she puts madness upon the creatures, and also upon some humans, so that they go down to the river. They see her, so it is said, or they receive a sign which in some way points to the manner of her death. If they see her, she comes for them once, twice, thrice, and the third time they are bound to follow."

This was a gruesome story, I thought as I listened, though not of the sort I could believe. I hoped Freda did not believe it, but of this I was not sure.

"What does she look like?" I asked. "If human beings see her as you say, do they give any account?"

"The story goes that they see foam rising from the water, floating away and dissolving, vaguely in form at first, but afterwards more like the woman she was once; and some say there is a hand that beckons. But I have never seen her, Miss Larcomb, nor spoken to one who has: first hand evidence of this sort is rare, as I daresay you know. So I can tell you no more."

And I was glad there was no more for me to hear, for the story was too tragic for my liking. The happenings of that afternoon left me discomforted—annoyed with Dr. Vickers, which perhaps was unreasonable—with poor Freda, whose fancies had thus proved contagious—annoyed, and here more justly, with myself. Somehow, with such tales going about, Roscawen seemed a far from desirable residence for a nervous invalid; and I was also vaguely conscious of an undercurrent I did not understand. It gave me the feeling you have when you stumble against something unexpected blindfold, or in the dark, and cannot define its shape.

Dr. Vickers accepted a cup of tea when the tray was brought to us, and then he took his departure, which was as well, seeing we had no gentleman at home to entertain him.

"So Larcomb is away again for a whole week? Is that so?" he said to Freda as he made his adieux.

There was no need for the question, I thought impatiently, as he must very well have known when he was required again to put up Captain Falkner.

"Yes, for a whole week," Freda answered, with again that flush on her cheek; and as soon as we were alone she put up her hand, as if the hot colour burned.

III

I DID NOT LIKE DR. VICKERS and his Italian lessons, and I had the impression Freda would have been better pleased by their inter-mission. On the third day she had a headache and charged me to make her excuses, so it fell to me to receive this friend of Robert's, who seemed quite unruffled by her absence. He took advantage of the opportunity to cross-examine me about the water-dropping: had I heard it again since that first occasion, and what explana-tion of the sounds appeared satisfactory to myself?

The fact was, I had heard it again, twice when I was alone in my room, and once more when sitting with Freda. Then we both sat listening—listening, such small nothings as we had to say to each other dying away, waiting to see which of us would first ad-mit it to the other, and this went on for more than an hour. At last Freda broke out into hysterical crying, the result of over-strained nerves, and with her outburst the sounds ceased. I had been in-clined to entertain a notion of the spiritist order, that they might be connected with her presence as medium; but I suppose that must be held disproved, as I also heard them when alone in my own room.

I admitted as little as possible to Dr. Vickers, and was stout in asserting that a natural cause would and must be found, if the ex-planation were diligently sought for. But I confess I was posed when confronted with the fact that these sounds heard by Freda were inaudible to her husband, also present—to Robert, who has excel-lent hearing, in common with all our family. Until I came, and was also an auditor, no one in the house but Freda had noticed the dropping, so there was reason for assuming it to be hallucination. Yes, I was sorry for her trouble (answering a question pressed on me), but I maintained that, pending discovery, the best course was to take no notice of drops that wet nothing and left no stain, and did not proceed from overflowing cisterns or faulty pipes.

"They will leave off doing it if not noticed; is that what you think, Miss Larcomb?" And when I rashly assented—"Now perhaps you will define for me what you mean by *they*? Is it the 'natural cause'?"

Here again was a poser: I had formulated no idea that I cared to define. Probably the visitor divined the subject was unwelcome, for he turned to others, conversing agreeably enough for another quarter of an hour. Then he departed, leaving a message of concern for Freda's headache. He hoped it would have amended by next day, when he would call to inquire.

He did call on the following day, when the Italian lesson was mainly conversational, and I had again a feeling Freda was distressed by what was said, though I could only guess at what passed between them under the disguise of a foreign tongue. But at the end I recognised the words "not to-morrow" as spoken by her, and when some protest appeared to follow, she dumbly shook her head.

Dr. Vickers did not stay on for tea as before. Did Freda think she had offended him, for some time later I noticed she had been crying?

That night I had an odd dream that the Roscawen house was sliding down from its foundations into the river at the call of the white woman, and I woke suddenly with the fright.

The next day was the last of Robert's stay at Shepstow. In the evening he and Captain Falkner returned, and at once a different atmosphere seemed to pervade the house. Freda recovered cheerfulness, I heard no more dropping water, and except at dinner on the second evening we saw nothing of Dr. Vickers. But he sent an Italian book with many scored passages, and a note in it, also in Italian, which I saw her open and read, and then immediately tear up into the minutest pieces. I supposed he wished her to keep up her studies, though the lessons were for a while suspended; I heard him say at dinner that he was busy correcting proofs.

So passed four days out of the seven Robert should have spent at Roscawen. But on the fourth evening came a telegraphic summons: his presence was needed in London, at the office, and he was bound to go up to town by the early express next day. And the arrangement was that in returning he should go straight to Shepstow and join Captain Falkner there; this distant moor was to be reached from a station on another line.

Freda must have known that Robert could not help himself, but it was easy to see how her temporarily restored spirits fell again to zero. I hope I shall never be so dependent on another person's society as she seemed to be on Robert's. I got up to give him his early breakfast, but Freda did not appear; she had a headache, he said, and had passed a restless night. She would not rise till later: perhaps I would go up and see her by-and-bye.

I did go later in the morning, to find her lying like a child that had sobbed itself to sleep, her eyelashes still wet, and a tear sliding down her cheek. So I took a book, and drew a chair to the bedside, waiting for her to wake.

It was a long waiting; she slept on, and slept heavily. And as I sat and watched, there began again the dropping of water, and, for the first time in my experience of them, the drops were wet.

I could find traces now on the carpet of where they fell, and on the spread linen of the sheet; were they made, I wondered fantastically, out of Freda's tears? But they had ceased before she woke, and I did not remark on them to her. Yes, she had a headache, she said, answering my question: it was better, but not gone: she would lie quietly where she was for the present. The servants might bring her a cup of tea when I had luncheon, and she would get up later in the afternoon.

So, as I was not needed, I went out after lunch for a solitary walk. Not being governed by Freda's choice of direction, I determined to explore the course of the river, and especially how it flowed under the steep bank below the house, where I saw the wreath of foam rise in the air on my first evening at Roscawen. I expected to find a fall at this spot, but there was only broken water and rapids, alternating with smoother reaches and deep pools, one of which, I concluded, had been the death-trap of the Elliotts' cow. It was a still, perfect autumn day, warm, but not with the oppression of summer heat, and I walked with enjoyment, following the stream upward to where it issued from the miniature lake among the hills, in which it slept for a while in mid-course. Then I turned homewards, and was within sight of our dwelling when I again beheld the phenomenon of the pillar of foam.

It rose above the rapids, as nearly as I could guess in the same spot as before; and as there was now little or no wind, it did not so quickly spread out and dissipate. I could imagine that at early morning, or in the dimness of evening, it might be taken for a figure of the ghostly sort, especially as, in dissolving, it seemed to move and beckon. I smiled to myself to think that, according to local superstition, I too had seen the white woman; but I felt no least inclination to rush to the river and precipitate myself into its depths. Nor would I gratify Dr. Vickers by telling him what had been my experience, or confide in Freda lest she should tell again.

On reaching home, I turned into the snuggery to see if Freda was downstairs; it must, I thought, be nearly tea-time. She was there; and, as I pushed the door open and was still behind the screen, I heard Dr. Vickers' voice. "Mind," he was saying in English "I do not press you to decide at once. Wait till you are convinced he does not care. To my thinking he has already made it plain."

I stood arrested, not intending to play eavesdropper, but stricken with surprise. As I moved into sight, the two were standing face to face, and the doctor's figure hid Freda from me. I think his hands were on her shoulders, holding her before him, but of this I am not sure. He was quick of hearing as a cat, and he turned on me at once.

"Ah, how do you do, Miss Larcomb? I was just bidding adieu to your sister-in-law, for I do not think she is well enough to-day to take her lesson. In fact, I think she is very far from well. These headaches spell slow progress with our study, but we must put up with delay."

He took up the slim book from the table and bestowed it in his pocket, bowed over my hand and was gone.

If Freda had been agitated she concealed any disturbance, and we talked as usual over tea, of my walk, and even of Robert's journey. But she surprised me later in the evening by an unexpected proposition.

"Do you think Mrs. Larcomb would have me to stay at Aston Bury? It would be very kind of her if she would take me in while Robert has these shootings. I do not like Roscawen, and I am not well here. Will you ask her, Mary?"

I answered that I was sure mother would have her if she wished to come to us; but what would Robert say when he had asked me to companion her here? If Robert was willing, I would write—of course. Did he know what she proposed?

No, she said, and there would be no time to consult him. She would like to go as soon as to-morrow. Could we send a telegram, and set out in the morning, staying the night in York; to receive an answer there? That she was very much in earnest about this wish of hers there could be no doubt. She was trembling visibly, and a red fever-spot burned on her cheek.

I wish I had done as she asked. But my Larcomb common-sense was up in arms, and required to know the reason why. Mother would think it strange if we rushed off to her so, and Robert might not like it; but, given time to make the arrangement, she could certainly pay the visit, and would be received as a welcome guest. I would write to mother and post on the morrow, and she could write to Robert and send the letter by Captain Falkner. Then I said: "Are you nervous here, Freda? Is it because these water-droppings are unexplained?" And when she made a sort of dumb assent, I went on: "You ought not to dwell on anything so trivial; it isn't fair to Robert. It cannot be only this. Surely there is something more?"

The question seemed to increase her distress.

"I want to be a good wife to Robert; oh, I want that, Mary. I can do my duty if I go away; if you will keep me safe at Aston Bury for only a little while. Robert does not understand; he thinks me crazed with delusions. I tried to tell him—I did indeed; hard as it was to tell." While this was spoken she was torn with sobs. "I am terrified to be alone. What is compelling me is too strong. Oh Mary, take me away."

I could get no fuller explanation than this of what was at the root of the trouble. We agreed at last that the two letters should be written and sent on the morrow, and we would hold ourselves in readiness to set out as soon as answers were received. It might be no more than an hysterical fancy on Freda's part, but I was not without suspicion of another sort. But she never mentioned their neighbour's name, and I could not insult her by the suggestion.

The letters were written early on that Thursday morrow, and then Grey Madam was brought round for Freda's drive. The direction chosen took us past the cross-roads in the outward going, and also in return. I remember Freda talked more cheerfully and freely than usual, asking questions about Aston Bury, as if relieved at the prospect of taking refuge there with us. As we went, Grey Madam shied badly at the same spot as before, though there was no visible cause for her terror. I suggested we had better go home a different way; but this appeared impracticable, as the other direction involved an added distance of several miles, and the crossing of a bridge which was thought to be unsafe. In returning, the mare went unwillingly, and, though our pace had been a sober one and the day was not warm, I could see she had broken out into a lather of sweat. As we came to the cross-roads for the second time, the poor creature again shied away from the invisible object which terrified her, and then, seizing the bit between her teeth, she set off at a furious gallop.

Freda was tugging at the reins, but it was beyond her power to stop that mad career, or even guide it; but the mare kept by instinct to the middle of the road. The home gate was open, and I expected she would turn in stablewards; but instead she dashed on to the open moor, making for the river.

We might possibly have jumped out, but there was no time even for thought before we were swaying on the edge of the steep bank. The next moment there was a plunge, a crash, and I remember no more.

The accident was witnessed from the further side—so I heard later. A man left his digging and ran, and it was he who dragged me out, stunned, but not suffocated by the immersion. I came to myself quickly on the bank, and my instant thought was of Freda, but she, entangled with the reins, had been swept down with the mare into the deeper pool. When I staggered up, dizzy and half-blind, begging she might be sought for, he ran on down stream, and there he and Dr. Vickers and another man drew her from the water—lifeless it seemed at first, and it was long before any spark of animation repaid their utmost efforts.

That was a strange return to Roscawen house, she tenderly carried, I able to walk thither; both of us dripping water, real drops, of which the ghostly ones may have been some mysterious forecast, if that is not too fantastic for belief!

It was impossible to shut Dr. Vickers out, and of course he accompanied us; for all my doubt of him, I welcomed the service of his skill when Freda's life was hanging in the balance, and she herself was too remote from this world to recognise who was beside her. But I would have preferred to owe that debt of service to any other; and the feeling I had against him deepened as I witnessed his anguished concern, and caught some unguarded expressions he let fall.

I wired to Robert to acquaint him with what had happened, and he replied, "I am coming." And upon that I resolved to speak out, and tell him what I had guessed as the true cause of Freda's trouble, and why she must be removed, not so much from a haunted house, as from an overmastering influence which she dreaded.

Did the risk of loss—the peril barely surmounted, restore the old tenderness between these two? I think it did, at any rate for the time, when Robert found her lying white as a broken lily, and when her weak hands clung about his neck. Perhaps this made him more patient than he would have been otherwise with what I had to say.

He could hardly tax me with being fancy-ridden, but he was aghast—angry—incredulous, all in one. Vickers, of all people in the world; and Freda so worked upon as to be afraid to tell him—afraid to claim the protection that was hers by right. And now the situation was complicated by the fact that Vickers had saved her life, so that thanks were due to him as well as a kicking out of doors. And there was dignity to be thought of too: Freda's dignity as well as his own. Any open scandal must be avoided; she must neither be shamed nor pained.

I do not know what passed between him and Dr. Vickers when they met, but the latter came no more to Roscawen, and after a while I heard incidentally that he had gone abroad. As soon as Freda could be moved, her wish was fulfilled, and I took her to Aston Bury. Mother was very gentle with her, and I think before the end a genuine affection grew up between the two.

The end was not long delayed; a few months passed, and then she faded out of life in a sort of decline; the shock to the system, so they said, had been greater than her vitality could repair. Robert was a free man again, war had been declared, and he was one of the earliest volunteers for service.

That service won distinction, as everybody knows; and now he is convalescent from his second wound, and here at Aston Bury on leave. And I think the wiser choice his sisters made for him in the first place is now likely to be his own. A much more suitable person than Frederica, and her name is quite a plain one—a real Larcomb name: it is Mary, like my own. I am glad; but in spite of all, poor Freda has a soft place in my memory and my heart. Whatever were her faults and failings, I believe she strove hard to be loyal. And I am sure that she loved Robert well.

THE LONELY ROAD

"I AM AWFULLY SORRY, TOM, I am indeed, and after all your kindness in coming down to see me about that tiresome business, but we can't drive you to the station this evening as I promised. The mare has been kicking in the stable again, and Summers has just discovered she is dead lame. You must really make up your mind to stay another night, and we will get a conveyance over from Ardkellar first thing to-morrow. If I write at once I shall catch the post: we haven't a telegraph office in the village, or I would wire. Summers has only just made the discovery, so he tells me. Now do be reasonable, and say you'll stay."

"That is kind of you, Margaret."

Tom Pulteney fixed again in his left eye the single eyeglass that was always dropping out. This so that he might look at his widowed cousin with the right expression, and she was good to look at, though no longer in her first youth.

"A few more hours here is a temptation; a greater one than I can say. But I'm positively bound to get back to Dublin to-night, and somehow or other I must contrive to catch the 8-50. I'm not such a weakling that I can't walk the distance. How far do you call it to the station?"

"It is eight miles good from here to Ardkellar. And it is a lonely road—"

"Well—I shan't need company for that short distance. I shall be too full of regrets after tearing myself away from you—to say nothing of Adelaide. Though you know very well that Adelaide does not count."

"I don't know anything of the sort. But I hate you going—all that way on foot, and at such an hour."

"Hate my going by all means—I'd wish nothing better. But for a different reason."

"Oh, Tom, do be serious: but if you must go, take care. The road has had a bad character of late; there have been assaults and robberies. Of course you don't go about with a revolver—here. But do you carry a heavy stick?"

"I didn't bring one. But I've got my fists, and I know how to use them."

"You must have a stick. I will lend you Laurence's; it is loaded at the head. I know you will sometime let me have it back."

"If it will make you easy about me—"

"It will make me easier. I am vexed about the mare—and not knowing till the last minute. I am afraid you will have to set off at once if that train is to be caught. And it is getting dusk even now."

The farewells followed, which Tom Pulteney made as affectionate as he dared. It was something of a triumph to him that Margaret was really concerned about the possible risk he was running, on a lonely stretch of road where there had been at least one attempted murder; and he set out with that conviction kept warm at heart.

To him an eight mile walk was truly a light matter, but he happened to be burdened carrying a suit-case made heavy by expensive fittings, and before the end of the first half mile, he began to wish he had slipped his pet razors into his pocket, and asked his cousin to send the case after him, which without doubt she would have done. And for a reason other than the weight: if thieves were abroad, and he was attacked by two, it would be easily snatched by a confederate while one of them knocked him on the head. And a good sound leather suit-case, all but new, is worth stealing now-a-days apart from what it may contain. The contents of Tom's were also of value, things that he could ill spare—among other oddments a handsome finger-ring which he had brought from town, hoping he might find courage to offer it to Margaret as a *gage d'amour*.

The parcel had not been opened: opportunity had not served, or else he had feared to damage his own cause by speaking too early in her widowhood. These articles would, he reflected, be safer if carried on his person, and then he could abandon the suit-case with less reluctance should there be need.

He was now far beyond Ballymacor, and the road before him was solitary. On a sudden impulse he deposited the case under the hedge, unsnapped the locks, and sought in the fast-fading light for his more treasured possessions. These he secured in innermost pockets, again shouldered his burden, and went on whistling under his breath, as might a man light-hearted and unafraid.

But was he unafraid? Was he not assuming the pretence of a boldness he did not possess? In the midst of that search into his luggage, a doubt beset him that the action there and then had been unwise; for at the same time he heard, or thought he heard, a rustle of movement behind the hedge. There was nothing for it then but to go on, and trust he had been mistaken, or the presence and movement wholly innocent. But presently he imagined—imagination first, but soon there was no doubt—that he heard footsteps following. He swung round twice and glanced behind him, but so far as he could see in the dusk the road was clear.

The sound went on, and now the footsteps approached nearer, quickening upon his, and he was already bracing every nerve, preparing for the encounter he expected.

At this critical moment a huge white dog leaped over the fence on the right.

"Why, Boris," he exclaimed unthinking, and the creature came beside him with wagging tail: surely in the event of attack, here would be a formidable ally.

The dog was friendly, and appeared to answer to the name called. Margaret had had such a dog in her husband's lifetime, a Russian wolf-hound of which she had been fond; Pulteney had often seen them together, the tall elegant woman followed by the noble hound. Surely this must be Boris; and yet he had a dim recollection of some mischance mentioned in a letter of Adelaide's, an accident in which the dog had been injured, and he thought killed. Certainly he had not seen Boris on any recent visit to Ballymacor. If only he could keep the dog beside him, he would, he thought, be safe. So he spoke to the creature by name, and spoke again; and each time Boris responded in dog fashion, pleased by the recognition, or so it seemed.

The footsteps still were following; and now, bolder because accompanied, he glanced over his shoulder. Yes, there were two men, and they were close behind, of villainous aspect in the dusk. The dog also looked round and growled, showing his teeth, formidable white fangs, set in a jaw like an alligator's: if the creature was strong enough and fierce enough to pull down a wolf, he would surely be a match for any man. But supposing the followers were armed, and their object murder and not mere robbery, what then?

The sky by this time was clearing, and behind the breaking clouds there came some shining of the moon, showing the way in front and the white hound beside him, and, as he remembered after, both their shadows. From time to time he spoke to his four-footed companion, and also put out his hand to pat the dogs neck; but somehow he never succeeded in touching him—the white rough coat seemed always just beyond reach, though there was no shrinking away to avoid contact.

Pulteney all the while was on the strain to listen, and though he still heard the following footsteps, double footsteps, it seemed to him that they were falling further behind. He could not now be far from Ardkellar, his destination; the railway-line here crossed the road high up on bridge and embankment, and a luggage train lumbered over before him, with gleaming lights and a long rattle of trucks. Not far beyond there was a crossroads, and here the footsteps stopped. Pulteney glanced again over his shoulder, and saw that the two men had halted there, and seemed to be consulting together.

He turned and went on, and now he heard no more the pursuing feet. He was close to the outskirts of the country town, and, he concluded, in comparative safety. He could still see the dog beside him, and was beginning to wonder how he could best dispose of his companion in safety, and contrive to let Margaret know; as

Boris who had befriended him, must certainly have strayed from Ballymacor. They had reached the first row of houses and the outpost of street lights, when he noticed that the form of the dog was altering, becoming shadowy in outline, instead of substantial as before. Still the creature kept step by step beside him, though a figure compacted of white mist growing more and more transparent, till at last, at the passing of the third lamp, this ghostly likeness of Boris faded into nothing and was gone. Tom Pulteney walked into the station of Ardkellar, grateful for his escape, but a bewildered man.

He wrote the history of that night's adventure to his cousin Margaret.

"Upon my word of honour, this is the literal truth, though you will find it difficult to believe. I made sure the dog was yours, as he seemed to know me, and evidently would have shown fight had I been attacked. And I believe the men saw him just as I did, and were deterred from carrying out their plan. It is true I could not touch him, though I tried; but no one could have been more astonished than I was when be dissolved into something like white smoke and then was gone. It was an experience I shall never forget."

To him, Margaret in reply.

"I do believe your story, and to me it is altogether convincing, though so strange. My dear Boris died two years ago: there was an accident I cannot bear to think of, even now. He was caught by a touring car going at speed, and caring nothing for the life or safety of a dog. I had him shot in mercy; I never say destroyed. And what you saw that night is witness that under other conditions he is in existence still. He was so good, so faithful: I never called on him in vain, and he knew almost my thought before I spoke. I was thinking of him that evening. I said to Adelaide—she will tell you—how I wished I had had Boris here, for I would have sent him with you on that lonely walk, and then you would have been safe. For I was very anxious. I believe my thought, my wish, did send him, dear, dear fellow. But I cannot expect you to receive this as I do, or think that it explains."

Tom Pulteney to Margaret.

"I am convinced, indeed. It was you who worked the miracle, and you worked it for me. Your letter, which explains so much, tells me one thing more: may I hope it is the one thing I would give the world to know? You were anxious—you cared what became of me. Could you care always—could you care enough? I pray that the post may bring me the answer I long for; but I am ever your devoted lover, however you reply."

A GIRL IN WHITE

I

IN TELLING THE FOLLOWING STORY I give fictitious names. I do not wish the little house to be identified, nor would I do the owner of the property the slightest injury. It is, doubtless, a harmless place, where people have lived happily in the past, and will again in the future—ninety-nine people out of every hundred. That I happened to be the hundredth man who there underwent a notable experience, may have had nothing to do with local influence. I write this, but add a query: perhaps one wiser than I will answer, and unravel the mystery which I merely present. I do not pretend to explain.

I took Riverside Cottage for my mother and widowed sister, for three months of the summer of 1914—mid-June to mid September. They had both passed through a time of trial with which my story has nothing to do; quiet and change of scene became desirable, and mother wished to be within easy reach of London and of me. That was why I explored the Thames valley on their behalf, and was at once attracted to this house—a modern villa, with gay garden sloping to the water's edge, and boat moored at a small landing-stage overhung with trees: the stage and mooring-place shared, I may mention, with the villa next along the road, the garden of which joined with ours.

As soon as my mother and Lydia were settled in, I ran down for the week-end. They were satisfied with the place, and indeed could not praise it sufficiently, or the wisdom of my choice. The quiet delighted them, the privacy, as well as the outlook over the broad stream, which seemed to exercise a tranquilising influence in its flow. Also the small house was sufficiently convenient; the two elderly servants were pleased, as well as the joint mistresses: what more could be desired?

Needless to say, I agreed with the encomiums and swallowed the reflected praise; but somehow there was a note which jarred. I was the discoverer of the cottage, its original admirer; but the very first night I slept under its roof, I began to wonder what attracted me to the place, and why I had thought it the right sort of nest for mother, who was old and tired, and Lydia, who was middle-aged and particular.

What was the jarring note? Did the softness of the valley, the near neighbourhood of a vast body of moving water, depress my spirits? No, for when we sat out in the garden, bright with flowers, and when I rowed Lydia a mile or so up stream, for the sake of floating down in the cool evening, I felt as usual. It was the house which overpowered me with its influence (I use the word in a non-committal sense)—the house where I became oppressed and ill at ease.

It is just the place where a fellow would cut his throat: that was my reflection the next morning, after a night of broken rest and uneasy dreams. My mother remarked at breakfast that I was not looking well, and Lydia made some joke to the effect that it did not suit me to be off the pavements. I went to church with the two women; for, as a matter of course, the dear souls were punctual church-goers, and expected me to be the same: returned to eat a light and digestible mid-day meal; and enjoyed a post-prandial nap in a basket chair under the trees, which made up for the disturbed night. Where could be a passing of time more commonplace, and less likely to foster morbid fancies? Yet it was after this, while still broad daylight of a summer afternoon, that I had my first glimpse of the white girl.

The staircase came down into the square entrance hall, close to the door of the dining-room (it will be understood that in the cottage there were no wide spaces; all was small and cramped). As

I was descending the stairs, the figure of a girl in white passed quickly before me, from left to right, entering the dining-room. I felt a distinct shock of surprise, and, gaining the open doorway scarcely a minute later, paused to look into the room. There were no screens or recesses in which to hide, the room was plainly vacant, and here the bow-window did not open to the floor as in the other parlour. The latticed casements were set wide to admit the air, but they were narrow and high from the floor, and it would have needed a distinct effort for a grown person to squeeze through. I was still standing astonished in the doorway, when Lydia called to me from the garden. I was to make haste, for tea was ready; it had been carried out of doors.

Now the natural impulse would have been to tell out my uncanny experience, and inquire who was this girl in white who intruded upon us; but a curious reticence shackled my tongue and kept me mute. An inner voice might have been whispering— This is our secret, yours and mine, and you must reveal it to no other. I did not consider then the scruple about alarming my mother; that developed later. As I took the seat placed for me under the tree, the servant emerged from the house carrying hot scones covered by a napkin; she wore the usual black gown and white apron, and I knew the other domestic was similarly attired. Lydia and my mother both wore black; it could have been no mistake for any lawful inmate; none of them were in the least like my white girl. I drank my tea and kept up an indifferent conversation, but all the while I was trying to reconstruct the picture of what I had seen.

It was not easy. As a rule, I pride myself on quick perception and ready memory, receiving clear imprints, which are correctly retained; but in this case it was as if the surprise of the vision had blurred its details. The slender figure of a girl in white, no touch of colour in her array, which seemed of ordinary modern fashion— quickly passing the foot of the stairs, and disappearing into the room beyond. I had seen no face, that must have been turned from me; but I thought I could recall fair hair, so fair as to be almost flaxen, swept up smoothly from the nape of the neck, into twists worn high upon the head.

Again at night I was ill at ease. The period of absolute darkness is brief at midsummer, and the first grey light was making
lawn and flowerbeds visible when I drew away the screens from
the window and looked out. There behind a rosebush, at the edge of
the shrubbed border, was the same white figure. The girl might be
stealing flowers before their owners were awake; I thought her action
looked like it. Presently I saw her more distinctly, as she moved
across the lawn to a heavy-topped standard, which had its own
circle of root-room cut round it in the grass. She was welcome to our
hired roses; but a desire beset me to accost her, and find out who
she was, and whence she came. So I hurriedly flung on my clothes.

A last glance from the window showed her still in sight. I went
down to the drawing-room, opened shutters and glass door, and
stepped out into the garden; but, as will have been divined, in vain.
There was no girl in white, nor did the lawn show any track of footsteps, though my own were plainly traceable in the morning dew.

I was glad that morning to get back to London and my work;
and felt distinctly reluctant to view the approach of Saturday, when
I was again pledged to spend the weekend at Riverside. But on this,
my second visit, I experienced nothing more abnormal than the
burden of melancholy and foreboding which the Cottage imposed
on me before, weighing on my spirits and driving away sleep. I
saw no white girl, and evidently my mother and Lydia had seen
nothing, for they seemed wholly contented and at ease. For the
third week-end I was engaged elsewhere; but the fourth, a Saturday late in July, found me again at the Cottage.

Expectant attention is supposed by some people to account for
psychical happenings. I went thither prepared to see the figure,
and I did see it, but under new conditions; no repetition of what
occurred before.

My broken night repeated itself, though through the previous
fortnight I had been sleeping well. I could get no rest in bed, and
tossed there till I was almost in a fever. Plainly it was the house
which affected me with this insomnia; and as soon as daylight began, I resolved to dress, take out a couple of cushions, and see if I
could get to sleep lying in the boat. I crept softly downstairs,

crossed the solitary garden, where all was wrapped in the Sabbath stillness of the early dawn, and, once in the boat; swinging to the silent flow of the great river, I slept delightfully and woke refreshed.

The servants were busy in the house when I went back, to bathe and shave and dress again, and doubtless they regarded me with wonder. To shave! I was presently at the glass, intent on chin-scraping—turned to moisten the lather—and, looking back, the face presented to me was not my own. Instead of the expected image, this was the countenance of a lovely girl, who looked at me with dark eyes full of sadness and appeal, whose lips moved as if to speak.

I cannot calculate how long the vision lasted; I only know it gave me full time to see—to note my own figure reflected behind her, shirt-sleeved and razor in hand, my head overtopping hers—to imprint on memory every feature of that face. Yes, I had been right; she was fair, the ghost girl, with hair so light as to be almost flaxen, which curled in rings on her forehead, while—an unusual combination—her eyes and eyebrows were of the darkest brown. My ghost was pale, but it was not the pallor of death; her lips were warmly red, and on the left cheek there was a dimple ready to deepen had she smiled. Her dress was white. So far I can describe her, though there is poverty about the written words. I stood frozen, gazing; and then the image melted into a haze of mist, which in its turn disappeared, and the mirror gave back nothing but my own swart reflection in the common way.

My hand shook, and I cut myself over the shaving which came after, which perhaps was not wonderful. The vision was not repeated, though several times that day I stood to gaze. And the second night was sleepless, like the first.

The experiment of the boat had answered well, so at dawn I betook myself thither as before. I fell asleep easily, but woke after the first hour, before the light was full. But it was sufficient to show plainly the slope of the garden, and there, wandering among the flower beds, was the white girl.

I did not spring up at once to confront her, something seemed to hold me paralysed and still. She came on towards me, walking uncertainly with spread hands, as I have seen the blind! On, till she stepped upon the wooden stage, and then, light as a feather, over the side into the boat.

It did not sway under the added burden. I lay in the stern, as I say, paralysed; and she went on to the bow, there turning to look back at me, and wringing her hands together as if in a passion of distress. Then—it all passed in a moment—she plunged into the river and was gone.

I was on my feet the instant after, but there was nothing to be seen. No swirling eddies, no bubbles coming to the surface, no human creature struggling and sinking in those dark depths. Then I remembered that I had heard no splash—all had passed in absolute silence—the boat had not wayed, as it must have done under a material weight. I was awake, I had not dreamed; but the being of my vision was not girl but ghost.

II

CLOSE UPON THIS LAST INCIDENT came the cataclysm we all remember, the outbreak of the war. I volunteered to rejoin my old regiment, was accepted, and in the hurry of preparation and equipment, last days in England slipped rapidly away. But I found time to prosecute certain inquiries about the past history of the river cottage. I could not ascertain that it had ever been the scene of a tragedy, but people are not always candid in answering such questions put by a tenant. It was built some forty years ago, and the original owner died there, peacefully in her bed, and at an age exceeding the threescore years and ten. It was now the property of two middle-aged spinsters, who let it every year to cover the expenses of their autumn tour. All this was prosaic enough; the girl in white was not to be accounted for. And, moreover, she seemed to have been visible to no one else; the vision was to me alone.

Of my own fortunes during the following twelvemonth, I shall speak only briefly. I was in the great Retreat, and was twice wounded, but so slightly as to be able to return to duty after a brief sojourn in hospital. But in the early spring I received a third wound, which was a more serious matter, and sent me back to England for doubtful and difficult repair. My mother and Lydia came to London, where I was in hospital, occupying lodgings near me, and anxious, so soon as I should be pronounced convalescent, to have me handed over to their care. I was better, able to sit up, and discharge was well in sight, when my mother sprang upon me what she felt sure would be a pleasant surprise.

"Can you guess, Dick, where we are going so soon as you can be moved? We were so happy last year, Lydia and I, in the little house you found for us at G—, that I thought we could not do better than engage it again this summer, if it is still to be had."

And here the dear soul paused, plainly expecting my expressions of delight. I could not spoil her pleasure by avowing I hated the place, the cottage and its surroundings, and of my free will would never have set foot in it again. So I swallowed down my distaste.

"And was it to let, mother?" I asked in my turn.

"Alas! no. Riverside Cottage had been snapped up before we inquired—and I don't wonder, it is so sweet a place. But I have taken the house next along the road, the one they call the Lodge, and I hope we shall like it as well. If you remember, the gardens join, and the landing-stage is shared between the two. The rooms are larger than at Riverside, and that will be an advantage when you are with us too."

Not Riverside Cottage after all, but the house next door. That was something of a reprieve, for I did not know how, under invalid conditions, my jarred nerves would stand the reappearance of the girl in white. But it was not probable, at least I thought not, that two houses could be made uninhabitable by one ghost.

I did not leave the hospital so soon as was expected—complications arose, and healing was deferred. So I had time to receive a report, this time from my sister, of the neighbours at Riverside. The Tressidys were pleasant people, so I gathered; an old General who was subject to gout, and his maiden sister who kept house for him; also two unmarried daughters, both pretty and one charming, and the name of the charmer was Emily. The other daughter was, I gathered, something of an invalid; and Emily was the mainspring of the family, full of spirits and fun. Lydia so evidently intended me to fall captive to Emily, that the spirit of resistance quickened, and I was not sorry to hear, on my arrival, that Emily was away on a visit, and the introduction would be deferred.

The Lodge appeared cheerful and comfortable that first evening, and I was not visited with the depression of the year before; also, in my airy bedroom overlooking the river, I slept well and undisturbed. It was not until the second day that I was introduced to the Tressidy family. Lydia came to summon me from the small sitting-room which was styled the library. The General had called especially on me, bringing with him his elderly sister, and the younger daughter, Grace. A pretty girl, Lydia said, preparing me, but not to be compared with Emily. So I was ushered into the room, halting with my stick.

There I was presented to a grizzled, choleric-looking old soldier, a meek elderly female, also grizzled; lastly to the girl. And how shall I describe my sensations, when from her seat in the background and the shadow, she turned on me the face of my ghost, and faintly smiled?

It was the very same face which looked at me out of the glass at Riverside Cottage, the dark eyes and eyebrows, the almost flaxen hair, even the hinted dimple on the cheek, which became more evident with her smile. Was it wonderful that I felt myself stricken dumb in those first moments, and then that I answered with some odd mis-statements in replying to General Tressidy, when he asked, as everybody does, about conditions at the Front, the service I had seen, and my wound. What the old man thought of my confusion I do not know; perhaps he concluded that the marring bullet had impaired, not body only, but also mind.

I had a chance to speak to Grace Tressidy later on when tea was served. The likeness persisted; it was no temporary hallucination. I wished she would have removed her hat, simple as it was, the ghost having been hatless; but in other ways she was dressed for the part, as her gown was white. She wished to relieve me of handing the cake, because I moved lamely, but this I would not allow; and when her wants were supplied, I sat down by her; the

General was now talking to my mother. Did she like the river valley, I asked, and did she know it well? I wanted to ascertain if she had been in the neighbourhood last year, but could not put so bold a question. It was all new to her, she replied, and all delightful; and then she caught her breath, and looked at me with the dark eyes of the vision, eyes with a question in them on her side: was it possible she remembered me, as I recognised her?

"You will think me very silly," she went on. "Emily laughs at me. I have never been here before, and yet it seems as if this place was familiar—even the house where we are staying. I knew every nook of the garden, and every turn of the road. It is as if I had visited it in a dream."

Was that in truth the explanation, and was my ghost nothing more than a perception of Grace Tressidy's dreams? I saw her several times in the days that followed, sometimes hatless, and twice I tried to draw the conversation again to this point, that I might ask her further, and perhaps confess; but each time she avoided it with timidity: had she taken herself to task for so unguardedly speaking out to a stranger, or was she afraid of what I might have to tell? The charming Emily was still away, and I was told, among her other virtues and merits, that she had been a constant nurse and guardian to this younger sister during a period of ill-health. My informant did not say the nature of Grace's illness, and she appeared now to have completely recovered. She walked and bicycled, and was as active as other girls; but the aunt would not let her go on the water, so the boat at the landing-stage was left to us.

I was disturbed by no ghost at River Lodge, but again I took to resting ill at night, though, up to now, mine had been the deep sleep of healthy convalescence. Perhaps I was thinking rather more of Grace Tressidy than was good for me, or would have pleased Lydia, who wished me to be attracted to her favourite, Emily. But, however caused, my insomnia returned; and the night it was at its worst, after tossing feverishly for a couple of hours, I recollected how, the year before, I had been able to sleep in the boat. There it still was, moored to the landing-stage between the two gardens, and a longing beset me to try anew the experiment which succeeded before. So again I armed myself with cushions and went out, and, lying there in the stern, expected to find drowsy peace.

The summer was not so far advanced as when I slept out the previous year, and the early mornings were somewhat chill. It seemed to be the chill which waked me, and, raising myself for a change of position, I looked up the slope of garden to the River-side house with its drawn blinds. And lo! there again was my vision, on the lawn among the rose-bushes, recognised with a shock of heart which curdled through nerves and blood.

My white girl, who so strangely resembled Grace Tressidy; or was it this time Grace Tressidy herself? She moved away from the bushes, and came slowly towards me with her hands spread out, like a blind person feeling her way.

Was I dreaming or awake? The ghost had acted so; the figure was but repeating the scene of a year before. I lay as if spell-bound, and could neither move nor speak. She came on, and as she crossed the stage I saw that her feet were bare. Then, as before, she stepped into the boat.

This time it rocked and swayed under a material weight. The spell was broken. I sprang up, but not soon enough to prevent what followed. The figure at the prow made the despairing gesture I well remembered, and then plunged into the water, now with a splash and scream.

The current in shore was slow, and what there was carried her past me. I seized her as she rose for the second time, and dragged her out drenched and gasping, but, thank Heaven, alive.

"I was asleep," she sobbed; and then— "What will Emily say!" and she fell again to weeping.

I could seek no explanation then and there. My task was to hurry her back at once, and rouse the inmates of Riverside for those ministrations of which she stood in need—hot bath, dry rubbing, bed. I could see that the accident caused all that household deep dismay, but it was everything that the girl was saved.

When I went round later to inquire, I was told Miss Tressidy wished to see me: this was not Grace, but the aunt.

"We have no words to express our thanks, Captain Blake," she began. "I speak for the General too, for he is laid up in his room; the agitation has brought on a fit of gout. Our poor child would have been lost to us, but for you. It was just God's Providence that you happened to be there."

Then followed her story. Grace was a somnambulist. She had walked in her sleep as a child, but the tendency seemed to be out-grown, till it returned after an illness early in last year. Then it caused grave anxiety for a time, but the sister, Emily, was con-stantly at hand to watch, and so prevented harm. Grace was now well again as they believed; the trouble had not recurred for nearly a twelvemonth, so it was thought safe for Emily to leave.

The troubled period was, I gathered, in June and July of 1914, and so coincident with the appearance of my ghost, in a place un-known to Grace Tressidy, but where she was in the future to run so grave a risk to life.

Does this afford an explanation of the story I have told? It may, or it may not; but it is the only one I have to offer.

Some day I may tell the whole of my experience to Grace her-self; but first there must be the telling of another tale I have in mind, and all will depend on whether she is disposed to listen. I think—I hope—she will be favourable to a war-worn soldier, but I do not know. Then I shall perhaps discover correspondences closer than those of which I am aware, and divine how it came about that we were drawn together, I as her preserver, she to yield the life I saved, to my care for days to come.

A PERPLEXING CASE

HE OPENED HIS EYES; consciously opened them for the first time since the blow and roar of the explosion which had seemed to blot him out of life; and looked about him, wondering. He was lying on his back in a narrow hospital bed, next but one to the wall, and in the next bed somebody was groaning: that was the first sound received by his understanding ears. His right side appeared to be stiff with bandages, but felt benumbed rather than painful;—he seemed to have no use in that arm. But his left arm lay out upon the covering, and he could move it without difficulty, and the fingers of the hand. And it was his hand which he was presently regarding with surprise.

If you had looked at the board hung over the head of the bed, you would have seen his name entered as Henri de Hochepied Latour, sous-lieutenant in a French regiment which co-operated with the British in a recent attack. His name as I have written it; his injury, wounds from shell-burst, and shock to brain—this a free translation of the surgical terms: and the date, five days before, on which he had been transferred from the dressing-station to this hospital behind the lines. Could the patient have lifted and turned himself to read, he might have challenged more than one item in this account; what these were will be apparent later. But for such an effort he had not the strength; he could only stare at his left hand, holding it before his face.

In this mischance that had befallen him, which he recognised as fortune of war, what had happened to alter that unwounded member? What he expected to see was a big brawny fist, with knotted joints and hard muscles; the hand of a working man, who, somewhat reluctantly and at the call of duty, had taken to shouldering a rifle. It might be whitened and attenuated by illness, but surely it still would be the same in form. What he did see was a hand delicately slender, olive in hue of skin, strong no doubt in a determined grip, but not with navvy's strength; the nails almond-shaped, daintily manicured and tended; in all these details unlike his own. How could such a change have come about? He opened and shut the hand before his face, staring stupidly at it in his surprise.

Presently a nurse, who had been attending to the moaning patient in the next bed, bent over him and noticed that consciousness had returned.

"I will bring you presently some tea, monsieur," she said, to test whether he understood, speaking in slow careful French, the French of an Englishwoman.

The dark head moved on the pillow. "Have you no English, Sister?" This man had been in hospital before.

"Yes, of course I have. I am English. But I thought you would better understand my French, though I know it is not good."

"Good or bad, it would be all the same to me. I can say *bon jour*, and ask for bread and cheese, and that's about all. What did you say to me?"

"Only that I would bring you tea as soon as it is ready."

Sister Bennett glanced again at the board hung over the bed before she turned away. There must have been some mistake, for certainly sous-lieutenant Henri Latour ought to be able to speak his own language, and understand it when spoken, even by an Englishwoman. And he was a thorough Frenchman to look at, this wounded soldier, though he had an English tongue in his head, and not the most refined intonation of speech. But she made no comment in reporting to the doctor that Number Forty-nine had come to himself. If there had been a mistake, they would find it out soon enough without intervention of hers. And doctors and nurses were all closely engaged that night, as a fresh batch of wounded had come in.

But the next day there was further trouble. Number. Forty-nine indignantly denied his identity with the French officer Henri Latour, declaring that he was one Richard Adams, lance-corporal, attached to the London Scottish. He persisted in this assertion with so much ruffled temper, that the doctor gave direction that he should be humored. Confusion was a common enough consequence of shell-shock, so said the man of experience; but, for all that, this was not quite a common case. It was an odd coincidence that Richard Adams of the London regiment was lying unconscious in that very hospital. He had been injured, so it was believed, at the same time as young Latour, and by the bursting of the self-same shell; and, though his wounds were not considered serious, he had not yet come to himself. Sous-lieutenant Latour would be all right in a day or two, so Senhouse, the captain-doctor, forecasted. No doubt this young man had been in touch with Corporal Adams immediately before the catastrophe, and somehow—though how was unexplained—the impression of Adams' personality persisted in this condition of temporary aberration. That there could have been any actual mistake between the two was out of the question; the identification discs in each case furnished proof. And, beyond this, a friend of Latour's, visiting the hospital, had recognised him when he was carried unconscious from the ambulance.

Here was testimony enough, but further witness was forthcoming. The French lieutenant was presently inquired for by two ladies: Mademoiselle Ottilie Latour, his elder sister, and with her a charming girl whom she addressed as Julie, who was the young officer's betrothed. Might they be admitted to his bedside, such was Mademoiselle Latour's petition, just to look at him as he lay asleep, if they might do no more.

Senhouse the doctor was not hard-hearted enough to refuse. If the ladies could promise self-command, they could see the patient awake or asleep. His wounds were not serious, and recovery might certainly be hoped for. The shock of the explosion, however, had to a certain extent affected his mind. For this they must be prepared.

Mademoiselle Latour promised that neither she nor her companion would betray alarm or distress, and she held Julie's quivering hand fast in hers as they passed through the temporary ward, the eyes of broken men turning on them from their pillows of pain.

The young lieutenant was awake: he lay staring at the ceiling, still with a puzzled frown upon his brow, though he had thrust the slender olive hand, which was not the hand of Richard Adams, away under the bed-coverings: he could not bear the sight of it, it perplexed him too much

Senhouse paused by the bed as the two women came beside it, standing opposite, and he glanced up at them from the face on the pillow. Yes, there could be no doubt that this was Henri Latour, the likeness between brother and sister was so strong; the clear-cut distinguished features seemed to have been struck from the same die. This Henri might have been thought somewhat effeminate-looking when clean-shaven: now his chin was disfigured by an eight days' growth of beard: but there could be no doubt that Ottilie, the sister who resembled him, was beautiful, of the very type of womanhood that Captain Senhouse most fervently admired, noble-looking now in her calmness and her grief.

"He is awake," she breathed in the lowest of whispers. "May I speak to him?"

Assent was signified.

"*Mon frere*," she began, bending nearer, with the younger girl also pressing close and leaning on her arm. The face which was Latour's turned to regard them, but his air of sullen indifference did not alter or lighten into recognition. He looked coldly at the anxious sister, and the tremulous young beauty who was his betrothed, made a slight movement of negation, and closed his eyes.

"These ladies have come to see you. They are speaking: don't you hear them?" Thus the doctor, in English.

The man addressed replied in the same tongue.

"I am obliged to them, but I don't know them. And I speak no French."

His manner suggested obstinacy as well as indifference. He did not know these people; he was annoyed by the emotion with which they seemed to regard him, and in his maimed state he was sensitive about pity: he wished they would go away. Ottilie Latour made another effort, naming the familiar home, the early interests they had shared; surely at such a hearing, the shattered memory would light up into renewed being, as might a smouldering fire! The younger lady fell on her knees, and her voice was broken by sobs.

"Ah, Henri—ah, Henri," she cried. "Don't you remember how we parted and what you said? Have you quite forgotten?"

The man opened his eyes again, but turned to Senhouse without notice of the appeal. He was fingering his chin, which showed a dark stubble of beard.

"Doctor," he said, "is there anybody here who can shave me? Nurse says I'm bound to ask you for the order. I hate to be like this."

English again, and rough-toned English to boot.

"It is of no use at present," Senhouse said to Mademoiselle Latour. "You are only distressing yourselves needlessly. Better to come away."

There were friends waiting who took the weeping Julie in charge, but the sister lingered behind.

"It is very strange," she said to Senhouse. "Do you often have such cases? Without doubt that is my brother, but it is not his voice. He would never speak like that; he is a cultivated gentleman. How is it that he forgets his native tongue? I could understand shock stripping off later acquirements for the time, but not what is the bed-rock of nature." Here she paused, her earnest gaze striving to read the doctor's countenance, on which was written deep concern. "Do you think—really think—there is any hope?"

"We do not give up hope, we doctors, and you must not. The case is a peculiar one, that I grant; but others which have come under my notice have displayed equal confusion. Much may yet be done; we must have patience. Have you any knowledge of the man he seems to personate: one Richard Adams, a private soldier in the British army? Can you suggest any possible link between him and your brother in the past?"

Mademoiselle Latour shook her head, but she appeared to be considering.

"No, I recollect nothing. Of course Henri may have known him. He was in England two years ago, and made many acquaintances; but not army ones, so far as I am aware."

"Oddly enough, a man of that name was wounded by the same shell-burst as Lieutenant Latour, and now lies in this hospital, also suffering from shock. Would it distress you too much—could you spare the time—to look at him? He is here, in this lower ward; the door on the right. You may recognise his face: if not likely, it is possible. I shall be greatly obliged."

Senhouse had a special reason for this urgency, one he did not avow. There seemed little or no ground for supposing the inspection could be of use. Mademoiselle Latour, however, assented willingly. She was quite at leisure; she would do whatever was wished. So together they entered the second ward.

Richard Adams was conscious and very restless, the Sister in charge said when interrogated; he had been talking strangely all the afternoon, as if delirious. There seemed no sense in it, but what he jabbered was in French. She was glad the doctor had come. That was Adams, in the middle bed.

Adams was a herculean young fellow of the Saxon type, fair and blue-eyed, and in the eyes was a cloud of trouble. He was tossing restlessly on his narrow couch, as if no position could be easy; but when he caught sight of the lady-visitor, his countenance became radiant with joy.

"Ottilie—Ottilie!" he exclaimed, stretching out two eager hands burning with fever. "This is good, to see some one from home. How did you come? Have you been anxious about me at Les Bochers? Tell me, how is mother? And my Julie; how, is she? You don't know what it is to lie here, and long to have word of them, if only a word. Now you are here, my dear sister, how long can you stay? Give me every moment you are able."

For a brief instant the sister seemed on the verge of fainting, but she yielded her hands to the grasp of those others which were strange to her. The voice was familiar, and the questions: who could have questioned her so, but Henri only?

"Mademoiselle Latour cannot stay long," said the doctor, bending down to him. "No doubt she will come again. And now you must not excite yourself."

"I want to hear of them all," the man went on; this rough English private soldier. "All of them—old Francois, and Madelon and Ninette: all, down to Ponto the dog. I dream of them at night, and I see them when I dream. Has mother been anxious about me? I feel sure she has."

The sister at last recovered power of speech.

"Yes, yes—indeed—she has been anxious: she is. She talks of nothing but Henri. I am here to bring her news."

"Tell her my last thought was of her. There was a blow which struck me—a great rushing, and a noise that stunned. The rush sent me spinning with it, as if I had been a bullet from a gun: spinning—spinning through space. I thought I was going to her—to Rochers la Vallière, and I cried out her name. But I did not get to La Vallière: I did not go so far. Everything went dark, and I remember no more. I woke in this place, and I cannot make them understand what I want. Take me with you, Ottilie; take me home. Are they well there? The invasion has not touched them? Is mother well?"

"They are all well, and safe, and hoping for news of—of you—of Henri." As she spoke, she looked across at Senhouse in appeal: she knew not how much longer she could trust her self-command to keep up this farce: farce, was it, or fact and truth?

Not many more words were exchanged before the doctor asserted authority and led her away; and now she needed the support of his arm. Outside the ward she was thankful to sink into a chair, and drink the water he presently held to her lips.

"You did not know this Adams?"

"Not his face. But it was my brother speaking with his lips. My brother's body is in the other ward—his spirit here. M. le docteur, it is terrible. Body and soul apart! What can be done?"

"You must forgive me for exposing you to such an ordeal. I suspected what was the matter, but I wanted to be sure. I wanted to see if this Adams, as he is called, would recognise you. Plainly he did so: he spoke to you at once by name. It will be easier to treat, now that we understand. There may be need of long patience. But, to my thinking, there is no reason for despair."

Mademoiselle Latour was gathering back her shaken self-control; she set down the glass of water.

"What can be done? " she repeated.

It was the question Senhouse had asked himself, and still he was groping in the dark after an answer. But he desired above all to reassure this noble-looking woman, who had been so sorely tried by his experiment. In replying, he assumed a confidence he was far from feeling, but hope was strong that it might be justified by the event.

"You will give me a free hand to do what I think best for M. Latour? There is a man, a Parisian doctor, who is great in these mysterious cases of—of brain-suspension, and confusion and all that. We will have him here in consultation, and he shall advise and treat the case. He has made some wonderful successes. You may be certain no pains will be spared by us to efface what now is wrong, and to restore the link of mind and body completely as before."

SENHOUSE DID NOT FORGET the apparent Latour's complaint about his sprouting beard, and he gave the required order that the lieutenant should be shaved—a simple matter, which had a somewhat unlooked-for result. The hospital orderly was sufficiently skilled to operate in this way upon the chins of the patients, and in due course of time he arrived with razor and lathering-bowl to shave the young French officer. He found the young French officer in sufficiently good spirits to be communicative. There was nothing, he averred, that did him so much good as a clean shave: it put him at once on right terms with himself and his world. And as (he hoped) his was a "Blighty" case of wounding, it would never do for him to go back to England with so much bristle showing. Liz, his wife, as good an old girl as ever stepped, would in that case have nothing to say to him.

"You think of crossing over to England, sir?" questioned the orderly, mindful of necessary respect when he was shaving an officer. But this officer had an odd way of talking, Frenchman as he was.

"Why, of course I shall be sent to England, and I hope it will be to a London hospital: That will be convenient for Liz. She lives out Poplar way, and takes in fine sewing; and she has kept herself comfortable with that and the allowance—good old girl. And I know that, were it ever so, she'd never look at any one but me; not like some of the fellows' wives one hears of. We've got a kid, too; eight months old he is, and so far I've never set eyes on him. Liz'll bring him to the hospital when she comes to see me, you bet she does, for she's as proud of him as—as—"

The illustration failed, as the razor was now operating round the lower lip, and silence was only prudent. But in another couple of minutes he would be released.

"There, sir, there's a clean shave for you. And, though I say it as shouldn't, one it would be hard to beat."

The patient fingered his chin somewhat doubtfully, with the one hand he could move; the hand which had caused him so much disquietude when he came to himself.

"I've got a glass here," said the soldier-barber. "'Tis but a little one, but if you look in it you can see for yourself. It has freshened you up above a bit, and you can't fail to be pleased."

The small vanity-glass was produced, and held at the right angle. The patient looked, and, looking, gave a cry—a yell of horror which rang through the ward, so that all the heads on all the other pillows turned to gaze, and the sister in charge came hurrying to learn what was the matter. This Latour, usually quiet and biddable, was suddenly wrought up into a state of fierce excitement.

"What have they done to me," he demanded wildly, "to make me look like that? I never had that sort of (blank-blank) face. I'll have the law of the (blank-blank) doctors, (blank) me if I don't. If I go to England with that face, Liz'll never believe I'm her husband." And so forth, in the teeth of regulations, and despite all persuasion, the protest garnished with sundry very forcible oaths which we omit, until excitement stilled away into exhaustion, and the sick man lost himself in sleep.

THE PARISIAN DOCTOR who had become the referee in shock cases which do not yield to ordinary treatment, we will call Despard for the purpose of this narrative; it is not his real name. It became known very shortly that he had been summoned to the perplexing case at the B— hospital, which some rumour had gone abroad. Despard was supposed to pin his faith on hypnotism and such-like uncanny nostrums, and in consequence his name stank in the nostrils of one half of the surgical staff. He was going to hypnotise the shock case, that was the assumption; and some surprise was evidenced when it crept out through certain preparations, that Latour was to be treated by the more ordinary method of the transfusion of blood.

"I hope you've got a healthy subject to be donor," said the C.M.O., meeting Senhouse on the stairs. "And don't forget the saltwater admixture; for, whatever Despard says, I hold that to be essential." And then the C.M.O. bethought him to ask: "Who is the donor?"

"Well, sir, it is the other shock man, Adams. M. Despard has chosen him. He is healthy, enough, I think, and a young Hercules for strength."

"Tut-tut," said the great man, who very plainly disapproved, and to whom the hypnotist and his methods were anathema maranatha. "What!—two shock cases, and transfuse their blood! Never heard of such a proceeding in my life. What possibly can be gained by it but an aggravation of both their symptoms?" And so forth; and the C.M.O. may be written down as "left objecting."

THE EXPERIMENT WAS TRIED next day in the operating-room of the hospital, Senhouse acting as one of Despard's assistants, the other being a coadjutor who accompanied him. The door was of course barred against intrusion, and what took place within was never precisely known. The process was a long one, and once while it was in progress Senhouse managed to slip away, so as to convey a modicum of comfort to the room below, where Ottilie Latour had been allowed to wait. She looked up at his entrance, eagerly expectant. She was pale to the lips with anxiety, but as beautiful as ever—at least Senhouse thought so.

"Is it over?" she asked.

"Not yet, and will not be for another hour. But I thought you would be relieved to know all is going well, and Despard is quite hopeful. He says it is a simple case compared to some which have passed through his hands, and he expects complete success. They went off into trance without difficulty, both of them, and neither saw the other, as a screen was put up between them. And they will be moved into fresh quarters directly after, so that there will be nothing to revive former impressions. I am sorry you have so long to wait."

"I do not mind how long; it is everything to be on the spot, and I thank you from my heart for getting me permission to wait here. I know you will bring me the earliest news."

"I will come to you the instant certainty is assured. But I don't expect Despard will give leave for you to see your brother to-day. Don't let that disappoint you."

Upon this, the messenger went back to his post at the theatre. There a certain amount of vital fluid was in process of interchange, and two spirits wrongly housed in their tenements of flesh were brought into touch by a force only partially recognised, though of existence coeval with human life.

After a while one of the patients began to stir and moan, and then to utter some querulous complaint.

"The young gentleman is coming round," said the assistant, calling Despard's attention. "*And he is speaking French.*"

Despard gave a grunt of satisfaction.

"Ah," he said, "if that is so, we have done well."

Some half hour later Senhouse went back to Ottilie.

"It is over, successfully over, and M. Despard confidently hopes the confusion will never be renewed. Your brother is in bed in the new ward, quite composed, and he remembers that you visited him. 'When is my sister coming again; my sister Ottilie?' he asked me. I told you had been here to-day, but the doctor thought it unwise to permit a visitor on the day of operation. He said: 'Tell her to give my devotion to Julie and mother, and a message of remembrance to all at Rochers la Vallière.' And then he turned his face away on the pillow and fell asleep. That was your brother in his true form, not as before. You understand?"

Yes, Ottilie Latour understood, and her eyes were full of grateful tears.

FOUR DAYS AFTER, the second shock case was entrained for Blighty. Another shave had smartened him sufficiently to appear as Liz would wish and expect; and now when the glass was presented he saw his own face in it—the face she would recognise and that he knew. And his hand was broad and muscular again, not the slim olive member the sight of which was his first perplexity. What had been the matter with him he queried, and was told on the doctor's authority he had suffered from shell-shock. And that to the victims of shock, confusion and dementia manifest themselves in many forms, including distorted vision, all owing to the temporary loss of balance by the brain.

BEYOND THE PALE

WITHOUT DOUBT the Hennikers' was a love-match. They had been married a couple of years, and it may fairly be said that neither party had found cause to repent. Rupert Henniker was sincerely attached to his wife, and she positively idolised him. The French proverb says that in all such unions there is one who kisses, and the other who permits the embrace. In this case Henniker was the one kissed, but he willingly yielded the cheek, and felt that Joan's adoration was well placed.

Joan began her married life with high ideals. She determined so to identify herself with her husband's pursuits, that she might everywhere be his unfailing companion; and to this young wife the nursery interests, which frequently alter such a programme, had not been vouchsafed by Providence. So when Henniker laid his plans for a season's shooting in the wilds of Western America, Joan, as a matter of course, expected to go

She did not claim to shoulder a rifle beside him; that was not her way: but she could keep the rough little mountain dwelling which had been placed at their disposal, cosy and home-like for Rupert, and see that he missed no comfort that her care could supply. If on the spot, she could see that he changed into dry foot-wear when he came back of an evening; she could wash his socks and darn them, and contrive the best imitation possible of his favourite dishes over the stove, which there would be the sole substitute for an English kitchen-range. She had some practical knowledge of these matters, though it was slight and inadequate; but

348

she determined it should be sufficient, and everything in the adventure before them was seen through the rose-coloured medium of romance. The separation which might have been had she held back, was now no longer to be feared; and a prolonged tête-à-tête in the wilds would draw them together even nearer than before. Henniker had expressed himself as proud of his little woman's pluck, and she was determined to justify that pride and that praise.

Their solitude would not be absolute, as Arnott's ranch was distant only half a mile, which in that land of prairie wastes and wide distances, seemed almost as close as next door. Arnott and Henniker had been boys together and schoolmates, and it was upon his suggestion they were going out. Arnott's wife was said to be a good sort, and on Joan's arrival she would equip her with all needful knowledge.

So young Mrs. Henniker set out on her sea and land journey with a brave heart and bright anticipations, and her courage did not fail when at last they traveled on beyond railways and civilisation, into the great solitudes; climbing the spurs of the foot-hills, and looking up at the huge mountain wall and the high snows behind which the sun sank in the west. Perhaps the adobe hut when reached was something of a disillusion, though it was fairly commodious and not absolutely bare; the Arnotts had put in necessaries in the way of furniture, and had done their best to make it habitable. It would look more home-like when Joan had had time to unpack and arrange her possessions and his—other than the precious rifles, which were not for feminine handling: and about all this Joan would have the aid of a "help" Mrs. Arnott had engaged for her, to soften the edge of hardship in this strange new housekeeping in the wilds. Nita, the half-bred Indian girl, could at least manage the stove, and wash and scrub the place down, if she could do no more.

Mrs. Arnott had of course her own establishment to look after, where a couple of pretty children added to the domestic cares and joys, so she could give Joan only occasional assistance; though a fount of practical advice was at her service whenever she cared to come up to the ranch. So the next day Joan was left alone with her wild-looking "help" when Henniker went off to the bills.

Nita had a double tongue in her head, Spanish and Indian, on which a very little English had been grafted; and it was by the help of the very little English, that she and her new mistress were to exchange ideas and commands. Joan would have scorned to confess that from the beginning she stood in some awe of her assistant, but it was so in fact. Nita's service was utterly unlike any to which she had been accustomed, and there was something disconcerting about the girl's sudden lithe movements, and the keen regard of her black eyes. At first mistress and maid were on good terms; and though Nita's ideas of necessary cleanliness were far from satisfying Joan, the young housekeeper hoped that admonition and instruction would have their due effect in time; and greater energy was displayed after the gift of a gay ribbon out of one of the Henniker traveling trunks.

But with the unpacking of these trunks came the development of an intense curiosity on the part of Nita concerning all kinds of civilised belongings, and, as Joan began uncomfortably to suspect, of a cupidity equally intense. The girl longed to deck herself out in imitation of her mistress, and pile on the few ornaments that were in evidence: Joan had, as a matter of course, left her jewel-case in the custody of an English bank.

Nita was nominally assisting arrangement upon shelves and drawers, and fingering the possessions that were laid away, when Joan first noticed the peculiar scar on her right wrist. Such a slender brown wrist it was, and at some time or other it must have been frightfully hurt. A deeply-seamed scar ran the whole way round the arm, or almost the whole way, as only about an inch of smooth skin was free from the ghastly indentation; and below this, nearer the hand, were a couple of lines of blue tattooing, twisted together at the back into a sort of device. Joan asked her how she had been hurt, but evidently Nita's English was not equal to the task of explanation; she frowned and drew back, pouring out a torrent of bastard Spanish, which left her mistress as wise as before.

Joan did not inquire further, but, thinking to please her, offered as a gift a string of coral beads which matched the ribbon. To her surprise Nita refused it, but snatched up a small miniature portrait taken from the trunk.

"Not those," she said, "I don't want those: I have beads enough. I will have this instead: give me this!"

The miniature was one of Joan's dead mother, and greatly valued by her; unluckily it was framed in a glittering oval of Paris paste. Joan was shocked at the greed and the demand, and wrenched the portrait out of those brown fingers which closed and clutched against her; there was indeed a struggle over it between the two.

"No, you cannot have that," she said, trying to disguise her displeasure—for what was the use of being angry with this child of nature? "You may have the corals if you care for them, but not this. It is the only portrait I have of my mother, and I value it more than all the world."

The girl looked sulky, but no more was said. Of course it was not the picture that she wanted, but the oval of shining mock gems. The attraction of this to one who had never before looked upon diamonds, real or imitation, was greater than Joan could divine. Yet civilised women have before now succumbed to such lures, so to covet possession may be reckoned less surprising in one beyond the pale. Joan was prudent enough again to lock the miniature in her traveling trunk, and when the key was turned she dismissed the matter from her mind. But it was by no means blotted out of Nita's by that closed lid and turned key.

Several days went by, full of small jarring discomforts which need not be enumerated here. One afternoon Joan went up to the ranch to take counsel with Mrs. Arnott, and on her return she found the place deserted, her boxes broken open and ransacked, and, what specially moved her to wrath, the precious miniature was forced out of its frame and cracked across, while the glittering oval had altogether disappeared.

This was an outrage indeed. The actual thefts were of small account measured against this damage, the wrong of the disfiguring crack which split the beloved face in two. Joan cried out that the offender must be caught and punished, and Henniker was of the same mind; so he and Arnott, who was sheriff's delegate for that part of the district, rode up into the hills in search of Nita, making their errand known.

The girl was supposed to have her abode with the old Indian woman her grandmother, who received them with wrath and curses, and swore to Nita's innocence—as doubtless she would have sworn to any statement which suited her, having small regard for truth. Also she declared that she knew nothing of the grand-daughter's whereabouts, so the pursuing party returned baffled, after breathing forth vain threatenings.

Mrs. Arnott was with Joan when her husband and his friend returned.

"Did you really beard old Rachel in her den?" she asked, and looked more than a little concerned.

"Why of course we did. What else were we to do?" was his rejoinder.

"I suppose it was a matter of duty, but the old crone is what they call about here ill to cross and likely to put ill luck upon you both. It was all very well for you to be out to catch a thief, but I wish you and Mr. Henniker had left old Rachel alone. You must know," she said, turning to Joan, "deserved or not, this grand-mother of Nita's has the reputation of being a witch."

Of course they laughed at this as at an excellent joke, Joan and the two men, but there was an air about Mrs. Arnott as if she more than half believed in Rachel's malignant powers.

"I am more sorry than I can say that I sent Nita to you," she went on. "But the girl seemed teachable and promised to do well. There is nobody else but old Mercy Clew, our herdsman's wife, and she is coming up to you to-morrow. She is a rough specimen, but I have always thought her honest, and I believe your possessions will be safe with her."

The foregoing may be taken as the prologue to the drama, all of it commonplace enough, but needful to make clear what will follow.

Joan had spent a busy morning shepherding Mercy Clew—who was both deaf and obstinate—in the way of the help she required.

It had been a strenuous time: a trial of patience as well as of physical strength in unaccustomed labours; and she had withdrawn into their living-room for a few minutes breathing-space and rest, throwing herself into the one cushioned chair with a gasp of relief. Her eyes were closed, her muscles all relaxed, when tap-tap came behind her—the rapping of impatient fingers on the glass. Mrs. Arnott sometimes tapped like that on her way to the entrance door; and Joan started round to face the window, feeling rather aggrieved by the intrusion. But Mrs. Arnott was not there. The tapping came again, and now she saw something where the glass was struck; only a shadow, but the shadow of a hand.

A hand reaching down from above. If the shadow was of any real substance, the intruder must be crouched upon the roof; the hut had, of course, no storey above the ground-floor. It must be Nita; that was her instant conviction: Nita playing some annoying trick: but with a warrant out against her it was surprising that she dared. Joan ran outside to see. No, there was no one on the roof, either above the smitten window or behind—no one hiding round the chimney-stack, no one within sight; but, passing it on her return, she discovered that the smitten glass retained the print of a hand.

The hand had been pressed flat against the pane, palm and outspread fingers, and it seemed to have been dipped in something viscous and sticky, faintly streaked with blood. She looked at it from time to time during the day, and watched the gradual drying off of the mark in the keen hill air; but it was still faintly visible when Henniker returned, and his attention was called to it.

"Yes," he said, "whoever made that mark must have stretched down to do it from the roof. A daring trick, and likely, enough to be Nita's, unless indeed she has an accomplice. We shall catch her at it if she is foolhardy enough to come again."

There was no more tapping on the glass that night, to call attention to what was going forward; but when they got up the next morning a second window was marked. This one lighted the bedroom and looked to the other side of the house. Here there was no roof-slope above it but a gable, so it would have been more difficult, well-nigh impossible, to reach down to the glass from above.

The print of the hand, however, was made precisely as before; wrist upwards and fingers downwards, a sticky impression streaked with blood. It was Henniker this time who discovered it when he drew aside the window screen to shave; he called to his wife, who was kindling a fire in the stove, and they both regarded it together.

"Somebody is trying to take a rise out of us"—such was Henniker's ultimatum. "No doubt it is supposed we shall be scared by these cursings of the witch. I'd like to get to the bottom of it before anything is known, so do not let us appear to take notice. I shall not say anything to Jack Arnott—yet, and do not you to his wife."

It was all very well to resolve on this course of action—or inaction, and easy to, take no notice of a sticky mark on the outside of a window, which was presently effaced with a wet cloth. But the next demonstration, if it can be so called, was of a different nature and less possible to ignore. Mercy Clew came rushing in from her wash-bucket to where Joan was stirring a saucepan over the stove.

"Come you out here, Mis' Henniker. I cannot go on in the yard. They have been throwing stones at me this half hour!"

The woman had an air of passionate indignation, but together with the anger there was fear. Mrs. Clew's command of English was superior to Nita's, but Joan found her almost as difficult to understand.

"Do you mean that somebody is throwing stones, and at you? Who would dare to do such a thing? It must be a mistake."

"Come you out and see"—taking hold of Joan by the arm. "I wouldn't like to have you hurt, but I want you to believe. And if it is the doing of old madam, like enough she'll stone you too."

It was true that stones and pieces of rock were scattered over the beaten earth of the yard; but, for all Joan knew, they might have been there since the beginning of time. The woman showed the spot where she was standing, and the direction from which they struck her; and, the moment after, another stone fell plump into the water-bucket, and a second bruised Joan on the shoulder. Nobody was in sight.

"It is horrible of them. What have we done that we should be so persecuted! We must find out who is doing this."

She was angry rather than dismayed, and eager in searching round the dwelling-house and outbuildings. Except for these possible screens, Hunter's End stood in the open, away from trees and rocks. There seemed no possible cover to conceal the thrower of the stones, and yet again, immediately on their return, one was tossed into the yard.

"Bring your pail indoors into the kitchen," Joan commanded. "We shall be safe there."

But safe they were not, though shut in by walls and doors. The stones still struck them both, and fell within on the floor. The elderly "help" reached for her shawl and bonnet, which were hanging on the pegs.

"I'm sorry to leave you, marm, but stay I can't where there are such goings on. It's all through the old madam that your place has got bewitched. And, if I'm not mistaken, you'll have no more peace here, day nor night."

"Who is this old madam, and what do you mean about bewitching?" Joan held her back, almost by force, till she answered.

Mercy Clew dropped her voice to a whisper.

"'Tis not well to say the name of her, but she is kin to the girl you had here, her you sent after with a sheriff's warrant. It is well known that madam puts spells upon people, and has laid a spell upon the girl herself, if what one hears is true. She's an awful woman when she is angered, and you will have to get quit of her one way or another, or there will be no peace for this house. Mis' Arnott, she knows something of what has been done elsewhere, enough to pass her word to you that I am telling truth. And until madam's quit of you, I can tell you this. Not a soul about will come nigh the place, or drive their beasts past it. I'm sorry from my heart for what's before you, but you'll have to fend for yourselves."

And the Hennikers had in fact to "fend for themselves" in the days that followed. The witch, if truly a witch was in fault, had contrived to put upon them a boycott as stringent as any that existed in Ireland. And it was not only that the report of the stone-throwing had gone abroad, and the superstitious were afraid to venture into the bewitched quarter, animals, who could not be affected by hearsay, were also a prey to terror. Arnott's dog, who was used to accompany him in visiting Hunter's End, on the first occasion after these events began, hesitated when within twenty yards of the door, and appeared to scent danger: he then turned tail and fled for home, despite the calls of his master. And one of the ranch horses, drawing a load of logs for the Hennikers' use, and led by Arnott, jibbed determinedly at about the same distance, and neither blows nor coaxing could induce it to approach nearer. It was impossible to get help for Joan, other than what Mrs. Arnott could occasionally give; and Henniker did not like to leave her uncompanioned in the midst of such eerie happenings, so the guns were idle in their rack, except for the shooting of some rock pigeons and conies in the near neighbourhood of the hut.

Henniker's opinion had altered from the scornful disbelief professed in the beginning, to a mood of unwilling and annoyed conviction. The stone-throwing against old Mercy in the yard he had dismissed as nothing more than a spiteful trick; the tapping on the glass fell into the same category, and the impression of a human hand in an impossible position, might even have been made by a dummy pressed against the pane. But when it came to later experiences which he shared, occurrences when he and Joan were alone in the house, stone-throwing within shut doors which went on at intervals, the affair assumed a different complexion. Stones—it is true they were small ones—were thrown when the two were sitting at supper, first from one side of the room and then from the other; and a good-sized pebble was dropped from above into his coffee-cup, breaking the cup and spilling the contents. Even at night they were allowed no peace; articles left in the kitchen were brought through the shut door into their room and hurled upon the beds; the coverlets were grasped and dragged by something which remained invisible; fingers rapped a tattoo against the window; and, what seemed more extraordinary than all, running footsteps passed backwards and forwards overhead, where was nothing but the sloping roof.

Henniker started out again and again, gun in hand, but there was no target for his shot. Joan kept her courage wonderfully through those harassed days and nights; but when at last her husband accorded her a well-deserved meed of praise, she broke down and shed tears.

"I don't mind—that is, I can bear it so long as it only what we hear and feel. But if it should come to seeing anything dreadful, I am sure I could not go on being brave—"

It was after this avowal that Henniker asked advice of Arnott, who had come down to see how they were faring; and it may be noted here that this friend had now been taken into the full confidence which was at first withheld.

"What would you do in my place? It's beyond endurance that we should be driven out by sheer devilry—for devilry it must be; but how can I stay on here when it is killing my wife? She won't leave me, or I would send her away, and stay and brave it out by myself."

"What would I do? Why, I'd be inclined to try what the half-breeds resort to in similar cases. Rank superstition you will say, and so do I; but it is possible there may be something in it as they say that it succeeds. They pit one witch against another, and let the two of them battle it out. There's a man up the river who goes by the name of the witch-doctor. If I were you I'd have him over, and pay the dollars of his fee. I understand it is a big one."

"If we can be freed from this, I don't mind what I pay, or what absurdity I have to put up with."

"You will have to put up with absurdity, if his rites are of the sort I imagine. I have heard of them of course, living here, but I have never seen the thing done. I may as well say this is Cora's advice as well as mine" (Cora was his wife). "Very well, as you are willing, I will send Clew with the buggy at dawn to-morrow to fetch down Hill-of-the-Raven, and you must be prepared to receive him here."

Hill-of-the-Raven professed himself willing to undertake the job, and soon after mid-day Arnott brought him to Hunter's End. He was a very lean, very tall old Indian, who looked inappropriately garbed in European dress instead of his native paint and feathers. Arnott acted as interpreter, as his English was of the smallest; and he also mounted guard over the old man's bag of conjuring tools while Hill-of-the-Raven made first the outer round of the house, and then entered every room, standing and snuffing the air as a stag might who perceives a taint to windward, all the while muttering incantations to himself. Finally he confabulated again with Arnott, who looked distinctly annoyed.

"Hill-of-the-Raven wants more money," he informed Henniker. "The old rascal says it is a worse job than he expected, and of a different sort: 'plenty magic here, and bad magic.' He was to have cleared you out for ten dollars, but now he says he must have five and twenty."

For answer, Henniker counted the bills into his friend's hand.

"No doubt he is scoundrel enough for anything, but I will not stint the money. Tell him to go ahead with what he has to do."

"And he says the senora must help him. There is a woman in it, and there must be a woman against. Will Mrs. Henniker mind?"

Joan raised no objection, and the preparations went forward. The man stripped himself to the waist, wearing only his leather breeches. He then laid a sheet of iron on the wooden top of their table, and produced an odd-looking bowl of beaten metal, which he required Joan to fill with spring water, dipping into it the forefinger of each of her hands, first one and then the other, and stirring the water from left to right. He gazed into the bowl for a few minutes in silence, and then spoke rapidly to Arnott, who translated.

"He is enumerating the articles you have lost and wish restored. Some blouse-waists and a skirt, a belt and buckle, a scarf, and a circle of stones that glitter. That is right, is it not? But nothing more than he could have learnt from Clew."

This seemed only the preliminary. The witch-doctor now built up with great care four little pyramids of some stuff which looked like dried herbs, one at each corner of the iron sheet, the water bowl still occupying the centre. He took a hot coal from the fire and lighted these pyramids, one after another. As they smouldered he began to speak, as if in conversation with some person invisible, upbraiding, commanding, threatening; and now the sweat stood in beads on his brow and rained from him with the effort he was making, though it appeared to be mental rather than bodily.

At intervals he sprinkled water round him in the room, finally snatching up the bowl and emptying it by tossing the whole contents upwards into the air. This in itself was a conjuror's marvel, as the water totally disappeared and nothing was wetted by it; but this crowning action had a result which astonished the three spectators. A material object fell from the ceiling and dropped upon the iron sheet. A woman's hand.

They all looked in amaze at this product of Hill-of-the-Raven's incantation.

"I have succeeded," the witch-doctor announced to Arnott. "The senor and senora will have no more trouble. But they must fold the hand in a fair white cloth, and bury it at sundown under the nearest tree. The senora will receive again what she has lost, but she will be asked to give back something in return. And that something she would do unwisely to refuse."

The Hennikers were by no means anxious to detain Hill-of-the-Raven, and he departed with Arnott to set out on his return journey in the buggy. Joan and her husband were left possessors of the strange Thing which had fallen from the ceiling: could it really have been this slight small hand, now lying limp and dead, which had caused all the disturbance and trouble. A human hand, of natural flesh at least, though drained of blood; and—wonder the more, as Joan presently cried out in recognition, it was Nita's hand. It bore the double line of blue tattooing twisted into a knot, which she well remembered on the girl's wrist; and the hand appeared to have been severed exactly where Nita bore on her fore-arm that deeply indented scar. That the hand should have been hers, seemed to make the whole thing more horrible even than before. Joan shuddered away from the touch of it.

"Let us do what the man said: let us bury it out of sight."

"Yes, but not till sundown," replied her husband. "We had better keep to the letter of the instructions, absurd as they may seem. Find the white cloth he spoke of, and have it wrapped in readiness, and I will go and dig the hole under the tree."

So the burial of the small limp hand took place exactly as Hill-of-the-Raven had enjoined, hastily and almost furtively conducted, at least to the consciousness of these two people; they felt almost as if they had been concerned in a murder, and were now hiding away the corpse. There was something solemn, too, in that still evening in which hardly a breath of air stirred, with sunset flush still lingering behind the mountain peaks, and a few faint stars beginning to look forth.

Henniker smoothed over the disturbed ground, and then shouldered his spade.

"That ends the trouble we will hope," he said.

Joan had kept her courage well in hand through the long strain upon it, but the events of that day had overtaxed her nerves.

"I am ready to hate *out west*," she sobbed. "When we have turned our backs on it, and are again in safe England, shall we ever believe that these things really happened, and were not from beginning to end an evil dream?"

A quiet night followed for the inhabiters of Hunter's End; there were no more tapping fingers, nor scampering feet above upon the roof. The next morning Mercy Clew came back to work, unafraid of further peltings, as she had full confidence in the witch-doctor's power of exorcism, and belief that all would now be well. And, more notable still, Arnott's horses driven by, no longer held back and sweated in terror, nor did the dog refuse to accompany his master. Whatever it was that had scared them from the place, was plainly removed and gone; and, now Joan had the companionship of Mrs. Clew, Henniker was released to carry his gun to the hills. This seems like the end of the story, but it is not. There is one more episode to be related, stranger than all.

Six days had gone by, and the seventh had dawned. It had been an undisturbed week, and the first vivid impressions of the witch diablerie were beginning to fade.

The first change that came was in the weather, which recently had been oppressive, heavy with heat, and scarcely a breath of air fanning down into the valley from blue heights and distant snows. The cup of it had doubtless been charged to the brim for a crisis of electrical disturbance. Never had Joan in her English experience witnessed such lightning or heard such thunder: the jagged flashes seemed to leap from peak to peak, and the thunder was caught up by the mountain echoes and doubled and redoubled, rolling like a cannonade among the hills. Then followed torrential rain, driving and pitiless, scourging all before it, and creating, as it seemed in a moment, streams and rivulets where all had been as dry as dust. In the midst of this downpour a hail came from without: a buggy and pair of mules had halted at the gate, and two people were craving shelter, a boon that could hardly be denied.

Henniker opened the door, and a man staggered in supporting a woman wrapped in a hooded cloak, who seemed to be ill or faint. He placed her in a chair, and cleared the wet, lank hair out of his own eyes; he was a good-looking young half-breed, about twenty years of age, and he had some broken English.

"This Hunter's End?" he asked, looking round. "And your name Henniker? My sister here is ill, having lost her hand. She has come to claim it again from you. And she has brought back the things she took away."

The fainting woman in the chair was Nita. The man opened a bundle on the table, and there, crumpled and soiled, were Joan's possessions, and rolled within them the oval frame of paste. As he took the bundle from her knee, the cloak that covered her fell apart, and showed that her right arm ended in a stump, about which a linen bandage was twisted, and the bandage was stained with blood.

"My sister's hand?" he continued, looking from Joan to Henniker, and back again to Joan. "You have it here. I bring you these in exchange: you have no claim to keep. If you do not restore her hand, she will die."

Joan whispered hurriedly to her husband.

"This was what Hill-of-the-Raven meant. *The thing* we were to give back if it was demanded of us. You will have to dig it up."

"Are you afraid to be left with them?" he queried.

She shook her head, so he shouldered his spade and went forth to the tree-root to open again that small and uncanny grave, which was dug and filled in seven days before. He brought back the parcel in its folds of fair linen, from which he had shaken the dry earth; the rain which still fell without had not penetrated so deep.

The hand when unrolled from the cloth appeared to be unchanged, corruption had not set in. All this time Nita sat with closed eyes, leaning back in the chair, as if barely conscious of what was taking place. Now she moved when her brother addressed her in their native tongue, and held out the maimed stump of her right arm, from which he unwound the binding cloth, exposing the raw wound. He then united the severed parts, and Joan used afterwards to aver that she heard the bones grate together as they met. And when the bandage was re-wound (a couple of pieces of bark folded in it to keep straight the wrist) she saw the dead fingers move, and the hue of life suffuse them once again.

This was the last of madam Rachel's magic, and of the uncanny events at Hunter's End. The brother lifted Nita to her feet, and half carried, half supported her to the waiting buggy, where his mules were hitched to the post. Both of them were apparently indifferent to the still falling sheets of rain, through which they presently disappeared in the direction of the hills.

COACHWHIP PUBLICATIONS
ALSO AVAILABLE

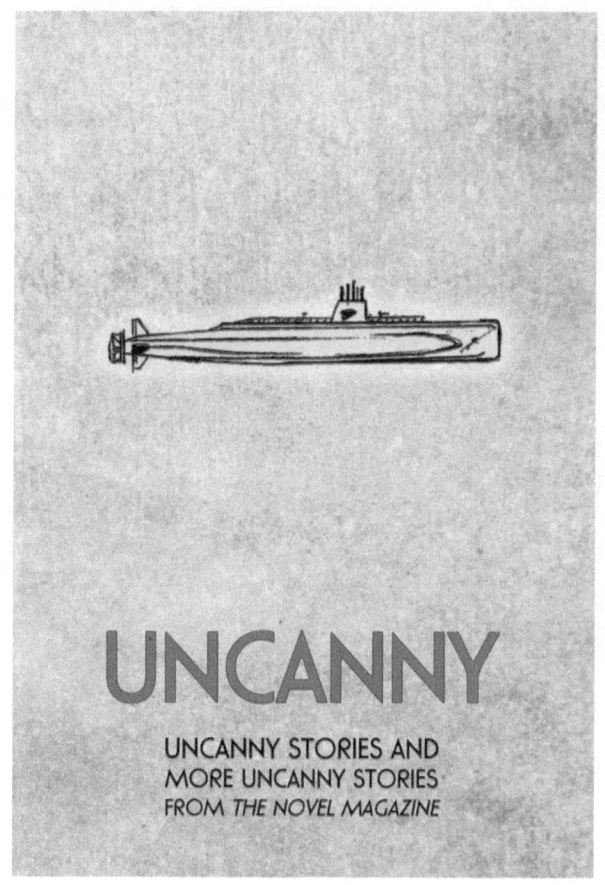

UNCANNY

UNCANNY STORIES AND
MORE UNCANNY STORIES
FROM *THE NOVEL MAGAZINE*

ISBN 1-61646-244-2

COACHWHIP PUBLICATIONS

COACHWHIPBOOKS.COM

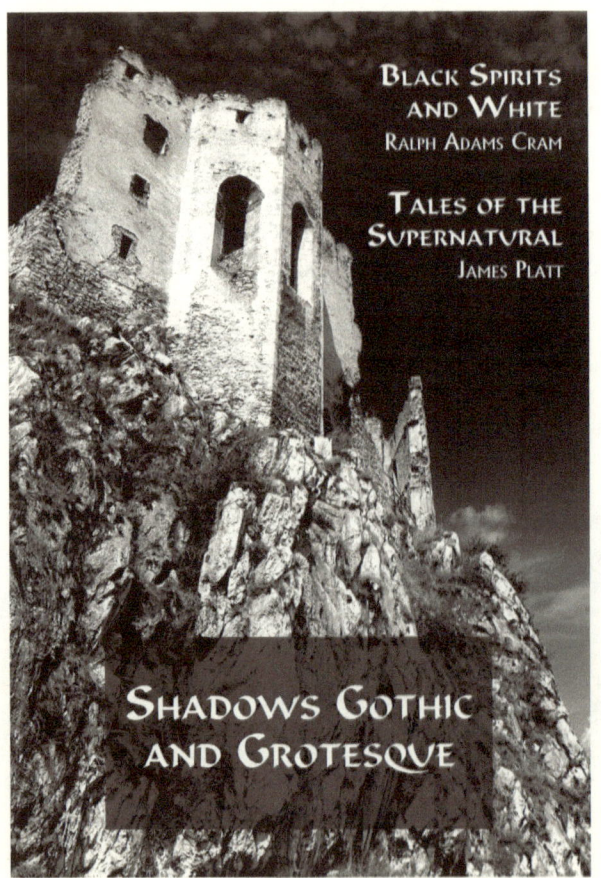

BLACK SPIRITS
AND WHITE
Ralph Adams Cram

TALES OF THE
SUPERNATURAL
James Platt

SHADOWS GOTHIC
AND GROTESQUE

ISBN 1-61646-059-8

COACHWHIP PUBLICATIONS

ALSO AVAILABLE

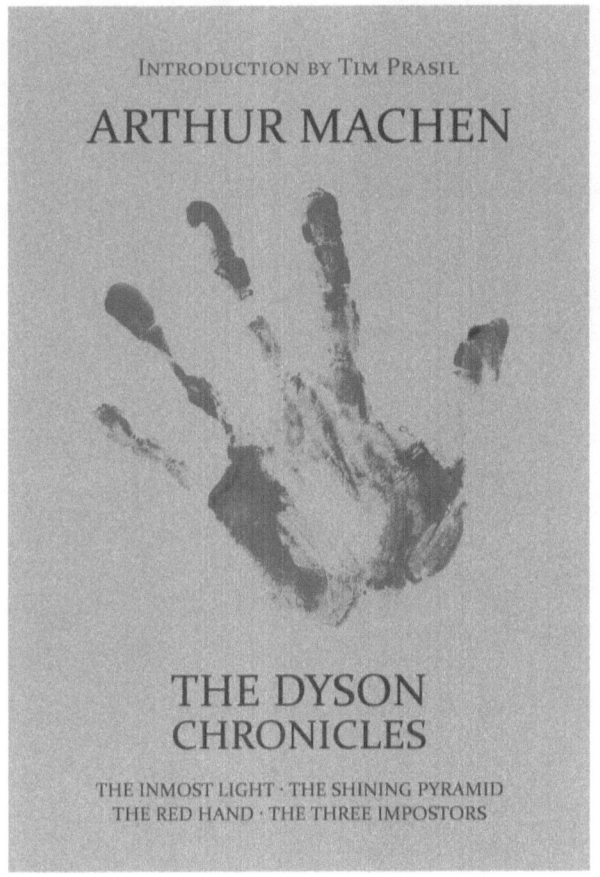

INTRODUCTION BY TIM PRASIL

ARTHUR MACHEN

THE DYSON
CHRONICLES

THE INMOST LIGHT · THE SHINING PYRAMID
THE RED HAND · THE THREE IMPOSTORS

ISBN 1-61646-227-2

COACHWHIP PUBLICATIONS

COACHWHIPBOOKS.COM

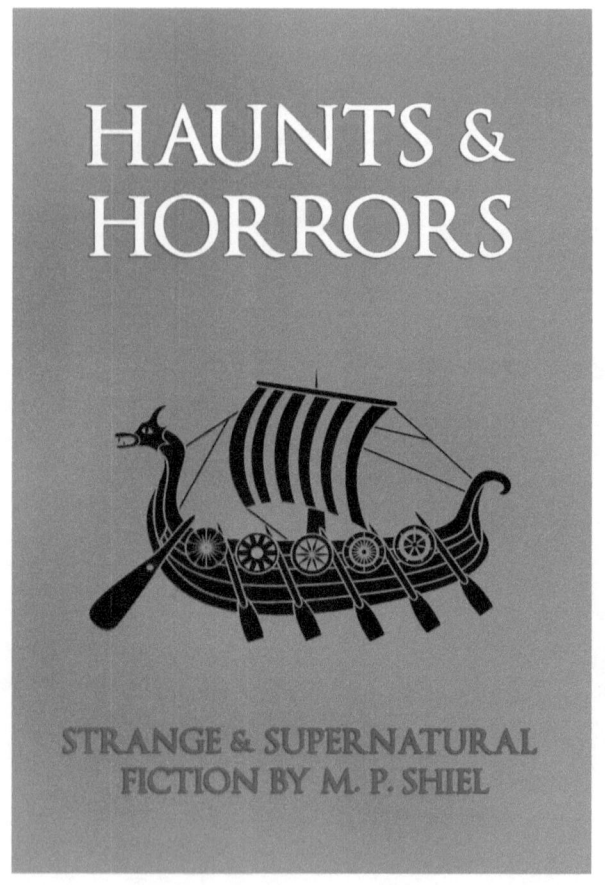

HAUNTS &
HORRORS

STRANGE & SUPERNATURAL
FICTION BY M. P. SHIEL

ISBN 1-61646-119-5

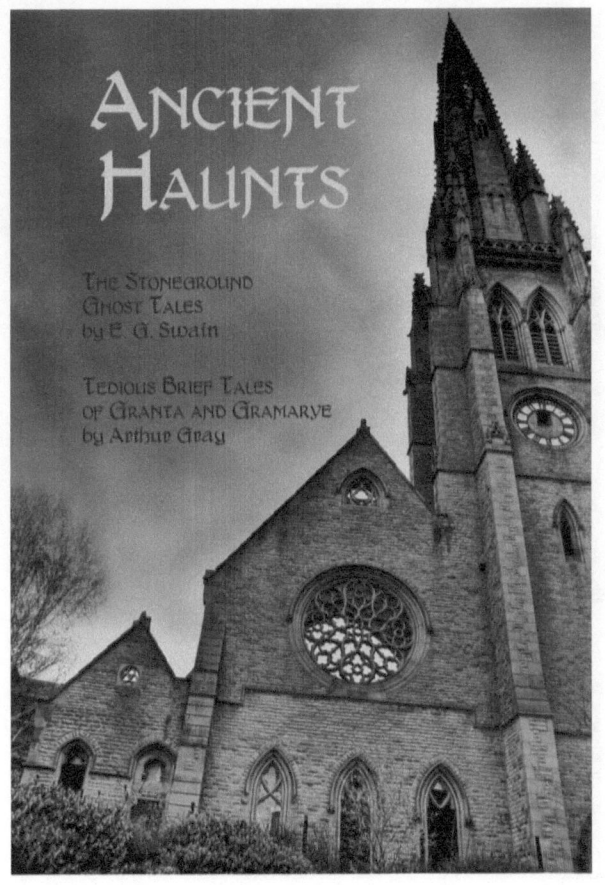

ANCIENT
HAUNTS

The Stoneground
Ghost Tales
by E. G. Swain

Tedious Brief Tales
of Granta and Gramarye
by Arthur Gray

ISBN 1-61646-005-9

COACHWHIP PUBLICATIONS

COACHWHIPBOOKS.COM

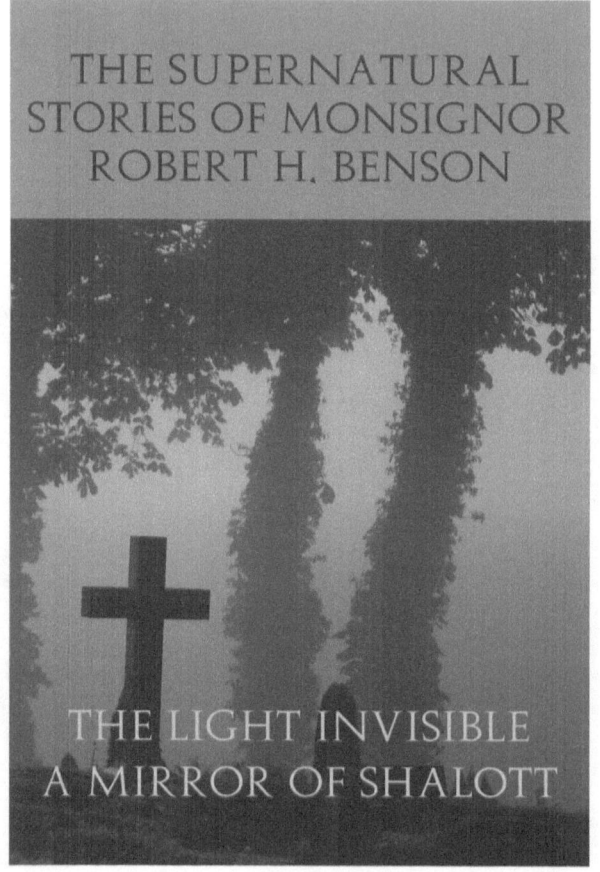

THE SUPERNATURAL
STORIES OF MONSIGNOR
ROBERT H. BENSON

THE LIGHT INVISIBLE
A MIRROR OF SHALOTT

ISBN 1-61646-004-0

COACHWHIP PUBLICATIONS

ALSO AVAILABLE

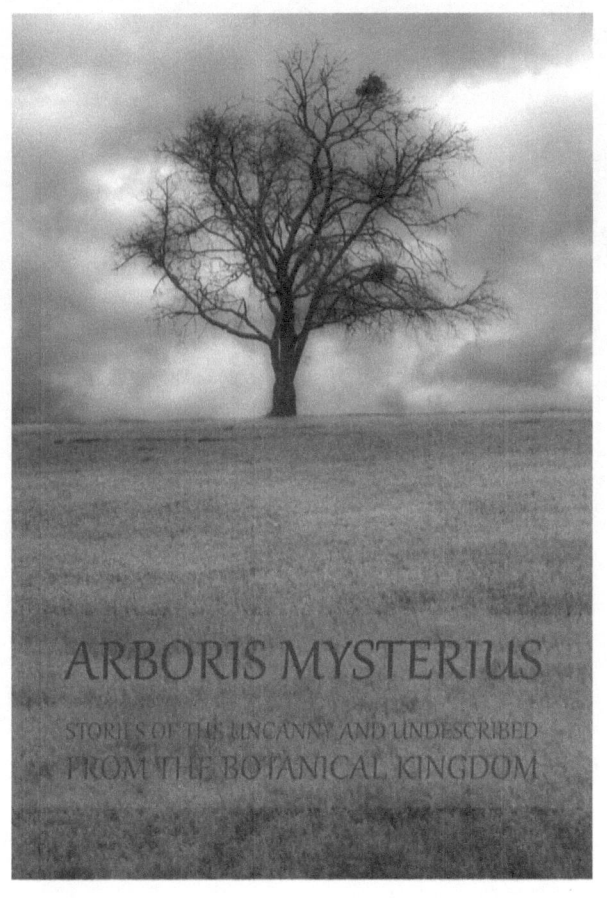

ARBORIS MYSTERIUS

STORIES OF THE UNCANNY AND UNDESCRIBED
FROM THE BOTANICAL KINGDOM

ISBN 1-61646-246-9